DANCE OF THE APPRENTICES

TO DR O. H. MAVOR
A GLASGOW MAN

Edward Gaitens (1897–1966), was born in the Gorbals of Glasgow. Leaving school at fourteen, he undertook a variety of casual jobs to support himself over the years. When the First World War broke out he became a conscientious objector and was imprisoned for two years in Wormwood Scrubs. In the 1930s he started to write, and his early attempts in this field were greatly encouraged by his fellow Glaswegian, the successful dramatist James Bridie, who had become chairman of the Glasgow Citizens' Theatre at that time.

A number of Gaitens' short stories were first published in the *Scots Magazine*. Mostly based on his own life in the Gorbals, these were later collected as *Growing Up and Other Stories* (1942). Six of these stories were incorporated into *Dance of the Apprentices* (1948), a novel of city life and the turbulent years between the First World War and the Depression. Gaitens continued to write from time to time during the years in which he lived—virtually anonymously—in London and Dublin. *Growing Up* . . . and *Dance of the Apprentices* remain his only published books.

Edward Gaitens

DANCE OF THE
APPRENTICES

Introduced by James Campbell

CANONGATE
CLASSICS
31

First published in 1948 by William McLellan &
Co (Publishers), first published as a Canongate
Classic in 1990 by Canongate Publishing Limi-
ted, 17 Jeffrey Street, Edinburgh EH1 1DR.
Copyright Edward Gaitens 1948. Introduction
copyright James Campbell 1990.

The publishers gratefully acknowledge general
subsidy from the Scottish Arts Council towards
the Canongate Classics series and a specific grant
towards the publication of this title.

Set in 10pt Plantin by Hewer Text Composition
Services, Edinburgh. Printed and bound in
Denmark by Norhaven Rotation.

Canongate Classics
Series Editor: Roderick Watson
Editorial Board: Tom Crawford, John Pick

British Library Cataloguing in Publication Data
Gaitens, Edward, *1897–1966*
Dance of the apprentices.—(Canongate classics)
I. Title
823.912

ISBN 0-86241-297-8

It is with the kind permission of Jonathan Cape
that some of the material included in *Growing
Up and Other Stories* has been incorporated in
this novel.

Introduction

Edward Gaitens is an enigmatic presence in Scottish literature. He made his debut with *Growing Up and other stories* in inauspicious circumstances—in the middle of the Second World War—then was silent for six years until *Dance of the Apprentices* appeared in 1948. After that, he wrote little. His stories crop up in modern anthologies (usually the same one: 'Growing Up' itself), but neither of his two books has been in print for decades. Nor is much known about his life; and, according to a note in a recent anthology which quoted his literary executor, that was how Gaitens wanted it.

Gaitens was a Gorbals man—a Gorbals hard-man, in fact, though his razor was his pen. He was hard on the place itself, and hard on its inhabitants, whom he portrayed as mostly the perpetrators of their own misery. But hardest of all was his reluctance to offer his characters an escape from their prison. You can take the boy out of the slum, he seems to say, but you can't take the slum out of the boy.

Of course, there would be no drama in Gaitens's work were it not for the refusal of people to believe that, and their stubborn insistence on trying to transcend circumstances. The Gaitens hero is the Idealist as a Young Man, the apprentice who is striving to turn a chaotic urban world to coherence. At the close of the short story 'The Sailing Ship', for example—a work which displays Gaitens's craft at its best—Johnny Regan watches a handsome windjammer unfurl her sails at the mouth of the Clyde estuary. He has come all the way out to Dumbarton Rock to see it: the *France* contains everything his life lacks—adventure, wealth, power—and now is sailing into the world without him, 'away from unemployment and wretchedness, from the ignorance and misunderstanding of his parents, to the infinite nobility of the sea!' So long does Johnny stand on the shore, however, that 'darkness, with the small rain and a cold wind, had enveloped his transported body'. That 'darkness' is more than just the dusk: it is Johnny's lot in life.

Johnny Regan is simply another name for Eddy Mac-donnel, protagonist of most of the tales in *Growing Up*, and of *Dance of the Apprentices*. And Eddy is not too distantly related to Edward Gaitens. Like Johnny, Eddy tries to spring himself from his slum prison—into poetry, philosophy, socialism—only to be dumped in a real prison for his idealistic opposition to the Great War. This was precisely Gaitens's fate in life: two years in Wormwood Scrubs as a conscientious objector.

Elusive though he was, Gaitens's talent was not unrecognised in his lifetime. He began writing at the behest of his friend, the playwright, James Bridie. In spite of its badly timed publication, *Growing Up* received a favourable press, and H.G. Wells sent a letter to the author comparing his stories to the best in English literature. In 1946, there was sufficient public interest for it to be announced in the *Glasgow Herald* that Gaitens (then working as a night telephonist) was writing a novel, to be published by the Glasgow firm of MacLellan.

When it duly appeared two years later as *Dance of the Apprentices*, Gaitens's admirers were surely a mite surprised, not to say disappointed, for he had scarcely produced a new book at all—rather, he had written the same one again. This complaint is made of many authors, but it is more literally true in Gaitens's case than in most; of the twelve chapters of *Dance of the Apprentices*, six are taken directly from *Growing Up*.

Yet, between them, novel and stories probably contain the best writing that exists about Glasgow's badlands. Most of the action of *Dance of the Apprentices* is divided among 'the three apprentices of idealism': Eddy himself, the boorish Donald Hamilton, who knows all the answers without ever having asked a question, and his opposite, Neil Mudge, a serious fellow with a genuine devotion to learning. The quest for a higher form of life than is to be found on Gowan

Street begins on the opening page. Eddy is reading a poem
by Robert Herrick:

> Fair Daffodils, we weep to see
> You haste away so soon . . .

The 'power and harmony of Poetry' are suddenly made real
to him, as they never had been in school; the words of the
poets, 'that once were dead were, every one, living, flashing
like luminous beads of rain'.

But then Gaitens plays a devastating hand: this eighteen-
year-old youth, four years out of school, 'was not sure
what daffodils were like; they were not often seen in
back-streets when their time came round'. As he reads,
his mother is in bed drunk; his baby sister lies at her
feet, her hair 'lustreless from lack of proper attention';
soon his father will appear, drunk and noisy and spoiling
for a fight, if not with his wife then with one of Eddy's
elder brothers; the strongest of those brothers, Francie,
will soon go mad; another, spurning the opportunity for
a better life, will inherit the family's only heirloom, the
bottle, and eventually die in the trenches; neighbouring
girls, beautiful now, will lose their bloom, if not their
reputations, by the age of twenty. The initially trite-seeming
sentiment, 'we weep to see / You haste away so soon', will
have gathered a grievous resonance by the time the story
closes.

Yet this hard-man never committed the artist's sin of
despising his own creations. That Gaitens wrote out of
a bitter, contradictory love of place and people is plain
from almost every page of his novel. One of the moral
triumphs of *Dance of the Apprentices* is to show how people
suffer under the weight of their own ignorance, and how
confusion turns to waste. The scenes of lethargy in the
Macdonnel kitchen present big, strong men labouring in
the mire of their own resourcelessness. Eddy's father, not
a bad person, has only his fists to withstand what the world
flings at him. The highest feeling of which his mother is
capable is a self-pitying sentimentality, displayed usually as
a means of getting money from her sons for drink. Here
Gaitens meets Edwin Muir: his people are orphans from
the land (Catholic Ireland in Gaitens's case), drawn to

an industrial jungle which requires only their labour, and sometimes cannot even use that.

The inclusion of the world of ideas into the book is reminiscent of the Muir of the *Autobiography*, of course, and it also brings to mind Muir's novel of 1932, *Poor Tom*, which *Dance of the Apprentices* in some ways resembles. Muir's 'apprentices', Tom and Mansie, also live on Glasgow's south side, are inspired by Nietzsche and other European thinkers, and take refuge in concepts of socialism current at the time. Eddy and his friends likewise read widely (without always understanding what they are reading) and discuss the ideas of 'individualism' and 'free wull'. And here Eddy Macdonnel comes face to face with other heroes, in what can be seen as a tradition in Glasgow fiction, such as Mat Craig of *The Dear Green Place*, Duncan Thaw of *Lanark*, and even the outlaw Joe Necchi of Alexander Trocchi's *Cain's Book*; in all of the above novels, the theme is of an artist who cannot get his work done, an idealist whose dreams convert to rubble, a tree that never grew.

Gaitens's Gorbals is full of buried talent, most of it doomed to unfulfilment or worse. Take, for example, the tender portrait of the flyweight boxer Terence Mooney, surely drawn with the outline of Benny Lynch in mind:

> Except to professional eyes, he did not look like a pugilist, yet he was in the first class of flyweights, with a brilliant original style, seven stone of exquisite poise and quickness in the ring, and he had given a world's champion two of the hardest fights of his career. He was very popular in the Gorbals for his unassuming manner, and they said he could have been a world's champion if he had left the drink alone.

The pre-First World War Gorbals Gaitens wrote about was frozen until the mid-1960s, when it was swept away. One of the pleasures of this book, to anyone with a passing acquaintance with Crown Street and Florence Street, is the sense of reunion in its pages, with brown-painted closes and corner pubs and the insides of a room-and-kitchen, with types and with language—the minodge, the jawbox and the ran-dan. There were still in the 1960s, and no doubt still are, boys like Terence Mooney who can only make it in sport, and others who turn their considerable wits to crime; there are still illegal prize-fights on Sundays, if not on the banks of the River Clyde then somewhere else, and still Italian cafés, though they no longer serve hot peas. There are people who 'mix the tongues of Eire and Scotland', and others whose respect for learning is matched only by their want of it, and there is never any shortage of 'unemployment and wretchedness . . . ignorance and misunderstanding'.

Gaitens was less at ease in the longer narrative than the short one; but his readers are amply compensated. No other novel is so deeply dyed in the colours of this still-familiar world. In describing it, Edward Gaitens lights up the gloomy night through which the apprentices try, and try again, to dance away to freedom.

James Campbell

Book One

Wahn, wahn, überall wahn . . .

CHAPTER ONE

Fair Daffodils, we weep to see
You haste away so soon;
As yet the early-rising sun
Has not attain'd his noon—

In a low voice the lad recited again and again those simple
lines, all his senses reaching out like glistening April buds,
enthralled by the unaffected passion and grace of the lyric
which he had met for the first time.

Stay, stay,
Until the hasting day
Has run,
But to the evensong;
And having pray'd together, we
Will go with you along.

He had discovered Poetry.

When he left school at fourteen, four years ago, the word
was meaningless to him, though he had learned many poems
for school lessons, memorizing them easily, and was always
word-perfect when asked to stand up in class and recite,
but the rhymes sounded to him like gabbling jingle, and
the words fell through his empty head like pebbles tossed
in the air. But tonight, from the book his friend had given
him, in an instant, the radiance, power and harmony of
Poetry rose like a sunrise within him, and all those words
that once were dead were, every one, living, flashing like
luminous beads of rain from the crafty settings of the poets.
So, mingled of awe and delight, he muttered:

We have short time to stay as you,
We have as short a Spring,
As quick a growth to meet decay
As you or anything . . .

And, so to the end:

3

We die as your hours do
And dry
Away,
Like to the Summer's rain
Or as the pearls of morning's dew,
Ne'er to be found again.

He fell silent at last, with a silence intensely alive.

He was nòt sure what daffodils were like; they were not often seen in back-streets when their time came round, but in this moment of inspiration he was surrounded by their ecstatic movements and atmosphere of eternal youth. Through the open window facing him, where he sat at the kitchen range, grime from the dozen foul back-courts of this colossal oblong of tenements drifted in on a momentary breeze of a heat-wave. The kitchen reeked of beer and cheap whisky. Behind him, in a small, set-in bed, his mother, a woman of fifty, snored in drunken sleep, her head reclined ungracefully, her mouth open; against the bed stood a table, unpicturesque with scraps of a coarse meal. But all this had utterly passed away from him. He was outside these narrow walls, solitary, in secret glades and woods where Creation's gaiety was born, lived and died, unsullied by human presence, year after year; he was striding vigorously, alone, over Scottish moors and scaling sheer, high places on mountains where rare flowers hung.

To him, in his absent state, the moan of a child sounded far away, uncanny, like a bodiless, wandering voice. He turned his head from staring into the world and gazed vaguely awhile at the bed, where a six-year-old girl, his sister, lay at his mother's feet. The sultry midnight had made her rest feverish and she had tossed the dirty, hot blankets from her. A violent motion of her mother had pushed her half-naked form against the wall and her head was pressed hard against the bed's inside corner.

The child moaned again and the lad rose from his seat, a chair cushioned with a pile of old newspapers and coverless magazines, and placed there his book, a Collins's pocket edition of *The Golden Treasury*. Two paces across the diminutive floor brought him to the bedside, where he stepped lightly on a chair and leant over to ease his sister's sleep. As he touched her flushed cheek his fingers glowed with kindness, suffused by the mysterious currents of imagery. He smoothed back her red hair, lustreless from lack of proper attention, that had fallen about her eyes, drew her head up on the pillow and spread a covering round her. Then he held aside the curtain which he had drawn across his mother's face to prevent the lowered gaslight from waking her and whispered, softly touching her shoulder: 'Move over! You're crushin' Mary!'

His mother woke, regarded him through drink-hazed eyes and, with a vacuous smile, slept again. She was unlovely. Her hair was haggish, her face inflamed by debauchery. Six years ago his father had broken her nose with a blow of his fist.

A flame of hatred of his father leapt in him as he looked at her mutilated face, then in painful wonder he tried to reason out why his parents' marriage had failed so miserably. His mother had been pretty in her youth. They used to talk about her bonny red hair—how it shone in the sun; and the lad saw his elders young again as he had so often studied them in the massive gilt-edged Victorian album that lay at this moment alongside the big, Douay Family-Bible on the parlour table. From dim daguerrotypes, sharp-edged tin photos, growing fainter with time, his parents, in their twenties, smiled at him like the receding figures of a dream; and in brown-toned pictures of a later period of photography he saw them on their honeymoon in Ireland, in Killarney, in Edinburgh and Scottish seaside places, his father smiling, grave or pompous, his mother naive, in sentimental attitudes or as she had looked up at the photographer, with a foolish smile, set for her picture.

When had it begun, the bitter discord that made each hate the other as a burden, the lad asked himself. They had set out together happy, fairly well-off, according to back-street standards, eager with plans to enrich them- selves and rear a family that would be proud of them. But their love was soon dead, and their children came into an atmosphere of petty hatred, dissipation and violence. Baffled by the riddle of their failure, his imagination roved through that world in the album among the people who begot them and those who were young with them.

He saw her English father, the old packman, a curly-headed, kind, humorous man, who used to travel up and down the country, selling silks, satins and cloths to farmers' wives. He would suddenly arrive with golden half-sovereigns and big, round wooden boxes filled with coloured ju-jubes, fruit drops or crystallized ginger for his daughter's boys. He used to drink away his well-earned money with everyone, set off penniless on the roads and write from distant places to borrow small loans from his daughter. She had loved her father.

He saw his father's Highland mother, a handsome, big-bosomed dark woman, resolute of feature, soft-eyed; she had something of his father's dominance. She had left her son a small but thriving chandler's shop, but he had loved books and company, had no head for business and soon lost the shop with giving on credit goods that were never paid for and drinking up the profits with customers and friends.

The lad wondered if that was the time when his parents' resolution and integrity had crumbled away, when his father had to return to work in the shipyards and engineering-shops at his trade as a brass-finisher, making parts of nautical instruments—skilled, delicate work which he had soon to give up because his eyesight slightly failed. After that he became dock-labourer, navvy, went to sea for spells as an ordinary seaman, or took any kind of labouring job he was lucky enough to get, while his wife, when he was unemployed, earned a little scrubbing the floors of churches and dance-halls and, on Monday mornings, big public-houses, where crowds of rough men drank till midnight on the Saturday, spitting tobacco-spit on the sawdust-sprinkled floor, sometimes spewing up their drink on it.

A procession of dead people out of the album marched alive through the lad's mind. Ladies with corkscrew curls, in crinolines, archly holding silken fans, with big white cameo brooches at the throats of black bodices; ladies in long skirts with impertinent bustles; all the men with burly moustaches, tightly waxed or loose, in tall silk hats, swallow-tail coats, and spats, with heavy gold alberts across their waistcoats; in bell-bottom trousers, jackets with high lapels and tight, cocky little bowlers. Very few of them had realized the aims of their youth; the majority had ended, like his parents, in a wasteland of weak resignation, but in the faces of those few who had risen out of the back-streets he had never discovered more courage and determination than was in his father's youthful face, and he always puzzled over why they had succeeded where his father had failed.

He had stared so long and intently at his mother's face that a mist of staring had risen in his eyes through which he saw her countenance softened, with much of its worry and fears, spite and pettiness smoothed away; and in the false tranquillity that his staring, his wish for well-being, had given her, there came to him the queer idea that she and his father were also dead, like those departed people in the album, because the charm of beginning was lost to them and the inward peace and freshness which sweetens in ageing people who have always tried to live up to the highest in themselves, was not in them. They could never start afresh now.

He stepped with cat-like quietness down from the bedside chair and stood looking around the dirty, neglected kitchen with a sense that here was life's evil dream and that the immortal experience from which his sister's moans had called him away was true reality. He shuddered as he remembered how narrowly manslaughter and murder had been missed in the many family fights he had seen, when heavy blows were struck and weapons raised. His imagination, fired and clarified by poetry, plunged him back through time to the night when his mother was disfigured, and with agonizing vividness he lived through every incident, movement and violent emotion of the fight that had begun in this kitchen.

Eddy Macdonnel, a boy of twelve, had just run home that evening hugging a big volume of *Pickwick Papers* which he had borrowed from the local Carnegie Library. He sat on a chair against the small wall-space between the end of the dresser and the sink and opened the book with delightful excitement, not knowing what to do first—whether to look at all the comic drawings of Cruickshank and 'Phiz,' or to start reading and come upon each illustration in its place. Thrilled with happy indecision he smiled at the engraved frontispiece and decided to start the story.

His mother, stirring pots at the range, was letting him read in peace for once, because he had run all her errands after school and she was nicely ahead with her men's dinners. She seemed very content, too, and he foresaw a long, luxurious evening lost in his new book.

The cries of playing children in the back-court below gradually faded as dusk mooned into the kitchen, filling first the square alcove of the bed, which was farthest from the window, tranquilly wiping all colour from the wallpaper and every bright ornament, powerless only against the fire's glow, which radiated brighter by contrast.

Eddy leant his head back against the wall, the open book on his knees, and waited for his mother to light the gas. However, she had one of her 'saving' fits on her and she took her time about it, finding enough light for her work in the gleam from the range. At last she thrust a spill of paper between the firebars, lit the incandescent mantle, pulled down the window-blind, and the half of the kitchen that seemed to have vanished into space reappeared.

Eddy dived headlong into his book, but he had only read a few more pages, stumbling over difficult words, when he had to rise and let his father in. He knew immediately, by the way his father thrust brusquely past him into the kitchen as he held the stairhead door open, that there was small hope of peace in the house tonight. He closed the door timidly and sat down again, tensing up with apprehension, a constricted, nervous sensation in his stomach, a greyish feeling round his heart.

Mr Macdonnel wasn't drunk. It was mid-week, equally too far-distant from last pay-day and the coming one for him to have spare money to spend on liquor. In his own favourite phrase he was 'as sober as a judge.' But the boy knew it was dangerous to make even a pleasant remark to him in his present state, when his eyes bleakened and seemed to dart sombre, unnatural light, when the jerky movements of his powerful, uneasy body seemed to sputter malice and ill-will as a naked live-wire crackles sparks.

Mr Macdonnel, looking marvellously fit and untired after a long, hard day's shovelling on the concrete-board of a big navvying job, greeted neither his wife nor boy, but stood a moment with his head dominantly posed looking wryly at Mrs Macdonnel, who sensing his temper, became glum and engrossed herself fussily at the range, not even turning her head. They were both primed with petty self-righteousness, ready to nag.

Mr Macdonnel strode with unnecessary, frenzied haste into the lobby, divested himself of cap, jacket and waistcoat, and dashed back towards the jawbox, rolling up his shirt-sleeves, baring his breast, his hobnailed boots, streaked with clay, whitish with concrete, thudding violently the floor. His every motion bragged that he was the breadwinner; his hefty gestures, as he soaped and splashed at the tap, were like shouts of 'I'm heid o' the hoose! I'm boss here!' his tough, middle-sized physique hummed with self-esteem which egregiously pervaded the little kitchen. And his wife, with whom every night he lay close, who had borne him eight children, bored his expressive back with hateful looks as she shifted off the hob a long-handled, iron pot of potatoes, furiously billowing steam, and waited behind him, sullen with ill-will.

Eddy looked up nervously from his book at his mother, who grimaced scorn at her husband, asking the boy's support, expecting him also to grimace annoyance at his father's prolonged washing, but he only looked scared, fearing his father might see he was taking sides; and he bowed over his book, feeling, like hot coal on his head, her resentful stare at his evasion of sympathy with her.

A stranger, unaware of the intense, hateful emotions alive in the room, might have smiled at the queer faces the elder people made, but the boy knew they were always a prelude to senseless quarrelling between them, which ended in blows, screams, the running-in of neighbours, sometimes the police. He had seen so many such times when the streets were more friendly than home.

The vibrations of hate were astir, blurring the words of Dickens. Feeling the dangerous mood of his parents, he stared unnerved, stupidly at the page, jumping when his mother said petulantly: 'Will ye let me pour these taties?'

Mr Macdonnel lingered, silent, spiteful, and splashed more vigorously. Suddenly he turned off the tall, curved brass tap, swung round, snarled in her face: 'Ach, can ye not give a man a minnit tae wash himself!' then he made a hideous rattle wrenching the family-towel from the roller on the food-press door and pushed brutally past her to the middle of the floor, where he savagely dried himself.

The boy, now miserable with apprehension, stealthily eyed his mother as she tipped the water from the potatoes, her movements irascible, spasmodic, nerved with hatred as she turned a murderous look at her husband. Like some ancient witch incantating over a fire, he saw her red face writhing vindictively through a cloud of steam. She always protruded the right corner of her lower lip over the upper with a chewing motion when she was angry and the habit had moulded a permanent expression of offence. Eddy felt his father near him and turned his head slightly to escape the smell of his new moleskin trousers, which always sickened him. His delight in the crowded stage of *Pickwick Papers* was dead; the rasps of the coarse towel on his father's flesh, magnified by fear, rankled in his ears; towel fringes flicked his book; he edged about trying to read, too terrified of his father to tell him he stood in the light. Scalding tears sprang to his eyes; he closed the book and hung his head in sullen muteness.

The kitchen was stuffed with the heat of cooking, the smells of a sour towel, coarse soap and wet skin, but it was the ignoble anger throbbing through the room that made Eddy feel the oppression of these things, his natural atmosphere since childhood, which would not have weighed on him had he been happily reading. He would have liked to walk the streets but was afraid something tragic would happen, and he remained with the tremulous, valiant idea of protecting his mother; he wanted to go and read in the parlour, known as 'ben the hoose' or 'ben the room,' but he knew his mother would forbid him to have light. She did not regard reading as a good excuse for consuming gas. When she sobered up after weeks of drinking she was fanatically economical.

Through a silence that had lasted for ten minutes, Mrs Macdonnel's voice, haunted with fear and defiance, cut sharply: 'Shure ye'll be wantin' yer dinner!' Mr Macdonnel buried his tough head in the towel and scrubbed viciously. This seemed to scald her with irritation and she repeated the remark, thudding a pot on the hob to announce her anger. Her husband whipped the towel away, glared, and shouted harshly, mimicking her voice: 'Ach, whit the hell's the matter with ye? Of course Ah'll be wantin' ma dinner!' which began a contest of nagging that quickly increased in spite and virulence.

Eddy ran with relief to answer a knock at the door and admit one of his elder brothers, a young man of twenty-four, who had heard his parents from the stairhead and entered with a scowl on his fresh-complexioned face. He stood dumbly for a few moments in the raw silence of his parents' glowers with head morosely hung, then threw his cap, blackened with shipyard dust and oil, on to a hook behind the door and went into the parlour, where he sat in darkness at the window, chin in palm, staring out at a Glasgow street.

In another few moments, with his fears diminished by the thought that there would be assistance if his father became violent, the lad opened the door again for the eldest son, home from his work at a rabbit-and-hare-skin curing works, a tall, slight, dark young man of twenty-seven, whose clothes exhaled a disgusting stench. A whitish rime from the chemicals with which the skins were treated and thousands of minute hairs on his coat and trousers gave him a frosty look as he entered briskly with head up and distended nostrils, turning a hungry eye on the table. Seeing how his parents were he leant negligently for a minute against the dresser, his posture expressing disgust, and looked angrily at them, his most venomous glance being for his father, at whose back he sneered before turning to leave the kitchen. John did not look up as James came into the parlour, lit the gas and straddled before the grate, hands thrust in his trousers-pockets, fixing his gaze on the empty firebars. Both young men were looking at nothing so much as their frustrated meal and the wreck of their whole evening. Their parents' quarrel became louder; words charged through the short lobby. The man's voice bawled: 'Shure the bloody towel stinks like a water-closet;' the woman's skirled passionately: 'Ye're a liar! It wis fresh two days ago!' and her husband roared: 'Dirty Trollop! Ye're not fit tae keep a house!' and Mrs Macdonnel, her shriek becoming inarticulate: 'Jimmy! Are ye goin' tae let 'im call yer mother that? Ay, hit me! Dare tae pit yer haun oan me an' Ah'll land ye in the Nick! Jimmy!'

Eddy ran into the parlour, pale and trembling, crying to his brothers: 'Oh, me da's gaun tae hit me maw! Will ye no' come ben?' They received him in bored silence, then John swung his head round sharply and bellowed: 'Ach, stoap greetin'! Let thim fight it oot, shure wan's as bad as the other!' John was the dandy of the family, the darling of many girls. His curled, gold hair, glinting above full, round cheeks smudged with labour, gave him a cherubic look, his raucous shout contrasting with his boyish mouth. At length he said softly: 'Ach, stoap greetin'! Ah'll see naebuddy gets hurt!' and stuck out his chin.

At that moment Mrs Macdonnel rushed in, screeching back at her husband while jabbing hairpins in her greyish, red hair, her eyes bloodshot with passion, her body quivering with vindictiveness. From the kitchen volleyed after her: 'Dirty trollop! Dirty trollop!' and a peal of gibing laughter. She yelled enraged at her sons till the veins of her neck bulged, asking them if they were 'her sons or no'?' and screamed through the lobby: 'Ye bloody whoremaister!' then Eddy lost touch with reality in a nightmare of violence. Mr Macdonnel dashed into the parlour; Jimmy and John jumped to their mother's side and their father thrust his head in their faces, sneering, mocking: 'Whit are ye goin' to do, eh? My, Ah'm frightened o' ye'se! Ah'm shakin' like a leaf!' and he sniggered, malicious, provoking, balancing his hands on his hips, his shirtsleeves rolled to the armpits, his shirt still tucked in his braces, showing his breast as white as a woman's. Over Jimmy's shoulder he shouted at his wife: 'Dirty trollop, yer face scunners me! Ah wish tae God Ah'd never seen it!' As he half-turned to make for the kitchen, Jimmy said loudly, 'Och, da, ye shouldnae call her that! She's sober an' made yer dinner!' and he wheeled round with death-pale face, shouting: 'Ye young whelp, Ah'll smash ye!' Jimmy parried his blow and Mr Macdonnel, maddened at his defiance, launched his fists at his breast. They grappled as hatefully as enemies; John leapt on his father; fists swung and thrust wildly, smashing on flesh and bone; the parlour table crashed to the floor; Mrs Macdonnel egged on her sons; Eddy wailed, pleading with his da not to fight, while alarmed neighbours thumped on the stairhead door and under the window in the street a crowd gathered.

Mrs Macdonnel screamed repeatedly at Eddy: 'Go an' fetch the polis!' but he stood panic-struck, expecting every moment to see Jimmy lift the heavy poker from the fender. Maybe his da's skull would be smashed! Maybe Jimmy would be hung! Pressing away from the fight, into the corner against the bedboard of the cavity bed, he vividly saw a scene of his father stretched on the floor in a pool of blood and his brothers kneeling over him, moaning: 'Rise up, da! Rise up!' and he felt the silence that follows murder.

His mother clawed her hot nails into his neck, pushing him out of the room, yelling to him to 'Get the polis!' Then she rushed back to the fight, pummelling her husband's back. Infuriated by her treacherous blows, Mr Macdonnel wrenched away from his sons, turned with hatred in his eyes and dashed his fist full in her face. She hurtled into an armchair of imitation leather standing by the window and clapped her hands over her eyes, wailing hideously, as the brothers rushed on their father, Jimmy shouting: 'Ye bastard! I'll kill ye for that!'

Eddy rushed terrified into the street to find a constable, and three neighbours hurried in past him as he opened the door. The badly-lit landing was crowded with tenants from the upper two storeys and people from the street. Shame

mingled with Eddy's panic and grief as he rushed downstairs followed by sympathetic, scandalized comments:
'Eh, it's wee Eddy Macdonnel.' 'Puir wee sowl!' 'Ach,
they Macdonnels are aye fightin'! They should be chucked
oot o' the proaperty!' and he asked crazily in his heart why
his da and maw weren't happy and peaceful like the parents
of other boys.

When he reached the closemouth the crowd on the pavement were craning their necks up at the Macdonnels' window, peering into the dark close hoping to see the fight
issue into the street. Some shipyard apprentices going home
from work were enjoying the fight, trying to surpass one
another in witty observations, and Eddy stood in tears
while their remarks riddled him with misery. In the calami-
tous, high-pitched Glasgow accent others were saying:
'The wumman'l be kilt! Sumbuddy oaght tae stoap it!'
'Whaur's the polis?' 'Ach, the polis are nivir haundy when
they're wantit!' Street-fights and tenement brawls were
commonplaces to them, and a squat, bow-legged apprentice
shouted after Eddy: 'Hi, wee yin! Wha's winnin'?' as
he broke through the group of shawled women, rough-clad
men and boys, with his mother's moans ringing in his head,
and ran to the corner of the opposite block, staring round
wildly for a policeman. A dwarfish woman of a size familiar
in Glasgow's poorer streets, with a blackened eye and other,
older marks of manhandling on her small, monkey face,
cried to him through broken yellow teeth: 'There's a polis
up yonner b' Teacher's pub! Rin quick, sonny, an' ye'll
catch 'im!' Eddy raced up to the cross street of louring
tenements, past low-browed gaslit shops, and sobbed his
news to an immensely tall constable who leaned against
the wall of a main-road public-house gazing vacantly at a
pub on the opposite corner.

The big Irishman listened coldly. Twenty years of arrest-
ing drunks and quieting family quarrels had not won him
promotion. He was hardened against demented urchins
accosting him with wails that murder would happen if
he 'didnae come the noo!' He eased up massively from
his slight lean, untucking thumbs from his belt. 'Two
hundert Gowan Street, ye said?' he observed stolidly.

'It's Macdonnel yer name is?' Eddy hung his head and the policeman said: 'Shure, Oi know yer house as well as the back of me han'. All right, Oi'll be down as soon as me mate arrives,' and he ambled away in the opposite direction. Eddy looked after him, then ran home. The crowd had gone from the close; that meant nothing tragic had happened and a great oppression lifted from his breast; the front-room was still alight; he rushed upstairs, found the door ajar, and entered the kitchen.

His mother had been put to bed and his Aunt Kate was shrilly calling down the law on Mr Macdonnel's head while she bathed her sister's injured face from a big basin of bloodstained, lukewarm water that stood on the crowded table with the loaf, the half-empty bottle of Worcester sauce, the dismembered cruet and the three men's dinners, which had congealed, cold on their plates, the sliced parboiled onions sticking out of the stiffened mincemeat like shards from sand.

Aunt Kate, spirting moisture from the piece of flannel she dipped and squeezed, keened: 'Oh, Mary! Oh, ma bonny wee sister, he's kilt ye! He's kilt ye!' while two neighbours lamented with her. 'Ay!' wheezed Mrs Houston, fourteen stone of dark Scotch matronhood tightly wedged in a grandfather chair at the fireplace, 'it'll be Goad's mercy if he hisnae marked her fur life, the puir saul!'; and, 'Ay!' contributed Mrs Brown, a wee, red-haired buxom woman, from her chair by the dresser. Their 'Ays' trailed, slow, comfortable, like strokes on Mrs Macdonnel's cheek.

Mrs Macdonnel was moaning: 'Oh, ma hied! Ma heid!' while Aunt Kate shot her hands to heaven in passionate anger, unaware of water streaming down her arm from the flannel clutched in her hand. 'My Christ! He widnae hiv laid a haun oan ye if Ah'd been here!' she screamed. 'Ah'll pit him in the nick fur six months if he daurs show his face here again! B' the Holy Mother o' God Ah wull! The dirty coward!' Her neat little figure trembled, she clenched her fists till the knuckles shone, then next moment she became maudlin and fired up again as she noticed her nephew.

Her restless, dark eyes blazed. 'Hiv ye no' broaght the

polis?' she cried; 'hiv ye nae hert fur yer mother?' She left the bedside and shook him hysterically by the shoulders. Eddy snuffled; 'Ah've tell't thim tae come. They said they'll be up the noo! Is me maw awful bad?' His mother groaned, Aunt Kate darted to her, but the injured woman pushed her hand fretfully away. 'Ye're hurtin' me, Katy! Pit a vinegar-cloath oan ma heid. It's loapin' like fire.' Aunt Kate searched vainly in the skirt-pocket under her apron while directing Mrs Houston to get a bottle of vinegar from the press, and Mrs Brown bounced from her chair, producing, like a conjuror, a big snow-white handkerchief from beneath her soiled, sour apron. She offered it proudly. Aunt Kate thanked her and unfolded and refolded it expertly, while Mrs Houston toddled up with an old whisky-bottle full of malt vinegar, labelled, 'McNish's Heather Dew. Full Strength;' and while she poured the brown liquid into the basin, Aunt Kate applied the popular remedy for every kind of headache.

'Ay, it's a gran' thing the vinegar!' obœed Mrs Houston.

There's naethin' like it when ye've been oan the ran-dan,' said Aunt Kate.

'Did Ah ever tell ye'se aboot ma auld man?' said Mrs Brown. 'Hoo he yince mistook a boatle o' vinegar for a boatle o' whisky? It was twa weeks syne come the morn's nicht . . . or was it three weeks come next Setterday?' Mrs Brown paused with a vague stare, straining at her memory; Aunt Kate, with a huge safety-pin in her teeth, looked alarmed at the ceiling and nodded to Mrs Houston. Mrs Brown was away on one of her endless, digressive stories and must be stopped. Mrs Houston, with unusual sharpness for her, saw the danger and said slyly: 'Mebbe yer sister wad be the better o' anither wee hauf, Katy,' and Aunt Kate sweetly asked Mrs Brown if she would mind running across to Reid's pub for 'a half-mutchkin.' Mrs Brown, having now completely forgotten she was going to tell a story, crossed the landing to her own house, reappeared in a fawn-coloured shawl, took a large hip-bottle from the press, went out and returned with it half-full of glowing liquid, her breath positively proving that she had drunk a hasty tot to her own health.

They all livened up at the prospect of 'anither wee drap' and a long gossip over the fight and Mrs Macdonnel's condition. Eddy approached the bed and looked at his mother. Her arm, red-raw with years of scrubbing in water filled with washing-soda, hung limply down the sideboard of the bed. Her eyes were bruised and puffed up, her lips swollen; blood had congealed in her nostrils. With the stained handkerchief round her forehead, her russet hair disarrayed, her crimson face, she was a horrible effigy of womanhood. Eddy began to sob bitterly and impulsively faced the three women, shaking clenched, small fists at them, at lunatic, incomprehensible cruel life. Burning with bitter desire to avenge his mother, he cried at them: 'Where's me da? Ah'll kill 'im!' and his mother mumbled sentimentally through her swollen lips: 'Och, ma ain wee son. He's greetin' fur me!' and she turned proud eyes to her neighbours. 'D'ye hear 'im? He's greetin' fur me!'

They all praised him for his loyalty to his mother; Aunt Kate took him against her breast but he pulled away from her, ashamed, and stumbled into the dark lobby, his fists crushed to his eyes, to shed his tears. Looking up, he saw his father's working cap, white with concrete-dust, hanging from a peg. The sight of it surged back his ebbing rage. He seized it and gazing at it hatefully, spat on it. His finger felt a rent in the inside and he tore at the lining, greased and soiled with the sweat of his father's head, till it hung from the cloth. He tried to tear the cap across but the thick, tough tweed resisted his strength. Cursing obscenely, he twisted the peak till he felt the cardboard softly snap in his grip. Then he quietly opened the stairhead door, threw the cap contemptuously out on the landing and stood awhile, gazing at it where it fell under the landing light, the torn lining trailing over, the twisted peak sticking up absurdly. With all his heart he wished it was his father lying there, beaten, broken and abject, like that rag of a cap.

He closed the door and returned to the kitchen. While the women gossiped he stood against the dresser looking at the big volume of *Pickwick Papers* which lay where he had thrown it down, beside a small wicker shopping-basket, two dirty cups and a quart milk-jug. The hours of delight it had promised had been ruthlessly torn out of his day. He thought no more of the jolly, human world enclosed in a book. After his tears, after all his tremblings and terror, he had fallen cold and dull. Aunt Kate, while serving cups of whisky, had distractedly placed her cup on the book and spilt some over it. A ring of whisky-wet and several small spatters were raising discoloured blisters on the blue cover, but Eddy turned indifferently away and watched his aunt putting the three dinners of mince and onions in the oven, saying she'd keep them nice and warm for his brothers, then he walked unhappily into the parlour and was surprised to find Jimmy sitting alone in the dark.

The brothers had lost sight of their father in the gaslit streets; John had gone to have a meal in some eating-house; Jimmy had slipped back home and had been sitting in the parlour for some time, on the utmost edge of a chair, hands firmly clasped between his knees, bent forward, his dark, aquiline face blank with pessimism. He sometimes sat like this for an hour or more, contemplating despair.

Startled by Eddy's entrance he leapt up, flung aloft his arms and tore at his hair, crying: 'Christ! There's never any peace in this hoose! Whit are they auld cows yammerin' at ben there? Yap! Yap! Yap! Night an' moarin' they're at it so that a fella canny get a decent wash or bite in cumfurt!' He wrenched off his stinking work-clothes, vociferating harshly: 'By Christ! Ah'll get away tae sea again! Ah'll get a ship taemorra an' never come back tae this lousy hole!'

The loud cries of his eldest brother ended the lad's evocation of the past. He had seen his brother sitting before him as plainly as he saw him six years ago. The whole mean tragedy had been re-enacted more vividly than any stage-drama because it had been played out in the immortal light of the soul, because within him was all the fear, hatred, pain and violence, the goodness and meanness of the principal actors. He had come out of their loins. They were in him; he was in them.

'Never any peace!' Every member of the family had cried so at one time or another but none had made an intelligent move to establish peace. He recalled how his mother had become really ill late that night. The doctor was summoned and discovered that her nose was broken. For three weeks she had to attend hospital daily and Eddy accompanied her through interminable vigils in the outpatient's waiting-room; vigils that began at noon and ended at five or six in the evening in a listless queue at the dispensary window. His father had shown up after a month, slouching in unkempt, unshaven, out of work, weeping in shoddy contrition, swearing he would make it up to his wife for all the harm he had done her. She had refused to prosecute him even though urged to do so by the doctor, in part because she quailed before the scandal of a police-court appearance, partly because she still had an inkling of tenderness for him, partly because she felt she now had a virtuous ascendancy over him if ever he returned. She had only to remind him of her disfigurement and threaten him with imprisonment if ever he showed signs of his old tyranny and for a long time she nagged him without fear. But he reasserted himself soon after he was in employment, though he never lashed out at her with the same reckless ferocity.

The lad heard his mother stir and mutter and turned to see her lift a hand to her eyes. He had forgotten to draw the curtain across her face and he stepped over and drew it. A spasm of bitterness against her flashed through him as he regarded the mean set of her mouth. She had often aroused violence by her niggardly behaviour at meals and her sheer inability to control her irritation at any time. But the peace of Poetry filled him again, quelling antagonism, and a great pity for his parents welled up. He exonerated both of them. They were victims of 'The System.' Capitalism created poverty. Poverty made brutes and wastrels of human beings. Socialism would bring plenty and freedom for all mankind. The pamphlets his friend had lent him proved it so clearly. With youthful enthusiasm he foresaw the end of social inequalities. There would be a 'Glorious Revolution.' All over the world 'wage-slaves would cast off their chains.' He saw the 'New Order' at work. Men and women, magically altered, living like clear-eyed, happy beings in whom love and courtesy never died. But he was a

Catholic. Could he be a Socialist also? Hanging from the centre wall of the whitewashed bed was a cheap, china Christ whose torso ended in a holy-water font, dry and dust-filled, from which dangled three strings of rosary-beads and a dirty scapular, misshapen with body-sweat. Over the head of his sleeping sister hung a companion figure of the Holy Virgin; her right hand disrobing a profusely bleeding heart, her left raised in benediction, she gazed with a silly simper on the drink-logged face of Mrs Macdonnel. He looked up at them guiltily; their tiny eyes seemed alive, seemed to accuse him of sacrilege. But a priest, he reminded himself, had written a pamphlet to show that Catholicism and Socialism were compatible. Was it true that the Pope had cast that priest from the Church? The terrible word 'Excommunication' thundered in his mind and he felt the frown of the mighty Pontiff bent on him. He had heard speakers at meetings say that Christ was just a man, that the Immaculate Conception was nonsense, that Religion was 'the dope of the people,' 'the safety-valve of Revolution,' but his slow mind still crawled among the terrors of purgatory and hell-fire. He imagined his mother's fury had she known his thoughts. For her the word 'Socialism' meant damnation. She had yelled at him insanely: 'A' they Socialists are bloody atheists. Ye canny be good if ye don't believe in a Goad! It's better tae turn Prodesan than be a Socialist,' just as she had railed when she discovered him reading a Labour pamphlet and when she shouted his friend Neil Mudge from her door.

He returned to the fireplace, picked up his book from the chair, and stood gazing through the open window into the brooding, blue darkness that pressed on the sleeping tenements, almost convinced that the eyes of the idols followed him, chiding him for his unstable faith, as he reopened the anthology, glad to escape the pains of thought. In Poetry he had only to see and feel things.

The night had become hotter so that the very stars seemed to hang listlessly, stifled by heat. Down in the back-court Corporation dustmen were tipping out the middens, loudly clanging the galvanized-iron bins as they emptied and replaced them in the square, stone shelters, filling the courts' well of quiet space with din and echoing talk as they bore away in creels on their backs, like fishwives, the garbage of fifty houses. The naked wick-lights on their hats fluttered as they carried their loads out to the street cart. A window squealed open and a man's voice shouted: 'Hi, doon there! Make less noayse! Ye've waken't the wean!' The dustmen laughed and one cried: 'Haud yer wheehst, man! Awa back tae bed an' keep yer wife warrm!' The window was slammed violently.

Young Macdonnel was chanting the verses of Herrick again with lowered voice. Shaping the words intensified his power of vision. He felt the higher lift of April skies, the mad race of clouds rushed by Spring winds, the stir of Earth to new life. The perfume, colour and music of rebirth flooded his senses, quickened by the lyric, a poem of death and ending, yet in its beauty, rich with immortality and human promise, because every lovely form, from whatever medium, shaped by man, is a little pace away from the brute to the Godhead in him. The beauty the lyric sang was more real to him than all the arguments and statistics of propaganda pamphlets, and all humanitarian platitudes. He did not reason, he felt and imaged the future. In his moment of illumination, over all the ugliness, misery and brutality he had seen in his home, that he knew malformed men's lives in his city and everywhere in the world, he saw the beauty, poise and nobility of Poetry triumph at last. Yes, man would learn the art of living, but for yet a long while he would wash out evil in his own blood, until at last, utterly weary of greed, mistrust and fear, hatred and murder, he would discover humility and gentleness. His heart knew that such loveliness would animate future mankind and, somehow, he associated it with his hazy, Socialist ideas as he felt the poet's intense appeal. Boldly, like a being defying evil and death, he lifted his head and held out his hands to the night.

A Macdonnel party was nearly always an informal affair. Guests were never invited by card or telephone. They just 'got to know' and drifted in, irresistibly drawn by the prospect of free drink and uproarious song. John Macdonnel always insisted that there were people in the Gorbals who possessed second-sight in the matter of parties. Fellows like Squinty Traynor, Baldy Flynn and bowlegged Rab Macpherson and ladies like wee Mrs Rombach, Tittering Tessie and wee Minnie Milligan—though why she always showed up at parties when she was a Rechabite and never touched a drop, he couldn't understand—could smell a wake or a wedding a mile off and always crept in at the exact moment when there was still plenty of drink going and everybody was too drunk to ask or care if they had been invited.

Sometimes the nucleus of a Macdonnel party was formed in the Ladies' Parlour of a local pub from which Mrs Macdonnel would emerge with some shawled cronies and confer on the pavement, deciding whether they should continue their tippling in another Ladies' Parlour or in one of their own kitchens. Owing to this erratic behaviour on the part of his wife, Mr Macdonnel occasionally returned from his day's work to find her absent—when he went round her friends' kitchens in search of her—or at home with several lady friends all jolly and mildly drunk. If he was hungry and in sober mood his icy glare sent all his wife's friends flying like snow in a wintry blast, but if he yearned for spirits he thawed and deferred his displeasure till the following morning when the mere thought of work was a nightmare to his aching head.

Every time Jimmy Macdonnel came home from sea there was a party and a few more after it till his pay of several

months was burned right up. Even if Mrs Macdonnel had
been six months teetotal she couldn't resist taking one wee
nip to celebrate her son's return and that wee nip somehow
multiplied, had bairns, as she would laughingly tell you
herself.

Returning from his last voyage before the Great War,
Jimmy Macdonnel, after a year's absence as cook on a
tramp steamship, was the originator of a famous Macdonnel
party. It was a bright July Saturday afternoon when Jimmy
unexpectedly arrived. A delicious smell of Irish stew was still
hanging around the Macdonnel kitchen. Mrs Macdonnel
was a rare cook and Mr Macdonnel who loved her cooking
had dropped into a smiling drowse, dazed by his enormous
meal. At the open window Eddy Macdonnel was seated on
the dishboard of the sink muttering to himself the Rules of
Syntax out of an English Grammar, asking himself how it
was that Donald Hamilton could repeat from memory whole
pages of the Grammar and yet couldn't write a grammatical
sentence, while he, who could hardly memorise a couple
of Rules, could write perfect English with the greatest
of ease. But he drove himself to the unpleasant exercise
of memorising, resisting the temptation to bask in the
powerful sunshine and listen to the children playing at
an old singing-game, The Bonny Hoose O' Airlie O. The
children were gathered near the back-court wash-house,
round the robber and his wife. First the little girl sang:

> *Ah'll no' be a robber's wife,*
> *Ah'll no' die wi' your penknife*
> *Ah'll no' be a robber's wife*
> *Doon b' the bonny hoose o' Airlie, O,*

then the boy answered, taking her hand,

> *Oh you sall be a robber's wife,*
> *An' ye'll die wi' my penknife*
> *You sall be a robber's wife*
> *Doon b' the bonny hoose o' Airlie, O.*

The old ballad tune seemed to come out of the heart of
young Scotland, out of the childhood of his country's life.
Eddy wanted to dream into that bygone poetry. Ach!
He drove his mind again to memorizing the lesson for
his nightschool class. Mr Henderson, the English teacher

had a biting tongue for lazy students. He turned back the page, started again, and his muttered Rules mingled with the snores of his father and his mother's whispers as she sat at the table scribbling a shopping-list on a scrap of paper and continually pausing to count the silver in her purse.

Just then there was a knock at the stairhead door and Mrs Macdonnel, touching back her greying, reddish hair, rose in a fluster to open, exclaimed, 'My Goad, it's Jimmy!' and returned followed by a slim, dapper young man of twenty-nine, with bronzed features, in the uniform of a petty-officer of the Merchant Service and carrying a sailor's kitbag which he dumped on the floor.

'Did ye no' ken Ah was comin' hame the day?' he asked resentfully; 'Ah, sent ye a postcard fae Marsels.'

'Och, no son!' said his mother, blaming in her heart those 'forrin' postcairds' which always bewildered her. 'Shure yer da would hiv come tae meet the boat. Ye said the twenty-seeventh,' and she began searching in a midget bureau on the dresser to prove her words, then she gazed mystified at the 'Carte Postale' with the view of Marseilles Harbour. 'Och, Ah'm haverin'!' she cried, 'it says here the seeventeenth!'

'Ach away! Ye're daft!' said Jimmy, 'How could ye mistake a "one" for a "two"?'

Mr Macdonnel woke up, rubbing his eyes, Eddy got down from the dishboard, closing his Grammar; and they all stared at Jimmy in silent wonder. He certainly looked trim as a yacht in his blue reefer suit, white shirt, collar and black tie, but they weren't amazed at his spruceness nor by his unexpected arrival but by the fact that he stood there as sober as a priest. For ten years Jimmy had been coming home from sea at varying intervals and had never been able to get up the stairs unassisted; and here he was, after a six months' voyage, not even giving off a smell of spirits. Mr Macdonnel put on his glasses to have a better look at him. What was wrong with Jimmy? They wondered if he was ill, then the agonizing thought that he had been robbed occurred simultaneously to the old folk, and Jimmy was about to ask them what they were all looking at when his mother collected herself and embraced him and his father shook his hand, patting his shoulder.

Jimmy flushed with annoyance at his mother's sentiment as he produced from his kitbag a large plug of ship's tobacco for his da, a Spanish shawl of green silk, with big crimson roses on it for his mother, and a coloured plaster-of-paris plaque of Cologne Cathedral for his Aunt Kate, then, blushing slightly, he took his seaman's book from his pocket and showed them the photograph of a young woman, 'That's Meg,' he said, 'Meg Macgregor. She's a fisher-girl. I met her at the herring-boats when me ship called in at Peterhead.'

His mother was delighted with his taste and knew immediately why he had arrived sober. She passed the photograph to her husband, who beamed at it and said heartily, 'My, she's a stunner, Jimmy boy! A proper stunner! She'll create a sensation roun' here!' Mr Macdonnel usually awoke ill-tempered from his after-dinner naps, but his indigestion vanished like magic as he imagined the glorious spree they were going to have on Jimmy's six months' pay; and he swore he had never seen such a beautiful young woman as Meg Macgregor. Then Jimmy startled them all by announcing, as if he was forcing it out of himself: 'Meg's awfu' good-livin', mother, an' she's asked me tae stoap drinkin' for the rest o' ma life. Ah've promised her Ah will.'

Mr Macdonnel glared wildly at his son, then gave a sour look at the portrait and, handing it back without a word, rolled down his sleeves and pulled up his braces. He was dumbfounded. What had come over his son Jimmy? Teetotal for the rest of his life! Was he going to lose his head over that silly-faced girl? Mrs Macdonnel studied Jimmy with plaintive anxiety while he described Meg's beauty and goodness. 'Ach, she was made tae be adored b' everybody!' he said, and warned his mother to steer clear of the drink and keep her house in order to receive his beloved, whom he had invited to come and stay with the family.

His mother promised to love Meg as a daughter and silently hoped that the girl would stay at home. She was too old now to be bothered by a healthy young woman with managing ways. Jimmy swore he hadn't touched a drop since he had sailed from Peterhead and described the tortures of his two-days' self-denial so vividly that his father shivered and hurried into the parlour to get his coat and vest. Jimmy said he was finished with the sea and booze; sick of squandering money. He was determined to settle on shore, get married, and spend all his money on Meg's happiness.

A miserly gleam beamed in his mother's eye when he said that and she wondered how much his new devotion would limit his contribution to her purse. Jimmy took a bundle of notes from his inside breast pocket and handed her thirty pounds, reminding her that she had already drawn advance-sums from his shipping-office. Mrs Macdonnel said he was too kind and offered to return five notes with a drawing-back movement, but Jimmy refused them with a bluff insincere gesture, for there was a flash of regret in his eye as she tucked the wad in her purse, but, with genuine feeling he invited her and his da out to drink him welcome home. 'Ah'll have a lemonade,' he said, gazing piously at the ceiling as though at the Holy Grail. His mother thought he was being too harsh with himself. 'Shure ye'll hiv a wee nip wi' me an' yer da, son. A wee nip won't kill ye!' she laughed slyly, and Jimmy promised to drink a shandygaff just to please her, sighing with relief when he thought of the dash of beer in the lemonade. He called his father who came in from the parlour wrestling with a white dickey which he was trying to dispose evenly on his chest. 'Ah won't keep ye a jiffy, laddie!' he said, facing the mirror and fervently praying that the smell of the pub would restore poor Jimmy to his senses.

As she put on her old brown shawl Mrs Macdonnel was disappointed at Jimmy's insistence that they should go to an out-of-the-way pub. She wanted to show off her bonny son; he was so braw; so like a captain! She imagined the greetings they would get going down the long street.

'Ay, ye've won hame, Jimmy, boay? My, ye're lookin' fine, mun! Goash, ye oaght tae be a prood wumman the day, Mrs Macdonnel! Jimmy's a credit tae ye!' and she foretasted the old sweet thrill of envy and flattery. But Jimmy said he would never drink again with the corner-boys. Love had made a new man of him!

When they had all gone out Eddy Macdonnel hurried into the small side bedroom to read the book on PSYCHOLOGY AND MORALS he had borrowed from the Corporation Library. Inspired by Jimmy's miraculous conversion he crouched over the volume, concentrating fiercely on the chapters headed WILL POWER AND SIN, and his heart swelled with a reformer's zeal as he saw himself one day applying all these marvellous laws to the human race, hypnotizing countless millions of people into sobriety.

Three hours later he heard a loud clamour in the street below. Throwing his book on the bed he raised the window and looked over and his uplifted heart sank down, for he saw Jimmy stumbling happily up the street with his Aunt Kate's hat on his head and his arm round his father's neck. They were lustily singing 'The Bonny Lass O' Ballochmyle'. Mr Macdonnel's dickey was sticking out like the wings of a moulted swan and large bottles of whisky waggled from the pockets of the two men. Behind them, laughing like witches, came Mrs Macdonnel and Aunt Kate with the sailor's cap on, followed by six of Jimmy's pals who were carrying between them three large crates of bottled beer.

Eddy closed the window quickly and stared sadly at the wall. Jimmy, the idol of his dream, himself had shattered it! As he turned into the lobby, Jimmy opened the stairhead door and thrust his pals into the kitchen, which already seemed crowded with only two members of the family. John Macdonnel, now a fair young man of twenty-five, just home from overtime at the shipyards, leant in his oilstained working clothes against the gas stove, reading about the Celtic and Rangers match in the Glasgow *Evening Times* and regretting that he had missed a hard-fought game which his team had won. With a wild 'whoopee' Jimmy embraced his brothers, who smiled with embarrassment. John was proud of Jimmy's prestige with the corner boys, though he knew it was the worthless esteem for a fool and his money; Eddy saw Jimmy as a grand romantic figure, a great chef who had cooked for a millionaire on his yacht and had seen all the capital cities of the world, and Jimmy's kitbag, lying against a home-made stool by the dresser, stuffed with cook's caps and jackets, radiated the fascination of travel.

Aunt Kate, a tiny, dark woman of remarkable vitality, went kissing all her nephews in turn and the party got into full swing. Liquor was soon winking from tumblers, tea-cups, egg-cups—anything that could hold drink—and Aunt Kate, while directing the young men to bring chairs from the parlour, sang 'A Guid New Year Tae Ane An' A',' disregarding the fact that it was only summer time, and Jimmy, thinking a nautical song was expected from him, sang 'A Life On The Ocean Wave!' in a voice as flat as stale beer that drowned his Aunt's pleasant treble. But somebody shouted that he sang as well as John McCormack and he sat down with a large tumbler of whisky, looking as if he thought so himself.

Then Aunt Kate told everybody about her marvellous meeting with Jimmy whose voice she had heard through the partition as she sat in the Ladies' Parlour in The Rob Roy Arms and Eddy learned how his brother had fallen. Jimmy, it appeared, felt he must toast Meg Macgregor in just one glass of something strong; that dash of beer in lemonade had infuriated his thirst and in a few minutes he had downed several glasses of the right stuff to his sweetheart, proving to his aunt's delight that he was still the same old jovial Jimmy.

John Macdonnel, all this while, was going to and fro, stumbling over outthrust feet between the small bedroom and kitchen sprucing himself up to go out and meet his girl. From feet to waist he was ready for love. His best brown trousers with shoes to match adorned his lower half, while his torso was still robed in a shirt blackened with shipyard oil and rust. He washed himself at the sink, laughing at his Aunt's story, then turned, drying himself, to argue with his mother about his 'clean change.' Mrs Macdonnel waved her cup helplessly, saying she couldn't help the indifference of laundrymen and John implored Eddy to shoot downstairs and find if the family washing had arrived at the receiving-office of the Bonnyburn Laundries.

Visitors kept dropping in for a word with the sailor and delayed their departure while the drinks went round. Rumour had spread the report that Jimmy Macdonnel was home flush with money and a Macdonnel party was always a powerful attraction. The gathering was livening up. Two quart bottles of whisky had been absorbed and beer was frothing against every lip when Eddy returned triumphantly waving a big brown paper parcel in John's direction.

It was at the right psychological moment, when a slight lull in the merriment was threatening, that Rab Macpherson romped from his hiding-place in the doorway into the middle of the kitchen and suddenly burst out singing at the top of his voice:

> Le—et Kings an' courteers rise an' fa'
> This wurrld has minny turns,
> But brighter beams abune them a'
> The star o' Rabbie Burns!

Rab's legs were very bow and wee Tommy Mohan, who was talking to his pal John Macdonnel at the sink, sunk down on his hunkers and gazed under his palm, like a sailor looking over the sea, away through Rab's legs all the time he was singing. Everybody was convulsed with laughter and Mrs Macdonnel was so pleased with Rab, that she got up, still laughing, and with her arm around his neck, gave him a good measure of whisky in a small cream jug.

Suddenly everybody fell silent to listen to Jimmy Macdonnel, who had been up since three in the morning and half-asleep was trolling away to himself, 'The Lass That Made The Bed For Me' and Mrs Steedman, a big-bosomed Orangewoman, startled the company by shouting, 'Good aul' Rabbie Burns! He ken't whit a wumman likes the maist!' There was a roar of laughter at this reminder of the poet's lechery, then Aunt Kate insisted that Mr Macdonnel should sing, 'I Dreamt That I Dwelt In Marble Halls,' while her sister, Mrs Macdonnel, asked him for 'The Meeting Of The Waters' because it reminded her of their honeymoon in Ireland. Mr Macdonnel, assisted by the table, swayed to his feet as pompously as Signor Caruso, twirled his moustache, stuck his thumbs behind his lapels, like the buskers of Glasgow back-courts, and 'hemmed' very loudly to silence the arguing sisters. He always sang with his eyes closed and when the gaslight shone on his glasses he looked like a man with four eyes, one pair shut, the other brilliantly open. He honestly believed he had a fine tenor voice and with swelled chest he bellowed:

Yes! Let me like a soldier fall, upon some open plain!
Me breast boldly bared to meet the ball
That blots out every stain!

The china shivered on the shelves above the dresser and Eddy Macdonnel, lost in some vision of bravery, stared with pride at his father. Halfway through the ballad, Mr Macdonnel forgot the words but sang on, 'tra-laing' here, pushing in his own words there, and sat down well satisfied to a din of handclaps and stamping feet.

Jimmy was blasted into wakefulness by his father's song and he washed himself sober and led out all the young men to help him buy more drink. When they returned, well-stocked, half-an-hour later, Mr Macdonnel had the whole crowd singing.

I'll knock a hole in McCann for knocking a hole in
me can!
McCann knew me can was new
I'd only had it a day or two,
I gave McCann me can to fetch me a pint of stout
An' McCann came running in an' said
That me can was running out!

This was Mr Macdonnel's winning number at every spree and the refrain had echoed several times through the open windows to the street and back-court before the young men returned. In the comparative silence of clinking bottles and glasses, Jimmy told his laughing guests of the night when he had served up beer in chamber-pots to a party of corner-boys. A dozen chamber-pots were arrayed round the table and twelve youths sat gravely before them while Jimmy muttered a Turkish grace over the beer and told them that was the way the Turks drank their drink and they believed him because he had been six times round the world.

When Aunt Kate had recovered from her delight in this story she asked Eddy to run up and see if her 'bonny wee man' was home from the gasworks. Eddy raced up to the top storey, knocked on a door, and started back as his uncle's gargoyle face thrust out at him and barked, 'Where's Katey? Am Oi a man or a mouse? B' the Holy Saint Pathrick Oi'll murther the lazy cow!' Eddy said faintly, 'Jimmy's home an' we're having a party. Will ye come down?' and Mr Hewes followed him downstairs muttering threats of vengeance on his wife for neglecting his tea.

The gathering had overflowed into the parlour when Eddy returned with the gasworker behind him; the lobby was crowded with newly-arrived guests listening to Aunt Kate singing 'The Irish Emigrant's Farewell;' the eyes of all the women were wet with film-star tears and the singer herself seemed to be seeing a handsome Irish youth as she looked straight at her husband standing in the kitchen doorway and returning her stare with a malignant leer. Aunt Kate filled a large cup with whisky from a bottle on the dresser and, still singing, handed it to him with a mock bow. On similar occasions Mr Hewes had been known to dash the cup from her hand and walk out and desert her for six months, but this time he seized it, swallowed the drink in one gulp, hitched up his belt and joined the party.

Eddy crushed a way through to his seat on the sink and watched his uncle, who, seated beside Mr Macdonnel, eyed with hostility every move of his popular wife. There was an excess of spite in Mr Hewes and he loved to hate people. Time, accident and ill-nature had ruined his face. A livid scar streamed from his thin hair down his right temple to his lip; his broken nose had reset all to one side, his few teeth were black and his little moustache as harsh as barbed wire; and with a blackened sweatrag round his neck he looked like a being from some underworld come to spy on human revels. He was called upon for a song when the applause for his wife had ended, and he stood up and roared, glaring at her:

> Am Oi a man, or am Oi a mouse
> Or am I a common artful dodger?
> Oi want to know who is master of my house!
> Is ut me or Micky Flanagan the lodger?

Shouts of 'ongcore!' egged him on to sing the verse several

times, his glare at his smiling wife intensifying with each repetition. He was suspected of having composed the song himself and the neighbours always knew he was going to desert his wife when he came up the stairs singing it. His whole body was humming like a dynamo after two large cups of Heather Dew and as his wife began chanting an old Irish jig he started to dance. Throwing off his jacket he roared 'B' Jasus!' tightened his belt and rolled up his sleeves, revealing thick leather straps round his wrists, and his hob-nailed boots beat a rapid deafening tattoo on the spot of floor inside the surrounding feet. His wife's chant became shriller and the whole company began clapping hands, stamping and yelling wild 'hoochs!' that drove the little gasworker to frenzy. John Macdonnel, all dressed to go out with a new bowler hat perched on his head, lifted a poker from the grate and thrust it into the dancer's hand. Mr Hewes tried to twirl it round his head between finger and thumb like a drum-major, then smashed it on the floor in passionate chagrin at his failure. 'B' Jasus Oi could dance ye'se all under the table!' he yelled, and with head and torso held stiff and arms working like pistons across his middle, he pranced like an enraged cockerel.

Faster he hopped from heel to heel, still packed with energy after a hard day shovelling in a hot atmosphere; sweat glistened on his grey hair and beaded his blackened cheeks; he twisted his feet in and out in awkward attempts at fancy steps and looked as if he would fly asunder in his efforts to beat the pace of his accompanists; then, with a despairing yell of 'B' Jasus!' he stopped suddenly, gasped, 'Och, Oi 'm bate!' and hurled dizzily behind foremost into his chair.

It was a hefty piece of furniture but it couldn't stand up to his violence; with a loud crack its four legs splayed out and the gasworker crashed like a slung sack into the hearth, smashing the polished plate-shelf sticking out beneath the oven; his head struck heavily the shining bevel of the range; the snapped chair-back lay over his head, and there was a roar of laughter which stopped when he was seen to lie still among the wreckage.

His wife and Mr Macdonnel bent over him, but he pushed

them away, staggered erect and, shaking himself like a dog after a fight, snatched and swallowed the cup of whisky which Mrs Macdonnel had poured quickly for him while looking ruefully at her shattered chair and plate-shelf. The blow had hardly affected him and, as Mrs Hewes anxiously examined his head he pushed her rudely aside, shouting, 'B' Jasus! Oi'll give ye'se "The Enniskillen's Farewell!"' and he roared boastfully the Boer War song of an Irish regiment's departure. Suddenly he realized that attention was diverted from him; someone in the packed lobby was crying, 'Here's Big Mary! Make way for Blind Mary!' and Mr Hewes, grasping his jacket from Mr Macdonnel's hand, slung it across his shoulder, stared malignantly at everyone and pushed uncivilly out of the house.

The Widow Loughran, who was being guided in by Jerry Delaney and his wife, was a magnificent Irishwoman, well over six feet, round about forty, and round about considerably more at waist and bosom. The habit of raising the head in the manner of the blind made her appear taller and gave her a haughty look, but she was a jolly, kind woman in robust health, and her rosy face and glossy, jet hair, her good-humoured laughter, caused one to forget her blindness. Blind Mary was the wonder of the Gorbals. She drank hard and regularly and stood it better than the toughest men. 'Mary's never up nor doon,' they said, and she boasted that she had never known a 'bad moarnin' in her life. She also wore a tartan shouldershawl of the Gordon clan, a widow's bonnet, and a bright print apron over her skirt. Mrs Macdonnel led her to a seat and she stood up, her hands searching around for Jerry Delaney when she heard there wasn't a chair for him. He was pushed into her arms and she pulled him into a tight embrace on her ample knees. Mr Delaney, popularly known as 'One-Eyed Jerry' since a flying splinter, at his work as a ship's carpenter, had deprived him of his right eye, was no light weight, but Mary handled him like a baby, and Mrs Macdonnel shrieked with laughter: 'Blind Mary's stole yer man, Bridget!' and Mrs Delaney, a dark beauty of five-and-thirty, laughed back, 'Ach away! She's welcome tae him! Shure they're weel matched wi' yin eye atween them!' This so tickled Mary and Jerry that they almost rolled on the floor with helpless laughter, and Mrs Macdonnel looked very worried, expecting every minute to see another of her chairs smashed to smithereens.

Aunt Kate had vanished in pursuit of her man and returned at this moment, pale with anger, to announce publicly that he had skedaddled, but that she would set the police at his heels and make him support her; then she sang in her sweetest voice, 'O My Love Is Like A Red, Red Rose!' followed by a delicate rendering of 'Ae Fond Kiss.' But no one was surprised by her instant change from wrath to tenderness, except young Eddy, who felt that this was his most profitable 'psychological' evening as he watched Blind Mary with her hands boldly grasping Mr Delaney's thighs and began excitedly composing an essay on 'Psychology And The Blind' for his night-school class.

Someone called for a song from Blind Mary, and One-Eyed Jerry courteously handed her to her feet. She stood dominating the whole room, protesting that she couldn't sing a note, but everyone cried: 'Strike up, Mary! Ye sing like a lark!' and she began singing 'Bonny Mary O' Argyle' to the unfailing amazement of young Eddy, who could never understand why her voice that was so melodious in speech was so hideous when she sang. In his boyhood Eddy had always loved to see her in the house, finding a strange sense of comfort in her strength and cheerful vitality. Coming in from school his heart had always rippled with delight to see her gossiping and drinking with his mother and some neighbours. Her rich brogue always welcomed him, 'Ach, it's me wee Edward. Come here, ye darlin'!' and there was always a penny or sixpenny bit for him, hot from her fat hand, or a bag of sweets, warm from her placket-pocket, their colours blushing through the paper. He enjoyed the strong smell of snuff from her soft fingers when they fondled his hair or read his face and the smell of her kiss, scented with whisky or beer, had never repelled him.

Mary had only sung two lines when she was sensationally interrupted by Bridget Delaney, who suddenly leapt from her feet and shrieked indignantly: 'Ach, don't talk tae me aboot legs! Is there a wumman in this house has a better leg than meself? Tae hell wi' Bonny Mary O' Argyle!

I'll show ye'se the finest leg on the South Side this night!'
and she bent and pulled her stocking down her left leg to
the ankle, whipped up her blue satinette skirt and pulled
up a blue leg of bloomer so fiercely that she revealed a
handsome piece of behind. 'There ye are!' cried Bridget,
holding forth her leg. 'Ah defy a wumman among ye'se tae
shake as good a wan!'

Blind Mary stood silent and trembling in a strange listening attitude, thinking a fight had begun, and everyone was
astounded. Jerry Delaney, blushing with shame, plucked
nervously at his bedfellow's skirt, but Bridget pulled it up
more tightly and shouted: 'Awa! Ye've seen it oaften
enough! Are ye ashamed o' it?' while Jerry told her he
had always said she had the finest leg in Glasgow and acted
as if he had never beheld such a distressing sight. Beside
them a very dozy youth gazed dully at Bridget's fat, white
thigh, and from the rose-wreathed wallpaper Pope Pius X,
in a cheap print, looked sternly at the sinful limb.

Mrs Macdonnel hurried her hysterical sister-in-law into
the small bedroom, and the only comment on the incident was, 'Blimey! Wot a lark!' from Mrs Bills. Blind
Mary asked excitedly what had happened. Some of the
ladies, while affecting shocked modesty, trembled with
desire to take up Bridget's challenge; but no one could
have explained her hysteria, except, perhaps, Mr Delaney.
His one eye always glowed with admiration for a fine
woman and he had gazed warmly all evening at Blind
Mary. But Bridget's astonishing behaviour was superseded
for the moment by the arrival of Wee Danny Quinn 'wi' his
melodyin',' whom Jimmy Macdonnel himself introduced as
the guest of honour.

The street-musician, a pugnosed, dwarfish Glaswegian,
bowlegged and very muscular, drank two large glasses of
whisky, wiped his lips and began playing. The mother-o'-
pearl keys of his big Lombardi piano-accordion flashed in
the gaslight as his fingers danced skilfully among them, and
while he leant his ear to the instrument, his little dark eyes
looked up with a set smile, like a leprechaun listening to
the earth. He played jigs and reels and waltzes; all the
furniture in the kitchen was pushed to the wall and all

who could find room to crush around were soon dancing through the lobby and back again.

It was late in the night, when the dancers had paused for refreshment, that Willie McBride the bookmaker, a six-foot red-headed Highlandman, suddenly reappeared arm-in-arm with his wife, he dressed in her clothes and she in his. They had disappeared for fifteen minutes and affected the change with the connivance of Aunt Kate, who slipped them the key of her house. Mr McBride had somehow managed to crush his enormous chest into the blouse of his slim wife; between it and the skirt, his shirt looked out, and from the edge of the skirt, which reached his knees, his thick, pink woollen drawers were visible; Mrs McBride, drowned in his suit, floundered, bowing to the delighted company.

This wild whim of the McBrides heated everyone like an aphrodisiac, and very soon Aunt Kate's but-an'-ben became the dressing-room for the transformation of several ladies and gentlemen. The two Delaneys exchanged clothes and Bridget showed to advantage her splendid legs swelling out her husband's trousers; Aunt Kate retired with a slight youth and reappeared in his fifty-shilling suit as the neatest little man of the evening; then Mrs Macdonnel walked in disguised as her husband, even to his glasses and cap, and was followed by him gallantly wearing the Spanish shawl, in which, after filling out his wife's blouse with two towels, he danced what he imagined was a Spanish dance and sang a hashed-up version of the 'Toreador Song' from Carmen.

Danny Quinn's playing became inspired and his volume majestic as he laughed at the dressed-up couples dancing around. The house was throbbing like a battered drum when heavy thumps shook the stairhead door. 'It's the polis,' cried everyone with amused alarm. Mrs Macdonnel rushed to open and a soft Irish voice echoed along the lobby: 'Ye'se'll have to make less noise. The nayburs is complainin'!'

'Ach, come awa in, Tarry, an' have a wee deoch-an'-doris!' cried Mrs Macdonnel, holding the door wide for the portly constable who stood amazed at her masculine garb, while Willie McBride was roaring, 'Do Ah hear me aul' freend Boab Finnegan? Come ben an' have a drink, man! Shure you an' me's had many a dram when yer inspector wisnae lookin'!' and Mrs Macdonnel conducted into the parlour police-officer Finnegan followed by a tall, young Highland officer, a novice in the Force, with finger at chinstrap and a frown of disapproval. The two policemen were welcomed with full glasses, and Mr Finnegan, known all over The Gorbals as 'Tarry Bob' because his hair and big moustache were black as tar and his heavy jowls became more saturnine with every shave he had, surveyed the strange gathering with a clownish smile, while Mr McBride, the street bookie, told the company how often he had dodged the Law by giving Tarry Bob a friendly drink.

In five minutes both policemen sat down and laid their helmets on the sideboard among the numerous bottles and fifteen minutes later they had loosened their tunics and were dancing with the ladies, their heavy boots creating a louder rumpus than they had come to stop.

Eddy Macdonnel stood in the crowded lobby craning his head over to watch the lively scene. After a long while he heard his mother say to Tarry Bob, who was protesting he must go: 'Och, hiv another wee nip! Shure a wee nip won't kill ye!' then he saw the good-natured policeman drench himself in beer as he put on his helmet into which some playful guest had emptied a pint bottle.

Eddy's wits were staggering. 'Human behaviour' had passed his understanding. In a state of bewilderment he opened the stairhead door and wandered slowly down to the closemouth. His confused head was ringing with a medley of folk-songs and music-hall choruses and his heart held the streams and hills and the women of the poetry of Robert Burns. He was thinking of Jeannie Lindsay and wishing he might find her standing at her close in South Wellington Street. But it was very late. He hurried round the corner in a queer, emotional tangle of sexual shame and desire, his romantic thoughts of Jeannie mingled with the shameful memory of his mother and the women dressing up in men's clothes and Bridget Delaney pulling up her skirts to her hips to show her bare legs to the men.

WORKERS OF THE WORLD UNITE! YE HAVE NOTHING TO LOSE BUT YOUR CHAINS! YE HAVE A WORLD TO WIN! Eddy Macdonnel read the world-famous slogan of Karl Marx, in big white letters on a red streamer hung across the drop-scene of The Pavilion Music Hall. He had long known it by heart from Socialist pamphlets and many times he had read that scarlet streamer. Here among packed humanity the slogan roused him like a battle-cry. His heart flamed with enthusiasm, and he gazed intently forward lest the two companions he was crushed between should notice his emotion.

But they were unaware of him. On his right, a stoutish rawboned youth of nineteen puffed a clay pipe, emitting bitter fumes while he concentrated on a column of propaganda facts and figures under the heading 'Grapeshot' in the *Socialist Standard*; to the left of Eddy a rosy-cheeked young man of twenty, short, stocky and of clerkish aspect, studied with a conscious, intellectual frown, accentuated by pince-nez, the arguments of *Man And Superman* in a thick volume of Shavian plays and prefaces. Eddy Macdonnel held a *Labour Leader* and two new pamphlets he had bought from the bookstall at the entrance, but his elation surpassed his desire to read; the zoom of voices, the cries of paper-sellers at the exits and down the sides of the gallery, excited him like the surging of the sea.

The three youths were regular attenders at this winter series of ILP Sunday evening lectures which offered an open platform to all exponents of progressive political thought. Tonight Tom Mann was billed to speak and the three friends congratulated themselves on getting a front seat. They had anticipated this lecture with eager impatience. They all knew something of the lecturer's dynamic history, of his term of imprisonment for leading a great strike followed by his triumphant organisation of the dockers into a powerful union.

The cosy Pavilion was packed to its full capacity, though there was still a good half-hour to go before the meeting opened, and late-comers were shouldering for standing-room in the gallery promenade. Into the electric blaze from an enormous ungainly chandelier shining on a roof crowded with flying cupids chasing naked nymphs, tobacco smoke coiled into a thick blue fog through which the sound of voices ascended like the drone of countless insects. A few limp handclaps greeted the arrival of the deputy chairman and the usual thirty minutes musical prelude began. It was announced that a Miss Gunn would beguile the audience with the Celtic songs of Kennedy Fraser and a small, obese soprano toddled on to the stage, posed, beaming, by the piano and sang in a sweet spirited Scotch voice 'The Road To The Isles.'

Young Macdonnel was immediately transported to islands misted in purple heather and shimmering in opalescent seas; Donald Hamilton lifted his eyes from *Facts And Figures* and Neil Mudge closed *Man And Superman*. After two more songs of a sadder strain the vocalist was followed by a violinist, a sallow young man with long dark hair who looked like a genius in his velvet coat and Bohemian tie. Then the deputy chairman apologised for the lateness of the speaker, explaining that he had travelled from London and had already addressed two meetings in other parts of Scotland. The violinist received applause enough to please a Kreisler but the handclapping became thunderous as all heads on the stage turned simultaneously to the wings. Tom Mann appeared and Eddy Macdonnel committed one of the proudest audacities of his young life by springing to his feet and impetuously singing the first notes of 'The Red Flag'. Tom Mann waved the whole audience to its feet and swung it into the Workers' anthem and Eddy's confusion was drowned in the roar of a thousand voices.

But he simply perspired with pride throughout Tom Mann's speech. He felt he had inspired the whole audience and when Neil Mudge dug him in the ribs, saying: 'That was fine, Eddy! My, ye're coming out!' he foresaw himself in the near future as a great working-class leader. Fancy being praised like that by Neil Mudge. Neil, who had written essays. He had actually delivered two at the Study Circle of the Unitarian Church in Ross Street and he could talk easily about philosophers and Wagner and the plays of Bernard Shaw. Eddy wanted to cap his triumph by asking a question at discussion time. Trembling, he began to formulate one. Yes, he would ask: 'Will the Working Class ever be free while it is priest-ridden and doped by Catholicism?' Already he saw himself standing up, felt the gaze of the audience, and then he remembered when he had risen to ask a question at another meeting, his heart almost suffocating him, and the words had scattered from his head like frightened birds. The speaker had been kind, waited, signed and smiled encouragement and the audience smiled at his youth and embarrassment. The man beside him laughed: 'Go ahead, laddie, dinna be frichtit!' but he sat down in a hell of confusion, and for a week after went about with the shame on him.

Tom Mann got down to business without the formality of introduction, punching out his theme, 'Syndicalism And Socialism,' with two-fisted belligerence waving his arms and exhaling prodigious energy and confidence. Infected by his vigour the three youths leant excitedly over the gallery rail. 'By juv, he's great!' exclaimed Donald Hamilton, using his favourite expletive and forgetting in his excitement his affected adult manner. As the propagandist ranged the stage, smashing his thesis point by point with his right fist into his left palm, as though his ideas were concrete, tangible objects he was shaping there before them all, like a sculptor chiselling marble, Neil Mudge remarked in a tone of generous patronage: 'Ay, he's a rare oarator!' then settled in judicious calm lest his appreciation of oratory should be mistaken for agreement with extremist views.

Neil was a 'Constitutional Socialist' who regarded anti-parliamentarians with kindly aloofness, but Donald Hamilton and young Macdonnel wanted 'Blood-red Revolution' and they plunged into Tom Mann's enthusiasm like swimmers into a heaving sea. Eddy Macdonnel studied feverishly the agitator's slightest movement, his tossing leonine head and blazing eyes that flashed into every corner of the auditorium. Eddy loved him and the tall, dark intelligent chairman, thin and keen, who occasionally smiled sedately or lightly clapped his long slim hands. He loved all this gathering of Clydeside workers, boilermakers, moulders, hefty rivetters, platers and pattern-makers, pale clerks, rail-waymen and miners. They were all intelligent and fearless, while those 'others,' the great mass of the city's wage-slaves, who put their 'joabs' before the 'cause;' the proud, snob-bish middle-class that preferred property and comfort to ideals—were cowardly and ignorant.

Eddy's feelings were like a desire to embrace the world. Those 'others,' the Capitalists, the contented wage-slaves, his parents, were all blind. 'They have not seen the light. They listen, but they do not understand,' he quoted silently, thrilled by a condescending pity for misled human kind. Stuffed, as he was, with sentimental tags from the pam-phlets, he believed men would one day march in friend-ship 'Sunwards'—with every Capitalist converted to sharing 'The Fruits Of The Earth' which provided 'Plenty For All'—to end for ever the fester of slums and the beastliness of war. 'Rabbie Burns is right!' he thought, 'It's comin' yet for a' that! Man tae man the warld ower shall brithers be an' a' that!' He would have to be more courageous, more wholehearted, from now on. He felt ashamed of lying to his mother this morning that he had attended Mass, even inventing a sermon to convince her, though he had skulked miserably round the streets in the Mass-time hours. He admired the audacity of Donald Hamilton who recently had stopped going to Church and openly professed himself an atheist. Ay, he would have to defy even his parents for the 'Cause!'

Donald stirred beside him, eager to shoot his question across that intimidating abyss of the auditorium. Donald was up. 'Mister Chairman! I should like to ask the Speaker What is the present attitude of The International Trade Union Movement to war; also, if war broke out, would the International Strike make a decisive weapon for Peace!' Without a flicker of embarrassment, his clay pipe steadily poised, pronouncing clearly every word, Donald delivered his question, then sat down and leaned forward, pipe in mouth, elbow on knee, to consider like a thoughtful adult, the reply. Mr Mann replied, that despite dangerous warclouds piling up, Trades Unionism persisted in a very critical state of disunity and roared mightily that the International Strike would be a very decisive weapon indeed! At the close of deafening applause, Donald rose and said: 'Thank you, Mister Speaker!'

Eddy Macdonnel was mystified by Donald's self-confidence and despaired of ever equalling it. Nerved by his example he determined to ask a question and the intention surged hot waves of daring and timidity through him. He became alert and had sunk all his inhibitions when Neil Mudge moved violently at his side and exclaimed 'Damn!' and Eddy turned to see him, flushed and annoyed, groping among their feet for his notebook which he had dropped when snatching at his glasses when they slipped from his nose as he stood up. The Chairman's, 'Any further questions?' sailed up from the stage, but Neil's poise was ruined and Eddy, affected by his failure, lost his nerve. The little green bag for the collection came their way; Neil snappishly passed it on and Eddy nervously dropped in a threepenny bit.

The meeting was over, their opportunities to shine in discussion gone, and as they came out of the Pavilion they both looked enviously at Donald Hamilton's irritating mien of self-satisfaction. Bracing to a snell November wind they walked silently down Renfield Street, swung left into St Vincent Street and cut through Mitchell Lane into Buchanan Street. In the dark lane Donald Hamilton stayed behind to relight his pipe and came pounding after them with his big steps, shouting the beginning of a conversation. He was met with silence. Neil Mudge was still smarting with frustration and Eddy reverberated with enthusiasm, his mind a glorious entanglement of words, music and vague ideas about Syndicalism, Organisation, Revolution. He wanted to hear them talk, being too shy to open discussion. He invariably listened, sometimes dropped in a word or two and flushed with pleasure when Neil complimented him, surprised by an original phrase. 'My, that was damn well expressed, Eddy!' he would say. 'Ye oaght tae write something. Ye'll be giving us an essay up at Ross Street, next!' But he quailed at the image of himself calmly reading a paper to the Men's Study Circle of the little Unitarian Church in the Calton slums, coolly leading a discussion as Donald did when he delivered his 'Essay on Milton.' But he would often visualize himself doing all that, enjoying the effort and success, till some other imaginary triumph replaced it or he was exhausted by emotional imagery.

The three friends walked silently for twenty minutes in profound Scotch quiet, Donald holding his strong, Roman nose very aloof, his determined jaw rigid, as he swung along mannishly, imposing the pace from his mood, hands deeply plunged in a roughnapped brown overcoat, long thin lips clenching his pipe, his carriage expressing adult disdain of Neil's huff. They were passing Jail Square, opposite the unimposing façade of the Law Courts, a wide space opening on Glasgow Green, the ancient, dingy river-side park, where political and religious fanatics argued and orated and the Salvation Army recruited souls; where lively racehorse tipsters offered fortunes on threepenny and sixpenny slips of paper, and quack doctors, for a mere trifle, supplied all-comers with infallible cures for every known disease while amateur philosophers coiled endlessly in and out the labyrinths of Free Will and Determinism.

Lustily swinging the walking-stick he affected, Neil Mudge ended the twenty minutes' silence, looking straight ahead with a faint smile as he said, 'My, it's damn cold! It's no' sae warrm as it was in the Pavilion.'

Donald Hamilton plucked his pipe from his lips. 'What?' he said, and Neil, slightly turning his head, repeated his remark less gruffly. 'No, by juv! It isn't, by juv! It wid be a gran' night tae be hung, by juv!' cried Donald, his stony expression breaking up in a burst of uproarious laughter at his reminder of the Jail Square's ancient function as a place of public execution. 'Ye'd be blawn aff the gallows!' he shouted, stopping to guffaw helplessly while his pals paused and laughed.

My, ye're a soambre divil, Beefy,' said Neil, poking him with his stick.

Donald hated the nickname which had stuck to him since

schooldays, but he was so immoderately gratified with his wit that he took no offence.

Two sparse groups, like hangers-on of Learning, were gathered in the Square round two opponents whose contending voices struck feebly against the wind. They would linger there till the small hours in the bitter cold, drifting away in ones and twos, probably leaving the debaters, still loudly disputing, quoting chapter and verse. Donald suggested biding awhile to listen. In this way the three apprentices frequently livened up the suicidal dullness of Glasgow Sundays when Socialist meetings were few or they considered the speakers of those advertised as too 'moderate' for their recognition. But Neil pushed ahead, 'No thanks!' he said, 'Philosophy won't keep ye warrm. I want tae get home!'

The wind stung their cheeks like arrows as they left the Saltmarket and crossed Albert Bridge. Up the river to their left the two lights of the weir gleamed dim as glowworms where the weir fall thrashed the darkness. Fascinated, Eddy Macdonnel watched the beams of the parapet lamps thrill the black water, writing romantic signs on swirl and flow. His blue eyes laughed at the tortured shine as they hurried across, happier at his companions' resumed friendliness, for he lacked the skill to keep the conversation going. In eightpenny woollen gloves his hands tingled fervently, deep in the pockets of his flimsy overcoat, and the clink of his ironshod heels pealed through his body. Cars and trams crossing the bridge flashed cheer at him and as he looked happily heavenward he fancied that the keen stars of this brilliant November night glowed like a jewelled crown around his head and sang like a choir in his heart: 'Life is glorious! Glorious at seventeen!'

Leaving Albert Bridge they turned left into Adelphi Street and swung diagonally right into Rose Street, a long, straight dull thoroughfare, fouled at this end on one side with slums only fit for demolition, on the other side with the stony silence of a school playground and the blind gable of a factory. Eddy listened to his friends arguing: 'Well, anyway, Tom Mann's nut afraid tae speak out!' Donald was saying, 'It's a peety we haven't mair like him. The

Labour Movement wants more red blood in its veins. We've too many namby-pamby reformers crawlin' like snails tae the Millenyum!'

'Syndicalism presupposes violence; violence is anti-social,' said Neil Mudge, quietly authoritative. 'Revolution creates Revolution *and* Revolution. Consistent constitutional progress will eliminate Capitalism without bloodshed.'

Donald lifted his head, laughed pityingly and blew out a long, sarcastic curl of smoke, 'A foolish consistency is the hobgoblin o' little minds,' he sneered, quoting Ralph Waldo Emerson without acknowledgment. 'Capitalism bears within itself the seeds o' its own destruction,' he added with dogmatic finality, passing of the dictum of Marx as his own, original phrase.

'But, my dear chap!' said Neil in a tone which implied patient long-suffering with faulty reasoning, 'if Capitalism is self-destructive, whence the necessity for revolution?' He clutched the rim of his bowler as they turned into Govan Street against the wind and coughed a little cough expressing dialectic superiority.

'Revolution is The Historic Mission o' The Workers,' replied Donald, primed with a Marxian slogan for every argument. He flicked a used match from his fingers; it flashed a white curve in the darkness and vanished in a gutter stank. 'Damn guid shot that, eh? Did ye see it? Right across the pavement an' doon the stank, by juv!' he cried, more pleased with his dexterity than with his skill in debate.

Gowan Street surrounded them, a dreary main street running from east to west of the city. Massive blocks of tenements loured, their dark closes gaping, their hundreds of windows dimly aglow with gaslight, seeming to crush the life from the low-browed shops beneath, all shut and blinded except for the rare gleam of an Italian ice-cream or fish-supper saloon.

'We swear by the beard of the Prophet, Karl Marx,' sneered Neil, with a theatrical gesture at his chin.

'There is nae Goad but Compromise an' Ramsay MacDonald is his prophet!' counter-sneered Donald.

Tramcars swayed past them, galleons of light and humanity, their steps echoed by the wide, barred gateway of a big timber yard, gorged with deals of sweetsmelling pine, next to the Hairworks, the fur-curing factory that exhaled the smell of putrid rabbit-flesh. 'That beastly place always stinks enough tae knoack ye doon!' said Neil with a refined shudder.

'Ah don't smell anything,' said Donald cheerfully. 'Ah'm not surprised—wi' that filthy pipe o' yours!' Neil gibed as they crossed the road and walked alongside the school, where young Macdonnel had spent his boyhood. A square, ugly four-storeyed building of red sandstone, blackened by industrial smoke, it reared massively at the far side of its playground, open to the road; its ground-floor serving as the parish chapel, its three upper floors the parish school. Unaware of its ugliness, Eddy struggled between the influences of his religion and his new beliefs, resisting the impulse to bow his head and lift his cap like a good Catholic. In guilty anxiety he lost his companions' argument, heard only their voices. He knew they would have respected his gesture but strong with the teaching of the pamphlets he successfully resisted making it. He felt it would be a cowardly submission to superstition, but breathed relief when they were beyond the chapel-house, as if priestly eyes were spying on him. As they tramped under the shadow of a hideous cabinet-making factory, he exulted again in his friends' arguments. 'Compromise,' Neil was saying, 'is a social necessity! Without it there could be no progress. Society and Compromise are synonymous.'

Donald took his pipe from his mouth in manly disgust. 'That's the atteetude of your ILP, the skulkin'-place o' lily-livered Democrats, all theory an' no guts. We want more Action! Action is the life-blood o' the Movement!'

'What about the Vote?' said Neil. Donald took two prodigious puffs, his smoke ascending like amazement. 'The Vote!' He sniggered. 'The Vote! Well, what about the Vote!'

'Used intelligently it will eventually emancipate the proletariat,' Neil advanced coolly.

'Evenchilly! Evenchilly!' Donald returned sarcastically, 'An' when wud that be? Has the Worker ever used it intelligently? Doesn't the Capitalist Press instruct him how tae use it? The Vote is the red-herrin' drawn across the Worker's path b' the Powers That Be tae seeduce him fae his Historic Mission!'

At the corner of Commercial Road, another street of slums and small factories, ending here in an evil, narrow lane, Donald, who affected to be bored with the argument, suggested, 'Shall we call in at the Tallie's?' and they wheeled left into Rowanglen Road, and entered a small ice-cream saloon, their regular place of retirement from wandering round the blocks. A highly-coloured sign entitled the place THE THISTLE SALOON and on the lintel of the door minute letters said, Joe Boganny, Prop. In the narrow window, curtained at the back, a few bottles of wrapped and bare sweets reposed among several dummy chocolate boxes covered with ribbons and unnaturally charming ladies. A sturdy Italian of forty, with ornate moustaches beautifully curled, bright floral waistcoat, gold albert and fob, was leaning on the counter and gazing stolidly into the street as the youths entered. He greeted them in broad Glaswegian, 'Hullo, boays! Hoo's things? Ah hivnae seen ye fur a week.'

'How do, Joe?' said Neil brightly, 'ye're lookin' proasperous. Taking all the money? How's business?'

'Och, no' sae bad!' said the Italian, 'No' sae bad. It's the weather, ye ken. There's no' sae much ice-cream takkin' this cauld weather.'

'My, that's a rare fine waiskit ye've got, Joe,' said Donald. He saw Joe in the waistcoat every Sunday but he enjoyed the fun of titillating his memory, sometimes being rewarded with a long enthusiastic description of his life in Naples. Joe stuck his chest out, proudly floodlighting the thick, furry waistcoat with its design like a Brussels carpet, 'It's twenty years auld that waiskit an' as guid as the day it was boaght,' he said, 'It was ma faither's in Naples. Whit's yer oarder?'

The youths gave their order and sidled into one of the four stalls which furnished the accommodation of the saloon.

Each stall had a table of imitation marble and the partition panels were gaudily painted; above their heads Italian battle-pictures crowded the walls where the central place of honour was given to brilliant lithographs of Italian royalty, draped with the national flags. Joe Boganny looked more Italian than his king and talked broader Scotch than his customers. He called through to the kitchen: 'A Macallum, plate o' hoat peas, plenty bray, an' a hoat raspberry,' and immediately the shop echoed with a babble of female voices speaking in rapid Neapolitan and apparently raised in furious indignation. Eddy Macdonnel could never overcome a feeling of strangeness among these saloon keepers. He became simultaneously alarmed and interested, filled with violent visions of flashing knives and bloody struggle, convinced that they were murderously quarrelling. The apparent battle continued for five minutes, then Mrs Boganny, still talking backwards excitedly, sailed into view with a steaming tray and, smiling as if she had joyfully murdered someone, presented the refreshments to her husband who lifted the counterflap, came through, and served.

Mrs Boganny, a dark little woman in black, with a bright scarf round her neck, and heavy, glittering earrings, leant her handsome breasts on the rounded counter that curved out towards the door, and twinkled her eyes and earrings at the youths.

'Colda nighta!' she said.

'Ay, it's enough tae freeze the ears off a brass monkey!' said Donald Hamilton, as he took an enormous bite from his Macallum—two circular sponges sandwiching a thick slab of ice-cream and a bar of Fry's cream chocolate.

Neil Mudge winced, 'My Goad, I don't know how ye can bite through that stuff in this cauld!' he said.

'Ye want good teeth fur the job,' said Donald boastfully, taking another outsize bite. 'Look!' he gaped his long mouth and showed his large strong teeth, tainted with nicotine, 'Hiv ye ever tried bitin' through a lump o' ice?'

Neil shivered and took a long drink of hot raspberry, 'Donal' ye're disgusting!' he said emphatically.

'This pea-bray's champion!' said Eddy Macdonnel, spooning up the green peas and scalding gravy on which he had sprinkled clouds of pepper and salt with lashings of vinegar. 'I say,' he said, 'I hear Tom Mann's speaking away out at Partick next Sunday but one. I'd like to hear him again,' and he looked hopefully at his pals.

'Good! We'll go,' said Donald, then he stood at the counter and called through to the kitchen where the two Bogannys had retired for warmth, 'A Tallie's blood, Joe, an' a small Woodbine!' When Mrs Boganny had handed these over with smiles and quivers of her earrings, Donald presented the Woodbines to Eddy and attacked with refreshed appetite the Tallie's Blood, a big glass of gaudy ice-cream, scarlet with raspberry essence.

Neil Mudge toyed with his hot raspberry, coughed, flushed and fingered his pince-nez, his usual signs of embarrassment or grave delivery. 'H-hem!' A short pause followed his little cough, like the pause of a chairman when he rings his bell. 'I'll be giving my treetiz on "Individualism" to the Men's Study Circle on that morning. I thought you chaps would like to hear it.' Neil looked straight at Eddy, his pince-nez seeming to contract and jerk violently up his nose as if in sympathy with his acute frown of mortification. Neil had attended the reading of Donald's 'Essay On Milton' and he expected a return of the courtesy. He coughed meaningly again, removed his glasses, polished them with a small square of chamois leather and frowned up at the King of Italy.

Eddy reddened with confusion. He regarded Neil as far superior to himself and Donald in intellect and culture. Donald was a slater's apprentice, Eddy was a plater's apprentice in the shipyards, while Neil was a bookkeeper in a big city office, went to business every morning togged up in his best and was studying to become a chartered accountant, and his pince-nez gave him an air of refined authority which intimidated Eddy. He was hoping that Neil wouldn't press him to attend his reading because he wouldn't have the courage to refuse and the prospect of hearing Tom Mann tugged at his heart. He loved the great mass meetings, vibrating with human excitement, and was always painfully shy at the intimate Study Circle.

Donald let his spoon rattle into his finished glass and remarked in Neil's averted ear, 'Did ye speak?'

'Och, it doesn't matter,' said Neil, still glaring at Italy's king, 'I was just mentioning my treetiz!'

'Aw, that thing o' yours oan Indiveedulism,' said Donald, 'Sure ye could read it tae us next Saturday. Ah wouldn't miss hearin' Tom Mann for you or anybody.'

'It's a very difficult theeziz an' I'm putting my best into it,' Neil said impressively. 'It's sure tae cause treemendous discussion. Will you be at the Circle, Eddy?' he asked, and Eddy, amazed at himself, found the courage to say, 'I think I'd rather hear Tom Mann,' saying it almost naturally because he had become aware that Neil, who had not refixed his glasses, was less impressive without them. About his gaze lay that shadow of tiredness which dims the look of most short-sighted people when they take off their spectacles, and suddenly this devitalised look on Neil's face made Eddy feel regret at having refused him. But he was relieved to have got out of going to the Study Circle this time. He always worried going there in case his mother might get wind of it. She'd never let him hear the last of it. She'd tell him he'd committed a sacrilege going to a 'prodesan' church when he should have been at Mass!

'Jeez, that ice-cream was dandy!' said Donald, smacking his lips noisily as he shredded tobacco from a plug with his penknife and filled his pipe, 'Could ye no' read yer treetiz oan Indiveedulism tae us here some night?' He lit his pipe and eyed Neil narrowly through clouds of smoke.

'No, I'm afraid I couldn't!' said Neil, sharply emphatic, 'A place like this is no' the appropriate place for essays like mine!' He was hot with annoyance at the indifference of his pals. This was his thanks for introducing Donald to the Study Circle! If it hadn't been for his encouragement Donald would never have thought of writing an essay on anything. And look at the praise he got at the Circle for his Essay On Milton! More than it deserved! Neil felt like getting up and going home straight away. At least Eddy might have supported him! He looked away from his pals towards the bright doorway into the Bogannys' kitchen with a deeply offended look.

Donald's pipe was going fine and the word 'Individualism' was ringing in his head like a fire-bell. He was feeling in great form and itching to draw Neil into another debate. 'How can ye ca' yersel' an indivualist while you believe in parliamentarianism and the Constitution?' he said, disregarding Neil's offended silence. Neil couldn't resist this. Forgetting his offence he said, 'It's the soul that's individual an' nae authority or constitution can interfere wi' the soul, the spirit o' man!' He turned and looked straight at Donald, who challenged him to define 'soul,' and they plunged into an all-in debate on Anarchism, Spirit And Matter, Law And Order, The Individual And The State. Eddy lit a fresh Woodbine, sat back and listened excitedly while Donald and Neil slogged each other with chunks of quotation and dialectics from the books. At the end of a tidy set-to Neil said, 'What's your opinion, Joe?' to Mr Boganny who had returned to the counter with the warmth of the kitchen clinging to him.

Joe leaned over his counter, lazy and warm as a dog in the sun. 'Och, Ah'm no' interested in politics. Ah keep ma opinions tae masel'. Wha dae ye think'll win the Cup this season? Celtic staun a guid chance.'

Neil grinned and said, his voice hollow with doubt, 'What about Clyde? Good old Clyde! Ah'll never desert them.'

'Clyde!' Donald shouted, his laugh pouring gallons of contempt, 'Clyde! Away ye go. They'll be lucky if they crawl haufway up the Scottish League afore the Season's oot!' He began making Prince of Wales feathers, trying to blow three plumes of smoke at once. Neil made a friendly snatch at his pipe and knocked it from Donald's hand. It crashed on the marble table and the burning tobacco smouldered ragged threads. Donald bought a new clay pipe at once from Joe, saying it had taken him a month to get a colour on the broken one and it would be weeks before he'd season this new one, and Eddy and Neil sat grinning at each other as Joe, laughing, swiped the broken pipe and tobacco into his apron.

The three apprentices, buttoning up tightly and saying goodnight to Joe, went reluctantly into the cold. Donald parted from them at the next corner firing off at Neil, 'Well, anyway Ah'm sick o' your effeminate Fabians an' lily-livered

ILP'ers. Ah'm gaun tae resign an' join Guy Aldred's
Anarchist Communist Group!' He marched away up South
Wellington Street, swinging his arms like a racing-walker
and Eddy's eyes sparkled as he turned down the street
towards Clydeside with Neil. That was the talk! He also
was sick of Parliamentary Reform. Revolution! Direct
Action were what was needed! He had been one month
in the ILP but it was too moderate for him. It stifled his
limitless idealism. He would resign and join the Anarchist
Group with Donald. With only half the Workers sworn to
Direct Action, Revolution would soon come roaring like a
torrent through Scotland, through the World! Forward
The Social Revolution! Away with Wage Slavery! Eddy
saw quite clearly now that Neil was a Timid Reformer.

Neil and Eddy parted at Eddy's close in awkward
silence. Neil feared that his young friend was inclining
with Donald towards 'Extremism' and was coming too
much under Donald's raw influence. He sighed. Donald
was all right, of course, a good pal and all that but Neil
couldn't understand how Eddy couldn't see that Donald
was just a wee bit coarser-grained than themselves. Donald
was at his best when he was on the subject of economics or
politics, there he took some beating, Neil had to admit, but
when it came to poetry and spiritual things Donald lacked
that last wee touch of refinement, that—Neil searched for
a fitting phrase as he turned into his close, feeling in his
pocket for his check-key—'Well,' he thought. 'Donald just
hisnae the passport intae the holy-of-holies.' Neil smiled,
as he slipped his key in the door, at the subtle aptness of
his phrase and repeated it to himself, taking off his cap and
overcoat in the lobby.

Completely forgetting Neil, Eddy raced upstairs whistling
'The Road To The Isles'. He was now an Anarchist and a
Free Lover! To hell with all Law and Order, Parliamentary Reform and Marriage! Parliament only hoodwinked
the People, Marriage was legalised prostitution. There was
goodness in all men and women. They could live without
laws to make them good. Eddy stopped, searching in his
pockets for his ILP card to tear it up, oblivious in his
new enthusiasm of the stinking stairs. He was urging on

time to the moment when he and Donald together would join Guy Aldred's Anarchist Communist Group. His mind shone with the Gaelic song he had heard first a week ago sung by the Kennedy Frasers in St Andrew's Halls, when he sat charmed by the beauty of the singer in the Celtic gown whose long white fingers plucked glittering music from the harp. The freedom of wild Nature, of loch and moor and mountain, dazzled in sunlight, filled his consciousness, tuned with his embrace of Anarchism as the lively notes rippled through his head.

Mrs Macdonnel opened the door before he had time to knock, 'Wheesht!' She glared at him. 'Fancy whistlin' oan a Sunday. Yer da's asleep. He'll kill ye if ye wake 'im. Whaur hiv ye been so late? At yin o' they Socialish meetin's?' She was looking at his bulging overcoat pockets. 'Is that mair Socialish books ye've goat?' She let him pass in and he lied that he had just been walking over the Town with Neil Mudge. She resented his correct speech as a reflection on her homely way of speaking, sometimes believed he was being superior. She whispered angrily, telling him to stop going about with Neil Mudge. He was a 'prodesan' and Socialist and no good to him. She warned him again not to wake his father and went out, closing the door saying she was going up to see Aunt Katy.

Eddy entered the kitchen and began telling his brother Francie excitedly about Tom Mann's spellbinding oratory and the wonderful meeting at the Pavilion. Och, Francie should have been there! Francie looked up from his book on physical culture by Sandow and whispered, pointing at the bed, 'Tell me later oan!' then gently poked the fire and went on reading. Eddy realised with alarm that he had forgotten his father. He looked at him sound asleep in the kitchen cavity bed, washed, shaved and all ready for the morning. 'In apple-pie order,' as he was fond of saying. He had read himself to sleep. An open book, face downwards on his breast, rose and fell to his breathing and his glasses shone dully, like pieces of mica, in the shadow of the bed-curtain. Mr Macdonnel had to be up at five-thirty in the morning. Eddy knew he would display ill-temper if he was waked and he tiptoed into the parlour, slunk the literature from his pocket and slid it beneath the mattress of the bed where he had been hiding his books since the day he came in from work and found that his mother in a fit of insane rage had thrown the big tea-chest of books he and Francie had collected, into the back-court midden. Sometimes the memory of that summer evening flamed in resentment through him. Hating his mother he had rushed downstairs with black fury in his heart, his eyes scalding with enraged tears, to find the children kicking his books about the back-court. He rummaged in the midden and saved half of them, wiping the filth off them as he came upstairs. But he was not thinking of that time tonight. He kept back one pamphlet, Catholicism And Socialism, by Father Hagerty. The parlour fire had not been lit and the brightly blackleaded grate intensified the coldness of the room, but Eddy was unaware of cold as he stood considering the picture of a harmless-looking priest on the pink cover of the pamphlet. He had heard that the Pope had excommunicated this priest and he was feverish to begin reading the writing of this daring man. Every new pamphlet Eddy Macdonnel bought he read with the excitement and appetite of a boy reading an adventure story. Every argument, every fact against Capitalism was accepted as gospel, every remedy and promise of Socialism were sound. The Golden Age was a reality for Eddy while he read the pamphlet. The ex-priest opened his thesis with the argument of the humility of Jesus Christ and the pamphlet began with the words: 'Christ rode into Jerusalem on an ass and all the people came. . .'

Standing by the cavity bed in the bitterly cold room, Eddy Macdonnel read on, excited, exalted, entranced.

It was the Macdonnel kitchen on a Sunday morning, round about noon, a blazing July day in the prosperous year Nineteen Hundred and Thirteen. Four different kinds of activity were energizing the six by twelve feet room. Francie Macdonnel was washing a shirt for his brother John; Eddy Macdonnel sat at the range reading and keeping up a big fire to heat pressing irons to press the shirt; Uncle Wullie, after swallowing his last mouthful of breakfast, lit a Woodbine, aggravated his weak chest and went crimson in the face with a spasm of harsh coughing. With two paces Jimmy Macdonnel stepped out of the small side bedroom into this scene and looked sourly at his Uncle and his young brothers. He was dressed in socks, trousers and semmit, his braces over the light undervest, a style of undress he worked in on board ship, where cooking in the galley in tropic heat could make even a silk scarf unbearable. The only part of his light cooking-gear he wasn't wearing was the pair of thicksoled slippers he wore as protection against the iron decks of tramp steamers when they were scalding hot in those latitudes. He was fond of telling the family of the time he thoughtlessly stepped out barefoot from the galley onto the hot iron deck when the ship lay in a tropic port, with the captain's dinner on a tray. A fearful screech had disturbed the siesta of those members of the crew who were too prostrated by the heat to go ashore and they woke up to see their cook dance like a mad dervish, throw a tray of steaming food into the air and dart back, writhing, into his galley. The captain, a violent-tempered, resentful man, to whom the temperature had done its worst, didn't take the accident at all reasonably. He had threatened to shove Jimmy in irons and didn't spare him one kind look for the rest of the voyage. Jimmy elaborated that story from time to time and the captain's threat was the latest exciting detail he had worked in.

Anyway, said Jimmy, the first thing he bought after that was a pair of heavy slippers. They lay handy in his sailor's kitbag at the moment and would lie there till he went to sea again. It never occurred to him to wear them, though he would complain about the filthy state of his socks and his mother's feckless neglect while walking about picking up the household dust. All the men of the family trod all day in the summertime, socked or barefooted till pleasure or livelihood called them outdoors.

Jimmy's arms, naked in the armless vest, were brown as a negro's after his last voyage, and his tall, slight figure looked superbly fit, but he was in a bad way, because last night he had almost surpassed himself, drowning in a final grand spree with the corner-boys the last few pounds of his ship-money. And now it was Sunday, in Glasgow.

With one more pace Jimmy sat down on a home-made stool, his back against the open flap of the coal-bunker, which comprised half of the dresser, laying his head in his hands, because it was too heavy to hold up in the normal way and sighed a deep shuddering groan. It's Sunday in Glasgow, he thought. Sunday in Glasgow! Oh, Jesus!

Uncle Wullie and his brothers regarded him silently. After another painful groan he dragged up his head and looked hot-eyed round the kitchen and at them. Catching sight of his breakfast, a big plateful of black-pudding, ham and eggs, now greasy-cold, which Francie had made and laid on the table that always stood close against the bed, he stared at it with anguished resentment and looked in agony at the ceiling. The sight of the food made him feel as he had felt once on his first voyage when the ship was giving one of its highest heaves. He would have liked to seize that plate, send it whirling through the open window, watch it fly like a Greek discus through the bright air, while the bits of food flew off it like a scatter of birds. But Francie, the strongest member of the family, though only nineteen, a lad as strong as a mule, was busy at the sink, sunlight glinting on his tawny hair as he scrubbed with crazy vigour a shirt for his brother John. The thought of rising, moving

Francie aside, explaining to him, then venting his spleen on that breakfast, made Jimmy so weary that he dropped his head in his hands again.

Uncle Wullie, seated at the end of the table, raised his eyes from his book, a small volume in chocolate-brown covers, propped against his teacup and entitled *Racing And Form* for 1913, from which he was making notes in a notebook. He glanced in pity over at Jimmy, then eyed regretfully the cold breakfast half-a-foot away from his nose. Uncle Wullie, Mrs Macdonnel's brother, had lived with the family since boyhood and they were all, except Mr Macdonnel, fond of him. He was a Corporation lamplighter. Every morning he left home carrying a thick short stick with a nicked, iron head and turned out the gaslight on tenement landings; every evening he went out from the Corporation depot shouldering a fourstep ladder and carrying an old-style, policeman's wick-lamp with a small hole in the bottom, and with these re-illuminated the same landings. Insignificant of body and features he was, and his habit of having his hair cut close to the scalp, leaving only a tuft at the brow, rendered him rather unsightly, but his black eyes were deeply kind and in all his thirty-six years he had seldom had an ill-thought for anyone. He was profoundly good-natured and always trying to be friendly, no easy task in a family so often morose and quarrelsome. He was unlearned but very proud of knowing the meanings of the foreign phrases: 'Honi soit qui mal y pense,' 'In camera,' 'non compos mentis,' and 'Felo de se,' which he pronounced in his own peculiar way and which he had collected from *Pearson's Weekly*, *Tit-Bits* and *Answers*, where he steeped his mind in the rainpools of knowledge, and whenever one of these phrases cropped up in a newspaper it was his delight to translate it for the family. Sometimes he waded into the deeper wells of learning in *Marvels Of Science* and *History Of The World* in sevenpenny fortnightly parts whenever Messrs Newnes flared them in the public eye, and he had two stacks of these, tied in order, with a fourteen years' stack of *Racing And Form* under the parlour bed. But Uncle Wullie's knowledge of the pedigrees and form of Derby and Grand National winners and the victories and history of famous Scottish football teams—especially his favourite team, Glasgow Celtic, was really astonishing, and he was known in the Gorbals as 'the lucky tipster' who never charged for his tips. People stopped him in the street to ask him for the 'best thing' for the day and he nearly always gave them the winning horse and backed the loser himself, which kept him in a state of mild annoyance. Whenever he brought off a big win he generously shared it with the family, and he was always hoping to win enough to set up in a bookmaker's business for himself; but the money he won always returned piecemeal into the bookmaker's hands.

Wishing to share his sympathy for Jimmy, Uncle Wullie looked across at Eddy Macdonnel, who sat by the range, his auburn head bent over a Corporation Library volume of short stories by W. W. Jacobs. Every now and then Eddy burst into hearty quivering laughter which almost threw him off his chair, at which Uncle Wullie smiled delightedly, but he couldn't catch his eye. Eddy was perspiring with the heat of the fire he was keeping up to dry John's shirt which Francie had promised to have dried and ironed by twelve o'clock. Mr Macdonnel and his wife had been on the spree for a fortnight and everything, including the family washing, had been neglected. John had promised Francie a half-crown for doing the shirt which Francie would have washed for no other reward than his brother's pleasure at seeing the job well and truly done, just as he had scrubbed out the whole house that morning because he was strong and because he was happy at his mother's promise, before she went out to Mass, that she would sign the pledge at the chapel tonight and never touch the drink in her life again.

A smell of sweet cleanliness pervaded the house, a smell strongly scented with the soft, brown soap, which the Macdonnel's called 'black soap,' that Francie had lavishly used, and the kitchen, which always caught the full noontide sun, was dazzled with glancing sunshine, that flashed on everything bright it could lay its beams on and shone on the metal clasps of Francie's braces, flying off them with all his movements, like shimmering golden moths and butterflies up the walls to dance in flickering reflections on the whitewashed ceiling. It splashed on the big steel fender and burned along the bevels of the Macdonnels' range, that range, famous as the most expensive one in the tenement, which Mr Macdonnel was always telling people was 'a dandy range. A real dandy!' and which Francie had scoured this morning with emery paper till it stood up like a stack of bright bayonets. Over the shining sea-green tiles of that range, with their design of yellow primroses, the healing sunshine poured and it flickered around bowed Jimmy like the laughter of invisible people who were sorry for him but weren't taking his misery too seriously. It was hard to believe that the window of this charmed den of light overlooked a foul, hideously ugly back-court, paved with broken bricks, uneven with subsidences and littered with tin cans, bones, old boots and other garbage pulled from the overfilled midden by the children whose happy cries of play ascended.

And Jimmy was cursing the Glasgow Sabbath and thinking of the bright Continental Sunday, recalling the rollicking booze-ups he had enjoyed on Sundays in foreign ports. God! If only he could get just one drink! But he knew that every pub door outside was as inexorably closed as the closed mind of a rigid Presbyterian, in this city where the rich, lay and religious, were at this moment drinking their wines from cool cellars, their whiskies and liqueurs from cabinets on pleasant trays, in their homes or in clubs well away from the Gorbals, while wagging grave pows over the wastefulness of the poor; and the poor, if they had money, were slinking into sheebeens to pay exorbitant prices for methylated whisky or suffering their tortures of thirst till Monday morning threw open the pub doors. Jimmy was smelling the good, human smell of France while cursing callous Law and glaring in his mind's eye at the two constables who had moved him and his pals on last night. Shure, weren't Tarry Bob and Big Andy Devine notorious for taking backhanders from the sheebeen-keepers and the street-bookies, he thought, sharing the opinion of the back-streets, that all ranks of the police, being only human, took bribes, raiding a sheebeen or nicking a bookie occasionally to hoodwink the public.

Ach, the heat! God, it was like yon time in Africa! Suddenly Jimmy remembered a pleasant occasion and it gave him a moment's coolness and peace. Somewhere his ship lay idle and he leant in lazy pleasure on her rail eyeing the dappled sea. A light breeze winnowed a hot Mediterranean day. Was that the time? Och, he was all mixed up! Was that the night he met the wee French lassie? Staring into his past he saw himself threading through vague dark streets in Marseilles; a shipmate, an American, was urging him on; the electric words BAL and CABARET sparkled at them here and there like laughing temptation; they stood beneath a red lamp above a doorway; a bar of light shot across the pavement and vanished and he was inside amid the sounds of women's laughter, and soon two slim arms were twining his neck with a sensuous charm. In memory these arms curled about him like the soft sea-wind, and he sighed relief and whispered within himself, into the darkness against his palms where his fiery eyeballs shot stabbing lights: 'Fifi! Oh, ma wee Fifi!' Then the next moment he thought disgustedly: 'Och, tae hell wi' Fifi!' as he felt a sensation like the roof of his skull being lifted right off and smacked heavily on again, as if all his nerves had mustered there and given him a thud like the blow of a mallet. And he woke from his blissful dream to hear Eddy's loud, innocent laughter and Uncle Wullie saying: 'Ay, that's a good story but ye should read the yin aboot the boay that adopted a faither!'

Jimmy staggered to his feet, glared, and shouted: 'Ach whit the hell are ye laughin' like a wild hyeenya fur? D'ye no' ken ma heid's splittin'?' Eddy said he couldn't help it, the story was that funny. 'Well, laugh inside yersel'!' said Jimmy and turned round to the dresser to talk to a parakeet the size of a thrush which he had once brought from the West Indies and which dozed luxuriously on the outside of a large parrot-cage on top of the coal-bunker. It had one eye half-open as if it feared to miss anything going on in the kitchen, and its white eyelid against brilliant green plumage gave it a strangely old, sophisticated look. It stirred awake at Jimmy's 'Pritty Poally! Pritty Poally!' repeating his words in a tiny, slumbrous voice, then mounted his finger, walked up his arm to his shoulder and made friendly pecks at his ear. 'Is there ony tea in the poat?' Jimmy asked Eddy. Eddy shook the big, dented enamel teapot standing on the hob and lifted the lid, filling the kitchen with the smell of stewed tea. Jimmy poured a cupful, wet a crust of bread in it, dipped it in sugar and offered it to Polly, who had followed his actions with the wildest excitement and dug its beak greedily into the moist bread. Then Jimmy put the sop in his mouth and Polly scrambled madly after it, clinging to his semmit and pecking at his lips, while Francie, Eddy and Uncle Wullie looked on in delight as if they had never seen this before.

Jimmy had found occupation to lessen his misery. He began cleaning out Polly's cage, pulling out the mobile floor and scraping off the clotted seeds and mess into the coal-bunker. Then he made Polly do her star turn. He stood her on the dresser and walked smartly into the bedroom, calling her name. The parakeet hopped to the extreme verge over the coal-bunker, eyeing them all as though she was announcing her performance; then with a frightened squawk she fluttered to the floor and walked into the lobby exclaiming 'Pretty Polly,' a panic note in her little croak as if she had lost Jimmy for ever, and they heard her beak scrape at the bedroom door while Jimmy teasingly called her. Then they all three tiptoed to the kitchen door and craned round with a simultaneous grin at the excited parakeet, and Jimmy opened the door, took her on his finger and they heard the bedsprings ring as he lay down talking to her.

Uncle Wullie was always exquisitely tickled by this demonstration of parrot intelligence. He snapped his long thin fingers as he always did when highly amused and bent double with his left hand to his side, laughing his chesty laugh, saying Polly ought to be given a chance on the stage. Eddy let himself go in laughter, too, and Francie, who seldom laughed outright, gave one of his queer grins, a little sideways movement passing across his eyes, like a scowl struggling with a laugh.

Uncle Wullie and Eddy returned to their books and Francie to scrubbing John's fawn-coloured shirt, which, though it was only a seven-and-sixpenny one, must have been tough, because Francie had decimated a large bar of Sunlight and expended enough energy to move two pianos, in scrubbing it, yet it still held stoutly together; and now he sang as he rinsed it lavishly, scattering crystal sprays of sunlit water into the iron sink. He began wringing out the shirt, admiring his forearm muscles as they bulged to his powerful grip, and he was so carried away by their magnificence that he laid down the shirt and flexed his huge biceps, turning his head from side to side to look at each one. Eddy, who was testing the temperature of two pressing-irons that were heating on the hob to press the shirt, turned his head and saw him and came over to admire them also. He put out his hand and shyly felt Francie's left bicep. 'My,' he said, 'it's as hard as iron! It's harder than it was a week ago! It must be them Sandow spring-dumb-bells that's doin' it!'—and Francie beamed a gratified smile and raised his mighty chest. The two brothers had recently taken up the physical culture system of Sandow, The World's Strongest Man, and they were excited with enthusiasm over it, after throwing up in contempt the Maxick and Saldo system of muscle development by mental concentration, which they had found uninteresting and mystical. Eddy said hopelessly that he could never be as strong as Francie. His brother laughed and said, 'Flex yer biceps,' and Eddy tentatively rolled up his shirtsleeves, bent two slim white arms and revealed two biceps, round and small, like the budding breasts of a girl. 'Ach, they're nae good! They're like wee pimples,' he said, disappointed and ashamed. But Francie, whom Nature and hard work had given muscles which no system could ever have supplied, laughed with the confidence of the successful and encouraged him to carry on with the dumb-bells. At that moment the gong of the big eight-day clock above the mantelpiece struck twelve tinny notes; Eddy seized the shirt, which Francie had almost wrung dry with sheer strength, and hung it before the fire over the back of a chair; Francie took a blanket from the bed, folded it in four, cleared the table and spread the blanket there for pressing the shirt.

At exactly a quarter-past-twelve the shirt was ready as

John stumbled in from the parlour, rubbing the sleep from his eyes, looking like a nigger-minstrel who has partially removed his burnt-cork complexion, his blond hair bedimmed with dirt and machine-oil. On returning from work at six a.m. he had thrown himself half-dressed and unwashed on the bed and had fallen into a profound sleep. But he woke completely on seeing his beautifully ironed shirt, patted Francie on the shoulder and playfully tapped his chin with his fist, telling him he was a champion ironer. Then he asked what was the matter with Jimmy, having heard him talking to the parakeet as he came through the lobby. 'He keeps oan askin' Poally tae say "Ma wee feefee",' said John, 'the drink must have knoacked him daft!' They looked vague and Uncle Wullie grinned, showing a dental gap four teeth wide: 'Ach, ye should hiv seen Poally this moarnin'! She was in great form.' John smiled and his Uncle said kindly, 'Jimmy's had a bad moarnin'.'

'Och, it serves 'im right!' said John. 'He shouldnae go boozin' an' swankin' wi' the corner-boys,' then he stripped to the waist and began washing off the ingrained dirt and oil of two days and nights overtime at the shipyards. When he had finished he also stood posing and admiring his muscles, filling the small mirror by the window with a fatuous smile of satisfaction. He was a plater's labourer. He helped the platers to place in position for the riveters the steel plates on the hulls of ships. He said that work fairly put the muscles on a man. Francie said that kind of work mostly developed the back muscles and John twisted his neck round trying to see his back in the mirror. He was slightly taller than his brother with soft white skin and a good physique, but Francie's muscles were the wonder of the tenement and the pride of the Macdonnels. Even Mrs Macdonnel took shy, proud peeps at her big son when he swung his dumb-bells in the parlour.

The strains of a Catholic hymn crawled through the open window, and John said there was that big Irishman again; 'He kens where the maist Catholics live an' where the maist Prodesans. Eh, he's a proper twister!' They all laughed and looked into the court at the broken-booted busker, a tall, red-headed Irishman, collarless, in foul greasy clothes, his cap lying at his feet, thumbs stuck in waistcoat armholes, who sang in a catarrhal voice, whinish with begging; 'Hail Queen of Heaven, The Ocean Star, Guide of the wand'rer here below, Thrown on life's surge, We claim Thy care, Save us from peril and from woe,' while children passed from close to close across the court, and in the next back-court, twenty youths, visible through spiked iron railings, shouted wildly, playing a game of football with a huge shapeless ball, made of paper and string. 'He always starts off wi' that hymn,' said John.

'Ay, an' five minutes after ye'll hear him singing "Onward Christian Soldiers" in another back-court,' laughed Eddy.

The beggar's powerful voice triumphed over the noise and shouting as he continually turned about scanning every window. Every window was open today and the smells of Scotch broth and Irish and rabbit stew curled out of them and drifted along to tickle the Macdonnels' nostrils. Coins thrown from windows, whirled glittering through the clear light and tinkled and hopped on the broken paving of the back-court, and fat Irishwomen, leaning on window-sills, shouted compliments to the singer, while the hymn, so moving to Catholic hearts, was delivered in bits and pieces as the singer stopped in the middle of lines to pounce on contributions and thank each donor: 'Mother of Chri—Thank ye koindly, ma'am!' the beggar shouted, 'Star of the—Thank ye koindly, surr!—Say, Pray for the wand—Thank ye koindly!—sur, Pray for me!—Thank ye koindly!' and the children brought him far-rolling coins while he watched them sharply to see they did not run off with any; and then he dashed at them indignantly as they knocked against him and trod on his cap. The rogue then saw three pairs of eyes laughing at him from the Macdonnels' window and touched his forelock to them and caught neatly a wad of coppers in paper which John threw down. Then he decided that the rain of coppers had ceased and lifting his cap to the assembled windows, he strode sturdily from the back-court waving a hand to the brothers.

After his long spell of overtime, John said he felt as fresh as a daisy with only six hours' sleep. He looked at his moleskin trousers, stiff with rust, dirt and machine-oil, hanging like pipestems down his legs, and remarked that he had been three days in them without taking them off and what a fine pair they were. John was the dandy of the family. He worked all the overtime he could get so that he could have money to keep pace with every change in men's fashions. He had earned nearly a whole week's wages with his overtime and he was going to pay the final instalment on a spanking six-guinea suit which Wee Mister Hourigan, the tailor, was hurrying to complete at this very moment in his kitchen on the third landing.

The beggar's hymn seemed to have stirred pious feelings in John as he stood there half-naked enjoying the heat and a chat with his brothers after his wash, and he said his girl Norah hoped he was going to Holy Communion this morning. His remark dropped into an awkward silence. Eddy and Francie had become Revolutionary Socialists and with adolescent enthusiasm were determined to overthrow Religion, 'The Enemy of The People,' unfrock every priest and minister and turn every church and chapel into a warehouse, cinema or dance-hall. Whenever their parents were out they always tried to convert John and Jimmy, but lately they had desisted, shaking their heads over human obstinacy as they proceeded along The Path of Progress alone, sorrowfully leaving their brothers bogged in ignorance, because Jimmy never argued but listened to them with smiling tolerance, not caring what they did to chapels or churches so long as he had his beer and cigarettes, and John, in spite of the wide lofty brow above his big blue eyes, always lost his mental balance at the first attack and answered angrily, 'Och, ye canny dae wi'oot the Capitalist!' or 'There must be a Goad. Who made the world? Whit's the use o' argyin'?'

Eddy lit a Woodbine, handing one to each of his brothers. With the high scorn of seventeen years he wanted to say, having acquired an indelicate style of argument from propaganda literature and soap-box orators, that the Communion wafer which the snuff-scented fingers of the priest had so often handed them across the altar-rail with a gibber of Latin, wasn't the body and blood of Christ but only compressed flour and water, like the Jewish Passover biscuit. With an effort he suppressed the shattering argument though marvellous phrases flickered like electric signs through his mind, clamouring to be spoken, and with weary aloofness he heard John say lamely: 'Norah's awfu' good-livin'.'

'Ay, she's good-livin',' said Francie.

'These blackheids spile ma looks,' said John, facing the mirror, forgetting Norah and religion in concern about some blackheads which showed up vividly on his fair complexion. He took a watch-key from a drawer in the mirror and pressed some out of the bridge of his nose, frowning at the pain. 'It's the machine-oil that does it,' said Francie, 'It gets intae the pores.'

'Ah'll away ben an' smairten masel' up,' said John, taking the fawn shirt from the dresser and slinging it across his naked shoulder.

'Me da's goin' tae sign the pledge the night,' Francie told him.

'Him!' sneered John, "He'll sign it the night an' break it taemorra as soon as the pubs open. Well, he'll get none o' ma money,' and he walked into the parlour, his braces dangling behind him like a horse's harness.

Francie and Eddy puffed their Woodbines, looking at each other silently, their smoke starting snow-white from the glowing tips, then shading into a blue like the cloudless sky as it twined in the air. 'Och, it's nae good tryin' tae convert them,' said Francie, 'the Revolution'll have tae start wi'oot them. They'll jist be dragged intae it like sheep. They're adamant.' Eddy nodded sadly. 'They're non compis mentis,' said Francie, giving up his stubborn brothers and turning to pose his muscles before the mirror.

His last words had a startling effect on Uncle Wullie. Although he was slightly deaf and absorbed in studying horse-racing, they pierced his ear like a ringing alarm-clock. 'Non compos mentis!' he said delightedly, putting down his book and turning round, 'That means they're no' in their right minds!'

'Och, sure we know that,' said his nephews simultaneously, with a faint suggestion of superiority. 'They're benighted wage-slaves,' said Eddy and Uncle Wullie returned mortified to his books just as Jimmy walked in from the side bedroom, with Polly nestling close against his neck. 'Is John wakened yet?' he asked, glancing round the kitchen.

'He's ben the room,' said Eddy.

Jimmy had been desperately waiting for John to waken, hoping to borrow enough from him to buy a drink at a licensed Sunday club or a sheebeen.

'Ah wonder if he'll len' me five bob?' he said unhopefully and went into the parlour. In a few moments he returned through the lobby loudly exclaiming: 'Bloody jew! Did ye hear 'im, Poally? He canny len' me a haufcroon! Bloody Shylock!' and he sat on the stool, with Polly on his finger, her beak at his lips, saying to her 'Say bloody jew. Go on Poally! Say bloody Shylock. Come on Poally! Say bloody jew!' Polly cocked her head, closing an eye, and looking at him through the other, appeared to make efforts to say a new phrase, but she could only produce 'Pretty Polly' and Jimmy lost interest, returning to his gloom, and Polly, climbing up his arm sat on top of his head and fell asleep there as if in sympathy with him.

Suddenly John appeared in the kitchen doorway, shouting indignantly: 'Who's a bloody jew! Ah work for all Ah get, don't Ah? Ah can do what Ah like wi' ma own money. You spen' yours boozin' wi' the corner-boys, then come cadgin' from me. You've got a neck!' He stood glaring, agitatedly trying to fix his cuff-links, barefooted, his flies wide open, his shirt, which he had just put on, floundering over his trousers. Jimmy did not answer but took Polly on his finger, stroked her and exasperatingly crooned, 'Pritty Poally' and John, fixing a choleric stare on him, returned to his dressing.

Uncle Wullie, annoyed at this interference with his studies, rose and walked offendedly into the parlour with his notebook and *Racing And Form*, glad to get out of the kitchen into comparative coolness, and Francie, seated on the dishboard of the sink with his knees drawn-up, was laughing silently in himself at Jimmy's innuendos with

Polly, while Eddy broke again into helpless laughter over another Jacob's story.

In ten minutes John returned fully dressed, laid his bowler hat on the dresser, stood before the mirror, glueing his splendid hair tight down on his scalp with brilliantine and nicely arranging his tie. Francie studied him with wide-eyed admiration. Francie took a great pride in John's dressy appearance in the locality, and none in his own, for he was insanely shy. He had two new suits in the chest of drawers in the parlour, which he seldom put on, except that he sometimes walked abroad in one when the streets were dark. It was his habit to buy new clothes, and when the whole family had assured him that he looked like a lord and was fitted like a glove, to fold them carefully and put them away, then walk out in his old togs, terrified of facing the neighbourhood all dressed up.

He thought John looked spanking and followed all his movements as he brushed every single hair into precise position. Aware of Francie's admiration from the corner of his eye, John was at the top of his bent, feeling that life was very good and thinking his hair had never looked so brilliant. 'This suit's good for more wear yet,' he reflected aloud then: 'Is there ony dandruff oan me shouthers?' he asked Francie, 'it spills all over me collar. They say bear's grease is good for it.'

Francie got down from the dishboard, picked up a clothes brush and began vigorously brushing him. 'Ach, ye're well set now,' he said, standing back to look and admire; 'Ye should try lemon-juice. It stimulates the roots an' invigorates the scalp.'

'Ah'll try some,' said John absently, as he was anxious to be going now, having heard of a fight between two corner-boys, one a champion boxer, that was taking place this morning on the banks of the Clyde, out of the way of the police.

The sickly smell of brilliantine lingered in the close kitchen and, as if it had recalled Eddy to the actual world, he raised his head from his book and looked at his handsome brother. 'Yer collar wants pullin' up a bit, John,' he said, and stood up to ease John's coat-collar into symmetrical position. Then as John, a fair model of a Glasgow back-street dandy in a brown suit and tan shoes, his bowler hat carefully poised, stepped towards the door, delighted with all this admiration and attention, Jimmy, with Polly asleep on his head, rose from his stool with a look of superfine disgust and, holding his nose between finger and thumb, minced on tiptoe into the bedroom.

John stopped and looked after him, unable to find an answer to this crafty insult, then stifling his wrath he paused to talk to Francie and Eddy about Terence Mooney, the boxer, who was their neighbour and lived on the third storey. John said bookmakers would be taking bets on the fight, that the other man was a hooligan who butted with his head and he thought Mooney would get the worst of it because he was no good at the rough-and-tumble style. As he said that, Uncle Wullie rushed in excitedly from the parlour and told them that Terence Mooney had just turned in the close and looked as if he had been badly beaten. John swore, angry with himself. He had slept too long and delayed over his dressing and had missed a grand fight. He opened quickly the stairhead door in time to see the boxer turn up the flight to the second storey and called him over.

A young man of twenty-five in a dark grey suit wheeled back down the stair and, walking lightly like a woman, came, shyly doffing his cap, and stood just within the door, talking to John, against whom he looked small and slight. A black silk muffler was roughly knotted at his neck and his tight-waisted jacket, buttoned closely, revealed the perfect symmetry of his body. He was as slight as a girl, with very small hands and feet.

'Ah heard it was Big Baldy Flynn,' said John, 'he's always shootin' oot his neck. He's a dirty fighter. It's time somebody dressed 'im doon.' 'Ay,' said the boxer in his quiet voice. His dark eyes were kindly and there was a weak kindliness about his small chin. Except to professional eyes, he did not look like a pugilist, yet he was in the first class of flyweights, with a brilliant original style, seven stone of exquisite poise and quickness in the ring, and he had given a world's champion two of the hardest fights of his career. He was very popular in the Gorbals for his friendly, unassuming manner, and they said he could have been a world's champion if he had left the drink alone.

'Ah bet ye gave Baldy a fine wallopin',' John said heartily, trying not to show surprise at the boxer's terribly bruised face. But Mooney seemed unwilling to talk about the fight. He said it was over and done with and best forgotten. It was the drink, he said. He and Flynn got to arguing, one word led to another; the other men egged them on and their pride wouldn't let them back out.

Uncle Wullie and his nephews were crowded in the doorway listening and Eddy, seeing the horrible bruise on the boxer's right temple, his left eye puffed and almost closed, his lips cut and swelled, shuddered as he saw too vividly that butting head smashing into the kind little man's face. He loved clean boxing and hated that cowardly method of fighting used by the gangs and the lowest type of corner-boy, when a man seized another's lapels, quickly pulled his jacket back over his shoulders, making his arms helpless, and then—a wave of nausea passed through Eddy.

Eddy had joined The Scottish National Sporting Club two weeks before in a fit of physical culture enthusiasm; Terence Mooney had been there on his joining night and invited him into the ring for a boxing lesson. To Eddy's bewilderment the little man seemed to wield a hundred hands, yet he had not given him one hurtful blow. Eddy remembered gratefully how gently Mooney had taught him and he felt sorry for him and his mother, the small, feckless Irishwoman, never sober, devil-may-care, always happy, running the money her son won from boxing through her fingers like sand.

John was apologising that he couldn't give Terence a drink. 'Ye ken hoo it is oan a Sunday,' he said, 'there isnae a drap in the hoose.' The boxer's wave of the hand, was as delicate as the gesture of an actor. 'Never mind, Johnny. Ah'm quittin' the drink fur good, onyway,' he said with weak conviction.

'Ye should put a nice juicy steak tae that eye,' said John.

'Some hopes o' findin' steak in the hoose wi' the aul' wumman oan the ran-dan!' Mooney laughed sceptically,

turning up the stairs, and calling back to John that there
was a gambling-school going on over at Shawfield. John
shouted thanks, saying he would go, and turned back into
the kitchen to have a last look at the angle of his hat. He
felt he was going to be lucky at the cards.

At half-past-two the elder Macdonnels returned. After
attending ten o'clock Mass they had gone the round of
all their cronies' houses in the hope of obtaining a dram.
'Ah'm shair Blind Mary Loughran had a drap tae gie us,'
Mrs Macdonnel was complaining to her husband as they
came in; 'did ye see yon big boatle when her wee niece
opened the press tae get oot the breid?' but Mr Macdonnel
replied that Blind Mary wasn't the one to hold back a dram
if she had it to give. 'Mibbe yon was vinegar,' he said.

They came in so quietly, subdued by their distress, that
they surprised Uncle Wullie and their sons. Uncle Wullie
was seated by the table greedily reading the current issue of
Tit-Bits—which he had just bought from the newsagent's
at the closemouth—with the big green covers of the weekly
widespread close to his face; Eddy was leaning out of
the window shouting conversation to a young Socialist
acquaintance; and Francie was stretching himself face
downwards on the floor raising and lowering himself on his
hands in a chest-developing exercise, reciting rhythmically
as he rose and fell: 'You are old Father William, the young
man said.' He jumped to his feet in great confusion, facing
his parents with lowered head, while Eddy waved goodbye
to his pal and got down from the dishboard of the sink and
Uncle Wullie pushed his face closer into *Tit-Bits*.

The two old people were in a pitiable state, every nerve
in their bodies craving alcohol. Mr Macdonnel whined to
his wife asking her for God's sake to make sure if she
hadn't a few shillings, suspecting her of lying to him.
She reddened with annoyance, saying she had told him
a hundred times she had nothing, and opened her purse
to show him its ragged, empty interior. Then she turned
to praise Francie as she looked round the well-scrubbed
kitchen and lobby, the shining range, the floor covered with
newspapers which he had spread over the wet linoleum till
it dried. 'Ma bonny wee son!' she said, 'he's cleaned the

hoose fae tap tae boattom. God bless 'im!' and she hung her dark grey shawl behind the door and came over and embraced him, promising with tears that she would drink no more after this day. But Francie pulled away from her, one of his queer grins on his face, feeling sad and frustrated, disbelieving her. And Eddy looked dumbly at his parents, also, saying to himself that Francie was a fool to trouble, that they wouldn't change, no matter what you did for them. They never kept their promises. They would sober up for a few weeks, or a month or two, then break out again. Sure, he and Francie would do anything for them if they'd only keep off the drink. But what was the use! And he felt deeply weak with his parents' weakness; nerveless, irresolute, afraid with a reasonless fear of himself before oncoming life.

Mr Macdonnel began walking rapidly to and fro along the lobby from the parlour to the kitchen, like a wolf in a cage. He had pawned his best suit and his old working jacket swung slovenly each time he turned. Mrs Macdonnel cried to him for God's sake to sit down, and he said shakily, 'Och, it's me nerves, Mary. Ah'm tremblin' like a leaf! If Ah could only get wan hauf tae steady meself Ah'd take the lifelong pledge' and suddenly threw himself on his knees at the bedside, holding clenched hands towards the crucifix, moaning loudly: 'Sweet Jesus, forgive me! Holy Mother O' God, pray for me! O Sacred Heart O' Jesus make me good-livin' from this hour.' He snuffled, pressing his face against the bedclothes, his shoulders heaving, and his sons watched him in discomfort, knowing his contrition was shallow and despicable, because they had seen it repeated Sunday after Sunday for years. They called it 'the whisky-greetin',' a phenomenon which afflicted their mother only when she was drunk and their father when he had recovered from intoxication.

And Mrs Macdonnel looked at him contemptuously as he stood up, tears streaming from his eyes, moaning, 'Did ye hear what old Father Rooney said in his sermon, that if ye died in drink ye'd burn for all eternity?' Then his agony became practical and he asked his wife if she had tried Uncle Wullie for a few shillings. Mrs Macdonnel resented his question, knowing how he hated her brother, regarding him as an interloper in the family, and she snapped back that Wullie had had a bad week with the racehorses and hadn't a farthing.

John had been their one sure hope of obtaining money for a drink and they were distressed to find him gone. When she learned where he was, Mrs Macdonnel said in a shocked voice, 'Och, he shouldnae gamble oan a Sunday! It's a mortal sin!' Then she pleaded with Eddy to go and find him and ask him to send home some money, promising him a sixpence from whatever John was pleased to send. Francie gave him the tram-fare and Eddy went on the errand, sulky and unwilling.

For two miles he rode through the hot pressure of tenement streets, then left the tram and went down a long path alongside the high fencing of a famous football club till he reached a wide waste piece of ground, bounded by chemical works, factories and pits. A mob of men and youths were gathered in a circle near a high slagheap, profuse with dandelions and other weeds which had blown and seeded there. Eddy was hot with shyness at the thought of pushing through this crowd of a hundred men to bend over and whisper to John, and he stood on the edge of the crowd, listening to them talking about the fight which had taken place on this spot. They were saying that Baldy Flynn was a dirty fighter and that the boxer's art had been futile against his brutal methods, but that, luckily for Mooney, the fight had been stopped after ten minutes by someone raising the false alarm that the police were coming.

Pipe and cigarette smoke soared from the crowd watching the gamblers. High on the slagheap a barelegged, redheaded urchin, in torn breeks and jacket over a filthy shirt, set there to watch out for the police, looked sharply every way very proud of his post, and called out frequently in shrill Doric: 'Kerry oan! A's weel!' and Eddy heard his brother loudly repeating: 'Any mair stakes? Any mair oan the cards? Nae mair stakes? Right! Ah'll turn up!' A dwarfish corner-boy, whom Eddy knew, sidled up to him and told him excitedly that his brother had won ten pounds and still held the bank; then he roughly shouldered those nearest them out of the way and made a path for Eddy into the inner ring.

Eddy waited till this critical moment in the game was over for a chance to speak to John, looking over the heads of a close circle of twenty men, some in their rough, working togs, others in their Sunday best, squatting on their haunches or seated on the ground with newspapers under them, before each man a thin shuffle of cards on which lay a small pile of silver and coppers. Most of them had thrown off jacket and waistcoat because of the heat, and with rolled-up sleeves and open shirtnecks revealed shaggy arms and chests. A gasp and stir of excitement passed through the crowd as John turned up the ace of hearts. A huge miner rose to his feet with an obscene oath and left the ring, throwing his jacket round his shoulder, saying: 'Ah'm skinn't! Ah'm leavin' the school!' Three spectators rushed to take his place, and the successful man threw his cap on the ground, saying: 'Ah bet ten boab oan this card!' and placed some silver on the card before him. John Macdonnel was joyfully raking in the money off all the cards as Eddy stood close to him. His bowler hat lay on a newspaper by his side, perspiration poured down his face, and his tightly brilliantined hair shone like a skull sculptured in gold. His big face beamed hilariously as he turned at Eddy's touch on his shoulder; then his heavy eyebrows crunched in a frown as he listened to his brother's whispered message. He hesitated, then dived a hand in his trouser pocket. 'Here's fifteen shillin's,' he said, 'ten fur me da an' maw an' five fur Jimmy. Away hame wi' ye, but don't tell them hoo much Ah've won!'

Eddy left the crowd, pocketing the money, and took a short cut to the Clyde down a lane past a hedge of wild briar. He walked along the semi-rural, semi-industrial shores, jingling the wealth of fifteen shillings in his trouser pocket, feeling the coins thud against his thigh as he walked wishing they were his own. Here the river ran obscure, discoloured, stinking with the foul waste from chemical works; there it shone limpidly, reflecting trees and flying birds. Couples passed or lay on the grass and the laughter of a picnic party echoed round him. He was bitterly resentful of his parents.

For the past two weeks his da and maw had squandered nearly every penny of his and his brother's contributions from their wages; now she would be sober for a spell and make them all miserable with moans about trying to save. Supposing he kept back a shilling? How would she know? And John wouldn't remember, anyway! Well, he would spend the sixpence she had promised him, but he was afraid she would nag him for it, saying he ought to have waited till she gave it to him. He found the drab stub of a Woodbine in the torn lining of his waistcoat pocket, lit it then spat it out, disgusted by its taste; the picture of his father hasting feverishly to that sheebeen in Rose Street causing disgust in his soul. He could just see him slinking up those filthy, dark stairs, trembling for fear of the police, to the dirty house where the big squint-eyed Irishwoman and her fly, wizened husband sold illegal booze on Sundays, to pay three times the fair price for a drop of poisoned drink. Why should I hurry for them? Why should I? Let them suffer! And he walked slowly, spitefully delaying, in his anger with his parents, and stopped to watch an Italian ice-cream vendor, serving cornets and wafers to a gay crowd of youths, girls and children from his gaily-painted barrow. His palate sensed the cold sweetness; he was sorely tempted to spend some of the money, but he walked on, in a mood of burning resentment against John, puzzled by his brother's alternate fits of meanness and generosity, because John hadn't given him anything, not even when he gave Francie a half-crown for washing his shirt, which Eddy had helped to get ready as well. And he wondered if John's luck would last. John was lucky at cards. He might win twenty pounds, but if he lost he would come home and sit glowering at the parlour window, not going out because he was skinned.

His resentment wore down and suddenly he began to laugh, remembering John's remark about Jimmy trying to teach Polly to say 'Ma wee feefee.' Jimmy was always bringing funny words home from foreign countries. What was yon he used to say when he came home from America? Yes siree! That was it. Yes siree! Funny! Perhaps 'Ma wee feefee' is French, he thought, wishing he knew some French, like his pal, Donald Hamilton. Yes siree! Eddy smiled at the Clyde, black here, near the city, then walked along studying the throngs of paraders through Glasgow Green, happy in the fine day, and looked towards the all-glass roof of the People's Palace, flashing back the brilliant light. He turned left and crossed the small Suspension Bridge from The Green to McNeil Street, and leant on the parapet, enjoying his old delight in its airy swing, gazing steadily at the swift current till he hypnotized himself into the belief that he and the bridge were sailing away. Overhead, gulls wheeled; below, people in hired punts and rowboats splashed gold from the black water. There was a sudden commotion at Donaldson's boathouse near the bridge, and redfaced George Donaldson, the stout little Humane Society officer, in his nautical uniform, pushed out a rowboat accompanied by a policeman who stood at the stern swinging grappling-irons. They were about to drag the river for a suicide and the narrow bridge became quickly packed with excited people. Some of them were talking about who it might be, and a woman next to Eddy said she was sure it was a girl she knew whom some man had got in the family-way, and a man said he was sure it was a fellow who lived in McNeil Street who had been unemployed for a long time. The small boat reached the middle of the river, the policeman slid the rope, and the sharp hooks sank in flowing blackness.

Eddy crushed his way out, not wishing to see any more. People said that fat river rats ate out the eyes of the drowned and horror filled him as he imagined the eyeless corpse dragged over the boat's side, dripping with black slime and blood. The cheerful day became gruesome and Eddy thought with pity of his parents' wretched state; recalling his father's decent, sober days, his mother's many times of kindness, her hard work for them all, her deep affection—and his quickened steps thudded the wooden floor of the bridge as he hurried home with the money.

The close known as 150 South Wellington street was like thousands of other Glasgow slum closes, a short, narrow walled-in passage leading up to three landings and through to a grassless earthen or broken-bricked back-court, with its small, mean communal washhouse and open, insanitary midden. In such back-courts the women of the tenements, after taking their weekly turn in the washhouse, hang out the family washing and take it in dried with sunshine or strong seawind and half-dirtied with industrial smoke and grime. They are the only playground of many thousands of the city's children, where the youngsters play football and children's games, climb on the midden and washhouse roofs and escape death or injury from the perilous traffic of the streets.

They look like tunnels cut through solid cliffs of masonry, these closes, and in the slums are decorated in the crudest style. Halfway up their walls are painted a stone or chocolate colour which is separated from whitewash by a stencilled border of another shade. There are often great holes in the walls of these closes, left unplastered or, if filled in, left unpainted and presenting unsightly daubs of crudely plastered cement. As the walls are for long periods unrefreshed with new paint, the old paint cracks and peels and the dingy whitewash flakes and falls before factors will spend money on property renovation. Many tenement dwellers live indifferent to all this ugliness and those with some spirit, who are angered by it all, lose heart in their long, unequal struggle against the tight-fistedness of factors, and live on and die in homes too narrow for fuller life, from which it seems there is no escape. These closes, badly lit, with their dangerous broken-stepped stairs, often filthy and mal-odorous, smelling of catspiss and drunkards' spew, have been for generations of Glaswegians the favourite, and for thousands, the only, courting-place, and many hurried, unhappy marriages have originated there. 'Stonnin' at the close' or 'closemooth' is a social habit of tenement dwellers and at all hours lone individuals lounge, staring vacantly.

At 150 South Wellington Street, the recognised meeting-place of the three apprentices of idealism, Donald Hamilton was whistling up the stairs to Jeannie Lindsay, his girl. His signal, two notes, one high, one low, like the chirp of one of the commoner singing birds, was as tuneful as his long, ungifted lips could make it, but it sounded his peculiar call, different from that of all other males who were calling their sweethearts in a similar way at seven o'clock of this Tuesday evening.

Having whistled thrice, Donald turned from the stairfoot to walk down the close, then stopped to suck vigorously at his extinguishing clay pipe. He was about to strike another match when he felt the bowl warming in his hand and saw a worm of smoke. He nodded satisfaction and vented a long fart which ripped along the close. He looked startled. 'By juv, that was a beezer! By juv! Trumpeter what are ye soundin' now? Good thing Jeannie didnae hear that yin!' He grinned with real physical pleasure, wishing he could have held it till his pals arrived. At such times he always struck an attitude reciting, 'Wheresoever you may be always let your wind go free' while his pals darted aside from him sniggering, with fingers at nose, Neil Mudge saying with refined disgust, 'Beefy, you're a filthy stinker! while Eddy Macdonnel always looked up with a holy look saying, 'I heard an angel's whisper,' or put up his hand like a schoolkid, bleating, 'Please teacher, what is peas?' Teacher. 'Peas is musical fruit.' Och, Eddy's a proper comedian sometimes. You can't deny it. He should be on the stage. Must have been the peasoup Ah had for tea. Shouldn't have had a second plate. But it was that good. My mother's the best soup-maker in Glesca. There's naebuddy can beat her at Scotch broth. He ambled reflectively to the closemouth and stood there his big strong nose proudly aloft, smoking contentedly, whiling time away, watching the fascinating life of the street.

In a three-roomed tenement on the first storey Jeannie Lindsay was clearing away the tea-things. She heard Donald's whistle but did not run with fluttering heart to the stairhead.

'There's that Donald Hamilton. He's gey early!' said Mrs Lindsay in a cold voice. She was not an unkind woman but she did not appreciate the possibility of Donald as a son-in-law. She expected her daughter to hook something more promising than a young apprentice slater whose arrogant self-assurance antagonised her. Her three grown sons were all back-street dudes and the pride of her bosom. She had paid out willingly for the education of Maurice, her eldest, at a High School followed by his employment in a stockbroker's office. His friends were superior clerks who lived in respectable localities like Hillhead and Anniesland, Crosshill and Battlefield and sometimes walked down South Wellington Street with a condescending, high-nosed walk to call on Maurice and go with him to Stock Exchange dances, tennis and bridge parties. On these rare occasions 150 and neighbourhood were much impressed by Maurice's classy pals in spite of the fact that his mother kept one of the most cluttered and dirty second-hand furniture shops in all The Gorbals and always looked as cluttered and dirty herself. She bought cheap, sold dear, and did nicely thank you. Summer and winter, in her two-windowed shop, she sat all day long gossiping with neighbours, absorbing everybody's private affairs, buying, sometimes from people selling their last sticks for money to bet or drink with, laughing much and heartily, driving hard bargains, and her red, dusty face glowed through the murky window with its litter of second-hand magazines and stained, slatternly books. Jeannie brought her dinner and tea to her there and she dined in public, never without a drop of whisky in every cup of tea, 'A drap o' the cratur to keep oot the cauld' as she said, mixing the tongues of Eire and Scotland. She knew fine she was cluttered and dirty, but she was cosy that way, and the knowledge did not weaken her conviction that her family was several degrees above the social depths of the street.

She wiped her mouth with her apron, nodded a frown at her daughter and said.

'Ye'll hae tae tell Donal' ye canny go oot wi' 'im the night,' then she snuggled into her peculiar, high-backed rocking chair which she had bought at a sale and kept for herself. Her stout frame was drowned deep in content after her high tea of shrimps and salad, lavish bread and butter, solid Scotch pastries and several cups of tea. Balancing a last cup on the arm of the chair she rocked herself gently. If they told her she was good to herself she answered without shame, 'Ay, ye need a guid inside linin' tae dae a hard day's work.' Everybody knew she worked harder than her husband who had been unemployed for so long it was a terrible strain on his memory and that of his family and friends to try and remember when he was last in a job. Mrs Lindsay kept him and filled her life with throbbing interest by constantly complaining about the burden he was. She would have been very disappointed if he had found work and deprived her of martyrdom. He helped her to buy at the sales, hiring a man to wheel all purchases; sometimes soiled his hands moving a bit of furniture into the shop and when his wife's criticism got under his skin, condescended to wheel the barrow himself. But, according to the standards of the locality, he dressed too well for a man who enjoyed handling junk. Nevertheless he had his strenuous hours. Every morning all through the Racing Season he knit his brows in agonizing thought over the columns of the *Noon Record* and *Sporting Chronicle*, deciding his daily bet with Dublin Daly, his favourite bookmaker. That decided, he plunged every power of his intellect into study of Socialist and Labour papers whose opinions he spouted with enjoyable pomp to the corner-boys up in Meikle's pub where he dismissed the 'eefeet and idle rich' with lordly gestures of contempt, so blinded by pomposity he couldn't see the corner-boys were egging him on. Therefore nearly all the work of The Wellington Furniture Stores was done by Mrs Lindsay's father, a stout, cheerful easy-natured man who packed himself away at nights like an odd item of old furniture on a rackety iron bed in a room at the rear of the shop.

Donald Hamilton was daydreaming the fine imposing husband he was being for Jeannie and visualizing the whole locality admiring him when he heard a familiar voice exclaim,

'Blast an' bugger it!' He turned his head to the left and there was Mr Lindsay, shutting up The Wellington Furniture Stores, next door to the close, fiddling irritably with the padlock and the flat iron doorbar. Donald knew exactly what troubled his prospective father-in-law. He smiled and as Mr Lindsay turned his portly stomach into the close he said brightly, 'Did a' yer hoarses go doon the day.'

Mr Lindsay's red, big-chinned face hung with disappointment, 'Ay, Donal' boay, the two o' them. Right doon the pan. Right doon the pan, Donal'. It was cattystrophic. Ye couldnae ca' it naethin' else.' He snatched the *Evening Times* from his pocket and pointed a quivering finger at Racing Results, 'D'ye see that! Ah've been followin' that filly Sonsy Meg right through the season an' at the critical moment, she lets me doon! It's cattystrophic. Accordin' tae her form she should have won in a canter. Oot o' the best racin' stable in Scotland, sired b' Rob Roy an' through him oot o' Flora Macdonald that's never lost a race. Ah put ma shirt oan her the day an' doubled her up wi' Hielan' Laddie, and look at her!'

'Whaur is she?' said Donald, peering at the paper.

'There! Tenth in the race. An' Hielan' Laddie roamps hame at ten-tae-one. That would 'ave been twenty poon fur ma five bob.' As Mr Lindsay pronounced the attractive sum which had dinned in his big head since the four-thirty race, gloom showered over him again and his rather prominent beery eyes fixed hotly the paper as if he could still see Sonsy Meg there tripping leisurely down the course at Lanark.

'Mibbe she's still runnin',' said Donald, to joke him out of his misery, hooting his powerful laugh in his ear.

Mr Lindsay winced, frowned and exploded, 'Well she can run till she draps deid for all I care for Ah'm feenished wi' her an' the whole racin' game.'

'Och, ye've said that before,' said Donald, thinking he would have sung a different tune if his double had won, 'It's a mug's game. Sure the Bookie always wins, but he'll never see the colour o' ma money.'

'Ah've said it before, Donal' boay, an' Ah'm sayin' it again, but this time Ah mean it. The whole Racin' fraternity's nothing but a bunch o' prevaricators, prognosticators and accumulators,' as the ripe words rolled out in his best style, Mr Lindsay began to cheer up. He sidelong glanced at the fine curve of his stomach of whose imposing concave he was secretly proud and breezed, 'What is the Turf? It's nuthin' but a gang o' robbers an' parasites suckin' dry the life blood o' the Proletariat. Ah'm askin' ye, what is the Turf? The plaything o' the idle rich an' a snare o' the Capitalist System tae beguile the Worker fae his Historic Mission.'

'That's good sound reasonin',' said Donald, seriously nodding, 'It's a peety the whole workin' class disnae see it your way. The Revolution widnae be far off.'

With that twenty pounds in his pocket Mr Lindsay would have shaken Donald heartily by the hand for such intelligent appreciation of his eloquence but he could only summon enough interest to ask Donald if he was waiting for Jeannie and said he would give her the nod when he got upstairs. As he neared the door of his house, all his bluff passed out of him like air from a pricked balloon. Could he squeeze that shilling out of his wife which would get him the three pints and two nips he needed to help him drown his loss and face tomorrow with his usual confidence? Maybe she would only go the length of a tanner. He sighed heavily.

Mrs Lindsay knew what he was after the minute he came in and steeled herself to refuse him. He hung his cap on a lobby peg and walking into the kitchen whispered to Jeannie at the sink. Mrs Lindsay stopped rocking herself.

'Ay, we ken fine Donald's at the close,' she said, 'but he can kick his heels. It'll no' hurt him tae wait a wee. Jeannie was oot wi' him last night an' Sunday. She's no merrit tae him yet. She has Maurice's suit tae press for the dance at the Assembly Rooms an' she canny gang oot till efter eight.'

Mr Lindsay sat down and said nothing. He had no courage left to argue with. All he desired at the moment was to blow gently the froth off a pint and drink damnation to the Turf. He was vaguely interested in the disposal of his daughter but he liked Donald and stood up for him against his wife. He appreciated the respectful attention Donald always gave to his powerful and eloquent arguments, but he had nothing to say for him at the moment. He coughed pompously. Another time he would paint Donald's virtues with irresistible eloquence. At the moment he needed all his powers to borrow a shilling. If it hadn't been for Sonsy Meg, sod her, he would be surrounded now with a fascinated ring of corner-boys, admiring his brilliant speeches. He longed to be there. Even now, with a pint down him he could rally his powers and magnetize their attention. But his wife looked invincible tonight and his heart sank with the fear that the pub would close before he won her round.

Jeannie continued washing the dishes, the flush which had mantled her cheeks when she heard Donald's whistle, still lingering there. She was eighteen, a high-coloured thin but well-formed girl with bright, tender, clear blue eyes, glossy blonde hair and brisk, light movements acquired through her constant hurry from one domestic task to another. She had done all the work of the house since the moment she was capable of handling a broom and scrubber. She did not answer her mother. She would have defied her had her heart been warmer towards Donald but there was no male alive whom she loved better than her three brothers. She thrilled at the thought of preparing Maurice's cheap evening-dress suit and shirt for the Stock Exchange dance. He was her favourite. Smiling, she pictured him. Tall, sleek hair well-oiled, blond, acquiline countenance, so proud and conceited! He ordered her about and was never satisfied but she loved it. He would be sure to criticize her careful laundering. She had turned him out for many dances and commercial and social affairs but this one was very important. He was to meet his employer's daughter tonight.

She smiled secretly and hurried, her fingers itching to be at the suit. Delight made her wipe the last dish with a flourish. She lit a ring of the gas stove, put on the pressing iron and flew downstairs to tell Donald she couldn't be ready till after eight. She couldn't help it if he was angry. Let him be! Maurice would be home any minute and within the hour she would have him turned out as smart as one of those dummies in Fraser's window, the 'Eelyte' tailors as she called it, in Argyle Street.

As she left the kitchen she heard her father opening his campaign with a humble request for a sixpence which she knew would rise to a shilling or more with the least encouragement. She hoped he would get it then he would clear out and leave her more room in the kitchen to work for Maurice. When she reached the foot of the stairs she saw Eddy Macdonnel standing with Donald and her heart jumped at the sight of him. She liked him for his shyness and was sorry he had never asked her to walk out. She walked out with Donald, always under protest and wondering why she did it. His self-confidence overwhelmed her but she was determined not to marry him. It wasn't going that far. Never fear!

Donald took his pipe from his mouth, amazed at her. Keeping him waiting to please a big jessie like Maurice! 'Och, ye'll be merryin' him next. The big dude! I'm Burlington Bertie from Bow. Ah weesh some smart wee skirt wid get the haud o' him an' merry him, the big saftie!'

Jeannie flushed angrily, tossing her head, 'Ye can please yersel' if ye wait or no'!' she said and turned and walked upstairs.

Donald's self-esteem staggered. He stared open-mouthed and put his pipe in his pocket, then, collecting himself he ran after her taking three stairs at a time and caught her at the turn of the stairs by her slim bare arm. She struggled and he pushed her roughly against the door of the landing water-closet, threw his arms awkwardly round her and tried to kiss her. She was enraged at his derision of Maurice. She struggled fiercely. She would have slapped his face but her hands were held and she cried out, 'Leave me alane. Take yer hauns aff me, ye big daftie. Leave go of me!' then she burst into tears and Donald stepped away from her and stood redfaced, confused, offering her his hanky, telling her not to be daft.

From the closemouth Eddy watched them, deeply bewildered, seething with a romantic urge to hurl himself between them, push Donald scornfully aside, put his protective arm round Jeannie and with his head proudly up tell Donald he was a bully and coward to treat her like that. But Donald was his best pal and that fearless. He would face up to anybody, fight the best fighter anywhere. Sure hadn't he fought the champion of the Shamrock Boys gang yon Saturday night up in the Shamrock Billiard Rooms. Eddy held Donald's cap expecting every minute the whole gang would set on them but it was a fair fight and Donald was only saved from a bad beating by the billiard-room proprietor arriving suddenly and stopping the fight. And Donald was that generous, always treating him and his pals to ices and cigarettes up in Joe Boganny's, free with his money when he had overtime. But tonight Eddy had hoped for the bliss of talking to Jeannie with Donald out of the way. It was always delightful to meet Jeannie anywhere in the street in rain or shine with her birdlike step, the light bright way she carried herself, the smiling, lightsome toss of her head, never gloomy. She was entirely like a clean, frank smile and cheered him deep inside. Och, he had spent whole afternoons leaning against the lintel of the washhouse door in the back-court watching her, her slim legs in big rubber wellingtons and a rubber apron on, doing a huge family washing and him wondering where she got the strength, she was so slender. Her face half-vanishing and reappearing in steam as she worked at the boiling copper, her shapely arms plunging into crystal froth of soapsuds in the tub, raising a sappled hand now and then to touch back fallen strands of hair from her flushed face moist with sweat and steam. And all the while her pretty movements endeared her to him and he afraid to tell her so. And now, as she stood there weeping, brighter because of that ugly watercloset door and the brokenpaned filthy landing window, it was as if her tears were falling inside him. And Donald was wenching her. Ach! His fists clenched in his trouser pockets. He didn't know what to feel and a glimmering of the complexity of human relationships began to irritate his vague, slow head.

Suddenly Mrs Lindsay appeared, her red face, which she had washed this evening, shining like a polished apple, a bright new print blouse ballooned by her handsome breasts. The rattling of the closet door and Jeannie's cries had carried through the open house door which Jeannie had left ajar and Mrs Lindsay had heaved herself unwillingly out of her comfort to see what the trouble was. She bulked round the bend of the stairs and stared at Donald with one hand on her hip, the other round Jeannie, 'Oh ye big galoot,' she said, 'Ah could spin ye! Ah could just spin ye roon' till Ah birled some sense intae yer heid. Awa doon they stairs an' dinny show yer face up this close again. Awa wi' ye noo an' stoap upsettin' ma lassie!'

Donald flushed, without a word for himself. He had not bargained for this. When he threw his arms round Jeannie he was elated with mastery, now he felt like a chastised schoolboy, but he tried to appear more manly than ever by casting his head ridiculously high and taking out his pipe and rattling his matchbox when he knew fine it was full, then as he was about to light his pipe he was presented with Mr Lindsay, a figure of irascible dignity, his halfbald head sloped like a melon, his stomach impressively paraded and thumbs in his lapels, exasperated by this noisy intrusion at the critical opening of his case for the price of a drink.

'What's all this?' he boomed, 'What's goin' on here? Whit's a' the tears an' the tantrums aboot? Are ye'se all iggorant, standin' here makin' ma family a public spektikkle? Can a man nut get a drop o' rest tae think oot the pressin' problems o' life after a hard day's toil? Is naebuddy goin' tae answer me? Are ye'se goin' tae bring the whole property tae look intae oor private affairs?' as he said this he swung upstairs his most scornful gaze, metaphorically looking down on the two neighbours, an elderly and a young woman, listening carefully at their partly-open doors. They whisked inside, banging their doors and Mr Lindsay, pleased with his powerful glance, laying his hand imperiously on Jeannie's shoulder, pointed upwards, 'Get up they stairs!' and started back as Jeannie whirled round hysterically and cried, pointing at Donald, 'Och, it's no' me! It's him. He thinks he's Lord O' The Isles an' he's only—he's only Lord Mud!' and she ran upstairs with her handkerchief at her eyes.

Her mother turned and followed her and Mr Lindsay winked solemnly at Donald an understanding signal of the eye between man and man about these Women. Then he said loudly, 'As for you Donal' me boy, Ah'v nuthin' to

say to you except tae ask ye tae clear oot! Vamoose!' Mr
Lindsay waved him away and Donald with a half-smile at
him went down to the closemouth and joined Eddy.

They stood there in wordless, youthful confusion, edging
apart to let people come in and out the close. Donald was
staring with a grim set frown and handling his pipe with
exaggerated adult gestures. Eddy was eyeing his set face
with sidelong glances.

'Wimmen!' said Donald, 'Jeez!' then with an obscene
phrase he dismissed the whole sex and as if he was shaking
off the influence of Women, he gushed a mouthful of smoke,
shrugged his shoulders and manfully swung down the street.
Eddy followed him and as they walked Donald suggested
calling on Neil Mudge, 'He expected tae feenish his treetiz
oan "Individualism" the night. Ah'll see if we can get him
tae read it an' we'll find whit stuff it's made of.'

They drifted down South Wellington Street for a hundred
yards and as they crossed the burnished tramlines of Gowan
Street, Eddy said tactlessly.

'Jeannie was lookin' lovely the night.'

Donald flushed and curled his lip. Eddy's remark had
touched him on the raw, 'Och, wimmen are fast becomin'
ma beet noyer,' he said, proud of his piddle of French and
his nodding acquaintance with Nietzsche. He turned a dry
nod to the greeting called after him by one of the group of
corner-boys standing at Cochrane's the corner-grocers, 'It's
nae wunner that some o' the world's greatest men hiv been
misohgynists. Wimmin hiv nae souls. Their only purpose
in creation is tae breed the race an' when they've done that
they're aboot as interestin' as stripped bean-puds. There's
nut wan o' thim is fit mate for a Superman. They don't know
the meanin' o' the words, "Freedom an' Independence!"'

Eddy listened silently, studying Donald's supermanly
expression, envying him his arrogant way with girls. Women
were a mystery to Eddy. He could never find the things to
say that flattered or amused them, though he was always
dreaming of himself in triumphant situations with maidens
of fancy and the few girls he knew, situations in which he
delighted them with brilliant conversation, holding them
spellbound by his masterful personality, but when he was

actually with them he stood tongue-tied, burning with dumb desire.

They had turned into Mathieson Street that led down to the Clyde, where back-street life surged and shouted round them, making the mild Autumn evening stuffy and hot. Two distinct games of football were being played in this last portion of the street with about forty rough lads and youths wildly shouting as they kicked about an immense football made of paper and string. Knots of ragged children, crowding the pavement, played old Scottish singing games, dancing, clapping hands; boys whipped peeries, played jorries or ran madly with steel cleek and gird; with a rusty, rattling bike, some boys were learning to cycle; girls hopped under skipping ropes, played peever or tossed coloured chukkies; two boys on roller-skates sailed recklessly along the smooth macadam; the pavements were crudely chalked with juvenile games; from top storeys downward at every other window husbands and wives leant out on cushions or pillows, groups of youths and girls stood at the closes, old people sat there on stools and from first storey windows tenants shouted conversation with neighbours at the close.

'This is life with the lid off,' said Eddy as they crossed the street, threading among the rushing footballers.

'It's the Mob at play, the slaves o' ceevilisation seethin' on the dunghill o' Capitalism,' said Donald, relishing his phrases which he believed he had just invented.

They regarded the 'Mob' with tragic superiority, then suddenly laughed heartily as a little bowlegged goalkeeper in a desperate dash at the ball, tripped headlong over one of the goalposts, a pile of heaped jackets and caps.

'It must be hard fur wee Rabbie tae save the ba' wi' they bandy legs o' his,' said Donald, 'Ye could run a tramway through them!'

They turned right, into Adelphi Street and entered one of the closes, cleaner and quieter than those in South Wellington Street and Gowan Street. Mounting to the third storey they knocked at one of its three doors. It was opened by Mrs Mudge, an extremely small faded Scotswoman of the size locally referred to as 'a nice wee body.' She invited them into the infinitesimal square entrance hall and called through to Neil, who could be heard rustling papers in his bedroom, that his friends had arrived.

Eddy had prayed that the six Mudge sisters would be out because he always perspired with embarrassment among them. They were all studious, all prize-winners at school and disconcertingly intelligent. But the entire sextette was at home as he walked into the kitchen, hiding behind Donald. Janet, the eldest, a fat young woman of thirty, was washing her hair at the sink. She whipped a towel from a nail and pinned it round her bare shoulders but not before they saw her robust breasts, urging out of her stays. She greeted them with a bright, flushed smile and began drying her brown hair, her big, confident eyes, lively and intelligent, studying them. Charmed by that glimpse of nakedness, Eddy, glancing at her homely, russet complexion, thought her quite pretty, then his old confusion in this female kitchen overcame him while Donald was coolly putting his pipe away.

'Och, ye can smoke awa, Donal',' said Mrs Mudge, We're used tae it here. Sure Mr Mudge smokes like a lum!' and she offered to bring them chairs, but Donald said they wouldn't be staying.

Flora Mudge, a dark young woman of twenty-four sat at the window knitting and reading Galsworthy's *Man of Property*, raising her head now and then to look over Glasgow Green across the canal-straight strip of the Clyde at the gloomy Nelson monument and the terracotta coloured Victoria Jubilee fountain, which never played; two sisters, sixteen and seventeen respectively, sat reading at opposite sides of the fire while the two youngest, eleven and twelve, monopolised both ends of the table with copybooks and opened school-primers. The six sisters were all spectacled and bantam size, as though destiny had strictly forbidden them to grow beyond their mother. Suddenly the five who were reading, raised their hands and smiles at the visitors and the gaslight glancing on their glasses gave them an owlish look. With one simultaneous smile, they fixed their eyes on their books again.

Donald and Janet were political opponents and Donald

asked her if her essay on 'Feminism' which had been set as
a subject of a literary competition by the *New Statesman*,
had been accepted. She said with cheerful pride it was being
published as the second prize-winner and they began a lively
argument on 'Feminism.' Janet dried her hair and was easily
winning the argument when Neil entered and saved Donald
from shameful defeat.

Neil's hair, which sprouted like lawn grass was tousled
and implied that he had emerged from a terrific struggle
with thought. His mother asked him if he had finished his
essay. 'Yer eyes look tire't,' she said, 'Ye'd better gie them
a wee bit rest.'

Neil's stocky figure never at any time suggested intellectual asceticism, but he loved to act the man fatigued by
thought. He put his shirtsleeved arm round his mother's
shoulder and uttered with fond condescension, 'Ay, Ah've
just feenished the pairoration. Puir wee mither, of the
making of books there's nae end an' much study is a
weariness o' the flesh. We Thinkers plum' the very depths
o' misery an' scale the heights o' joy!' He sighed heavily,
passing his hand across his brow, removed his pince-nez,
dangled them for a moment as though plunged in fathomless
preoccupation, slowly put them in a case, slowly inserted
that in his waistcoat pocket and shook his head, muttering
audibly: 'Ay, Thoaght! Thoaght! It leads ye oan—tae
what?' Then, staring at space with a Faustlike stare, he
recited in a tragic voice:

> *Introspection's cancer,*
> *Baffling surgeon's knife,*
> *Hoping, groping, blinking, thinking,*
> *Some men Call it* LIFE!

Five sisters lifted heads to look at him in pride and
Janet, while she wrapped a towel turban-wise round her
hair, smiled with maternal possessiveness at the back of
his head.

'Yer hair's toozl't, son,' said his mother, 'Ye'll hae tae
brush it doon afore ye gang oot.'

'He's sicklied ower wi' the pale cast o' thoaght,' said
Donald impressively.

'What?' said the little woman, who was faintly deaf.

'It's fae *Hamlit*, ye ken,' said Donald repeating the quotation.

Mrs Mudge nodded her head. '*Hamlit*,' she echoed musingly, as if it was the name of an optical disease, 'Ay, *Hamlit*. Neil reads too much. It's no' guid for his een, d'ye think it is?' she inquired peering anxiously at the youths.

'Och, there's naething wrong wi' ma hair nor ma een, mother,' Neil exclaimed irritably. He was proud of the literary disorder of his hair and her suggestion that it was untidy always irritated him. In a state of great annoyance he walked into his bedroom to get his jacket, his head slightly inclined to the right, a posture that, beginning as an affectation, had become a habit.

He came out again still looking intellectually wearied and preoccupied.

'Have ye goat yer treetiz?' asked Donald.

Neil struck a modest air. 'Och, I'll not bring it the night,' he said, ' I don't feel I'd do it justice. Composin' the pairoration has left me exhausted.'

His pals offered the encouragement he was hoping for and he threw off the mask of modesty and produced his essay. All its power and glory were concealed between the glossy blue covers of a twopenny copy-book which he stuffed into his pocket as they went downstairs. Turning into the street he said, beaming innocent enthusiasm, 'My, they pairorations always give me trouble, but, by jings, I think this is the finest I've ever done! Y'know, I sat starin' at the blank page till I thought my reason had gone. It was like "Waitin' for the star from Heaven tae fall"—now who was it wrote that?' he mused, pausing—'then it just rushed oan me like a sudden stoarm an' words poured through me like a torrent. By jings, inspiration's a wonderful thing!'

Neil mentally patted Eddy on the shoulder, gratified by his look of awe. 'Ay, there's something in young Macdonnel, though he's so quiet,' he thought, deciding to present Eddy with a volume of 'Keats,' judging after 'mature reflection' that 'Coleridge' would be too intellectual for him.

'Och, Ah never find essays difficult, once Ah get past the start,' said Donald nonchalantly, 'It's the first sentence that jiggers me; once Ah've wrote that Ah carry oan like a hoose oan fire. Noo, Ah remember when Ah wrote ma study o' Milton; Ah began it at twelve o'cloack at night efter tryin' for three hoors tae get the op'nin' words an' Ah feenished it at three o'clock in the moarnin' an' was up at six as fresh as a daisy.' He took three gratified puffs at his pipe, drawing himself up while Neil frowned, nettled by his cocksureness.

The three apprentices went through the gaslit streets for an hour's walk over the Town, saying little. Neil was conning over his essay, finding it faultless in composition and devoid of fallacies; Donald was collecting all his well-used arguments, quotations and slogans to riddle it with criticism, convinced that Neil wouldn't produce anything original; Eddy was darting ardent futile glances at all the prettiest girls in the crowds of workers parading brilliantly-lit Argyle Street, wondering if they were smitten with his amazing wealth of hair. They meandered, identified with the noise the lights and the crowd-life, drawn into, thrilled by it in spite of their view of themselves as thinkers superior to it, up Renfield and along Sauchiehall Streets to Charing Cross where they turned back along the quieter ways of Elmbank and Bothwell streets, down Hope Street, round by The Broomielaw, over the Suspension Bridge and through The Gorbals to South Wellington Street. As they approached 150, Donald looked eagerly ahead hoping to see Jeannie Lindsay there and was disappointed at seeing only Paddy Maguire and Bobby Logan, their unintellectual pals, who made no pretensions to politics, poetry or culture, but who always listened respectfully when the other three debated, exclaiming in amusement at the immensely long words they lavished.

Bobby Logan, a youth of nineteen, with thick pasty features and silvery light hair, almost albino, was a counterhand in the local Co-operative Stores. The ambition of his life was to become the Stores manager, but he reckoned he would have to wait about twenty years. Happily he was a patient youth and did not goad Time on but served dutifully the Co-operative ladies of The Gorbals with goods and dividends, knowing well that the grave in due course would swallow down a manager or two and then he would stand victorious in the dead man's shoes as sole director of the Butchery, Bakery, Grocery, Dairy and Provisions.

Paddy Maguire was a dark, sturdy young rivetter of twenty, Glasgow born of an Irish farmer. His father's dairy, which scraped a living from a portion of South Wellington Street, competing with nine other dairies there, and where rancid cheese, sour milk, cats and fly-paper caused an outstanding smell, stood opposite the close 150. Paddy worked in the shipyards and helped to eke out his father's income which was sadly reduced every week by bad credit customers.

The five friends met with cheerful greetings and stood around humming snatches of ragtime songs, then sooty Glasgow rain, loaded with smoke and grime, began to fall and they drew farther into the close where Neil, longing painfully to be asked to deliver the bundle of great thoughts that were bulging out his pocket said with a look of despair, 'My Goad, here's that aul' blether Lindsay comin' doon, we're for it now!' and they all looked upstairs at Mr Lindsay, who had just emerged from the landing watercloset and stood there inserting himself with slow dignity into an overcoat and pulling his cap closer down on his head while regarding them with a grave careworn gaze. He was a holy terror to the youths for he never met them in the close without starting a political argument which always ended as a long wordy lecture while they stood shifting from foot to foot itching with boredom.

'Try an' look as if we're not here an' he'll pass by' said Eddy Macdonnel, smiling at Neil who was too woestruck to return his smile. But Mr Lindsay relieved them all by passing without a word or a nod. At the moment they were all beneath his notice. His vocal chords were as dry as a truss of sunburned hay and his mental faculties were under a cloud. He had used the cream of his talents to extract that shilling from his wife. All he had left now was his thirst and his desire to get back at the Capitalist System for which he blamed everything, even the disgraceful defeat of Sonsy Meg. He could see it all now. She had been held in so as to get longer odds at another race-meeting. Ay, there was some jiggerypokery there. Some more Capitalist trickery. As he butted into the heavy rain he was stringing together the blackest propaganda facts he could fish out of his memory to tear down before the corner-boys the whole 'rotten structure of Capitalist Society.'

'Thank Goad Ah wasn't readin' my essay when that aul' gasbag came doon,' said Neil.

'Och, when are ye gaun' tae start readin' it? Ye're haudin' back like a wee lassie that's asked tae sing at a party!' said Donald.

Neil flushed but flashed his essay out of his pocket, 'Ah didn't know ye were so anxious tae hear it,' he said.

'Ach, Ah want tae hear whit stuff it's made o'. Ye've been dingin' in oor ears aboot it's wonderful style an' arguments for weeks noo.' Donald said.

'"Essay?"' What's that?' asked Paddy Maguire.

'Och, ye'll hear what it is in a minnit,' said Donald, 'Come intae the foot o' the stairs an' listen,' and they all grouped beneath the broken entry lamp, where Neil turned the glossy, blue exercise book, glinting in the drear light, folded back its covers with trembling fingers and revealed the word INDIVIDUALISM written in large block letters at the top of the first page.

'It's no' very long,' he said modestly.

'Och, it disnae matter,' said Donald, 'We've goat a' night.'

Neil coughed and uttered 'Individualism' in a small nervous voice and at that moment six children rushed downstairs screaming in play, skeltered back into the close, alarmed by the rain, and gathered curious round the youths, till Donald drove them away, when they ran and sat staring, halfway up the stairs.

'Damn they kids!' exclaimed Neil, proceeding with his introduction. His voice was acquiring power as he turned the third page when a happy drunkard rolled into the close, shaking off the rain like a dog and stopping to leer fatuously at them all.

'My, it's wat enough tae droon the nine lives o' a cat!' he solemnly assured them, bowing and raising a battered, mouldy bowler, then he staggered upstairs singing, 'Ah luv a lassie, A bonny Hielan' lassie!' and the children ran before him amused and afraid, while the essayist sighed, frowned, resumed and read for ten minutes uninterrupted. Paddy Maguire and Bobby Logan were becoming restive, eyeing each other with lowbrowed sympathy; Eddy Macdonnel listened engrossed, while Donald Hamilton folded his arms and puffed his pipe, looking very wise. Neil's 'treetiz' was concerned with the relations of the individual to the State and it threatened every kind of State, Communist, Socialist, Conservative or Ecclesiastical with dire consequences if it dared to make unreasonable inroads on personal liberty, and Donald condemned its logic with lordly scorn, for it was evident that Neil was refusing the State any rights at all.

Donald was so staggered by the essay's theories that he was about to interrupt the entranced reader when a stout hawker with a huge packsheet bundle of cast-off garments, her day's collection from middle-class houses, waddled into the close, her burden hanging down her back, swinging from side to side. The listeners made way for her but Neil read on mesmerized by the glory of his composition and the hawker's bundle, grazing the copybook, swept it from his hand while she puffed on upstairs unconscious of her interference with poetry and wisdom.

Paddy and Bobby laughed, but Eddy looked with sincere concern at Neil, rudely wakened from his self-imposed hypnotism. He snatched, startled, at his pince-nez, and as Donald handed him the copy-book he stuffed it indignantly into his pocket, walked rapidly to the closemouth and stood quivering with wrath, feeling that he had suffered the final indignity and toying with the suspicion that Donald had listened as indifferently as Paddy and Bobby despite his appearance of attention.

Donald strode after him, loudly asking if he wasn't going to finish the essay, for he didn't want to lose this glorious opportunity to lam into Neil's conglomeration of fallacious ideas. Neil glowered, silent, then said, 'Ach, it's rotten. It's no' worth reading!' and obstinately refused to continue till Eddy, whose mind had flown elated on the procession of words, happily indifferent to association of ideas, expressed his genuine appreciation of Neil's prose, and Neil, flattered and incited by a desire to rise on the wings of his 'pairoration,' consented to read the remaining pages.

They all returned to their stand under the lamp; Paddy and Bobby hovering near out of politeness, though they were feverish with boredom; Donald resumed his critical attitude; Eddy his look of eager attention. Neil began reading, flatly at first, but when he reached the last page he had warmed up and throwing his whole self into the last phrase, the crest of his 'pairoration,' he almost shouted, 'Individualism! We await Thy Glorious Dawn!' and tears glinted against his glasses as he stood for a moment with bent head and arms hung, like an exhausted orator.

'Ha, that was damn guid!' cried Paddy Maguire with terrific relief.

'My, that was great, Neil! Great!' cried Eddy aglow with Socialistic emotion and wanting to shake 'comrade' Neil by the hand, while Bobby Logan smiled his Punchlike smile, his long chin tilting up to meet his long curved nose.

As if he was forcing himself with a fearful effort back to reality, Neil shrugged his shoulders dramatically, pocketed the exercise-book, faced Donald with a challenging look and said quietly, apparently indifferent to Donald's and the world's opinion.

'Well, what did ye think of it?'

Donald slowly pointed his pipe, 'Ay, it was good,' he admitted in a hesitating, reflective voice, 'It didnae lose interest onywhere. Ah think it was an improvement oan yer treetiz oan Free Wull An' Determinism.' He suspected that the bulk of the essay had been contributed by Schopenhauer, Emerson, Thomas Carlyle and Bernard Shaw, though he had to allow that the plagiarisms had been well organised. 'Mind ye,' he hastened to add, 'Ah don't agree wi' the theeziz in wan particular!' and he shook his pipe at Neil like an elderly philosopher.

'I didn't expect ye would!' said Neil, resenting his knowing manner and thinking, 'Who is he tae pass literary judgments!'

Donald then made a scornful reference to one of the essay's major points and they began an argument on 'The Individual And The State,' with Neil vigorously attacking, heartened by his literary success. Eddy Macdonnel lit a Woodbine and listened with a broad amiable smile, drinking in their erudition; Paddy Maguire and Bobby Logan strayed to the middle of the close singing 'Alexander's Ragtime Band,' Paddy contributing a tuneless bass, Bobby's Punchlike features moving up and down crazily as he moaned a nasal tenor.

At that moment Jeannie Lindsay danced down the stairs her neat blonde hair gleaming beneath a gay, blue umbrella, wearing a shimmery rubber rainproof of emerald green and holding in her hand a highly-coloured quart jug as she was going to fetch her mother a quart of bedtime stout from the Jug and Bottle of The Shamrock Bar. Eddy saw her and immediately lost interest in the argument. She was the perfect little lady. Bent prettily beneath the umbrella she looked as if her hands had never in her life touched duster, sweeping brush or scrubber. Eddy ached with passionate desire to take her arm and escort her to the pub and imagined it so keenly that he felt the softness of her arm, the warmth of her side against his hand. She reached the foot of the stairs, gave Donald an injurious look, threw her whole heart into her eyes for Eddy and made him redden like a boiled carrot, replied with a little lyrical laugh to a naughty remark of Paddy Maguire's then her small seductive steps carried her into the pouring rain.

Donald, thunderstruck, realized that loveliness had passed by. Thrusting his glowing pipe in his pocket he shouted, 'Hi Jeannie! What the hell are ye scootin' away like that for? Hi, wait a minnit. Ah want tae talk tae ye!' and dashed furiously into the down-pour like a satyr pursuing a desirable nymph.

'Well! The ignorant buggar!' cried Neil, swallowing the torrent of eloquence that was gushing from his lips, 'What bloody manners' and he looked at Eddy with indignation inflaming his pince-nez.

'It wasn't exactly polite,' agreed Eddy, not wishing to be hard on a pal who shared his political outlook.

'Polite!' cried Neil, 'It was atavistic. It was uncouth!' Then with a theatrical shudder he waved his hand entirely discarding Donald, 'Och, what could ye expect from a

Materialist an' a Communist,' he said and went on talking
about higher things, mincing his young voice in the manner
of those Scotsmen who strangle their broad native tongue to
imitate upper-class English. Across the street an enormous
natural voice was booming, 'Hi! Paddy! Will ye come
an' look afthur the shop?' and Paddy Maguire ran across
to deputize for his father, who stood at his shop door, a tall
massive, blackbearded man, stooping and peering under a
streaming umbrella, impatient to be going to his evening
dram in the Snug of the Rob Roy Arms.

Bobby Logan sang on alone. He was secretly convinced
that his voice was exactly similar in volume and style to that
of a famous American ragtime singer and always wondered
why he was never asked to sing at parties. 'You made me
love you,' he crooned,

> *I didn't want to do it. I didn't want to do it!*
> *You made me want you.*
> *And all the time you knew it. I guess you always knew*
> *it!*
> *You made me happy sometimes,*
> *You made me sad,*
> *But there were times dear, you made me simply mad!*
> *I want some love that's true,*
> *Yes I do. 'Deed I do! You know I do!*
> *So give me, give me, what I sigh for,*
> *You know you've got the sort of kisses that I'd die*
> *for!*
> *You know you made me love you!*

Eddy Macdonnel was suddenly overcome by a great
weariness with learning and culture and Neil's genteel voice.
A deep longing for love and ragtime troubled his heart. Out
of the ghastly light shed by the broken mantle he glanced
impatiently from Neil to the end of the close that held the
drum of relentless rain and the echoes of song and debate. He
wanted to be standing there with Bobby, humming 'Itchy
Koo' and 'Casey Jones' and shuffling his feet to syncopation.
But Neil, taking his arm, said he was going home to finish
the evening reading. Eddy agreed to go with him as far as
his close, silently deciding to come back and join Bobby
and Donald when Neil was indoors and they left Bobby,

who lived on the second storey at 150, crooning away like a nonstop gramophone.

'Ah'm glad ye liked ma essay,' said Neil as they hurried through the slashing rain. He went on to say he was going to improve it and get it published and Eddy said simply he'd like to read it again. Neil handed it to him eagerly and told him he had a rare taste in words and ought to start reading poetry. 'Donald's a crude beast,' he said, 'He has nae finesse; only a good memory wi' which he sops up an' holds other men's ideas like a sponge holds water.' When they arrived at Neil's close and Neil delivered a brief monologue on the vital need for Poetry and Music in the Worker's life, while the furious rain slanted metallic lines past the closemouth, they became so cosy with mutual esteem that they shook hands warmly, an action they rarely performed when they were saying goodnight.

Five pairs of rubbersoled running shoes slapped the wet tiled sidewalk around the Greenhead Swimming Baths as the apprentices issued in running-kit out of their cubicles. For a few minutes they stood on the edge of the bath where there was hardly room to swim two yards in the surging, noisy crowd of naked men, youths and boys, from Oatlands, Bridgeton, Calton and The Gorbals, refreshing themselves after their day's work in pits, steelworks and tubeworks, tanneries, dyeworks and bakeries.

'Jeez, it's like a herrin'-shoal!' said Donald Hamilton, 'Ah hope hauf o' this crowd'll be gone b' the time we get back fae oor run.' He stooped, massaging his hips and calves, 'limbering-up' as he called it, telling the others to limber-up the way famous athletes and footballers always did. He always told them that and they invariably disregarded his advice but just stood, as they were standing now, smiling down at the clamorous pack of humanity that surged and crashed the leaping water.

It was the night following Neil's reading of his essay and the occasion of their bi-weekly run and swim. Paddy Maguire and Bobby Logan were crack forwards in the amateur Gorbals Rovers and kept in training with this run and swim on Wednesdays and Fridays. Their three pals joined them on these nights to keep 'Mens sana in corpore sano' as Neil and Donald expressed it. The first time they said that Paddy Maguire asked with a grin, 'An' whit aboot women's sano?' When their intellectual pals had recovered from their laughter they patiently explained that 'Mens' meant 'mind' but Paddy's question never failed to raise a laugh whenever they were hard-up for a joke.

They walked out in single file along the crowded bath-side, and at the office where they had left their money and valuables, edged past a queue of men and youths waiting to go in, and started off at a slow trot through a golden autumn evening cutting past the small railed greens of Glasgow Green and over the short McNeil Street suspension bridge to the south shore of the Clyde. They were a highly-coloured quintette. Donald Hamilton, a Ranger's supporter, wore a jersey of royal blue, Paddy Maguire, a supporter of Hibernians, one of dark green, Bobby Logan sported the white-trimmed crimson of Third Lanark and Neil Mudge the blood red jersey of The Clyde. Eddy Macdonnel, who had bought his first running-kit on the Saturday at Lumleys in Sauchiehall Street, ran in a white singlet trimmed at the neck and sleeves with bright blue. He was a Celtic supporter but at the last moment chose those neutral colours, convinced that while he was struggling between his Faith and atheism it would be hypocrisy to sport the green and white colours of a famous team supported by all the Catholics.

They all wore white running-shorts and every eye on the promenaded Green followed them, but they ran impervious to laughs, catcalls and the cries of boys, 'Hi! There's the Harriers!' Donald Hamilton smoked his clay pipe as he ran, to show off the power of his lungs and his pals cursed him for attracting unnecessary attention while he roared laughter at their confusion. Three prostitutes of the lowest social grade, who gave their unclean bodies to drunkards' fumblings beneath the railway arches of the Goosedubbs, Paddy's Market and Bridgegate in return for a drink or the price of a bed for the night in a women's Model, were sitting on a green near the bridge. Their faces, deprived of all womanly feature by cheap drink and beatings were grotesque with laughter at the procession of the running apprentices and one of them, pointing at Donald's thighs called out something about jigging balls. Donald laughed and Bobby Logan, with surprising brilliance remarked, 'She's one o' the ruins that Cromwell knocked about a bit. Did ye hear Marie Lloyd at the Pav, last week? Och, she was great!'

Neil Mudge coughed priggishly, 'Ah like my humour clean,' he said.

'Och, you're too parteecular!' said Donald, 'Sex is only a function. There's nae romance aboot it!'

'Ah wouldn't like to have it without romance,' said Neil and Paddy Maguire said 'Well, they're no' exactly Annie Lauries or Nellie Deans. Ye widnae say they were the tap o' the basket.'

'They're the products o' a city built oan sheer materialism an' industrial greed,' said Neil.

Their feet drummed the bridge's wooden floor whereover late seagulls languidly tossed, their wings touched with goldenred of sunset. Here, where the young Clyde loses its hawthorn beauty of Leadhills and the Falls Of Lanark, the gulls were always the loveliest objects in sight, like wild sea spirits come to call men out to sea-roving, weaving their silken grey through every season over Glasgow Town. And Eddy Macdonnel watching them, sensed a soaring lift in his breast as if he was flying and circling through the golden sunset. His limbs all at once became light and airy and he ran faster, as they wheeled left by the Co-operative Bakery, to join Neil who had spurted ahead of his companions.

For a while Neil and he ran together and Neil talked about his essay until he grew breathless, then outdistanced Eddy, his head inclined sideways, his hair attractively rumpled as though he had secretly ruffled it. He was now well ahead of the others and no longer could hear the gritty shuffle of their rubber shoes on the narrow, earthen towpath. On his inclined face there was a satisfied smile. He was thinking how faultlessly he had reasoned out his essay, in such beautiful style too, right on to its glorious 'pairoration!' Fleeting on wings of success he outpaced his companions and to their infinite surprise arrived at The Oatlands Sewage Pump, the end of their mile run, fifty yards ahead of them. He stood there waiting for them the blood buzzing in his veins, rippling internally with triumph, his eyes gleaming pride through his pince-nez.

Bobby Logan looked jealously at Neil as he came gasping alongside, well ahead of the other three. Bobby was champion among the five apprentices at the long distance run and the hundred yards sprint. It was the first night he had ever been beaten. He was always first to arrive at The Pump and he stood beside Neil feeling defeated, confused by Neil's triumphant grin. Donald and Paddy came up with Eddy Macdonnel many yards in the rear. They rested awhile all eyeing Neil with puzzled looks, wondering how he had done it, then they raced the hundred yards sprint, while Eddy timed them with Bobby's stopwatch, from The Pump to Polmadie Bridge, the distance to an inch, and again Neil created a sensation by beating Bobby Logan in every one of three trials.

They crossed the stone bridge of Rutherglen, half-a-mile further on and returned in the dusk to the swimming baths along the north shore of the Clyde. Bobby Logan padded gloomily in the rear along with Eddy Macdonnel. There was a leaden heaviness in his legs, his lips were tightly compressed, his punch and judy nose and chin nearly meeting in the dismal thought that he had lost for good and all his prestige as the unbeaten champion runner among his pals. The gaudy carpet-palace of Templeton's that seems to have given its architectural cue to the Co-operative Bakery on the opposite shore, gleamed garishly, dominating the evening with its bizarre design as the five apprentices passed it at a lagging pace on their way into the swimming-baths.

It was twenty minutes till closing time and in the swimming pool there were only a dozen bathers. The hot, tired bodies of the apprentices were reanimated and refreshed at the sight of the cool, clear water and they changed into bathing costumes and plunged into the pool. Neil Mudge was a poor swimmer and a timid ungraceful diver. He always dived from the bathside, but this evening, nerved by success, he posed almost gracefully on the third step of the diving board and the song in his head as it struck the water, was 'Individualism! We Await Thy Glorious Dawn!'

When James Macdonnel joined the Seventh Territorial Scottish Rifles in the Spring of 1913 to become a sparetime
soldier, like many thousands of young men in those fateful
days, he was not irresistibly driven by patriotism. He joined
because other corner-boys were doing it and because it
appealed to him as an interesting way of spending his
evenings. It brought him a free fortnight's holiday every
year with tons of good grub, plenty of company and sport.
The manoeuvres during the fortnight's summer camp at
Gailes were glorious fun. All the thrills of war without its
unromantic filth, butchery and death. Gymnastics, boxing
and rifle-practice in the regimental drill-hall filled-in those
evenings when his pockets were empty and the idea of
strolling round with a bunch of penniless corner-boys was
decidedly unattractive.

War seemed remote as the stars. He never dreamed of
it. When he changed on physical training nights from the
saturated, stinking togs he wore curing rabbit and other
skins at the factory known locally as the 'Hairworks' and,
dressed in his best and only other suit, jumped on a tram at
the closemouth, a rifle slung from his shoulder, his mind was
never lit up with visions of death and glory. He was thinking
of the pals he would meet and the laughs he would get when
he and other wits of the regiment discussed the oddities
of their short, fat sergeant, red and very bald, and their
business-man officer, tall, thin, hollow-cheeked and very
fierce when his tongue loosened and his opinions boomed
on the subject of those imperialist slogans of the times, The
Yellow Peril and The German Menace.

Route-marching on a bright Saturday afternoon helped
Jimmy to forget the comparison between the thick wad of
notes he collected from a shipping company at the end

of a few months' voyage and the slim pay-envelope the Hairworks gave him for a week's hard, stinking graft. He always called that envelope unseemly names then baptised it with a spit, for luck. It limited his big desire to get gloriously drunk and play the philanthropist in the pub to thirsty, admiring pals. But he could forget his exasperation when he marched with the Gorbals contingent along Gowan Street, up Crown Street and over Albert Bridge, grinning at his mother and Aunt Kate, his young brothers, his girl, Bella McAllister, glossy with smiles, waving their hankies and admiring him.

He was back repeatedly in the Hairworks, though he hated the job. When he got tired of waiting for a ship he hung round the shipyard gates from five in the mornings, looking for unskilled labouring work and when he got nothing there he turned in desperation to the curing of rabbit-skins, usually finding it easy to get taken on at the unpopular Hairworks.

But when real war was provided for half-a-world of young men, romantic, bored or workless, Jimmy was at home on a fortnight's leave from the yacht of a sewing-machine magnate who had come ashore to destroy grouse in the Highlands. Jimmy had an easy well-paid job on that miniature sailing-palace, but a two-months' cruise in the Mediterranean did not cure him of a nostalgia for the Gorbals nor prevent him from hating his employer whom he described as a pig at table and a bully on deck. When he had given his mother her share Jimmy burned up what was left of his two-months' wages in a spell of riotous living, over-stayed his leave and lost his grand position. All his mother's tears and pleadings as she urged him to stick to the finest job of his life, failed to move him. He wasn't going to kowtow any longer to any American millionaire.

Mrs Macdonnel's disappointment melted away when she watched Jimmy, as best man at the marriage of Aunt Kate's son, march up the aisle to the altar, still dressed in his officer's uniform which had been supplied by the hated millionaire. 'My, look at him! He's the star o' the weddin',' she said to herself, 'Ye wid think it was him the priest was merryin'.' She took a sly look at her sister, Aunt Kate, to see if she was impressed with Jimmy but Aunt Kate was looking with streaming eyes at her son and daughter-in-law whom Mrs Macdonnel thought commonplace up against Jimmy and she decided to make him get his 'photy' taken before, as she feared, the millionaire demanded the return of that bonny uniform.

Everyone at the wedding praised Jimmy up to the nines, but he was not a happy man. Bella McAllister had thrown him up because he loved whisky better than her and it was a year now since he had lost the bonny fisher-lass from Peterhead. He would never forget the devoted way she had followed him to Glasgow to be received with open arms by his mother. Ay, she would have been the wife for him! He sighed as he recalled the offhanded way he forgot her. Two days after she arrived he and his da and mother went on the spree. The fisher-lass waited patiently for the spree to end, then at the end of a fortnight, she went home sadder and wiser to marry a Hielan' fisherman. Jimmy forgave himself at the time with the false thought that he really didn't care for her and resumed walking-out with Bella McAllister.

So when the Great War was only a few days old Jimmy found himself unemployed, unloved and deeply out of tone with life. There was only one way of escape from it all. He would join up and ask for immediate foreign service on the strength of his Territorial training. He would serve his country and forget his thwarted love and environment of failure. He wasn't going to hide in a shipyard or munition factory. No fear! He would get into the thick of the fighting right away. He would show them. He pictured himself fearlessly charging the enemy, putting a dozen to the bayonet, saving the lives of several comrades and falling at last with a heroic smile on his face, crying Bella's name and clutching her bloodstained picture to his breast. Ay, she would be sorry!

The evening after the wedding he grinned and swayed, lord of the hour, in a slum pub called The Shieling, only in name like a lone Highland cottage. 'Come oan, boays!' cried Jimmy, 'Name yer drinks. Ah'm payin'! Ah'm jynin' up the night tae fight fur King an' Country far fae hame. Name yer poison, boays!' Drunken hands caressed his shoulder. 'Thaz right, Jimmy man. Thaz right, Jimmy boay. King an' Country! Smash they bloody Germans! We'll jyne up wi' ye!' And Jimmy struck up hs favourite song:

Cumrades, cumrades, ever since we were boys,
Sharing each other's sorrows, sharing each other's joys.

Voices thick with emotion and alcohol harmonized with him as he ended,

When danger was threatening my darling ole cumrade
Was there by my side.

But they didn't join up that night. They were all too romantically preoccupied with the idea to carry it out. But when Jimmy woke painfully at noon of the next day he remembered his vows of the night before. Well, nobody would ever say that he drew back at the last moment. He tried to lift his chin proudly and groaned at the weight of his head, then he called through to his mother for a glass of water and a cup of strong tea.

That night he joined up with Tom Kinney and walked out of the packed recruiting office along Bath Street and down West Nile Street arm in arm with him. Two of his pals had been rejected as unfit, the other four had waited outside. Jimmy regarded those four with silent scorn. They were cowards, betrayers of their promise. All their fine do or die oaths of comradeship were just talk. Afraid of foreign service! He wasn't afraid. Sure he had persisted in joining up when the recruiting officer told him his mercantile service would be as good as service in the trenches!

He told his mother next morning and consoled her as she wept and cried why should her bonny son go out when so many were staying at home in safe jobs. He would never come back, she said, clinging to him. Jimmy agreed he had been a bit hasty but it was for King and Country and he wasn't going to be a stay-at-home soldier. He felt regretful now. Maybe his mother was right and he wouldn't have joined if the others hadn't sworn to be with him, but when his Aunt Kate came in and hugged him and went out for whisky for him and when neighbour women and girls smiled at him on the stairs and in the street he enjoyed the pride of being a hero.

Being so full of glory Jimmy couldn't resist arguing with Eddy about the War. With his untutored mind, incurious about literature or politics, argument with Francie or Eddy was an activity he scrupulously avoided because they always first stunned him with long words and abstruse references, then tangled him up in a couple of seconds with a peppering of propaganda facts. He admired his young brothers for their learning but didn't desire to be like them. He caught Eddy eyeing him with sorrowful looks while he was wondering what like it would be over there. Real war! He and Eddy were alone in the kitchen, Francie sat by himself in the front room in one of his invincible silences and suddenly Jimmy said loudly, relieving his tense feeling, 'Och, Ah weesh Ah was batterin' intae they bloody Germans noo!'

Eddy was reading an article on War And Secret Diplomacy in *Forward*. He laid the paper on the table and said it was a pity Jimmy was sacrificing himself as cannon-fodder to the Juggernaut of Mammon and Militarism. Jimmy was at sea right away. He had never heard of Juggernaut or Mammon and was vague about the term Militarism. He didn't want to argue tonight. He wanted action. He wanted to rush headlong into the unknown violent life of war. He shouted triumphantly thinking he had at last an argument with which to silence Eddy, 'What aboot poor little Belgium and they German atrocities?' and Eddy's answer came back that Belgium had been sacrificed to the great Capitalist Powers and as for those atrocities well war itself was an atrocity inflicted on the whole human race by the Capitalist Class. And then Jimmy asked him what he would do if the Germans came over and bayoneted our mothers and sisters. Eddy hated that question. Who could answer it? People who hadn't an argument to save their lives before the War were bringing it up everywhere now and looking at you triumphantly as they asked it. Ach it was a stupid question! It was a hypothetical question. Nobody could properly answer a hypothetical question. He tossed his head and looked at Jimmy with a flushed angry face. He didn't know what he would do. He just didn't know. It was a hypothetical question. He didn't know. He just didn't know! And Jimmy looked at him triumphantly taking no notice of 'hypothetical' and swaggered into the lobby to get his cap and returned pulling it on and smiling condescendingly at Eddy. He had cornered Eddy at last. Eddy had no answer. He wished Francie had been in the kitchen as well. He would have cornered the two of them. Eddy was looking through the kitchen window thinking of the millions of young men now marching and singing towards the fields of France with their hearts flying on before them, dashing as moths dash into a candle flame, millions of wild hearts flying eagerly, like crimson-plumaged birds, into the red flame of war.

But Jimmy didn't want to argue any more. He was satisfied. He had won. He wanted action. He was going out to borrow the price of a couple of pints from one of his pals. He was surprised when Eddy stood up and grasped him warmly by the hand and shone his gaze intently on him and said tremulously,

'Ah hope ye'll come back safe, James!'

'Och, Ah'm no' away yet!' said Jimmy, not wanting to think of that side of war, 'Sure Ah'll come back!' Eddy had ruined a new stirring vision of himself as James Macdonnel The Gorbals vc. He had been seeing himself limping about The Gorbals with a wee leg wound, not bad enough to have his leg off, just enough to keep him at home a few months, being admired and treated everywhere with people pointing him out, 'That's Jimmy Macdonnel the first Glesca vc. He kil't twenty Germans single-handed an' saved his officer an' whole company.'

Jimmy patted his young brother patronizingly on the shoulder, 'Ach, ye'll be jynin' up like me as soon as ye're of age,' he said.

Two evenings after this, Jimmy Macdonnel, drunk and singing, linked in the arms of his mother and Aunt Kate and followed by a crowd of corner-boys, marched over to Central Station through the excited Glasgow streets where the very stones seemed to be throbbing with the news of war. John Macdonnel with a good few pints and nips in him marched behind them supported by a laughing Norah and after them hunched Francie, silent, gloomy, alongside Eddy who had compromised, after a struggle with his conscience, by carrying Jimmy's kit-bag, convinced that to carry the rifle would have violated his Socialist and Pacifist principles.

Jimmy came back two months later on a brief leave from training camp before leaving for the Eastern Front and a crazy Macdonnel party was flung in his honour. And again, one midnight, a wild emotional group saw him off at Central Station that for the next four years would be filled with women's tearful cries and the laughter and deep silence of fated men. And only a week after he had gone Jimmy sent a dramatic letter which Mrs Macdonnel read half in tears, half-joyfully, telling them how his train had missed by a few hours the terrible troop-train disaster at Gretna Green.

John, Francie and Eddy Macdonnel were left to represent the opposing attitudes of the Macdonnel family to the Great War. John lived in his usual way when he had time. He was working in the shipyards earning big money, more than he had ever earned or would ever earn again. Eddy drifted from one job to another trying to find one that wouldn't help on the War, while Francie, who believed in Marxian Expediency and undermining the power of the Capitalist Class by working along with it, taking all it had to give even if you were forced to make weapons for a Capitalist war, worked also in the shipyards but not so hard as John, only working overtime when he wanted a new suit or something special.

John Macdonnel knocked himself out every week working overtime, saving money hand over fist, sometimes getting drunk when Norah's watchful eye was off him, sometimes, on one of his rare free Sundays, adding to his pile with money won at pitch-and-toss or cards away out on the banks of the Clyde at Shawfield or Cambuslang. But his fat pay pokes brought him no real pleasure. He was always too tired to get fun out of his wages and he wasn't seeing much of Norah who was working nearly as hard as himself on munition work.

When it was well into 1915 and 'The-War-To-End-War' was thriving in popularity, John Macdonnel began to worry. Upstanding young men with 'Work Of National Importance' badges were receiving sour, suspicious looks. Brainless women were accosting in the streets men of apparent

military age and presenting them with white feathers. John
began to think the whole of The Gorbals was watching him.
Everywhere he passed groups of women at the closes he
fancied they were talking about him, saying what right had
he to swank about all togged up on Sundays while their
'puir wee laddies were awa at The Front.' He was as vague
as Jimmy on the question of how wars came. 'Politics,'
'Economics,' 'Armaments Race,' 'Territorial Expansion'
were for him words of maddening emptiness. Every time
Francie and Eddy fired them at him in arguments he felt
like a mad bull teased by two toreadors. His thick, fair
eyebrows beetled in pathetic bewilderment and he shouted,
'Ach, shut up argyin'! Sure there must be wars. There's
wars in the Bible. There's been wars since the beginnin' o'
the wurrld an' nothin' you can dae can stoap them. Who
startit the War? Wis it us? Naw it wisnae. It was they
bloody Germans invadin' Belgium,' and he walked angrily
out of the house leaving his young brothers agreeing sadly
that he was a benighted wage-slave doped by Religion and
The Capitalist Press into believing that Britain was the
saviour of the world. Of course they were sorry for him
but if he wanted to join up they couldn't stop him, and
they tried not to feel superior, but it was very hard not to
with all their reading and learning.

And John went downstairs thinking maybe they were
right about the German workers not wanting war. But those
atrocities! Sure they were in the papers every day. They
Germans are fiends. Have they not tortured children? But
his brothers said atrocities were newspaper lies. He cooled
off, then got hot again trying to think, muttering, shaking
his head like a puzzled animal, 'Ach, Ah don't know who's
right!' Elementary thought irritated him like the sting of
a nettle. He brushed thought aside and walked along in a
comfortable physical glow to meet Norah.

One night as they walked late in the streets Norah kept
on talking about the War and saying it would look better
if he joined up while he, burning with healthy longing,
wished she would come up a close with him, get it over
and stop obstinately refusing and saying no not till after
we're married. It was one of her most obstinate nights but

at length he led her into a close and they stood at the dark stairfoot in awkward embrace, unconscious of the smell of cats, stale dampness and pipeclay, their hot bodies pulsing with the desire they were afraid to satisfy. And Norah kept on tiresomely refusing him, saying she could only stay out another half-hour as she had to be up at five, saying again it would look better if he joined up.

'But Ah'm oan Work O' National Importance,' said John. 'Ay, but ye see,' said Norah, 'there's three o' ye'se at hame an' they're sayin' that aulder men can dae the joabs that young men are daein'. Of course Ah don't want ye tae go but it wid look better.' Their flushed faces were turned from each other, their troubled eyes looked stolidly into the darkness while Norah persistently turned away his fumbling hands until John, sour with frustration, said, 'Ach, mibbe ye're right. Ah'll jyne up taemorra.'

He saw Norah home to her close in Hospital Street and before he went to bed talked it over with his mother. Mrs Macdonnel wept and asked him why he should join up. Hadn't she given one braw son already? Wasn't that enough? Let other mothers give a son, them that had whole families making big money on munitions. And John said cheerfully that the War would soon be over and he would get sent out East, find Jimmy and watch over him.

John Macdonnel had always sickened at the sight of blood. Once in the shipyards a flying fragment of steel had slashed his wrist. He felt no pain but when the warm blood spurted over his hand he fainted. He was ashamed and puzzled at this phenomenon in the likes of him with his big, strong body and his capacity for hard work. Now he thought as he went to bed he might be mutilated for life like some of the Gorbals boys who were home already without an arm, a foot or a leg but when he stood waiting his turn in the crowded recruiting office next morning he had forgotten his fear and was thinking only of the fun of camp life. He was sent to a training camp near Glasgow and for a brief while paraded the Gorbals in the kilts of the Argyle and Sutherlands, relishing the admiration he attracted. Mrs Macdonnel leant out of their first-storey window to watch him every time he went out, with his sporran swinging, his spats pipeclayed

snowy white, his braw tobermory at a gallant angle, his cane
tucked jauntily under his arm. Aunt Kate leaned out with
her and shouted down, 'Ye've the brawest pair o' knees in
the raigiment!' and Mrs Macdonnel sighed as he turned
the corner and said maybe he'd never come back from the
War and lifting her apron to her eyes said she'd lose her
sons, her bonny wee sons.

'Ach, stoap yer greetin', Mary!' Aunt Katy always said,
'Hiv Ah no' goat twa sons away fae me? Ye'll hae tae keep
yer hert up!' and then they would sit opposite each other
in the bay of the window, keening about their sons before
going over to the Ladies Room in The Clachan to continue
their lamentations in liquor.

At last the time came for John Macdonnel's send-off
party, the night he left for Mesopotamia, in his puttees
and khaki kilts, ready for Active Service. The family and
friends marched through the dark streets with him over to
Central Station where troop-trains were daily departing and
ambulance trains full of wounded men pulled in again and
again. This time Mr Macdonnel, carrying his son's rifle,
walked behind John, and Eddy walked along with him
shouldering John's kitbag. And at last after being hugged
and kissed and cried over by the women, he passed through
the barrier.

Next morning a letter from Jimmy, in Gallipoli, came
for John. It was reposted, went astray, and two years later
John received it on the night of his return to France after
a short spell at home with slight wounds. The letter said
it was hell out there and urged John not to join up.

Francie Macdonnel became steadily more peculiar and solitary, burrowing deeper into a self-centredness that utterly
shut him away and left him unaffected by war-fever. His
periods of gluttonous reading of revolutionary pamphlets
and books on philosophy, Marxian economics and Anarchism, his attempts to forget his nameless fears by getting
drunk, sometimes in company but often alone, his passionate arguments against the War among his shipyard mates
were futile against the hypnotism of introspection. He seized
by the idea of making his powerful body stronger by dieting

himself and began buying every kind of health magazine he saw in the bookshops. He tried fasting and became alarmed when he felt discomfort after a few hours without food. Vegetarianism took his fancy and he would try it for about a week or so, fascinated with the wonderful cures he read of in the magazines, telling Eddy and his parents with shining eyes that it was the only way to get a strong body and a clear, supreme intellect, becoming angry when his father told him he was one of the strongest men in Glasgow and didn't need to fad about with all this exercise and dieting. From health-food stores he brought home packets of patent foods, mostly American, which promised abounding health if consistently eaten. Such foods had never before been seen in the Macdonnel kitchen and when Francie came home excitely with a packet of a new food and said he was going to live on it from now on it looked very queer on the homely table. Sometimes he brought three or four different foods in a week and as suddenly he would abandon vegetarianism and his confidence in esoteric cereals and swing round to as powerful a belief in thick, underdone Pope's-eye steaks, beer and meaty Scotch broth which he got his mother to make thick enough to stand a spoon in. Then one morning his mother, exasperated by the way he was wasting his hard-earned money, would be cleaning out the press and find it stuffed, she said, with these fancy foods, all stale and mouldy, in packets unbroken or less than half-eaten, so that there was no room for anything else, and after trying to read their puzzling names and promises of virility and longevity, she would throw them in the back-court midden.

Eddy was the only one Francie could interest in these enthusiasms which soon developed in Francie a neurotic anxiety about his health. Then his mind twisted towards persecution-mania. Sometimes Eddy, his father or Mrs Macdonnel would find him tensely holding the handle of the partly open stairhead door or the door of the parlour and listening, his eyes darting about, his brows knitted in an expression of cunning and fear, convinced that someone or something intending him injury, hovered behind. When they stumbled into him he would look at them insanely and walk away and only once could Eddy get out of him what he feared, what he listened for. He said his enemies were after him and would get him.

One morning, without warning or explanation he left home and for three months tramped Scottish roads, working in farms and quarries, drinking alone and sleeping in the fields and hills. As unexpectedly he returned, wild and ragged, a haunted look in his eyes, to labour again in the shipyards. When his calling-up papers came he threw them contempt-usously aside and among his shipyard mates openly declared his opposition to the War whenever he was challenged. He never received calling-up papers again. By some clerical error his name was passed over. On New Year's Eve he disappeared again after getting wildly drunk with some mates whom he deserted with savage abruptness. Late on that Hogmanay night he stumbled into a bright, crowded confectioners under the thronged Umbrella, the wide Argyle Street railway arch carrying trains loaded with people who had been away from home coming back to Glasgow to first-foot, and celebrate with families and friends. Francie stood with his back against the wall of the busy shop, alone with the loneliness of a man utterly locked within himself. He had come in to buy a big box of chocolates for John's girl, Norah, and one for his mother and Aunt Kate, but he couldn't remember what he had come for. He rubbed his brow hard with the palm of his hand, but he couldn't remember. He couldn't remember. The nameless fear that drove him so often away from friend-ship and life was stabbing his head. His brow felt frozen and in the hollow at the back of his head there was a constant sharp pain. He was tired after a hard day's work and a night's hard drinking, but he was more tired with fear, the fear of life he was afraid to leave. For a moment he stood stupidly swaying and humming 'Shenandoah' in sentimental memory of his brother, Jimmy, then he stopped, stiff, tensed and glaring within himself. And the people waiting, coming and going, smiled and laughed at him in friendliness.

Suddenly Francie became aware of their smiling stares and lacking the will to move to crush out through the packed people, hung his head in confusion. The manageress, a stout, cheerful young woman, her rosy complexion flushed by hurry, found a moment to come round to him, 'Come awa noo,' she said, 'ye canny staun here. Whaur's yer wife an' weans? Hae ye loast them?' She held his arm, smiling at him as a big, burly Scot said, 'Och, he's gie'n them the slip tae hae a nicht oot oan his lane.'

The little manageress swam in Francie's vision, small, far off, then very near, unnaturally huge and fabulously beautiful. He wanted to kiss her but was afraid of her beauty. Her stout, homely figure seemed to him fair as the apparition of a dream and within his fumed brain he was aware only of her floating in some airy void. She sat him on a chair behind a tall showcase at the end of the shop, 'Bide a wee there an' we'll serve ye when the shoap's quieter,' she said, hurrying back to the counter to serve.

Francie's head slopped on his breast, the whole place instantly faded and he slept, dead to the sound of footsteps and voices, crackle of wrapping paper and unending ping of the cash register. He woke during the cold, last hours of 1915, shivering, peering at a high tier of fancy chocolate boxes above his head. His waking was unnoticed by the shopgirls talking busily as they put on hats and coats to go home. He peered at his surroundings, puzzled, amazed, till the sound of girls' voices reminded him of his arrival here. In a panic of real fear that they might surround him and question him and with a sudden loathing for all mankind, he rose quickly and lurched out of the shop. The girls shrieked as he appeared and vanished then grouped in the door to look after him striding swiftly, keeping to the wall, trying to avoid the shouting, singing people who were sheltering from the rain beneath The Umbrella, seeing in the New Year in the streets.

As he pushed on blindly, with downcast head, he brushed against four young women in bright, new plaid shawls, marching along with linked arms, their voices echoing down The Umbrella, merrily singing:

A Guid New Year
And mony may ye see,
A Happy Guid New Year,
I'd pawn my plaid
Tae get a hauf-a-gill
For a Happy, Guid New Year!

He was swallowed up in the crowds and no one knew where he went.

Donald Hamilton, crouched in absorption by the kitchen fire was reading *Das Kapital*, but no one acquainted with the literature of Economics would have imagined for a moment that he was really reading Marx's monumental analysis of Capitalist Society because Donald was rushing through it with the speed of an errand boy reading a detective weekly, getting more excited as he saw the end approaching for he would soon be able to tell everybody with pride that he had read *Das Kapital*. In the same way, though he hated poetry, he had read 'Paradise Lost' and 'Paradise Regained', sitting up several nights to do it, at the time he wrote his famous essay on Milton.

Mr Hamilton, a tailor to trade, was squatted crosslegged on the floor with a suit in the making spread before him, and his needle, darting in and out with astonishing celerity, flashed like a tiny silver fly. Occasionally, he paused to smooth out some irregularity in the stuff or glance at the wag-at-the-wa' clock above the mantelshelf. Donald's rapid flick of the pages in the big Sonnenschein volume and the rapid blink of his father's needle, seemed like a race between them, a quiet breathless, race which the needle was winning with ease.

It was well after midnight and Mr Hamilton, a small vital, ruddycheeked man with thick, grey-streaked sandy hair, worked in unbuttoned waistcoat and rolled-up shirtsleeves for more ease in the warm kitchen. He sometimes made a suit at home for a neighbour or friend and supplemented the poor wages he got from a big Jewish tailors in Argyle Street. He was now hurrying to finish an outsize suit for a tall, broad Highlandman, a widower on the top storey who worked in the Corporation gasworks and was getting married again in a few days. From time to time, Mr Hamilton held his needle up to the light and peered through his glasses, threading it, or took a quiet look at Donald and Mrs Hamilton who was sitting on the other side of the fire mending a pile of socks and boys' stockings. Finally, Mr Hamilton decided to put away the suit for the night. With a sigh of fatigue he dipped a finger in his dangling waistcoat pocket, extracted half a clay pipe, looked into it, shook his head and punched the charred, unsmoked remains into his palm. Smiling, he eyed it and said, 'My, whit a wee doatle. There's no many mair puffs left in that. Jings, Ah've run oot o' baccy again. Have ye a fill tae spare, Donal'?'

Donald hardly looked up from his book, fumbled in his jacket pocket and handed his father a length of thick black twist rolled in white paper, 'Och, ye're aye smokin' OPT these days,' he said cheerfully, 'Whit dae ye dae wi' a' yer money?'

'It's the best an' cheapest brand Ah can find,' said Mr Hamilton coolly, 'Other People's Tibacca is aye ma favourite. It's a real Socialist tibacca.' He cut himself a generous plug and returned the twist to his son. Donald looked at it with simulated astonishment, 'My, it's no' a pipe you smoke, faither, it's a lum!' he said, 'You musta been studyin' eeconoamics. You're a Socialist all right. Your motto is, "Whit's his is mine an' whit's mine's ma ain!"' Donald laughed at this stale joke as freshly as he laughed the first time he ever made it and his father's small, rosy face creased in a delighted smile, 'Oh, ay,' he said cannily lighting his pipe, 'Ah widnae foarbid ony man the plaishir o' sharin' his proaperty wi' me. It widnae be actin' like a cumrade!'

Mrs Hamilton laughed as heartily as themselves at their cross-talk though it was as familiar as every object in her kitchen. She was a short but very fat woman who had grown steadily fatter in spite of years of loyal hard work rearing a family of five sons and five daughters. Her good-nature had increased in ratio to the worry and anxiety she had fought through many times of unemployment and illness. She was always the first up in the morning and the last to go to bed, never unoccupied, concerned about her family even in dreams. She was slightly asthmatic. She breathed uneasily as she moved and wheezed sometimes as she talked. Her amiable temperament created an indestructible atmosphere of kindness and welcome in her little kitchen.

At this moment, shortly after midnight of an Autumn

day in 1916 Mrs Hamilton was bravely hiding her anxiety while her son and husband blarneyed. She knew that it was in the small hours that deserters and men objecting to military service were arrested, surprised and taken from their beds. For over a week now she had been expecting the appearance of a policeman come to arrest Donald and when the evenings grew late her heart jumped at every knock on the stairhead door.

Donald read with apparent unconcern, but he was not entirely at ease. Though he assisted regularly at anti-war meetings and defied the disapproval of the neighbours, he was wondering how he would shape when his turn came to witness his loyalty to 'his Class.' He had decided that if Neil Mudge could face the ordeal of arrest and court-martial it wouldn't frighten him. He had visited Neil in the guardroom at Hamilton Barracks and he was hoping he would be drafted also into the Highland Light Infantry so that he could join Neil before they were both court-martialled as conscientious objectors and sent to jail. Neil had been very nervous and he had steadied him by his coolness. He foresaw himself nonchalantly facing his trial and conducting his own defence with a brilliance that would astonish the court.

Mrs Hamilton intercepted his gallant notions of himself by saying, 'Hiv ye heard how Neil Mudge has goat oan since he went tae prison?' and Donald answered confidently to prepare her for his own arrest, 'Och, Neil's no' in prison yet, but once he's there he'll be all right. He'll be a ceevil prisoner wi' ceevil rights an' the Army'll hae nae mair control over him.' Mrs Hamilton looked at him, unconvinced and worried as she rose to lay the big workbasket of mended socks on the dresser, 'Mibbe ye'da been better tae hiv goat a joab in the shipyards an' claimed exemption for Work O' National Importance,' she said. Her two eldest sons were at the Front, she had foggy but disturbing ideas about prison-life and had no desire to have a third son taken to meet a fate which might be more terrible than life in the trenches. She thought of Donald shut up for years in a prison cell and waited hopefully, wishing he would agree to the suggestion she had often made since the passing of conscription.

Donald read unsteadily. He did not wish to hurt her but unnerved by her nervousness he said more loudly than he had intended, 'Och, Ah've told ye Ah won't compromise! Ah'm nut goan tae hide behind a badge an' Ah'm nut goan tae fight in a war o' Capitalist Imperialism. Ah don't see the difference between makin' munitions an' firin' them at the Germans. Ah might as well go for a soldier as make shells or help tae build a warship!'

Mr Hamilton stopped on his way to the parlour with the suit and darted a concerned look at his wife, 'Ay, Meg, Ah think Donal's right. It's pusheelaneemous tae sit oan the fence an' a cooard's pairt tae make money fae the things o' destruction if ye dinny believe in war. Noo that we're in it Ah think we oaght tae see it through, but Donal's goat a right tae his opeenions an' Ah hope he'll staun up fur thim. Mibbe if there had been coanshyenshus objaictors in the past we widny be havin' a war noo. Noo, ye needna fret, Meg,' he continued hastily as his wife lifted her apron to her eyes, 'There's nae mair ill-treatment o' objaictors. There's too influential a public opeenion supportin' thim. The authorities are jist pittin' thim oot o' the way in coancentration camps so they canna mak pacifist speeches while the War's oan.'

Mrs Hamilton walked silently into the lobby, hiding her eyes and at that moment several heavy knocks rattled the stairhead door. She paled and started violently, then composed herself and opened the door. The constable who appeared erased his official frown when he saw the mother. He did not relish the job he was on. It looked as if this arrest was going to be like many others, an emotional affair with a terrible lot of argument.

Mr Hamilton placed the unfinished suit on the dresser, laid his pipe on the mantel and said nervously, 'It's for you, Donal'. Ye'd better go an' see him yersel'.' The policeman's, 'Does Donald Hamilton live here?' and Mrs Hamilton's shaky reply, 'Ay, whit did ye want? Will ye come in?' came clearly to their ears and Mrs Hamilton returned to the kitchen followed by a very tall, broad Highland policeman, the metal posy on top of his helmet and the badge of

Glasgow Corporation on the front of it, gleaming silvery in the gaslight.

Donald calmly marked his place in *Das Kapital*, scribbled some notes on a small pad, then lit his pipe and stood up casually and faced the middle-aged policeman, 'I'm Donald Hamilton,' he said coolly, with his head very high, 'Whit's yer business.'

Flushing with resentment at Donald's coolness, the policeman said gruffly, 'Ach ye ken fine what's ma business! Ye'll have tae come along wi' me, young man. Ye haven't answered yer callin'-up papers an' I've got authority tae apprehen' ye. Ye'd be as weel tae come quietly for yer ain guid.'

Donald was glad he had lit his pipe. It made him feel older, gave him poise. The uneasy policeman was taking sidelong glances at Mrs Hamilton hoping she wouldn't burst into tears like other mothers he had to face. But Mrs Hamilton, now that the moment had come was tearless and steady, looking calmly at her husband. Donald was now in his element. This was a supreme moment for propaganda. 'Law,' he said, gesturing his pipe at the policeman, 'is the enemy o' Liberty. It's the Capitalist Weapon of Might against Right. Every policeman sells his soul tae be a well-paid, well-fed Capitalist thug who's used tae suppress his own class, the Workin' Class!' He blew out a puff of smoke and looked steadily into the hostile, older eyes, empty of humour or sentiment. A flush of deeper anger reddened the policeman's face and he said roughly.

'Ah'm nut interested in your opinions an' I'm nut here tae listen tae a lecture. Ah've goat twa laddies at the Front an' that's where every decent young man oaght tae be. Noo come along wi' me an' nae mair argyin'. Ah've goat twa mair like you tae arrest tonight. Ye can keep yer opinions fur the court-martial an' save yer braith.'

Mr Hamilton tugged Donald's sleeve, saying quietly, 'Ye'd better gang alang wi' him, Donal'. He's only daein' his duty.'

The sound of voices so late in the night had wakened Donald's two young brothers and five sisters who stood in the unlit lobby like a small audience looking from a dark auditorium at a scene on a stage. The two eldest daughters with raincoats thrown round their nightdresses ran into the kitchen and embraced Donald. Donald lost his poise, and pushed them away awkwardly, fussing with his pipe to steady himself. Mrs Hamilton going into the lobby, told the children to get back to bed as she put on a dark hat and coat. Donald and her husband followed her and took their overcoats and bowlers from the lobby pegs. Then Mr Hamilton signed to the policemen and they all went downstairs gravely, walking through the sleeping streets and along Clydeside over Albert Bridge to Central Police Station where Donald was formally charged and lodged in a cell to await the arrival of a military escort in the morning.

During the three months that Francie Macdonnel was tramping the roads, wandering God only knew where, Eddy was busy all his spare time helping at pacifist and No Conscription Fellowship meetings, constantly at strife with his mother, who hated him more for deserting his Faith than for his conscientious objection. When she wasn't drinking and was attending the chapel herself she would ask him if he had been to an early or late Mass and what was the sermon about. He was sorry for the distress he was causing her but stubbornly resisted lying. Mr Macdonnel secretly admired Eddy's independence and book-learning but, when urged to do so by his wife, would mildly tell him he ought to attend Mass more regularly. One Sunday morning at the end of 1915, in a fit of adolescent enthusiasm, Eddy told his mother he would never attend chapel again. She screamed him out of the house and he spent the day selling pamphlets at meetings and came home very late, hungry and tired, and opening the door quietly with the check key crept into the parlour. His Uncle Wullie was still up and he tiptoed into the kitchen where Mr and Mrs Macdonnel were asleep in bed and brought Eddy some food and tea. While he ate Eddy relieved his pent-up feelings by telling his Uncle he wasn't going to go through another Sunday like the last when he sat quivering with anger as the priest appealed for recruits from the pulpit and but for the restraint of his superstitious upbringing would have risen to protest against this profanation of the Mass. He had walked angrily out at the end, past the throng at the door dipping their fingers in the holy-water font with Christ's command, 'Thou Shalt Not Kill!' echoing in his heart. 'Priests and ministers are traitors!' he cried, 'They have sold their souls! They cannot believe in Christ and encourage men to kill.' As he lay awake that night beside his Uncle who snored or breathed gruntingly because of his weak chest, he was making up his mind to leave home. He knew his mother's rage would have subsided by the morning to a silent resentment that would break out at any moment in shrieks and lamentations about his atheism and Socialism. It was becoming unbearable.

Shortly after that Sunday he heard that Donald Hamilton had been arrested. Burning with hatred of all uniformed authority he called at Donald's home eager for details, thinking his own time must be near and he wouldn't have to decide about leaving home but would be arrested, like Donald. While he talked to Mrs Hamilton, comforting her, he hoped he would be arrested next day and be thrown among his comrades into the fight against Capitalist war. He felt sublime when he was helping at outdoor anti-war meetings, believing he was risking injury and possibly death for his ideals, like the millions, he argued, who were giving their lives in France. One Sunday morning in 1916 he reached the pinnacle of enthusiasm when a hostile crowd of soldiers and civilians, incited by a paid agitator of the Empire League, broke up their small meeting, smashed their portable platform and scattered their literature to the winds. As two powerful Canadian soldiers rushed at the speaker Eddy stood before him with outstretched arms and dared them to hurt him. The big soldiers stopped a yard or two in front of them, staring like puzzled bulls, calling them lousy bastards and cowards and the tall, dark speaker, six foot in height, overtopping Eddy by several inches, patted him on the shoulder, 'It's all right, youngster! You look after yourself. Let them do their worst. They don't understand.' Two of their comrades were thrown into the Kelvin, others were badly manhandled, but the mob left him and the speaker unmolested. Sad but exultant he carried the broken platform and a bundle of muddied books and pamphlets back to the small Labour Hall.

His heart poised on a torrent of enthusiasm on the Saturday afternoon he visited Neil Mudge who had been court-martialled and was waiting to be transferred to a civil prison. He shimmered with excitement during the short railway journey from Glasgow to Hamilton with Neil's two eldest sisters. 'We're in the enemy camp!' he laughed proudly as Janet showed her permit and they entered the barracks and crossed the vast square to the guardroom. He was heady with pride in the thought that his turn would soon come to defy this Militarism. He thrilled and frightened the two girls by his loud, elated talk, and they cried, 'Wheesht! Ye'll be arrested an' kept here.' He tossed his head gaily, 'I don't care. I want to be arrested and get into the fight with Neil and Donald.' Ach, if only he'd been a public speaker he would have satisfied his wild desire to address the squads of raw recruits being drilled by bawling sergeants and those groups at bayonet practice, shouted ferociously on by instructors, dashing with fixed bayonets at sandbags dangling from gallows. In imagination he saw them mangled with wounds, reeling in death, heard their cries of agony. Phrases leapt to his mind, 'Comrades! Fellow-Workers! Throw down your rifles! Revolt! Refuse to fight in a Capitalist War! You have no quarrel with your German fellow-worker!' Playacting the heroic agitator, he saw the busy soldiers, astounded by his shout, turn and listen to his passionate speech, throw down their rifles and follow him into the streets, the nucleus of a world-wide mutiny that would stop the War. They were allowed ten minutes each to speak with Neil and Eddy gazed challengingly at the guardroom sergeant while waiting his turn to see his pal.

Neil was alone in the bare room with the barred windows, dressed in ill-fitting khaki and his trousers concertina-ed down to his big Army boots. 'Hullo, Neil. Och, it's great tae see ye again!' Eddy's voice trembled with emotion and pleasure. They gripped hands fervently, their shining eyes saying, 'It is the Cause!'

Neil stood silent a moment, with dramatically lowered head; his tousled hair was at its best romantic disarray, his chubby face was pale and there was a slight swelling on his right cheek which gave him a childish look. He raised his head, touching the swelling with his finger and told Eddy it was a cyst and he'd have to have it operated on. Then he shot his hands deeply in his trousers pockets, lifting the tail of his jacket above his behind and began striding rapidly to and fro with a thoughtful frown, his bluff little buttocks popping up and down tight against coarse khaki. Eddy Macdonnel, in a guinea suit of some sickly compromise between blue and mauve, a washable rubber collar and a sixpenny knitted tie, walked with him, feeling grave and grand. 'I'm the only one here now,' said Neil, 'There was a dozen men in here yesterday for desertion. They'd all been "out there" and didn't want to go back. The whole bunch left for France this morning under guard. It's awful the way war ruins youth. It kills a' the charm o' adolescence. There were boys o' nineteen here just like coarse, experienced men of thirty, after a few months in the trenches. An' ye should have heard their language! The place was like a sewer! An' they had dozens o' dirty postcards from France. The poor devils were a' drafted back this mornin' under heavy guard, an' some o' them handcuffed. They all advised me to stick it out an' swore they'd be objectors in the next war if they cam through this one.'

Eddy listened avidly and told him of Donald's arrest.

'Ay, ma sister wrote to me about it,' said Neil, 'Ah hear they've sent him tae Edinburgh. Ah was hopin' they'd send him here. The court gave me three months. Ah think Ah'm bein' transferred tae Barlinnie Prison on Monday. I'll be glad o' the solitude o' a cell after the sound an' fury o' this place.'

'The soul must have respite from the mob to refresh itself,' said Eddy. 'Remember what ye said in your letter? "Stone walls do not a prison make." They can't imprison our spirits. The Cause'll go on if we die.'

Neil admitted he hadn't been roughly treated, 'except when Ah refused to put on the uniform,' he said. 'Then four Tommies set on me an' forcibly dressed me an' Ah goat a few hard knocks. Ah might as well have spared masel' the pains. These wee coampromises don't matter, though I've heard that some o' oor chaps went aboot naked for days before they'd submit. Being in uniform doesn't make ye a soldier.' Eddy confessed he was worried by the question of compromise and said he was still labouring at the shipyards, 'Of course Ah'm only helpin' to build a merchant ship,' he explained hastily.

Neil told him not to worry, 'The only logical way to escape participation in a Capitalist war is tae live oan a desert island or commit suicide. Under the Capitalist system a penny spent oan the sheerest necessity o' life indirectly assists a war. An' don't you be anxious tae get arrested. Keep them oan the run as long as ye can. It's outside the prison walls we need revolutionaries. No' inside.' A young corporal put his head in at the door, grinned at them for a moment then shouted, 'Time's up, you twa!' and Neil shouted back, 'Och, gie us another five meenits, Mac!' The corporal, after a quick look up and down the passage outside put his head in again and said, 'Aricht. But ye'll hae tae skedaddle vite if the sergeant comes!'

'Ah've converted him tae Socialism,' said Neil beaming triumph, 'Ah gave him some Marxian an' anti-war pamphlets an' he's asked for more. He's remarkably intelligent an' him an' I have some rare arguments when he's oan guard-duty.'

They walked up and down in silence for the last few moments. 'I hear they're shooting co's in France an' Germany,' said Eddy solemnly.

'The Militarists in this country would shoot us too if they weren't prevented b' Liberal an' Labour opinion in the Church an' Cabinet,' said Neil and Eddy wished he was among the objectors in France and Germany. He fancied himself making the supreme sacrifice, facing a firing squad and protesting and defying to the end.

Heavy, quick steps rang along the passage; the corporal sprang to attention in the doorway and a burly sergeant stepped in past him and said gruffly, 'Time's up.' Eddy and Neil shook hands emotionally. 'Keep smiling, Neil,' said Eddy and they posed with hands clasped in dramatic silence for a moment. Then Neil rustled a letter from his tunic pocket, 'Post this for me. Ah couldnae give it tae

Janet. It's for a lady in Dundee!' Neil smiled a Don Juan smile and Eddy waved the letter in farewell as he turned out of the door.

Eddy Macdonnel had read in novels of men who went out to commune with Nature when faced with a critical turn in their lives. For long hours they walked by field or river seeking in solitude for guidance and strength. Sometimes such men carried with them a book, their favourite essayist or poet, or the writings of a saint.

Eddy lay against the wall of the stuffy, cavity bed smoking a Woodbine and gazing at the blotched and cracked white-wash of the bedceiling, pleased by the vision of himself as a wrestler with his soul. His Uncle Wullie lay along the front of the bed. His dark, bullet head had slipped from the dirty pillow and reclined awkwardly on the edge of the bedboard. He snored loudly, with wide open mouth, his four nicotined molars showing. Eddy at last was annoyed by his Uncle's invincible snore which penetrated and spoiled his daydreaming. 'Poor Wullie,' he thought, 'I wonder when they'll take him.' The little lamplighter had been twice rejected by the Army for unsatisfactory lungs. 'Well, they say the third time's lucky. Mibbe it'll be unlucky for him!' Eddy reflected sadly. He leant over and lifted his Uncle's lolling head back on to the pillow and the snoring stopped. He heard the dim chime of the kitchen clock through the small square ventilator high on the bedwall and tried to follow its count. Was that eleven or twelve?

He had laid awake half the night urging himself to the decision to give himself up to the military authorities. He had mentally acted over and over the manner in which he would stride into the recruiting office, throw down his calling-up papers and announce his opposition to the War. He had composed and recomposed the speech he intended to make, thrilled by the ring of revolutionary phrases. He called, 'What's the time?' hoping Francie would hear him through the ventilator that opened into the kitchen bed. There was no answer and he stood up, stepping carefully over his Uncle and reaching the floor by means of a bedside chair.

The unswept linoleum, warm with the heat of mid-summer, felt mild and gritty to his feet. Newspapers lay scattered about, clothes were slopped on the seats and backs of chairs. Eddy picked up that morning's *War Bulletin* which his Uncle had bought coming home from his morning shift. 'More victories!' he said scornfully, 'Och, it's nothing but Allied victories. The Workers'll never get the truth!' He threw down the small sheet contemptuously on a chair and poked his finger into a pocket of his Uncle's greasy, working waistcoat hanging on the back of it and pulled out a half-crown Ingersoll watch which had lost its electroplate shine with constant rubbing. It was half-past-twelve. Eddy picked up a copy of Jack London's *The Iron Hell* from an oval table littered with magazines, newspapers, caps and socks. Standing in front of the window in his shirt he read again the chapter from which he had borrowed ideas and phrases for his intended speech. He waved the book in the air and his eyes blazed, 'Long Live The Revolution!' he cried, quoting from the book.

A top storey window of the opposite tenement opened and a young woman leant out and looked full at him. He dodged aside, blushing with shame, and sitting down, pulled on his trousers. Then he stood before the window again and began doing deep breathing exercises. Yes, he would tramp along the banks of the Clyde and make his decision today. He would have to miss John McLean's Sunday Men's Class and one of McLean's lectures on The History Of The Working Class Movement and break for the first time his regular appearance at the No Conscription Fellowship Meetings. A running newsboy's voice echoed along Gowan Street and wound and wavered round the tenements. It always carried clear on the quiet Sunday streets, the voice of calamity that had risen night and day since the War began: *Bull'tin! War Bull'tin!—Speshul!—Cashulties!—War Bull'tin!—Speshul!* The ominous cry thinned away, wavering, fading, as tremulous sheepcries fade in the mountains.

Well, the wage-slaves of the tenement warrens were getting all the sensation they wanted now! Murder wholesale instead of an odd one or two here and there. Eddy smiled at his original thought and walked barefoot through to the kitchen, where a wet smell of strong soap mingled with the odours of blacklead and fried ham and eggs. Francie was standing looking at the shining kitchen-range like an artist admiring his masterpiece. Soothed by two hours of furious cleaning he had just cooked his breakfast and Dietzgen's *Positive Outcome Of Philosophy* shared the table with a pot of tea and a considerable grill of ham, eggs and black-pudding piled on a small tea-plate.

'My, ye've made the range like it was new,' said Eddy.

'Mind ye step on the papers. The floor's wet,' said Francie, pointing at old newspapers spread on the damp linoleum, then sitting down he started his breakfast, knitting his brows at his book as if he was glaring at an enemy. Eddy had resolved to go out in a high spiritual mood without breakfast, but the smell of food was too tempting and he cooked and ate a hearty meal of ham and eggs. Francie stopped reading to complain of their parents' behaviour, 'Ah pleaded wi' them this moarnin' tae stay teetotal. Ah'd do anything fur them if they'd stoap the drink. If they go oan the spree again Ah'll leave hame fur the road. Ah'm sick o' dirt an' drink an' fightin'!'

The brothers seldom discussed their deeper feelings and while he was tying his tie Eddy said half-shyly, 'I've decided to give myself up to the Military,' then he coughed, looking intently into the mirror. There was a brief silence then Francie said, 'That's no' the best way tae serve Socialism. Let them come an' fetch ye! Ye'll serve the Cause better b' spreadin' propaganda among shipyard wage-slaves than b' languishin' in a jail. Why should ye sacrifice yerself oan the altars o' Moloch?'

Eddy answered, 'I don't think it's right for me to be safe in a job while men are suffering and dying in France and our Socialist comrades lie in prison for opposing the War. James an' John went to fight for what they believe in, I want to suffer for Socialism. The only way to stop war is to refuse to take part in it.'

Francie closed his book, 'Ye'll only be a futile martyr. Wance the Juggernaut starts rollin' there's naebuddy can stop it. The Materialist Philosophy teaches us tae undermine Capitalism wi' its own weapons an' methods. The Boss

Class uses guile as well as force; we can only destroy
the System b' the same means. Marx has proved that the
time is no' ripe for The Dictatorship o' The Proletariat.
If millions o' fools want tae blow themselves tae bits, let
them. Shelterin' in a joab, even oan muneetions, is no'
cowardice, but expediency. James jyned up at the outbreak fur the adventure; John went partly because he was
afraid o' the neebors an' public opinion an' now the Derby
Scheme's ropin' in them that'll only go b' compulsion!'

Eddy brushed back his tuft of auburn hair that sprung
up again like bristles of a bass broom, 'I know all that,' he
said, 'but I believe in the power of the individual protest!'
Francie tossed his book on the bed, nicked his cigarette, laid
it on the edge of the mantelpiece and said contemptuously:

'Ach, under the System the individual disnae count.
Marx proves it's only Mass Action that'll smash Capitalism.
Mass Action in a' the belligerent countries would have
nipped the War in the bud.' Still wearing the damped,
packsheet apron in which he had scrubbed out the kitchen,
he faced the mirror on the wall beside the window and posed,
admiring his biceps, grinning at his feeling of wellbeing,
then he said irrelevantly, 'Och, Ah think Ah'll scrub oot
the front room. Me biceps are no' so big now. Maybe Ah
should take up vegetarianism again. Ah didnae gie it a
proaper trial.'

Eddy continued dressing, unsurprised by his brother's
whimsies as Francie nervously lit the stub of cigarette
he had laid on the mantel and recited in a chuckling
voice, '"'Twas brillig an' the slithy toves did gyre an'
wimble in the wabe!" My it's a rare book yon *Alice
In Wonderlan'*. D'ye mind Alice at the tea-pairty?' He
stood grinning at his memory of the book then strode suddenly into the lobby, which he began sweeping with mind-
less vigour as if his life depended on it, and shouting.

> *You are old Father William, the young man said,*
> *And your hair has become very white*
> *And yet you incessantly stand on your head!*
> *Do you think, at your age, it is right?*

Eddy, polishing his shoes on the edge of a chair, turned
his head and recited back,

At the first, Father William replied to his son,
I thought it might injure my brain,
But now that I'm perfectly sure I have none,
Why I do it again and again!

They both laughed themselves red in the face at Lewis Carroll's nonsense, then Francie repeated the first verse and shot out breathlessly, stopping his violent sweeping, 'Are ye going tae Johnny McLean's Class the day?'

Eddy collected his volume of Keats' Poems from the parlour sideboard and said he was going for a walk. As he went out Francie called after him, 'Ah'd come wi' ye but Ah want tae hear Johnny McLean oan "The Seegnificance O' The Paris Commune"!'

Feeling half-proud, half-ashamed of his studious appearance, with the poems beneath his arm, Eddy walked through the streets as far as Bridgeton Cross and from there took a car to Cambuslang terminus. He left the tram and walked away out along the banks of the Clyde, trying to quiet the fear of what he was going to do. After some vigorous miles he flung himself on the grass and read and smoked, looking sometimes down on the clear waters of the young Clyde. Some people said you could hear the guns in France on hot still days like these. He put his ear to the ground and sprang up enraged at the image he saw of the colossal destruction and agony of war. The utter peace of the cloudless sky intensified his pain. They were bleeding and dying in their thousands at this moment to defend their tenements, their slums, their dirt and drunkenness, their lives of toil and thwarted love.

That men should live in friendliness in the beauty of the world, seemed so simple to him. He read Keats again and again, intoxicating himself with rhythm and words. Wild ducks flew overhead across the river, glimmering blue and grey, and rainbow coloured. He followed their flight in mind to places lonelier, where reeds whispered at night and waters were black and still. He was filled with loneliness and Nature suddenly appeared strange and hostile. He rose and hurried from the quiet place and ended his adventure with solitude in the reeking habble of an ILP Sunday evening lecture in the Pavilion where a half-antagonistic audience listened restlessly to an anti-war speech verging on sedition.

The following evening, when he came home, tired and grimy from the shipyards he trembled and paled at the sight of an OHMS envelope staring at him from the mantel-piece. The four fateful letters loomed huge to his eyes, threatening, solid, inescapable, symbols of the Power he had resolved to defy. The rapid thud of his heart drummed in his ears while he stood with exaggeratedly upheld head looking at the letter, as though he was facing a court-martial. He took it down quickly, opened it and ran a contemptuous eye through the questionnaire. Then he found a penny bottle of ink in a midget chest of drawers on the dresser and after a long search a pen, among a heap of dusters and rags in the dresser-drawer. Dust had turned the half-inch of ink in the bottle to mud; the pen was rusty and useless. He rejected pencil as unfit for his high purpose and went downstairs and bought a pen and bottle of ink in the newspaper shop at the closemouth.

He came in again, sat down at the table and wrote across the form in a bold, ungainly hand, 'I believe in The Brotherhood Of Man! I refuse to fight in a Capitalist War! I have no quarrel with the German Worker! To hell with Imperialism!' His heart was beating wildly as he looked with timorous satisfaction at what he had written. He decided to add another exclamation mark to the word 'Imperialism' then he pushed the form roughly into the envelope and sealed it by pasting on the gummed re-addressing slip. His mother entered at that moment, stumbling and spilling odours of whisky and snuff. She flung her shawl carelessly on a chair, frowned darkly and girned at him.

'Yer Army papers came the day. Whit are ye goin' tae do?'

'Nothing!' said Eddy, sharply.

'Ye'd shame me afore the neebors!' she shouted, 'Why don't ye be a hero like ma twa braw sons instead o' a coanshense objector an' atheist?'

Ach, he was heartsorry for her! She also was a victim of ignorance, and poverty, like himself. Ay, just like himself! He looked at her swaying, glaring at him, working up rage in herself. Never would she understand him. He would have liked to stay and wash her face, tidy her hair, then get her to lie down and make her a cup of tea, as he sometimes did. But he couldn't face what was coming. She would yell and scream at him till she was worn out while he sat without a word to say. Ach, no, he couldn't face it! He ran out, and closing the stairhead door quietly, walked the streets till dusk before he found the courage to post the form. At last he pushed it quickly into a street-corner pillar-box and immediately his fear and despondency vanished. 'Well,' he thought, I won't shame her by having the polis come to fetch me. I'll give myself up tomorrow!'

But he spent another week of irresolution, accusing himself of cowardice while carrying on anti-war propaganda among his mates on the ship and in the workshops. He imagined that the scrawled form would land like a bombshell in the recruiting-office and almost at once a big escort would be sent to arrest him. A final calling-up paper arrived on the following Saturday and he told Francie he would present himself with his papers at the recruiting-office on Monday morning. Francie did not try to dissuade him any longer but said he wouldn't start work till the breakfast hour at nine o'clock. On the Monday morning Eddy went down to Clydebank with his brother and outside the gates of John Brown's they parted in silence, shyly, without a handshake. Francie pressed his last half-crown on his brother 'Ye'll mibbe be needin' it,' he said, turning to go as the shipyard buzzer sounded, then he passed through the big gates with a crowd of late-comers, his powerful shoulders stooped, his head indrawn. Half-turning, with a shamefaced glance at Eddy, he disappeared.

Eddy jumped on a tram and rode back to Glasgow, eager to carry out his resolve lest his courage should fail. When he arrived at the auxiliary recruiting station in Bath Street he stood watching the conscripts constantly passing in and out, studying their faces, trying to glean from their varied expressions their secret feelings. A little greyhaired pale-faced man ran lightly down the steps and nodded to Eddy, chuckling and rubbing his hands. 'Fine day! My it's guid tae be alive oan a day like this. They've rejected me! They say ma hert's no' strong enough.' He looked, smiling, up at the sky, 'Jeez, it's a gran' day!' then he walked trippingly down Renfield Street, and Eddy watched him till he was out of sight, shaking his head and bouncing his steps like a man who has just won a sweepstake.

A dark stoutish young man passing in said shakily, 'Goad, it's a game, eh? Ah suppose we'll hae tae go noo? If ye're AI there's nae dodgin' it. Have you been in there yet?' He offered Eddy a cigarette in trembling fingers, seeming anxious to stay and talk to ease his fear. Eddy regarded him with contemptuous pity, 'You can refuse to fight if ye don't believe in war!' he said. The young man looked blankly at him then went up the steps nervously clutching his calling-up papers.

Eddy paced up and down the pavement before the recruiting-office for half-an-hour then with impulsive decision he sprang up the steps and walked swiftly inside. He saw a long queue of youths and men extending along the passage from an open door and without hesitation walked through the door to the head of it. Three Army clerks sat at a green-baize trestle table busily dealing with the papers of each man in turn and directing him to a room on the right. At Eddy's abrupt appearance at the head of the queue they shot at him a simultaneous glance of amazement. Eddy threw his papers on the table and looked at them defiantly, 'I believe you sent me these,' he said, trying to speak loudly and firmly, 'Well, I've come to tell you I shall refuse to fight whatever be the consequences!' Then he completely forgot the fiery speech he had composed.

The queue was electrified by his audacity. It stirred, thrust forward heads. He looked straight at the three clerks but he felt the commotion in the queue and ardently desired coolness and eloquence to turn the moment into one of glorious propaganda. The three clerks were momentarily speechless, then the pale, sharpfeatured sergeant with thinning hair and pince-nez who was at the centre of the table, flushed and thrust the papers back at him, 'Go to the end of that queue!' he shouted. Eddy drew himself up to his full height and with thrown-back head said loudly, 'I refuse to obey military orders.' The sergeant, a worried-looking, kind-eyed man became indignant. 'So you're a conscientious objector?' he said sarcastically, 'Let's have a look at your papers.' He pulled Eddy's papers towards him, gave them a quick glance, then looked up with an expression of controlled impatience. 'Now look here, young fella-me-lad! You're only just nineteen, and you're a damned nuisance. You won't be drafted for some time yet and I advise you to go home now while the going's good.' But Eddy had turned and was addressing the queue in a loud shaky voice, 'Fellow Workers! Don't join up an' become conscripted cannon-fodder! Refuse to fight in a war made by Capitalists for the benefit of Capitalists! When it's all over you'll be thrown on the scrap-heap and forgotten! The German worker is your friend, not the British Capitalist!' The now infuriated sergeant struck a bell on the table, one of the clerks jumped up and caught Eddy by the arm and from a room on the right, where a doctor could be seen rapidly examining a line of men, placing his hand on their privates, sounding them with a stethoscope and passing them like cattle for slaughter, an orderly ran out and clapped a pair of handcuffs on Eddy's wrists. They hustled him, not roughly, along a passage and the orderly, a typical, middle-aged Glasgow workman, said, 'Noo, laddie, be sensible! Ye're only buttin' yer heid agin a stane wa'. Keep quiet, dae as ye're tell't an' ye'll mibbe no' be sent tae the Front.' Eddy smiled at him. 'I'm not afraid. I shall refuse to fight whatever they may do to me.' The soldier shook his head and shrugged his shoulders, 'A' weel, it's your funeral, laddie, no' mine!' They pushed Eddy into a small lumber-room and locked the door.

Eddy commenced marching from one side to the other of the small room singing The Red Flag at the top of his voice. He was shimmering with glory. He really believed his action was pregnant with historical significance, an inspiring impetus, a leap forward in the progress of Humanity. People were saying that there were mutinies everywhere in the ranks of the German and Allied armies. He believed the War would end suddenly, any time now, and the Workers all over the world would fraternize. He was convinced that the great Socialist Revolution would blaze up in Glasgow and sweep like wildfire through the world. John McLean had said it,

Book Two

Was gilt's, was ich dir sagen kann? . . .

CHAPTER ONE

Among Glasgow housewives, the 'Minodge' is a very important institution that provides them with frequent opportunities to call on each other for a gossip and a dram
and supplies them with footwear, hats, clothes, furniture,
household ornaments or utensils for a few coppers or a
shilling or so per week. Anyone, either the most improvident
poor or thriftiest well-to-do, can 'haud a minodge.'

The phrases, 'MENAGES SUPPLIED, ONLY FINEST
GOODS, BEST COMMISSION GIVEN,'can be seen on the
windows of small shops in dark back-streets and big stores in
the main thoroughfares. The organiser of this easy-payments
club receives a small commission from the shop at which each
member in turn, according to the number on her ticket, is
obliged to cash a voucher for a stipulated amount of goods.

Mrs Macdonnel was preparing to 'draw a minodge' one
winter afternoon in her little kitchen that glowed in firelight
like an old Dutch painting. Her range, famous in the
tenement, sparkled with immaculate steel and glistening
tiles and a riotous fire bellowed up the draught as if it meant
to hurl itself into the darkness outside. It flickered a pool of
light on new linoleum and illumined the coal-bunker in the
dresser opposite. Everything bright in the kitchen—the new
bedspread, the dazzling rubber tablecloth and the dishes on
the shelves above the dresser—got a blink from the terrific
blaze and returned it cheerfully.

Mrs Macdonnel sat a little away from the fire, musingly
cutting minute slips of paper from a page torn out of a
penny cash-book, and thinking it was time to be lighting
the gas. The snips fluttered into her lap; she stopped
cutting and slowly counted twelve pieces, three times to
make sure, then rose and placed them in a saucer in the
table and dropped the book into a dresser drawer. As she

lit the gas her eyes roved over her new belongings, shining with especial pleasure at the gaudy pattern of the linoleum and the expensive, greenish globe around the incandescent gas-mantle, and she foresaw the surprise of the women who were coming to join her minodge. 'Goash, they'll be gey envious!' she reflected, smiling, as she opened the stairhead door in answer to a timid knock and admitted a red-headed girl of twelve, home from school, her face and hands pink with cold.

'Oh, it's cauld, maw!' exclaimed the girl timidly—for she was never sure of her mother's temper—throwing down her ragged satchel and putting her hands to the heat.

'Ah want ye tae write oot they minodge tickets,' said her mother, pointing to the saucerful of slips, 'hae ye goat a pencil?' and she looked expectantly at her daughter. The child searched hurriedly in her satchel and said: 'Och, maw, Ah had a pencil an' it's drapped through a hole in me school-bag!'

'We'll need tae hurry!' said her mother, 'they'll be here the noo.' They both began an agitated search in holes and corners till they unearthed a two-inch pencil-stub from a dusty tangle of string, thread, wool, buttons and pins at the bottom of a big brass vase on the mantelshelf. 'It needs shairpnin'!' complained Mrs Macdonnel, slicing the stub unskilfully with a long bread-knife. The girl began writing numbers on the slips of paper with the reduced pencil, then ceased in a moment, crying: 'Och, maw, Ah canny write! Ma fingers are that stiff!'

'Come here an' warm thim.' Mrs Macdonnel sat back in her chair and received the small hands in her own. The girl smiled gratefully for the embrace and winced at the pain of quickening blood. 'Ma fingers are tinglin'!' she laughed.

'Whaur's yer wee gloves?' asked her mother. The child answered in a frighted voice: 'Oh, maw, Ah've loast thim! They were ta'en fae ma desk this moarnin'!' and Mrs Macdonnel echoed: 'My, it's an awfu' school, that Saint Peter's! The wee yins are aye stealin'!' Then she said, thinking of her commission: 'Never mind! Ah'll buy ye a nice new pair fae the minodge money,' and the girl smiled with relief.

'Ma ain pet! Ma ain wee lassie!' Mrs Macdonnel murmured, as she drew her daughter's red head to her breast
and bent her own greying, red head to it. 'Ah wonder whaur
Jimmy is the night? Ma brave wee son! Mibbe he's lyin'
oan a big field in yon Mespotamy wi' nae yin near him,
cryin' fur me!' She began weeping easily and the girl
drew away her head, scared by the gloomy vision. 'Naw
he isnae, maw!' she cried. 'Naw he isnae! He'll come
hame when the war's done. He's no deid!' There was a
knock at the stairhead door Mrs Macdonnel quickly wiped
her own and the girl's eyes with her apron. 'See wha 'tis,' she
urged, hastily tidying her hair. 'Mibbe it's Missis Glynn,'
said the girl, 'she aye comes first. It's like her chap.' But
Mrs Macdonnel, who, like all tenement housewives, knew
the individual peculiarities of the knocks of her friends and
neighbours, said with absolute certainty: 'Naw it isnae. It's
wee Minnie Milligan. Ah ken fine her sleekit wee chap!'
and she laughed slyly.

It was Mrs Milligan, who slipped in past the heavy girl,
after saying: Is yer mither in, Mary?' and greeted Mrs
Macdonnel with a shivering reference to the weather. She
sat down with her fawn-coloured shawl tightly hugged to
her breast and was not tempted to loosen it by the warmth
of the kitchen.

There was no admixture of Irish in Mrs Milligan. She
was a genuine Glaswegian, a small dark woman with a little
canny voice, which, in its flat cautiousness, suggested the
futility of all earthly doings and which, when she felt lively,
was high-pitched and skirled like the bagpipes. 'My it's an
awfu' war!' she remarked; then continued, pronouncing
the word like tush: 'They say the Alleys are goin' tae
give a Big Push next week. Ah hear the Kaiser's done a
bunk an' oor boays'll soon be dancin' through the streets
o' Berlin!'—and she laughed a dim, asthmatic laugh, like
the rustling of dry reeds.

Young Mary, who had resumed scribbling the minodge
tickets at a corner of the table, swung her stolid face
round in a look of annoyance at the visitor. She disliked
Mrs Milligan, who was always talking about the War and
making her mother cry about Jimmy. She was at it again!

'Hiv ye heard ony mair aboot yer son, Mrs Macdonnel?'
the little woman was saying: 'yer puir hert must be gey
heavy an' ye'll be thinkin' the postman's brocht ye bad
news every time he knoaks. Ay, it's a sad time!' Mrs
Macdonnel, who loved a 'good cry' and always seized on
the slightest excuse to indulge her weakness, hid her eyes in
her apron, and the girl, fearing her mother was going to be
maudlin again, hurriedly exclaimed: 'The tickets are ready,
maw!' But Mrs Macdonnel's mind was preoccupied with
her minodge; she dropped her apron, deciding she had
shown sufficient grief, and told her daughter to come and
stand by her chair at the fire.

Mrs Milligan eyed inquisitively the saucerful of slips and
announced: 'Ah see ye're haudin' a minodge. Hoo minny
are jinin'?'

'Twelve,' said Mrs Macdonnel, laconic and aloof. She
was alarmed by Mrs Milligan's manner and her pinched,
worried look. Her neighbour always hugged herself tightly
in her shawl and looked like that when she had come to
borrow money, and Mrs Macdonnel was determined not to
lend her a farthing. It would be unlucky to begin a minodge
by lending money, and anyway she hadn't got it, and besides
Mrs Milligan always took a long time to pay back! All these
negative reasons flashed through her mind as she looked
meaningly at the clock and hinted: 'Yer man'll shin be
hame fur his tea, Missis Milligan.' Looking more pinched
and worried, Mrs Milligan immediately poured out a sad,
desperate story about pawning the trousers of her man's best
suit which she would have to redeem this very night because
her husband was to be a very important delegate at a big
trade-union meeting in the morning. Could Mrs Macdonnel
lend her five shillings to get them out of pawn?

Mrs Macdonnel set her face and flatly refused to lend
her anything. She nodded secretly and significantly at her
daughter. She had guessed right!

Mrs Milligan rose at once, saying she would have to get
the money from somebody, pulled her shawl yet closer to
herself and with an offended look went out, closing the
stairhead door rather ungently. But she had hardly been
gone five minutes when Mrs Macdonnel, touched by the

vision of Mr Milligan facing his colleagues without his best trousers, sent her girl to inform the inveterate little borrower that she would give her the loan as soon as the minodge money was paid in; then she opened the door to admit the first arrivals for her club, two ladies oddly dissimilar—Mrs Laurie, a raw-boned woman six feet tall, and Mrs Kelly, a lady with abnormally small, screwed-up features, who barely reached five feet.

Mrs Macdonnel's delight increased as the members of her minodge steadily arrived, for it sometimes happened that one or two would exercise inconveniently the feminine right to change their minds and, notifying their decision at the eleventh hour, leave her with unwanted tickets on her hands. She was holding a 'three pound minodge' in which the twelve members would pay her five shillings weekly for twelve weeks and purchase their goods in the first or twelfth week, according to the luck of the draw. Her minodges were popular. Women could trust her to pay in their contributions and knew they would not meet with the awful experience of having their vouchers rejected when they went to cash them at warehouse or shop. Though she could drink away her family's wages during periods of moral weakness, she had a respectable horror of even the smallest debt and prided herself on owing no woman anything.

She smiled as she thought of the three pounds that would be paid in. She loved handling money and she greeted all comers with lively pleasure, delighted by their glances of surprise at her new belongings. Her kitchen was soon crowded with a mere knot of nine ladies. 'It's like "Maggie Murphy's Home"!' laughed Aunt Kate, who arrived last, her vitality heightened by a short dillydally with the bottle. They all talked about the War. Two of them had lost husbands and three given sons and they were all disgusted at the measly pensions they were receiving for the sacrifice of their dear ones—pensions which were small enough at the beginning (God knows!), they said, and which the Government had so often reduced it was now hardly worth the bother of going to the post office to draw them!

'Oi hear the Pope's thryin' to stop the War,' said Mrs Glynn, a dark little Irish woman with rosy cheeks and a squint. 'Shure His Holiness must be worn out intirely wid prayin' all the hours of the day an' noight for Payce! He would have to be stayin' till eternity on his bended knees to turn the heart of a man loike that Koiser!' A mutter that sounded like 'To Hell wi' the Pope!' was heard from the corner between the dresser and the window. Aunt Kate jumped to her feet and glared fanatically at the black head of Mrs McCleery, a stout Ulsterwoman who was whispering closely with a grey-haired elderly lady. 'Tae hell wi' the Pope, is it?' she cried, 'an' what wid ye be doin' without the Cathlic boys in the War? Heh!' Her voice rose as she rolled up the sleeves of her blue, print blouse and smacked her fists to her hips. 'Heh!' She tossed her raven head and her side-combs with the sham pearls glittered. 'Shure there's more Cathlics in the War than Prodesans! Shure isn't ma two big Cathlic sons fightin' fur King an' Country?' Then she began snuffling in her handkerchief. 'Ma wee Josie an' Peter! Ye'll no' come back again!'

Mrs Macdonnel, fearing her minodge was about to open with a battle, led her sister back to her chair, with furtive, annoyed glances at her and Mrs McCleery, whose face was inflamed with Protestant loyalty. 'Och, come oan, Katey!' she said, 'naebuddy's said onything. Haud yer wheesht an' Ah'll get ye a wee hauf!' The tension was eased and Mrs McCleery, apparently at peace with the Pope and all his flock, went on talking to the elderly lady.

Mrs Macpherson, a stout Highland woman with a large kind face and a small, soft voice, said gently: 'Och, what's the use of fighting about religion? Shure we all go to the same place, Catholic and Protestant, and God's the Father of us all!'

'Begob, ye're roight, Annie!' agreed Mrs Glynn, the innocent introducer of His Holiness, comfortably tucking folded arms within her shawl. 'Shure it's ayquil we'll all be before the Trone of The Almoighty God!' But the champions of Popery and Protestantism had only put their opinions aside for the time and at the rear of their minds were each firmly convinced that Hell was the destination of the other's soul.

Mrs Macpherson felt extremely pleased with her successful peacemaking. She was regarded as a simple body by her neighbours, who talked and smiled condescendingly about her. She loved cats, dogs and mice, and kept her working-man's Dining Rooms in Calder Street in such a profusion of cats that 'Macpherson's Eating House' was equally famous in the neighbourhood as 'The Cats' Home' because everyone swore that more cats than customers patronised her shop. She hadn't the heart to chase them and they knew it. Feline ladies and gentlemen of every class and colour walked in whenever they pleased and sat at her door licking their whiskers after the theft and digestion of a tasty bite, or walked forth calm and unhurried for an after-dinner stroll. It was said that the 'Sanitary Man' had called many times without result to complain about her four-legged lodgers, who rubbed against his legs and jumped on his shoulders while he put the case for the Corporation Cleansing Department, and it was common report that mice brought forth whole families and dined in leisure at her feet while a dozen cats sat on the big hob and talked to her as she lifted lids and stirred and tasted the contents of a dozen big iron pots.

Once a week, Mrs Macpherson cooked a fruit dumpling the size of a prize pumpkin which she retailed from her window at fourpence a pound. On the day it came from the pot to repose between a plate of salt ling and a trencher of houghs, two cats sat on either side the platter, staring in insolent ease into the street while steam billowed from the dumpling. Dogs were affected by this anarchy, admitted the cats' right to live, and simply didn't bother to fulfil their terrorist function.

'Ye hivnae broaght ony cats wi' ye the day, Annie!' cried Aunt Kate, 'shair the puir things'll be that lonely wi'oot ye!' and Mrs Macdonnel almost doubled up with laughter as she added: 'Weel, ye ken, Katey, she's left thim warrm an' comfortable oan yon hob! There's nae cat need want fur bite or sup while Annie Macpherson's alive!' A laugh went round, and Mrs McCleery cried: 'Goad, ye're right, Mary! Annie's goat a hert o' gold an' widnae herm a flea! The cats oaght tae gie her a Benefit Coancert!' Mrs

Macpherson laughed so vigorously at their fun that the two large black birds which dashed at each other's beaks across the front of her hat seemed to fly up and down to the tune of her laugh.

The arrival of two children, whom busy mothers had sent to draw their tickets, caused a pause in the chaff. They were an extremely small, bright girl and a small boy with a persistently wet nose, both painfully shy, the boy covering his embarrassment by repeatedly applying his sleeve to his nostrils. The women greeted them as 'puir wee lambs' and they looked grateful for their welcome into the warmth. 'It's wee Billy Quinn an' Maggie Magonigle,' explained Mrs Macdonnel; 'their mithers aye send them tae draw because they're luckier than theirsel's.' 'Ay, the wee yins are gey lucky,' agreed a toothless middle-aged lady whose wide mouth seemed to be the only mobile part of her enormous red face. She had a habit of champing her lips while she sat silent and resembled a cogitating ventriloquist's dummy; her lips snapped on her remark and disappeared entirely as she went on chewing, like a cow mouthing the cud.

Aunt Kate, with put-on sternness, ordered the boy, who was still engaged with his nose, to produce a handkerchief. 'Och, ye're no' a gaintleman tae come oot wi'oot a hanky!' she said, with a smiling frown. 'Look at wee Maggie's nose! There's a nice leddy's nose for ye!' The boy looked tearful at the women's laughter, and Mrs Macpherson fumbled in her handbag and produced a handkerchief so small that it tickled them all to further laughter; Mrs Macpherson's ladyish ways were always a source of fun. The boy promptly pocketed the dainty rag and used his sleeve as Aunt Kate embraced him and gave him a penny for sweeties.

A thin, nervous little woman, who was regarded as peculiar because she always sat silent in company with trembling hands on shaking knees, whispered anxiously to Mrs Macdonnel her desire to get home before her man returned from work, the agitation of her limbs increasing as she spoke. Mrs McCleery tittered to the grey lady beside her, and Aunt Kate remarked: 'Ye're gey nervous the day, Missis McGovern.' The thin woman gave a melancholy smile, while her knees clapped like castanets and Mrs

Macdonnel opened the draw, taking up the saucerful of slips and asking who would like to take it round.

A drymannered little woman, impatient to be going, nodded her shawled head sharply and suggested drawing the tickets from Mrs Macdonnel's apron, but Mrs McCleery and Aunt Kate demanded that Mrs Macpherson should draw them from her bonny hat. 'Come awa, Annie!' they cried 'turn yer wee burds upside-doon!'

Though its style was antique, Mrs Macpherson prized her hat as a marriage gift from her dead husband. She was the only one present with costume and hat and made an odd figure among the shawl-clad women. She unfastened her hat reluctantly by drawing out three blackheaded pins of fearsome length, which Mrs Macdonnel placed on the mantelshelf. The slips of paper were crushed into pellets and dropped in the hat, then Mrs Macdonnel shook it vigorously and put her hand inside and stirred the tickets round. 'That's roight, give thim a good sthirrin' an' ye'll have no complaints!' cried Mrs Glynn. 'Ay, steer the parritch weel an' ye'll hae nae lumps!' added the impatient woman, who regarded everyone and all the proceedings with suspicion.

Mrs Macdonnel returned the hat to its owner, saying the 'unlucky yins' wouldn't blame her if Mrs Macpherson took it round. Mrs Macpherson presented her hat to each member in turn, beginning with the children. As each one dipped out and read her ticket her expression betrayed her luck. The red-faced lady champed more excitedly; Mrs McCleery exclaimed 'Humph!' and threw the paper pellet on the floor as if it was some nasty insect; Mrs Glynn announced: 'Begod, the oul' man'll get his new boots next month!'; the dry woman's suspicion increased as she remarked: 'Ah've goat number eleeven, whit hae you drawn?' to her companion with the trembling knees, who complained in a husky, spectral voice: 'Och, Ah never hae ony luck! Ah've goat number ten!' while her hands danced on her lap; the boy had drawn number twelve and began to wail that his mother would beat him if he returned with such ill luck.

It was Mrs Macpherson's turn to pick, but ticket number one, the only number not yet drawn, had vanished. Mrs

Macdonnel accused her daughter of forgetting to write it out; young Mary asserted that she hadn't and joined the boy in crying; Mrs Macdonnel reddened with embarrassment, and the suspicious lady looked as if she was smelling out foul play; then Mrs Macpherson, after a deal of flushed fumbling, extracted the ticket from the ancient lining of her hat; she then said she was in no hurry for her goods and generously gave the boy her 'turn' for his; he paid his mother's five shillings and went home happily with the girl, who had also picked well for her mother.

Mrs Macdonnel produced a small bottle of whisky to wet the first week's contributions; the nervous lady and her suspicious friend, who had hung on hoping for a drink, drank their deoch-an-doris simultaneously, gathered in their shawls and departed with sharp nods. Mrs Macdonnel then told the remaining women, whose laughter skirled through the kitchen like screams of tropic birds, the story of Minnie Milligan and her man's best trousers, which she knew fine Minnie had pawned to bet unsuccessfully on a horse. She had a talent for telling a funny story, and, with the Glaswegian's habit of exaggeration, she larded the little punter's plight with fanciful details; her features wrinkled up like the face of a happy cat, her eyes closed tightly and she flushed an apoplectic red as her choking laughter interrupted her story. 'Goad, Mary, Minnie'll be sennin' her aul' man tae work wi'oot his troosers yin o' these moarnin's!' shrieked her sister. 'Ay, and thair she is, runnin' roon like a madwumman, fair distractit fur that five sheelin's!' concluded Mrs Macdonnel, who had enjoyed the story more than the audience.

Suddenly all their laughter was silenced by the postman's knock. Mrs Macdonnel's face went dead white, she clutched at her breast and her eyes stared like the eyes of a woman waking from a swoon. 'It's aboot James!' she cried. 'He's deid! Ah ken it! He's deid! Don't answer, Mary! Don't go!' but her girl had opened the stairhead door and taken the letter from the hand that pushed in. She rushed forward, crying: 'Oh maw, it's aboot James!' and stood before her mother weeping, with the letter trembling in her hand.

Mrs Macdonnel completely buried her head in her apron

and rocked to and fro in her chair wailing: 'Ma wee son, ma firstboarn!'; Aunt Kate embraced her and they keened loudly together with the girl crying violently by their side, still holding the letter. All the women stood and hovered round them, but no one thought of opening the buff envelope. Its message was taken for granted. Mrs Macdonnel had been expecting for many months the news of her son's death since he had been posted as 'missing.' Mrs Macpherson took the letter from the girl's hand; Mrs McCleery whispered: 'Dinny show it her, Annie! Puir saul, she's gey upset!'; the red faced woman ceased champing her lips and stared as if hypnotized; and Mrs Glynn began to relate how long she herself had sorrowed when they brought her son home dead, from an accident in the shipyards.

Mrs Macdonnel pushed her sister away, sprang up and seized the letter. 'Let me see it!' she cried; 'Whit dae they say aboot ma son? Ma wee Jimmy!' She tore open the envelope and tried to read the form, then thrust it weakly at her sister: 'You read it, Katey! Ah canny see!' Her sister puzzled over it, then handed it to Mrs Macpherson, who read out that 'No. 2044, Private James Macdonnel, The First Battalion, The 7th Cameronian Scottish Rifles,' had been 'Killed On Active Service.'

'But he's no deid! He'll come hame!' moaned Mrs Macdonnel, pointing dramatically at the set-in bed. 'Every night Ah lie there an' hear 'im runnin' up the stairs! He chaps at the door an' fa's in ma airms!' She turned and held out her hands to a framed enlargement of a photograph of her dead son which occupied the place of honour, facing everyone who entered the kitchen. One day a Jewish gentleman had called, canvassing for orders for enlargements of photographs—'in goylt frames, lady; ver' cheap!'—and had later returned with a bad copy of the excellent original. Jimmy looked into the bright room, neat and upright in a mercantile petty officer's uniform, a jaunty, foolish smile on his face, while his mother cried to him: 'Jimmy, can ye hear me awa oot there? Ah'll show ye the way hame, son! Ah'll show ye the way hame!' She stepped on a chair and took down the picture, hugging it to her breast, crooning over it. Her sister took it from her. 'Och, steedy yersel', Mary. Ye mustnae gie way. It's Goad's Wull! Mabbe be's at peace noo, lying in the airms o' the Blessed Virgin. Ah'll say a wee prayer fur 'im!' She rehung the picture and knelt at the bed, straining her hands to the nickel crucifix on the wall. 'Sacred Heart o' Jesus,' she prayed, 'watch ower Jimmy this night an' guide 'im tae Thy breist!' Mrs Glynn knelt near her, agitatedly repeating the sign of the cross, and Mrs McCleery, having forgotten her hatred of the Pope, stood weeping behind them.

Mrs Macdonnel started at the sound of a beggar singing in the back-court, saying the man was singing a favourite song of Jimmy's. She gave one of the women her purse to throw the busker a copper, then continued mourning, loving her dead son and hating her husband who had been hard on Jimmy. Mr Macdonnel, the petty, righteous man, had always been enraged at Jimmy's indulgence in drink, his own greatest weakness. Mrs Macdonnel remembered her son's first night of drunkenness and the savage fight between him and her husband that had sown undying hatred. Jimmy was throwing himself at the door, which had been locked against him, when her husband, with planned malice, had suddenly thrown it open and caused Jimmy to hurtle through and smash his forehead against the door-knob. When the house was asleep she had slipped Jimmy in and bathed his wounds.

All the women were now in tears, repeating after each other: 'Ay, it's Goad's Wull. He's at peace noo. He canny suffer nae mair. Goad's just!' Mrs McCleery recalled what great pals Jimmy and her son had been; Mrs Glynn remembered him as 'a broth of a boy' when he ran about the back-courts in his schooldays; and Aunt Kate said: 'Shure, Mary, minny's the time Ah've nursed 'im in these airms fur ye when ye warnae weel. He'll no furget his aunty up in Heevin!'; and everyone choroused: 'Ay, it's Goad's Wull!'

Aunt Kate put Mrs Macdonnel's shawl around her and they all urged her to come out. She must have 'a wee hauf' and try and forget, they said. They were thoroughly enjoying themselves.

They trailed out. Young Mary tugged at her mother's shawl, pleading: 'Ye won't drink a loat, will ye maw? Will Ah make ma da's tea?' Her mother pushed her aside. 'Dinny bother me! Ma hert's broken. Tae hell wi' yer da! He wisnae kind tae ma Jimmy!'; then she paused in the doorway and shrieked into the kitchen: 'Curse the bloody War! Whit right had they tae take ma son fae me? Ay, ma boay Eddy wis right tae be a coanshense objaictor!' Her sister and Mrs Macpherson put their arms round her and gently led her out, and the child shut the door on her voice echoing inanely on the stairs: 'A coanshense objaictor! Ay, a coanshense objaictor!'

Young Mary paused in the lobby with her ear against the crack of the door, then she opened it and stood on the stairhead leaning over the rusty iron banister listening to the women's voices as they stopped to argue and talk in the close. When they had moved into the street and she could hear them no longer, she returned to the kitchen and began making slices of toast and covering them with pieces of cheese which she melted before the fierce fire on the steel plate-rack fixed to the grate. The appetising odour filled the room as her Uncle Wullie came in from his evening round of lamplighting. He sniffed and grinned. 'Toastit cheese! Och, my, that's champion. Jist whit ye want oan a cauld night like this,' then he sat by the fire and rubbed his long hands close to it, cracking his bony fingers. He was feeling proud and pleased because he had been accepted at last by the Army, after being rejected. He had to report in a week's time to be drafted to a Labour Battalion for training. The promise of any kind of change after his long years of running up and down tenement stairs with his ladder and lamp, attracted him strongly. He began to cough harshly, gripping his weak chest and his dull complexion reddened. Young Mary, forgetting his deafness, said quietly while he coughed, 'James has been killed, Wullie.'

He held his head down to her, his palm curved round his ear. 'Whit?' he said.

The girl shouted tremulously, with tears starting to her eyes, 'James has been killed.'

He stared at her silently while sorrow at her news worked in his face.

'Hoo d'ye know?' he said.

'Me maw goat a letter fae the Govermint,' she said.

'Whaur is it?' said her uncle.

'She's ta'en it oot wi' her,' said the girl.

Uncle Wullie sat at the table and stared awhile with open mouth in depressed silence.

'Yer tea's ready,' said the girl, placing before him a plate of toasted bread and cheese and filling his cup. He stirred his tea slowly, then he said, 'Aw, poor James! it's a peety he wisnae a prisoner,' and he began wondering what would be his fate, his expectation of change and adventure darkened by dread. He took a few coppers from his waistcoat pocket and sent the girl to the corner bakery for some penny cakes. She returned along with the youngest son of the family, a pale, quiet boy of fifteen, home from his apprentice work at a jeweller's in Renfield Street. He had been ridiculously christened 'Egbert' because of his mother's affection for a venerable English priest of that name among the priests of Saint Peter's chapel. The name was ill-suited to him and he hated it because his schoolmates had nicknamed him 'Egg' and 'Ham and Egg.' Young Mary addressed him as 'Aigburt' and asked him if he wanted his tea. He went to the end of the table, facing his Uncle and pushed the door to with his behind as he sat down.

'Hiv ye heard aboot poor James?' said Uncle Wullie.

'Ay,' said the boy, his eyes fixed expressionless on the laid table.

'D'ye mind the wee parakeet he broaght hame fae sea yon time? My, yon was a rare wee burrd!' Uncle Wullie said laughing at the memory of the long-dead pet. 'D'ye mind hoo it used tae scrape at the door wi' its beak, tae get in? Och, it was gie'in it too much breed soaked in tea an'sugar that killed it. Wee Polly goat too fond o' that. She wid have lived longer wi' the right kind o' food.'

The children laughed with him. 'Ay, she wis a rare wee burrd!' said Egbert, his eyes shining as he remembered his dead brother's generosity when he came home from sea with pocketsful of money. He munched several mouthfuls, then said, 'Mibbe James is alive somewhere wi' a loast memory.'

'Ach, Ah doan't believe he's deid!' said Uncle Wullie, trying to make his voice sound hearty to cheer up himself and them.

Young Mary went to answer a timid knock at the door and Wee Minnie Milligan flustered in, saying, 'Goad, Mary, is yer maw no' in? She proamised tae sen' me that five sheelin's! If Ah dinnae get it soon the pawn'll be shut!' She nodded to Uncle Wullie. 'Yon was a bad tip ye gie'd me!' she said, shaking her fist at him with feigned annoyance.

Uncle Wullie leant across the table with his hand to his ear, his lower lip stupidly hanging. Minnie Milligan shouted, he nodded, smiled and seemed ashamed. 'Ay, Ah backed it masel',' he said. 'It wis a good hoarse but it didnae run up tae form.'

Minnie Milligan's feckless face looked silly with apprehension as she asked Mary where her mother could be.

'Mibbe she's over at The Shielin',' said the girl, 'an' if she's no' there, she'll be in The Clachan, but mibbe ye'll find her in the Rob Roy Arms.'

In desperation Mrs Milligan rushed away to thrust her head in at the swing doors of those public houses in search of the only woman who would lend her anything. As she went out, Uncle Wullie was frowning and pointing at the penny tin of pepper standing beside the sugar-basin. Egbert passed him the bottle of worcester sauce, then the salt at which Uncle Wullie frowned irritably and shook his head, then Egbert handed him the pepper. He grinned and nodded and began shaking it on his toasted cheese.

CHAPTER TWO

John Macdonnel waited for the end of the News and the commencement of the Sports Bulletin, the only wireless item that excited his deepest emotions. He glared at his big, hire-purchased Marconi set, inwardly cursing the voice that went round the world with such polite insistence. At the word 'Abyssinia' and the announcement of another Italian victory, he gave ear to the voice for a moment, then as it went on to quote the triumphant opinions of several distinguished Fascists on their country's cowardly invasion, he lost interest and anxiously considered his chances with the bets he had placed that morning.

He held in his hand a scrap of paper with the names of three horses written on it along with two large football pool coupons printed in green ink which announced in large print, SMEARS PENNY POOLS. FAIR AND RELIABLE! YOUR WINNINGS ON THE BREAKFAST TABLE! A FORTUNE FOR A PENNY! His eyes ran up and down twenty-four columns of tiny squares in each of which he had tried a forecast of the result of twelve football matches. Last year he had won a thirty shilling share and another of five pounds in the last week of the season. This season his hope of a fortune soared to dizzier heights. Supposing his was the only correct coupon sent in, he might win five thousand or maybe twenty thousand pounds!

By jees! Twenty thousand pounds! His feelings shot up like a rocket and buzzed round inside his head in a whirl of sparks that smouldered out in foggy plans when he reckoned what he could do with it. He would send Agnes and all his boys to college, buy a big self-contained house in a more respectable locality, Anniesland or Hyndland, say, and open a shop—a fried-fish shop! One shop! Sure Sir Thomas Lipton rose from nothing with one wee shop in

Crown Street and look how he finished up! Ach, with the rare start a few thousand pounds would give him he would soon have a chain of shops all over Glasgow and in every town in Scotland. Then, with a manager in each shop he could sit back and do nothing; just run about in a posh car visiting all his branches to see they were being properly run. Jeez! What a life! Money for jam!

He lifted his head and stared wide-eyed with a confident look as if he was a big-business man piling up a fortune and his bushy eyebrows danced up and down his forehead as he alternately frowned and stared. Ay, there's money in fish-supper shops! He and Norah had once managed one for her brother-in-law. Ay, yon was a rare time, busy every night in the brightly-lit crowded shop, slicing potatoes, dousing the fish in batter, plunging them into the smoking fat and wrapping up threepenny, sixpenny and shilling suppers while they talked and laughed with customers till midnight, when they counted up the evening's takings and went home about one in the morning, pleasantly tired, to a light supper and a quiet talk before going to bed. They had no time to get dull and they looked forward to the day when the shop would be their own. Norah's brother-in-law, the labour councillor, a generous Irishman, principal partner in an agency that supplied fats and oils to fish-friers, had promised to sell them the shop, goodwill, stock and fittings for a nominal price that practically made it a gift. Just about that time, his partner, who had been cheating him all along, had absconded with every penny of the agency's capital, leaving in his wake a mob of clamouring creditors. Their friend had struggled desperately to save the business, while suffering from internal cancer, and the hopeless struggle had hastened his early death.

John Macdonnel remembered how he had helped to nurse his dying friend and regretted again the glorious chance of success that fate had snatched from his grasp. He was bored to agony with his job as attendant in the Corporation Chambers and married life and the creation of children had become almost as tasteless as his job. At forty-five he was hardly recognisable as the once golden lad and dandy. His thick fair hair was streaked with grey and his deep frown, comprised of worry and dyspepsia, was exaggerated by his greyish complexion and tufted eyebrows.

He hunched forward in his chair at the announcement of Racing Results and his heart jumped as one of the horses he had backed was reported a winner. If the other two horses won he would have pulled off a three-cross-double and would lift twenty pounds from the bookie. His frown lightened, but when the two other horses were reported also-rans, he scowled and threw himself back hopelessly in his chair. At the announcement of Football Results he leaned forward again hopefully, studying his coupons and trying to check up with broadcast version the bewildering collection of crosses and figures in the twenty-four penny columns on which he had betted.

He could never succeed with this regular Saturday evening experiment but he invariably tried it before getting the *Evening Times* to verify his forecasts. 'Agnes!' he called, in a voice harsh with disappointment, and again, more loudly, 'Agnes!' when no one appeared.

A tall, sturdy girl of sixteen, with shiny auburn hair, dressed in a blue dress, her simple smile glimmering behind spectacles, walked in slowly and stood before him. There was a slight cast in her right eye, the result of an operation, which spoiled the homely comeliness of her face.

'Whaur's Norah?' said her father coldly.

'She's lyin' doon. Her heid's bad,' said the girl.

Mr Macdonnel handed her a penny, 'Ah want ye tae go fur the late *Times*!'

Agnes pouted. 'Och, da, let Philip go!' she said without taking the coin, 'He hisnae gaun ony messages the day!' and a queer smile glinted behind her glasses as if her father with his wild hair and worried frown looked very funny and she was trying hard not to burst out laughing at him.

Mr Macdonnel could seldom exercise his fatherhood without shouting and he said loudly, 'Bit Ah said you're tae go! Here, take the money an' don't staun there like a big galoot!'

Agnes took the penny and turned away, her sulky expression a comical sight against her fat cheeks and spectacles, but her father was too lost in self-pity to relieve his misery by laughing at her.

'Whaur's Philip?' he said, as she reached the door.

Agnes nodded towards the bedroom and said in a tearful voice that he was in there and Mr Macdonnel knitted his brows, asking her what he was doing, as if the question was tremendously important.

'He's writin' his essay for the Academy,' said Agnes.

'Good!' said Mr Macdonnel pompously, rising to switch off the wireless, 'then that settles it! You'll hiv tae go. He's goat tae stick tae his English. Bring me some watter before ye go doon.'

Agnes brought him a half-full tumbler of water from the kitchenette and went slowly downstairs as her father placed his closed fist in the pit of his stomach, leaned over with the glass of water in his other hand and gave the fire a look of dyspeptic resentment. He remained in this posture for some moments, thinking how bad he was and convinced that most of his forecasts were wrong. Then he took a round glass bottle of white powder from his waistcoat pocket, uncorked it, tipped half the powder into a tumbler, drank the clouded water smartly, shook his head in a shiver of nausea and placed the tumbler on a ledge under the mantelpiece.

'Ach, they can say what they like,' he thought, as though he was strenuously arguing with someone, 'ye can't beat bakin'-sody. Sure it hasn't done me ony hairm!' He had carried about a bottle of bicarbonate of soda for years, often taking it out in company, when conversation turned on stomach troubles, to praise the virtues of the powder and if anyone suggested that his dull grey colour was caused by the excessive use of it, he would irritably disagree. Sure a professor at the Western Infirmary had told him that he had doped himself with it for years. And a professor ought to know!

His daughter had returned and was silently offering him The *Evening Times*. He looked up, took it from her and began studying the football results and his coupons. A forecast of seven correct results was the highest he had made and for another long week his chance of a fortune had vanished. He threw the paper violently into the opposite armchair and sat back, recalling how happy he had been when working on those building jobs after the War. Always in the open air, eating well, sleeping well, never a minute's anxiety about his health and him a gaffer as well, over twenty men, with the power to engage or sack labourers at a minute's notice, helping to build yon big modern hotel by the lochside. He had carried the hod as sturdily as the biggest man on the job and could have done the bricklayer's work too if he had been asked. Och, they were dandy times, boy, when he laboured through long summer days in the glorious air of those mountains, with his brother Francie, who was in his right mind then for a few months. They had watched with real pride the gradual completion of the hotel, working overtime in the clear Highland nights and travelling down to Glasgow every Saturday for a smashing weekend with plenty of money in their pockets!

Ach, he knew fine! Let Norah say what she liked, he wouldn't have lost his health if he had stuck at building-work. Sure it was after he had been a year in the Corporation Chambers that his bad health had started. It was all her fault, asking her brother-in-law, after he was forced to sell that fish-supper shop, to get him a position because she thought labouring at building work wasn't a respectable job. Sure he might have been a master-builder by this time if he had stuck at the work. Builders were making pots of money these days with their contracts for the new housing-schemes. A man he knew as a bricklayer's labourer only a few years ago was a master-builder now and standing as a Liberal candidate in a municipal bye-election.

He felt guilty, knowing that if Norah came in she could tell with one look at him what he was thinking and would blow all his pessimism skyhigh with a few outspoken words, but he let his thoughts meander futilely back to the days when he was the best-dressed and handsomest man in Thistle Street. What was he now? Just an ordinary attendant toddling out every day to a monotonous job to open doors and cringe and touch his cap to the Provost and all the municipal big-wigs and their wives—the City Fathers—and Mothers! He hadn't been promoted because he was a Catholic. Oh, they couldn't jalouse him with their promises of something better later on. Employees of the True Faith weren't popular in this Protestant-run town. He would just go on in the same position till he was sixty then retire on a Superannuation Pension.

Holy God, every day of his life was the same! And there was Norah, after making him move to this more expensive Corporation house, saying that the neighbour-hood was losing respectability and that she felt isolated from her relations and old friends. Ach, ye can never satisfy women! He felt explosive with bewilderment. He was fed up with scraping and saving to meet instalments on hired furniture, pay electric light and gas bills, doctors' fees, buy new expensive books for Philip at Saint Anthony's Academy; he was mystified by the constantly recurring need for new boots and clothes for his children. And all on three pounds a week with Agnes, his eldest, on the dole, like thousands of other youngsters leaving school at fourteen and passing into their twenties unemployed.

His application for promotion was still on the shelf and he was sick of trying to please his mother and keep friendly with Norah at the same time. Spite and pride had pulled the two women apart through the years. Now, they never met. His mother resented Norah's outspoken tongue and energetic ambition, hating change, indignant with anyone who dared to criticize her way of life. Sometimes he sided with his mother, agreeing that Norah interfered too much, then, after a stand-up quarrel with Norah would agree with her that his mother was hopeless. Jeez, they kept him fairly on the hop! Between them he had never known a day's real peace since his marriage.

Weakly, he decided, as he always did in these stupors of pessimism, that Norah had been right after all in trying to make him rise above his family, in urging him to take an interest in Labour politics and get nominated for the Town Council. She had told him he was as clever as her brother-in-law, but he flinched still at the idea of addressing a public meeting. Hadn't he repeatedly told her he hadn't the head for the job? He was glad she had stopped egging him on to it and he didn't feel the shame he used to feel when she told him he had no gumption.

When was Norah going to rise and get the tea? He looked at the clock. It would soon be time to go down to his mother's. He wished he hadn't promised to go there tonight and uncomfortably decided to stay at home. He used to enjoy playing the dutiful son, going down every Saturday night with a present for her—a cake and a half-bottle of whisky when he was flush—knowing the neighbours said, 'My, Joahn Macdonnel's a guid son tae his mother!' But Norah frowned on his visits and when he stayed away for a few weeks his mother would meet his reappearance with a sulky silence that implied she knew very well who had stopped him. She was genuinely fond of the children and liked them to come and see her when they came from Sunday School. When they moved into this Corporation house Norah stopped her children's visits and deepened the hostility. He could never talk frankly about family affairs in either home. Ach, they were enough to drive a man daft the pair of them!

It was three weeks since he had seen his mother. Well, he wasn't going there tonight! He shook his head with stuck-out jaw as a boy of five years old, blue-eyed, soft-featured with a curly golden head, walked in smiling and aiming a long peashooter at the red curtains across the double-windows. 'Oh, da, Ah hit the tap o' the windy!' he cried, smiling at his father who turned to shout at him and then said quietly, trying to look stern, 'Hiv you been stealin' that barley again? Eh? Show me yer haun.' The boy, looking frightened, opened his fist which was full of pearl-barley. His father pointed dramatically towards the kitchenette, 'Go an' put that back in the jawr!' he said and turned to the fire, smiling at the boy's trembling mouth. Then he swung round and ruffled his silky hair, 'All right, ye can keep this loat, but if ye steal only mair, Ah'll . . .' He left unsaid the terrible things he would do and looked fondly after the child as he went out. Wee Frank, the spoiled one, his favourite, in whom he saw himself. He picked from the table an American dime magazine, lay slackly back and began reading a gangster story entitled, 'Scarface Wins Again.'

Agnes reappeared, grinning with anticipation, took a

bundle of film magazines from the long, narrow press by the side of the fireplace and sat opposite her father going through one magazine after another, poring over the pictures. She memorised all the nonsensical gush written around Hollywood stars, could talk about the most intimate details of their lives and never tired of gazing at her favourites during the long afternoons when her mother could find her no more housework.

The silence for the next half-hour was broken only by the silken flutter of the fire and the rustle of magazine pages. Then Philip, a tall slight boy of fourteen, his white clear skin flushed with excitement, ran in waving a copy-book and shouting, 'Oh da, Ah've finished my essay. Ah wrote it a' this afternoon!'

Mr Macdonnel was absorbed in a description of a savage machine-gun fight on a Chicago sidewalk. Machine-guns were stuttering like mad, bullets flew like hail, spattering walls, crashing through windows and motor-car screens, thudding dumbly into gangsters and upholstery of cars. He had forgotten his abortive football-coupons, his unsuccessful bets on horses, his life of failure, and he looked up extremely annoyed by his son's noisy interruption and told him he would look at the essay later on, then, noticing the lad's disappointment he laid his magazine aside and with a long-suffering expression took the copy-book from him, and read THE LIFE OF A PAIR OF SCISSORS in block letters at the top of the page.

Philip stood by shyly shuffling his foot and his father gazed vaguely at the opening sentence, then said testily, 'Och, stoap jiggin' yer feet. Hoo d'ye expect me tae concentrate wi' you doin' a stepdance beside me!'

Philip plunged his hands into the pockets of his shorts, tortured by the effort to keep still; Agnes tittered and Philip frowned at the crown of her head as she hid her face in her magazine.

Mr Macdonnel, who was still doubled up with dyspepsia, skimmed through the essay like a news-editor passing a proof and said in a lukewarm voice that it was fine and Philip would be a big writer one of these days and he must be careful to keep his essay clean for the Academy on Monday and pointed out that Philip had made the scissors singular, 'Should ye no' hiv made them plural?' he asked.

Proud of his grammatical knowledge, Philip explained that though the scissors sounded plural they were really singular. They had to tell their story in the first person singular. Mr Macdonnel said he saw the point and with a haughty stare at Agnes Philip returned to the bedroom, his head buzzing with vanity, to read over his essay.

Norah Macdonnel came in to hang up fresh window-curtains, putting on a bright print overall and looking as if she had just washed the sleep from her eyes. She was now a robust-complexioned, well-built woman of forty with a certain heavy attractiveness. Her faded auburn hair was fluffed about her broad, pleasant face, her brow was curiously bunched above her eyes, which, like Philip's eyes, were slanted and unimaginative but not hard. Her energy was slow but very determined. It was remarkable the amount of work she always made for herself in a one or two-roomed tenement house. Mr Macdonnel secretly called her 'hoose-prood.' He was content to sit back often amid dirt and untidiness and she had nearly driven him crazy with her mania for cleanliness.

Norah passed in and out without looking at her husband. They had just quarrelled about his mother. She was in a dreary mood after a rest to ease a headache caused by her weak eyes and she was thinking that John had always been the same unalterably dull man, that every day since their marriage had been exactly like today; with her doing the same work, cooking the same food, feeling similar emotions. She was not cheered by the thought of her children. At the moment she did not care for them at all. She was consumed by a fierce desire to escape into some vague region of freedom. She could not count on him to cheer her up. His self-concern blinded him to her boredom. She always fought her way back to cheerfulness by doggedly sticking at whatever work she was doing. She had tried, unsuccessfully with her rough words, 'Shake yersel' oot o' yersel' b' daein' something!' to galvanize him into a livelier interest in life.

Norah sighed seeing him sitting there, without a collar, his shirtsleeves rolled up and waistcoat unbuttoned, his mind partly occupied between reading and internal discomfort. He used to cheer up her Saturday afternoons by dashing home from work, changing into his best suit, snatching a meal and hurrying away to the Celtic match. Then in the evening he would hurry home excitedly pleased if the Celtic won or disappointed if they lost. Either way he was interesting and full of talk about the game, not half-dead like he was now.

She was asking herself why she had married him and blessed again the safe Corporation job that had turned up when he was thirty. It was far below what she hoped he'd have reached by now, if he'd had any gumption, but it was better than the dole or irregular earnings from casual labour.

As she propped a pair of steps by the window, Mr Macdonnel said distantly, 'We could be daein' wi' a nice cup o' tea. It's efter six!'

Norah mounted the steps and five minutes later said coldly, 'Ye had yer dinner at three o'clock. Ye canny be dyin' o' stairvation,' then she said loudly to Agnes, 'Here you, hiv ye naethin' better tae dae than make sheep's eyes at Ramon Novarra? Pit doon they magazines an' gie me a haun wi' these curtains!' Agnes came eagerly to help her mother while her father rose and lit a Woodbine then walked into the bedroom, shrugging his shoulders.

Norah frowned at his childish behaviour. His family were too thin-skinned to please her. But she was a stupid woman. Her natural frank manner, though not always malicious, was devoid of imagination. She slammed at moral problems like a navvy with a sledgehammer and she was always astonished and offended when her hefty interference was loudly resented. She invariably left trouble worse than she found it but she could never resist the itch to interfere in other people's lives and was always stamping in where wise folk fear to tread. She had tried to run the lives of all the men of the Macdonnel family whom she fundamentally misunderstood, then she finally washed her hands of them, fully satisfied that she had done her best and they weren't worth the trouble.

John was an Adonis among corner-boys when she first clapped eyes on him. His clean handsome look, his love of dress, manly stride and big cheery laugh won her heart and she dreamed right away of climbing with him to a prosperous social position. But he turned out to be a handful for some time after their marriage. He came home, like millions of other men, from three years in the trenches, three years he bitterly regretted and never talked about if he could help it, the same bundle of emotions and stupidities he had been when he went to the Front.

After the War he began drinking hard and playing the boss of the house and Norah decided to stop once for all his lordly behaviour, especially when he overturned a laid dinner-table just to show what a genuine he-man could do. He stalked boastfully out and returned at midnight to find the upset table, smashed crockery and mess of food as he had left it and there it lay till next morning when he got humbly on his knees and cleared it up. For a full fortnight Norah served him all his meals and cleaned her house without uttering a single word and by this stupendous exhibition of will-power John was stunned and subdued.

She recalled one Saturday night when he was drinking with his family and she plainly expressed her disgust with them for letting him get so hopelessly drunk. Later that night his mother had worked herself into a rage and called at her house to create a scene on the landing. Always his family in the way! She felt very tired as she felt many times with the struggle, for she had not found in him any stamina or eagerness.

She took the soiled curtains into the kitchenette and as she doused them in snow-white suds in the deep porcelain sink she seemed to wash her black mood away and began to think cheerfully about her father. There was a fine man for you now, though he did kill himself with the drink! At least he stuck to what he was good at till be became one of the finest french-polishers in Britain. Sure didn't he win a competition in polishing held by the trade when he beat some of the finest polishers from England? That was more than any of the Macdonnels had done. The work of Philip Larkin had been known everywhere as the best in the trade

and could be found to this day on the furniture and panels
of big Glasgow hotels. And her mother had hated the very
thought of poverty. When her husband was ill she carried
on his business and when he failed she felt shame to walk
down the street where they had lived so long, where every
window and closemouth was a comment. Norah couldn't
understand why the Macdonnels weren't deeply ashamed
of being nobodies. Philip Larkin had never lost pride in
his personal appearance. She never tired of telling the story
of the day he died, when he got up, quietly shaved and
dressed himself and with his gold albert and hat on, walked
into the kitchen where she sat with her mother and four
sisters, raised his hat with a deathly smile and collapsed. He
wouldn't go back to bed and died sitting there before their
eyes, saying with his last breath to his wife, 'Noo, Agnes,
ye wouldn't have wanted me to face me Maker without a
shave!'

After a year her mother married her father's friend,
the little Englishman, a Victorian dude and traveller in
furniture. All the girls disliked his foppish ways and soon
left home to make an independent living, working at their
father's trade. Och, yon were cheery days when she worked
as apprentice in a high-class factory turning out beautiful
furniture among a queer lot of foreign workmates, Poles,
Lithuanians, Jews, Germans, Swiss, Frenchmen. Norah
rinsed the curtains smiling as she remembered the timid
Lithuanian who had courted her and her sister with gifts of
food. One day she returned in the dinner-hour to find six
bottles of assorted aerated water hidden under her overall on
the bench; another day it was a dozen bunch of bananas, a
big bag of apples or sweets, then a large cake. She discovered
her admirer through a Polish workmate and when she went
to thank him he dived under his bench with fright and
shyness.

She wrung out the curtains and let down the pulley across
the kitchenette, wandering into memories of the War and
her three years on munitions when she stepped for the
first time, blushing with modesty, into overall trousers and
bobbed her long hair to hide it easier under the regulation
mob-cap. It hadn't been all jam, though she did earn big

money, in that factory where two explosions had happened with loss of many lives, what with the anxiety and strain in the long hours of day and nightshift, making the same movements all the time, like a machine, tipping measured portions of high explosive into parts of shells. She spent her big wages just like many others, feverishly buying expensive things and throwing them away on entertainments and pleasure. But she kept straight with John while he was at the Front and though they married on practically nothing when he was demobbed she was proud of the way she still kept their little home together and shuddered to think what might have happened if they had lived in the come-day-go-day-God-send-Sunday style of other young couples.

Houses were hard to get and they were lucky to be able to begin life in a single-end in a slum street with the patriotic name of Thistle Street. Their house was in the oldest, foulest part. Her lip curled with disgust at the aimless life she knew was lived by many in those tenements at this minute. She believed people like that didn't want to get on. Couples married, settled down and had families who married and reared families all in the same street and made wee clans of relations.

In their three years there she couldn't remember a Saturday night without a terrible fight in some part of the street when it was alive with people running at the sound of shrieks, shouts and the birl of police whistles. Och, she hated the memory of yon landing and its dirty, broken window without a single pane, its water-closet door with the broken lock, always wide open and smelling, its over-flowing pan drenching the landing and stairs with filth and the dark, badly-lit stairway where you had to be careful you didn't break your neck over a drunken man lying there. Facing her house was a shop with its window blinded by white boarding painted in black letters with the sign: PATRICK MURPHY. VERMIN SPECIALIST. FLEAS, BUGS, BEETLES, RATS AND MICE SUCCESSFULLY DEALT WITH. PROPERTIES AND ESTATES FUMIGATED. ESTIMATES GIVEN TO FACTORS.

Och, sure she minded it fine. Her fingers lingered, pinning the curtains on the pulley. It was as though she saw mirrored in the reflection from the electric light along the glistening edge of the sink, her young mating life in that brutal environment. She saw drunks every day, men and women crazing themselves with methylated spirit and Red Biddy; she had seen men taken away in the asylum van. Whenever she went in or out the close it was through a knot of shawled women clustered round a newspaper, discussing the day's horse racing. She had to shoulder her way past and knew they were talking about her, felt their hostile looks as she went upstairs. One day she told them she would complain to the authorities about the nuisance and impulsively that afternoon lodged a complaint at the local police-office.

Smoothing out the damp curtains she glowed with satisfaction remembering how she had changed yon filthy tenement kitchen into a fit place to live in; badgering the factor till he made all necessary repairs, then setting-to to rid the house of vermin and the stink of decay and foul living. For a whole month she worked day and night, with John's help after his day's labour, scrubbing, disinfecting, painting, varnishing, polishing, wrenching the rotted door off the concealed bed, scrubbing and plastering its bug-ridden walls before distempering them in white and green and afterwards buying an oaken four-poster bed for the cavity, which she hung with attractive curtains. 'My, Norah, ye've made it intae a wee palace!' said John when it was all finished.

What would have happened if her health hadn't been perfect when her first child was coming and she made that awful discovery. The little wife of the dark man who lived across the landing hadn't been seen for a week. It was rumoured that she had gone to visit her relatives in Ayrshire. Norah sensed again the putrid closeness of the tenements on that summer Sunday afternoon when she took across some dinner to the man and his four-year-old daughter. He opened the door narrowly and peered out at her pale and mad-looking. A disgusting stench came from the kitchen and she turned sick. The man opened the door wider and beckoned her in with gibbering sounds, pointing a shaking hand at the cavity bed. It needed all her courage to place the steaming dinner on the table and approach the bed. She knew what had happened before she knelt and lifted the blanket which hid his wife's dismembered body in a large box under the bed. The man and child had lived for a week with the body in that kitchen. The child stood whimpering, pulling at her father's hand while he sat insanely crying and Norah took her in her arms and went out, quietly closing the door and sent John for the police.

She moved heaven and earth after that to get away from the district, urging her councillor relation to agitate for the destruction of the property and provision of new homes for the tenants. When town councillors came a year later to inspect and condemn the whole property they praised her kitchen and said it was a pity to have to destroy it with the rest. My, that was something she kept under her hat to tell people!

Life was easier when they moved into the new slum-clearance tenements with their bathrooms and private water-closets, but she felt they hadn't got clear away from slum life. Some of their neighbours went on living in the old way. Children soon made the walls of closes and stairs ugly with chalk and scratched paint; landing windows were soon broken; women who seemed incapable of managing whether their husbands were working or idle, borrowed from her; she saw the fine new interiors being spoiled and some baths being used for coal and lumber. And John began to complain of his internal trouble and the long walk every day to his work to save tram fares. You couldn't depend on him to make the best of things. She soon found it dangerous to sympathize with him.

The pulley squealed as she pulled it up and twisted the rope deftly round the wall-hook. These new-style Corporation houses with private entrances were a great improvement. Here at last she had made a real big step away from slum life and closemouth loitering. Och, things weren't so bad. Still, she had to admit they had reached as high as they would ever reach. They would plod along like this to the end, going twice a week to the pictures and on Sundays to Mass, with very rare visits from friends or relations—till their family grew up and brought them the interest and excitement of their marriage. Well, she hadn't borrowed from people anyway!

Suddenly her youngest boy began to cry loudly from his cot in the bedroom. She ran to him and, returning to the parlour, hugged and soothed him, then sat by the fire and began applying zinc-ointment to his teething-rash. 'Ah'll hae nae mair wee yins!' she said angrily, 'this'll be ma last.' Oh, she wouldn't do anything forbidden by her religion but she was sure that God didn't want her to have any more and she wasn't going to let any priest encourage her to have a big family. The priests didn't have to rear the wee ones.

If only John had had the gumption he could have stepped up from being a town councillor to an MP. When she had sung her child to sleep again on her broad lap she sat gazing for awhile into the fire, dreaming of being in the company of men in snow-white shirt fronts and diamond-studs and ladies in tiaras and evening-dress, with long sweeping trains, fancying herself sending out gold-lettered invitation-cards, inviting people to balls and banquets, seeing herself and John in press photographs: 'John Macdonnel Discusses Unemployment With Prime Minister At 10 Downing Street.' 'Mrs Macdonnel and Lady Snowden Opening A Charity Bazaar For The Relief Of Children In The Distressed Areas.' She rose, smiling down at her infant, thinking how bonny he was as she took him back to his cot.

An hour later John Macdonnel came and sat down smiling broadly at the parlour-fire. He had escaped from dyspepsia in a deep sleep. He grinned amiably at Agnes when she entered with a card-table which she placed near the fire and covered with a white cloth to set the tea. Mr Macdonnel contemplated a large plateful of rich Scotch pastries and said cheerfully, 'My these are rare pastries. Ah weesh there was a Reception every night.' He was always claimed for extra duty at Corporation banquets and dinners and often brought home his share of the surplus from groaning tables, and sometimes he surprised his humble friends with a champagne supper when there was an unusually regal feast in the City Chambers.

'D'ye mind the time Ah took the wax elephant off the Duke's roast?' said John Macdonnel when his family was

seated and Norah was pouring out the tea, and he told
them again the ten-years' old story which always made them
laugh. It was one time when a visit of royalty to Glasgow was
being celebrated in the City Chambers and John on his usual
overtime duty walked into an ante-room where a huge roast,
intended for the guests of honour, lay waiting on a table.
John was so amazed by the crafty, imperial decoration on
that roast that he impulsively picked one off and crammed it
into his mouth, thinking it was a sweet-meat. When the roast
was being carried into the dining-hall an official examined
it and there was a fearful row while John went about in a
sweat with a headless wax elephant in his pocket.

'An' d'ye mind the night ye brought hame the big likker
jeely?' said Norah and John told them how he came home
one moonlit night after a Civic Ball with an immense liqueur
jelly under his overcoat. As he passed the Bridge-gate four
tough-looking men turned out of it and walked behind
him, appearing to dog his footsteps. He thought they were
waiting a chance to set on him and rob him and when he
was crossing Stockwell Bridge he placed the jelly on the
parapet, buttoned up his coat and turned to face them. At
that moment two policemen appeared at the other end of
the Bridge and the men passed on while John turned to
see the paper with which he had covered the jelly, sailing
down the Clyde.

Norah and the children laughed heartily at his description
of the shivering jelly glinting in the bright moonlight and Mr
Macdonnel hugged wee Frank, 'Ach ye're just goin' tae be
a big swell like yer da when ye grow up aren't ye, son?'

'Sure, he's a wee dude the noo!' said Norah, 'The way he
combs his hair ye wid think he was Maurice Chayvaler!'

'Ach, bit he disnae eat enough,' said John.

'You wait till he grows up. He'll be eatin' ye oot o' hoose
an' hame,' said Norah.

Mr Macdonnel told Philip to fetch his essay and asked
Norah to read it out. They all laughed when she read:
'A lady came in and bought me and the shopman wrapped
me up in a small parcel. The lady dropped me as she was
stepping on a bus and a poor boy found me lying in the
gutter and took me home. His mother was very pleased to

see me as she was mending his father's trousers and I came in very handy.'

Philip sat up flushed with pride, clutching his copy-book; Agnes switched on the wireless and Smetana's 'Vltava' boomed out its surging melody; she turned the knob and Beethoven's Fifth Symphony barged into the room, in a pandemonium of atmospherics, from some foreign station. Mr Macdonnel jumped from his chair, 'For Goad's sake turn aff that highbroo stuff! Here, Ah'll show ye hoo tae get stations. He dialled London and a hearty voice said, 'Hullo, folks!'

'Tommy Handley!' said John, 'That's the stuff tae gie the troops! Ah wonder if the aul' couple next door are listenin'?'

'Sure they listen in every night. They say they can hear it through the wa' as plain as oorsels,' said Norah.

John and Norah, who had lived in enmity for an afternoon, had come together over tea and Radio variety. Norah stole looks at John, thinking, 'Ach, mibbe it's no' his fault he has nae gumption. As ye get aulder ye don't blame people sae much.'

John eyed Norah thinking what a rare good wife and manager she was and wondering where he'd have been without her. The deathless human desire to live in creative happiness flowed through them in this moment as tranquilly as the great Bohemian river whose music they had turned away, serenely, like the triumphant Clyde, a world's river dug out by men's hands, streaming to the wide oceans, free, creative, carrying the means of life to international humanity.

A moment of the real happiness they had missed in life was granted to John and Norah in thoughts of their children's future.

At this time Mrs Macdonnel was sixty-two years old. It was thirty years since her last long railway journey when she went with her husband for a holiday in Ireland. Since that time she had only travelled twice on a train on short trips to places on the Scottish coast, and at the thought of going alone on such a long journey she felt timid and bewildered. But her family could only afford the one fare. Her husband and sons were on the dole, her daughter was earning a pittance as a machinist in a clothing factory and she had borrowed part of her fare from John, her married son.

On a raw November morning they saw her off at the station and as the train moved out she huddled up in a corner of the carriage, her mind full of working-class prejudice against asylums. She had heard stories of torture in strait-jackets, of the brutality of attendants and she convinced herself that her 'puir wee son' was being brutally treated. Her face writhed with rage against his persecutors, then streamed with tears of pity for him until the only other passenger, a small elderly woman seated opposite, leaned across smiling, asked her what her trouble was and produced from an attaché-case a glass and a small bottle of whisky.

It appeared that she was also on a sorrowful errand. Her son was lying in a north-country hospital and while Mrs Macdonnel sipped her drop from the glass the little woman told her all about him, describing his virtues from birthday to manhood with motherly exaggeration.

These friendly exchanges eased the dread in Mrs Macdonnel; her visions of Francie as a raving lunatic fighting with burly attendants were dispelled. She was sorry when her companion left the train just over the Border and before Carlisle was reached her terrors were returning. That taste of spirits had comforted her and she sat awhile looking out at the lights of the refreshment-room, dim in the afternoon fog, craving the warmth of another 'wee hauf' but unable to make up her mind to leave the carriage, fearing the train would start without her.

After some hesitation she timidly addressed a stout farmer, sitting in the far corner engrossed in a farming paper, and asked him how long the train was stopping. He assured her in a broad Lancastrian dialect that there would be a good ten minutes' wait and she went onto the platform, her heart jumping at the crash of a carriage door and the clanks of the wheel-tappers' hammers. She stopped midway to the buffet and half-turned to go back, then, deciding there would be time, she hurried in.

She stood extremely agitated in the warm bar, fumbling in her purse, and ordered a half of whisky. She told the barmaid why she was here and asked her when the train would start. The barmaid looked at the old figure in the plain, black hat and long dark coat, told her she would have time to enjoy her drink and said she was sorry to hear about her son.

At a sudden clamour of shouts and slamming carriage-doors Mrs Macdonnel drank off her dram and hurried anxiously onto the platform. It had been her habit for years, when out-of-doors, to carry her purse rapaciously clutched in her hand. As she sped down the long train she became aware of an unfamiliar sensation and found her fist tightly closed on nothing.

She stopped, breathless, sickened by the rapid thud of her heart, and searched feverishly about her person. She had lost her purse and the return-half of her ticket and the few shillings she had brought for Francie to get him cigarettes and any little comforts he could buy in the asylum. Half-fainting, she stumbled past hurrying passengers to the buffet. The barmaid looked astonished when she staggered in gasping, 'Ah've loast ma purse!' but she saw it lying against the counter by the glint of its metal clasps and stumbled forward to pick it up as the barmaid came round to help her.

She was now feeling ill and had to summon all her

strength to return to the platform. The barmaid assisted
her but the train was moving out as they reached the door.
Mrs Macdonnel sobbed bitterly that she would have to go
home without seeing her son as the barmaid led her gently
to a chair by the buffet fire and went out to enquire the
time of the next train. She returned to tell Mrs Macdonnel
that there would not be another one for three hours. She
advised the old lady to make herself comfortable and tried
to convince her that the asylum officials would not be so
callous as to refuse her admission to see her son.

Mrs Macdonnel reached her destination at seven o'clock
that night and walked out of the station bewildered by the
strangeness of the place, so unlike the streets of Glasgow.
She approached a policeman who helped her on to a bus
and told the conductor where to put her down. A long
dark road led to the institution. She crept along it timid
and heavy-hearted, peering at the names and numbers on
gates, till she came to a group of hospital-like buildings.

When she rang the bell the lodge-porter told her it was
many hours past visiting-time but as she had come from
Glasgow he would see what he could do. She felt chilled
and ill in spite of the lodge fire. Now that she was about
to see Francie her imaginations became terrifying. It was
over a year since he had left home and all that time she
never had word of him till this English County Asylum
wrote to inform his relatives that he was detained there.
She remembered him as a strong boy and powerful youth,
maundering about by himself, given to strange outbreaks
of rage but often radiant with laughter and kindness—the
strangest of all her sons. She recalled her pride in him on
that day he went and apprenticed himself to an engraver in
precious metals and her extreme pleasure when he brought
home the first sample of his work, her own initials engraved
on a sixpence rubbed smooth on one side and fastened with
a silver pin. She used to watch him at homework in the
evenings, bent over the kitchen table, skilfully plying his
small graving tools with his clumsy-seeming hands. She
recalled her grief when, driven by some morose impulse,
he left the job where he had been succeeding so well and
went away to tramp the roads. Her sons had been difficult,

Francie most of all, and secretly she knew she had reared them badly. But even as she wept over him she prided herself that nobody could say she hadn't been a good mother to them. This was God's Will, but not her fault.

The meeting of mother and son was emotional and painful. She could see no change in Francie. He was just the same as she had often seen him at home and she could not understand why they were keeping him. She wanted to take him home then and there, but the doctor shook his head and tried to explain. Francie was a violent case and his release might take some time.

Mrs Macdonnel returned home with a very confused story about Francie, but on her next three visits, when she was accompanied by her daughter, she gradually pieced together his rambling account. It appeared he had fallen ill with influenza in a country casual ward. When he got better he felt strange in the head and one day had violently attacked the workhouse master. He was overpowered and taken to the county asylum.

It never occurred to the family to contest the medical verdict and they settled down to a dense acceptance of the tragedy. Francie remained in the English asylum for a year during which he sent several demented letters appealing to them to bring him to a place nearer home, telling them that the authorities in London were playing invisible rays on his head and that he was surrounded by secret police who were out to arrest him for killing a man in Lockerbie. He would never get better, he told them, unless he was brought to an asylum in Glasgow. Moved at last to action by these letters and urged by his mother, John Macdonnel, with the help of a Labour councillor, began negotiations for his brother's transfer.

Several months passed before Francie was received as a patient in a mental-home in his native town. In their simplicity the family imagined that his transfer would only be a matter of a few days and they were astonished and angry at the long delay. But the people in authority at the English asylum raised the question of payment to the county ratepayers for expenses incurred by Francie Macdonnel, claiming that the Glasgow municipality should also meet the cost of sending him by train in charge of two attendants. The Glasgow authorities, unwilling to burden their already heavy rates with the expense of another incurable patient, resisted both claims. Finally, through the influence of a Labour MP, Francie was brought to his home town.

Every Sunday one or more of his relatives visited him, getting no nearer to him in spirit or understanding than when he was some hundred miles away. He was metamorphosed into something more pathetic than a trembling animal, for he was afraid of life, yet he continued to live, tortured by his misdirected physical strength. On some visits they found him, after an outbreak of violence, in the padded cell with an attendant close at hand. There he would stand, silent, like a dumb beast, or sit on the floor, hiding his face from them and grieving for the man he imagined he had murdered in Lockerbie. Sometimes he would walk with John and Egbert among the crowds of demented ex-servicemen and civilian patients, 'like his auld self,' said John, talking of his long tramps, his eyes animated as he described some wild, lovely place by sea or mountain; sometimes he would stride away from them, leaving them puzzled and helpless, with a look of disgust and despair, as if he considered them incapable of remotely understanding his trouble.

Mrs Macdonnel continued taking him parcels of food with cigarettes and pocket-money. It was her only way of expressing affection. In times of bereavement, sickness or celebration she had always given her children food. To her neighbours she gossiped about him after every visit, telling fond stories about him, enjoying her distinction in the role of unfortunate parent.

Towards the spring of the following year it seemed as if Francie was slowly emerging from his physical tomb. He was cheerful at visiting time, talked more sanely and said he would like to come home. Everyone was overjoyed by his improvement; John said he would get him out and applied right away to the medical superintendent, who agreed to allow Francie out on three days' parole.

On a brilliant May Sunday morning his two brothers hurried out to Hawkhead with a suitcase containing a new suit and clean underwear, cheered and excited at the prospect of bringing him home. But their hopes were shattered when they asked for him and were directed to the sick-ward. Since their visit he had refused to eat and was being forcibly fed. The doctor was unable to explain his relapse but he told them it would be some months before they could again consider a parole.

John's bowler hat bobbed less jauntily and Egbert's odd smile vanished when they entered the ward. Francie lay high up on the pillow in a bed opposite the door, his white, unshaven face expressionless. His eyes met theirs without recognition. John leant over him and said with feigned seriousness; 'My, you're a nice fella, lettin' us doon like this!' then he put the case on the bed, snapped it open and held up in turn a new cap and a bright tie and shirt; 'See what Ah've brought ye? Och, ye'd be a toff walkin' doon Gowan Street in these the night!' His rough eyes were moist, his hands jerked about like a Jewish hawker's trying to sell old clothes. He took off his hat, put on the cap and held his head at an angle to show off its dash and style; 'Look,' he said, 'It's a dandy! Ye'd hiv a' the lassies efter ye!'

Egbert smiled at his brother's antics, but Francie turned away his head, mumbling soundlessly and, as if he was coaxing a spoiled child, John hung the tie round Francie's neck and held the shirt against his breast. 'Don't ye want tae come hame?' he said, 'ach, ye'd look swell at the match the day. Celtic's playin' Rangers!' he announced as though it was news fit to wake the dead. 'It'll be the match o' the season, won't it Aigburt?' he winked at his young brother.

'Ay, it'll be a rare match,' said Egbert.

Then John told the sick man that his mother was breaking her heart to have him home, while he stared desperately into his sullen suspicious eyes as if he hoped by the power of his gaze to awake a glimmer of response. 'Look at the spankin' day!' he said, pointing at the wide ward window where the sun blazed in through the shimmering leaves of a young tree.

A smile, like an effort of his higher self to respond to his brother's appeal, passed across Francie's eyes, which seemed to have been dragged inward by indifference. Then his head turned wearily from them; he frowned, closing his eyes, and did not look at them again.

The brothers stood gazing at the still young face. John had exhausted his bag of tricks. They could think of no other way of communication with the unwilling life behind those closed lids. In the next bed a fair-headed boy sat up and pointed a finger at them, laughing ceaselessly; across the ward a powerful middle-aged man gibbered loudly at them, beating a soup-spoon on his bedrail like an infant. The brothers tried to smile at the imbeciles, then John shut the suitcase and they walked slowly from the ward.

At ten o'clock next morning as Mrs Macdonnel was going out with her daughter to Mass to say special prayers and light candles at the altars of saints for Francie, an unfamiliar rap sounded on the door. Mrs Macdonnel turned pale and sat down, her prayer-book falling on the floor, her mother-of-pearl rosary beads dangling from her trembling fingers, and in a scared, whispering voice told her husband to answer the door. Mary leant against the dresser looking at her father as he rose from his breakfast and walked into the lobby, leaving the kitchen door open; then the two women listened intently to the murmur of voices on the stairhead. When the old man returned to the kitchen there was no need for him to convey the caller's message. They had heard every word.

Mary embraced her mother and they wept together while Mr Macdonnel stood before them, his hands held weakly out, his grizzled head hung. 'It wis the polis,' he said, his toothless mouth awkwardly framing the words; 'he says Francie's ta'en a bad turn an' somebody'd better go an' see 'im,' then he sat and bowed his head on the table while his wife cried: 'Ma Francie's deid! Ma hert tell't me it was aboot him. It aye means death when the polis comes. It aye means death!' She looked resentfully at the bowed figure of her husband. They had lived in hatred for years and were now incapable of consoling one another.

Francie was dying when his father and John reached his bedside. A tall, bronzed young doctor stood there looking down in concern at the powerful man who writhed in pain before him. John was angered by his brother's moans and roughly asked the doctor to put him out of his pain. The young man stammered, embarrassed, that he had just given him an injection, that he was not in pain, and John was about to embrace Francie when the doctor said: 'Don't disturb him. He'll fall asleep now.'

Suddenly Francie died. His moans ceased and a smile came to his face like a gladness of one who has solved an exhausting problem. John flung his cap on the bed and pressed his cheek against the lifeless face; Mr Macdonnel removed his cap and kissed his son's forehead while tears fell from his hard eyes. At that moment Mrs Macdonnel entered the ward, and seeing from afar that all was over she threw off her shawl and ran crazily to the bed. For a moment John and her husband held her back, then they let her grieve over him.

A stout, severe-looking matron came in and spoke to the doctor, then told the little group that they would have to leave. John told her loudly, indignant at her grim discipline, that they had not been in ten minutes. She met his glare resolutely, then turned to give a young nurse instructions: 'You can see your brother in the mortuary in half-an-hour,' she said, her starched bosom upheld waiting for them to leave, like a sergeant of death.

They drifted mournfully down the ward where they were intercepted by Egbert, who had been walking round the blocks with the corner-boys and had heard the news by chance. He rushed forward in the uncontrolled family manner, his face strained with tragic expectation. John stopped him with a hand on his shoulder. 'Francie's deid!' he said and Egbert clapped a hand to his brow and crashed to the floor. John stared at him in astonishment as the matron ran forward to help raise him up, telling the nurse to bring water. Egbert recovered in a flash and refused the glass of water. 'Och, Ah'm all right,' he said. A glimmer of sweat damped his forehead, but his solid, pale colour was unaltered. They were all astonished. He was the silent one who had rarely spoken about Francie.

Mary took her mother home and the three men waited outside the mortuary. Hardly a word passed between them

as they walked to and fro in the May sunlight. They made
no attempt to cheer each other nor talk curiously about
the foolish wasted life, that but for some mental twist
might have been with them still in sane strength. They
did not speculate on the present or the hereafter; all their
movements suggested a weak fatalism; John and Egbert lit
Woodbines, nicking them and lighting them again several
times; John put a cigarette behind his ear, forgot it and
immediately took another from the packet. Egbert's strange
faint, the first in his life, had not altered him; he was the
same stiff, untalkative being. Fumbling with thick fingers
calloused and gnarled with years of pick and shovel labour,
Mr Macdonnel applied match after match to his broken clay
pipe and burned himself. 'Ach, Ah canny enjoy a smoke
the noo!' he said irritably, putting the pipe back in his
pocket. His massive, hobnailed boots crunched the gravel
as he walked with drooped shoulders, and the hair of his
unshaven cheeks gleamed like frost; whenever he looked
up his glasses flashed in the sun, which shone into his eyes
that were bleak, like stones under shallow, sunless water.

'Whit dae ye call yon the doctors dae tae ye efter ye're
deid? said John; then he said, 'An otopsy! Ay, an
otopsy. We don't know what Francie died o'. We oaght
tae demand an otopsy. Mibbe they doped 'im tae get rid o'
him.'

'Ay, we should demand an otopsy,' said Egbert.

'But mibbe me maw won't agree tae it,' said John.

'Naw, mibbe she won't agree,' said Egbert.

The mortuary door opened and a uniformed attendant
called them in. They filed into the narrow cell where Francie
lay on a wheeled stretcher under a white cloth, and bared
their heads in the cold silence as the attendant turned back
the cloth.

The faint smile of escape lay like moonlight on his face;
his distorted mouth had remoulded to graceful lines, his
brow was clear of the furrows of insane worry and terror,
his rest was like a deep sigh of relief. They looked at him
knowing not when or how the warped mind had begun to
crush the life from his strong body, unaware that he had
willed himself to die. Among them, in life, he had been

alone; now he was apart, with no further need to consider them or explain himself to anyone.

'He looks awfu' peaceful,' said Mr Macdonnel in a choked voice. John touched the cold brow. 'Ye canny suffer nae mair, can ye Francie?' he said.

'He's was gey young,' said the attendant.

'He was only thirty-four,' said John, 'an' the strongest yin in the family,' he added proudly, 'He could kerry a two hunnerweight bag o' cement as if it was a bag o' shavin's.'

'Ay, it's hard lines tae die sae young,' said the attendant, 'Bit we've a' goat tae come tae it sometime.' He covered the dead face.

The asylum doctors were willing, even anxious, to hold a post-mortem; they could not explain the death of this strong, healthy patient otherwise; but when 'autopsy' was translated into honest Glaswegian for Mrs Macdonnel she was horrified. 'Ah'll no let nae doactors cut ma bonny son open!' she said, and when John timidly suggested that Francie could be buried from Hawkhead she wanted to know what the neighbours would think if she let her son be laid in his grave by an institution. She would have Francie brought home and give him the very best funeral she could afford to pay for.

Insurance books and life-insurance policies were hurriedly examined for all the benefits due for Francie Macdonnel. Through years of unemployment, good times and periods of drunkenness, Mrs Macdonnel had seldom failed to put by for herself and all her family the few weekly coppers that assured them of respectable burial when it pleased God to call them. For thirty years the same 'wee Society man' had called at the same time every Monday and if she happened to go out she always left for him a little pile of coppers or a sixpence and threepenny bit lying on the three pink-covered books each entitled: 'Scottish Legal Life Assurance Society, Fire, Burglary, Accident, Death,' which she laid on the corner of the dresser near the door. With the help of the insurance money and one way and another, Mrs Macdonnel mustered twenty pounds to keep upsides with her pride and local conventions.

John promised his mother he'd get the best possible funeral for the money and he went to PATRICK HEWES, THE UNDERTAKER, whose bright shop beamed till late hours in Crown Street. Mr Hewes was a tall, broad, red-gilled Irishman, urbane and blue-eyed, who always boasted that he defied competition. He offered coffins at keenest prices and went about in a continuous state of brisk pleasure over his profession. He brought Francie home from Hawk head in a fine coffin costing twelve pounds and complimented Mrs Macdonnel, 'Sure he was a foine big man, yer son. It took four of me best men to carry him.' Mrs Macdonnel cried and treated him to a drop of the 'best Irish.'

Francie lay in state in the front room for a day and a half with two candles burning at his head. The white blind was down and the coffin rested on two slender trestles pressed close against the fire-place where he had so often sat and brooded. All day and late into the night the coffin trembled, shaken by passing tramcars and commercial lorries. When darkness fell the incandescent mantles of the globeless chandelier blazed purring light on his face. At the head of the coffin, the brass plate on the lid, propped upright against the press door, shone with the inscription: FRANCIE MACDONNEL, AGED 34 YEARS, DIED MAY 2ND, RIP.

From the closemouth below the voices of gossips and children echoed up; the choruses of crowds of singing corner-boys drifted by; in the small hours the footsteps of late walkers rang, as he had heard them when he lay sleepless or sat late reading, echoing along the straight silent gullies of tenement streets. They had brought him back to the cribbed, petty life of industrial back-streets, the life from which he had always longed to escape into his dreams of achievement and success.

Throughout the day neighbours, corner-boys and young men who had been at school with him called to pay their respects, humbly doffing caps and looking for a moment at the corpse. Those who were Catholics bowed their heads and made the sign of the cross or knelt to say a 'wee prayer'; those who were Protestants praised Francie to his mother while she acted the funeral hostess, weeping at the words of every other caller. Some brought wreaths and waxy, artificial flowers which were piled on the sideboard opposite the coffin. Willie McBride, the prosperous book-maker, sent his daughter with a large, glass-covered stone wreath of coloured flowers above two white birds on a marble tablet touching beaks across the words, GONE BUT NOT FORGOTTEN. The wreath from Mr and Mrs Macdonnel bore the verse, 'A Light Is From Our Household Gone. A Voice We Loved Is Still. In Affectionate Remembrance Of Our Dear Son.'

There was a one night's wake. The family and friends sat up till dawn with the dead, the men sitting stiff and awkward round the coffin, silent for whiles and hushing their voices when they talked; the women gathered in the kitchen, gossiping vitally about sickness and death and the bodies they had helped to lay out. Sometimes a quiet laugh echoed through the lobby; now and then a woman brought tea or whisky to the men.

Jerry and Sandy Delaney, sons of the woman who had once boastfully showed her leg at a drunken party in this same house, sat side by side. Jerry, a stout organ-builder, with dreary features and a kindly heart, began a political argument with Tommy Nolan who sat on his left. Tommy had been the white hope of the Gorbals in flyweight boxing but his love of strong drink had ruined his physique and talent and he was now a fat little man with a beery red complexion. He lived on the dole which he eked out by earning three to four pounds a week as a book-maker's collector of street bets. He was a Conservative and wanted to know why Jerry wanted to upset things. Jerry's pale, blue eyes were incapable of the visionary gleam, but he believed stoutly in what he called 'The Millenyum,' justifying revolutionary propaganda with the argument, 'It's no' the noo we've goat tae think o', it's the Future!' Tommy fell into a long silence apparently digesting this statement.

Jerry Delaney next startled John Macdonnel from sleep by suddenly addressing Mr Macdonnel who sat against the bed, staring constantly at the floor in a daze of feeling about his dead son. 'D'ye see that?' said Jerry, "twas your Francie made that.' He tiptoed past the coffin to show the sixpence on his watch-chain on one side of which his initials in intertwined script were finely engraved within a border of leaves. The old man peered stupidly at the coin and Jerry said; 'D'ye no' mind? Francie made it fur me twelve years ago.' Mr Macdonnel roused himself. 'Och, ay, Ah mind noo! Francie was a genius at the engravin',' he said and gazed again at the floor. In the kitchen, Aunt Kate was proudly showing a silver brooch which Francie had made; all the women said he had been a good son to her and Mrs Macdonnel smiled convinced that she had been 'a guid mother tae a' her sons.' No one was horrified by Francie's dismal end. Preventable sickness, poverty, madness, murder in their midst were accepted as inevitable. But behind her protective layers of self-pity Mrs Macdonnel suspected that all her sons had failed because she and her husband had lived in misunderstanding and hate.

The mourners went home at dawn to take a short rest before the funeral in the afternoon; the light was turned out; John and Uncle Wullie lay down fully dressed to sleep on the cavity bed; Mr Macdonnel huddled on a chair. In the subdued daylight through the white blind and the glow of two candles at the dead man's head the flowers and the brass handles of the coffin dimly bloomed.

At eleven o'clock, Mr Macdonnel slipped out unnoticed by anyone. He had forgotten to put on his cap and stood bare-headed at the closemouth, a black cotton muffler knotted at his neck. His right boot was unlaced, his trouser leg caught up on its gaping sides. Someone spoke to him about Francie, but he did not hear and walked down the road, trembling, the loose leather lace swishing as he walked. Somewhere he stumbled into the bar-parlour of a public-house, ordered a drink and sat alone there, staring at his glass for a long time without drinking. He was trying to make his stiff mind remember things about Francie, his favourite son. He accused himself. Ach, maybe he was to blame! He was selfish and hadn't taken enough interest in his sons. Ach, he and Mary hadn't been meant for each other. They should never have married. Then a scene from long ago came into his head. He lay in bed, young, healthy and sober, after a hard day's work. His two boys lay in the crooks of his arms and he told them stories from memory out of Grimm and Hans Andersen and stories he made up himself. Ay, he had been a rare story-teller and they wouldn't go to bed till he told them one of his own. Francie and his other son, away in London, were the only two who loved books like himself. Suddenly, out of the past, the laughter of children rang in his ears. He laughed, then buried his face in his hands.

He was absent when the priest arrived from Saint Peter's to read the Burial Service. A young Irish cleric, in seedy garb, he came in hurriedly, with a brief, distant word to Mrs Macdonnel, hardly glancing at the mourners crowded in the lobby and the room. He was irritated by Mrs Macdonnel who, fearing further expense refused to have Francie taken to the chapel and the service read from the altar. Someone took his hat; everyone knelt as he quickly hung a purple stole round his shoulders; then he sprinkled the coffin and mourners with holy water and murmured hastily some Latin prayers. All through the scamped service the disdainful look never left his face. The kneeling people responded: 'Christ have mercy on us! Lord have mercy on us! Eternal rest grant unto him O Lord, and let perpetual light shine upon him. May he rest in peace. Amen! Our Father Who Art In Heaven. . .' The prayer had scarcely ended when the priest took off his stole, snatched his hat from a hand, and left the house. Aunt Kate ran after him and knelt to kiss the hem of his overcoat as he left the house.

Mr Hewes arrived to screw down the coffin lid amid the loud, mournful cries of Mary and Mrs Macdonnel. John Macdonnel went in frantic search of his father, returned with him and hustled him into a second-hand blue suit, specially purchased for the funeral. Uncle Wullie, John, Egbert and Mr Macdonnel carried the coffin down the stairs and through the usual crowd of morbid watchers lined on both sides of the close. The women followed, carrying the wreaths, which were piled on the coffin in the motor-hearse. Only the men were going to the graveside, according to custom; the women stayed behind to prepare the funeral tea. Workmen were digging up the road before the close and the hearse stood by a gaping hole and mounds of dislodged paving-stones. At several tenement windows men and women leaned out to watch. This was an event in their lives. The hearse and four cars crawled forward; the navvies bared their heads and stood still holding long chisels; at the four nearby street-corners, groups of unemployed men and loafers doffed their caps.

For two hundred yards the hearse and cars moved at walking pace till they passed Saint Peter's chapel, when they raced ahead, avoiding the town's centre, speeding through the northern slums by narrow black turnings of factories and over the canal bridge till they reached Saint Kentigern's Cemetery. Inside the gates they stopped at the cemetery office which stands by Paupers' Corner, an allotment of nameless graves where the Parish buries the very poor. Mr Hewes jumped briskly from the hearse, delighted because he had covered the distance in twenty minutes. He handed papers to the cemetery warden and the funeral moved on up the slight hill.

Francie was laid in the family lair, where three Macdonnels slept the long sleep. It lay up a slope facing a line of gentle hills. When they lowered him the sunlight poured into his grave as if holding out warm hands.

'My, ye've been gey quick!' said the women when the men returned. The white blinds were up and tea was set in the room where the corpse had been. Some of the mourners went home. The meal was meagre, with scrappy helpings of boiled ham, baked beans, and a few pastries, and hungry guests sat to eat with ill-disguised looks of acute disappointment. Little was said about the little there was to eat beyond the remark of one famished guest who exclaimed, gloating on his spoonful of beans: 'My, these Heenz beans are champion!' and the reply of another, 'Och, Ah like butter beans the best. Ye ken; yon big saft yins that melt in yer mouth.' Some had to wait till the others had finished because the room and table were so small.

Everyone was impressed by the quickness of the burial; 'We've been there an' back inside foarty meenits!' said Jerry Delaney.

'Ay, he's a smart man, Mr Hewes,' said John Macdonnel. 'Y'know Ah met 'im the other day. "Hoo's business, Mister Hewes?" Ah ses. "Och, it's passin' me in the street boy!" ses he, "it's passin' me in the street!"' Everybody laughed and some of their awkwardness fell away. They began to chat and tell stories. John told a story about Francie, but he was soon forgotten.

That evening Mr Macdonnel sat alone at the front-room window staring at the street. He had just returned with two novels from the Public Library where he had three borrower's tickets. He was thinking that the Government ought to give old men like him some kind of work to do. He was tough and strong yet and could do a job as well as the young ones. There was nothing left to him but reading now. He stood up and expressed his boredom by yawning loudly, 'Ho hi ho!' He often startled people by suddenly yawning like this in company.

He took up one of the books, read twenty pages, and realized he had read the same book only two days ago. He rose with a heavy sigh and replaced it on the sideboard, mumbling: 'My damn't memory! It's no' what it was. No' what it was at all!' then he began fingering the stuff of the second-hand suit they had bought for him, wishing he had pawned it and wondering how much he could pledge it for. He would have liked to go out and buy himself a drink, but he had no money. He thought of the two long days till Friday, when he drew his Old Age Pension from the post office and determined he would slip out in the morning and pawn the suit, then, shame-faced, decided that would be too soon after his son's funeral.

He picked up the other book and sat at the window. The volume contained a crude bookmarker which he had shaped from a piece of wood with a penknife and sandpaper. It was a quarter of an inch thick and always left a book gaping an inch wide at the place where he left off. The young lady-librarian had recommended the novel to him. He peered at the title and the author's name. 'Ach, it'll be nae good. It's b' a wumman!' he said, and tossed it back on the sideboard, resolving to change both books next day. He walked into the kitchen to look at the clock, wishing it was the hour of Benediction at Saint Peter's. That would pass the time. For the last few years he had attended Morning Mass and Benediction every day and received Holy Communion every Sunday.

When he returned to the parlour he stood in his habitual manner in the middle of the floor for fully twenty minutes, dazed and staring at space, without a single thought in his head; then he pulled from under the bed a box of tools and began working on a small, crude gadget he was making for resharpening used safety-razor blades. He enjoyed making gadgets. It gave him something to do.

Donald Hamilton fingered the cicatrice under the right side of his chin and the one running from behind his left ear, wondering if people noticed them nowadays. Well, supposing they did, it was hardly likely that they could tell from a casual glance how they came there. They might think he was an ex-soldier and take them for war-wounds or assume that they were scars left by an operation. Ach, it was daft to worry about them after so many years. He seldom met those who might remember what he had tried to do twelve years ago.

Nevertheless, he was glad, at the moment, of his stoutness, of which he was usually sensitive. His chin had doubled, hiding the healed place and folds of flesh broke up the scar under his ear. Unless anyone ever alluded to it he could always say it was the mark of an operation for throat trouble. If he could prevent himself reddening, he could easily pass that tale.

He thrust away his uneasiness impatiently. Damn'd daft to think about it all all! And why tonight, anyway? In a flash he remembered that today was his birthday. Annie had forgotten it also. He felt hurt by her forgetfulness, though he never made any fuss about the day, especially since it reminded him of that night and all that followed it. That had happened on a birthday.

For the last two or three years he hadn't once thought about what he had tried to do and the sudden remembrance of it, shining so clearly in his head, chilled him to the heart.

He couldn't understand this intrusion of the past nor why he couldn't put it out of his mind. He hadn't been thinking of anything in particular when he started to shave himself and found himself gazing at the scar and fingering it, slowly, reflectively. He realised, alarmed, what he was doing and hastily picked up the shaving brush, rubbed it vigorously on the stick of soap and covered the place with a thick lather. But now that it was hidden he could still see the scar. Holding his chin up, soaping his neck, he could see it, stretched taut, waxy white, like the vaccination mark on his arm. And when he held his chin down tight, lathering his cheeks, he could still see it, and then he saw it as it was that night, a wide gash, pouring blood.

His hand trembled, then his whole body shook violently. He put down the safety-razor quickly, sat on a chair in the narrow space of the kitchenette and pressed his hands to his face.

The thick lather on his face squeezed through his fingers, but he did not feel it, was unaware of his wet skin. He was possessed by the unholy pessimism of that night and he began to fear that he might try to commit the frightful act again. He had read of sickly fascinations that drove men to crimes or morbid wounding of themselves. He closed his eyes tighter, pressed against his face till they hurt him but he could not shut out the picture of himself with those hands clasped to his neck and blood streaming over his fingers. As in a film he could see every detail of the old tenement kitchen in the house where he was born and reared, and himself sitting by the kitchen fire in the silence of two in the morning, working up his courage to do it.

He wished his wife and boy would return. He could talk to them and forget, but he knew they would not be home for nearly two hours, unless the boy became too troublesome and his wife came out of the cinema before the end, as sometimes happened.

A chill sweat oozed out of him, covering him like a coating of thin ice against which he felt the warmth of his underwear. He knew he was deadly pale but would not look in the mirror. Wild rain lashed the windows. If he went out he knew that the dismal memories would follow him.

He rose and went quickly into the front-room, forgetting to switch off the kitchenette light, and drew an armchair very close to the fire. Thick lather, imprinted with three fingers, frothed on his right jaw; his left cheek was shaved clean, his thick, black hair, streaked with grey, stood on end and a large towel, stuffed round his shirtneck, hung down in front of him. He wiped his face nervously with the end of the towel, then threw the towel behind him over the back of the chair.

A big fire was burning but he got up and fetched more coal, piling it on and listening to the draught tearing flame from the large, cold chunks. But he could not rid himself of deepening depression nor rein back his thoughts from the past. His thoughts crowded and shone more vividly, as if they were mocking him, forcing him to look at everything in his former self on that distant night. His head had never been so clear, yet the feeling all around him was one of oppressive, thickening darkness. Puzzled, he stared desperately at the long, streaming flames and shook his head drearily.

He saw himself sitting on the old, plain kitchen chair, heard the breathing of his father and youngest brother asleep in the cavity bed behind him. He was reading a volume of short stories by Jack London, taking in nothing, words and images passing him, his mind dark with the fear of life and the terror of death. He knew where his father's razor lay—on the top shelf in the press with the tin mug and brush next to the old meal crock. Even while he turned page after page, he felt himself lay his trembling hand on the black, cardboard case, felt himself draw the razor out stealthily. One quick sweep and it would be over. Ach, the pain wouldn't last! 'One brief mental pang.' He had read that phrase in a book by a famous Scottish singer where she told of the death of two of her relatives trapped in a burning opera-house in Italy when the burning roof fell in on hundreds of struggling, crazed, fighting people and she comforted her agonized heart with the hope that their death came with merciful suddenness, that perhaps they only knew 'One brief mental pang.' He repeated the phrase mentally, then he whispered, 'One brief mental pang an' Ah'll have nae mair trouble. Nae mair worry nor trouble!' He put down the book and half-started up, then sat back with blanched face, feeling sick.

He began reading again, now with more attention. He had

reached the story of the suicide who was rushed to a hospital with his throat cut and saved by the skill of a brilliant surgeon. On the day of his discharge, an hour after he had left the hospital he was brought back, having committed the act again and he laughed defiance and whispered as the same surgeon bent over him, 'It's you again? You won't mend me this time. I told you I'd beat you!' The foolish tale, larded with the suicide's arguments with the surgeon, proving the futility of life, nerved Donald to his purpose.

Why couldn't he do it, just like that, giving no chance to doubts or fears? He dropped the small book and stepped quietly the three paces to the press and in a moment was standing by the jawbox before the small wall-mirror with the open razor in his hand. The gemlike flashes of the keen blade as it moved in his unsteady hand, unnerved him. He tried to steady his hand and leant close to the mirror, looking at his thick neck. His heart was thumping and he could see the pulsing of his heart-beats in the veins of his neck. Terror overswept him again. He lowered his head and held the razor behind him, his eyes wildly roving the floor. Why was he afraid? He had never feared pain and this pain would end for ever the longer pain of life, the fear of living on with that foul disease, that before long would rot him; with the echo of his brother's trial and conviction for housebreaking still ringing in the neighbourhood; with the memory of Jeannie Lindsay's rejection of him and her seduction by another man with whom she had run away and who was leading her a rotten life.

Once he hadn't known the meaning of fear, but since the War and his return from the Work Centre for conscientious objectors, his nerves had slowly gone to pieces with long unemployment and this sickness he felt on him since his visit to a brothel with Francie Macdonnel when they worked together on a building job in Liverpool.

Ach, what's the use of hanging on to life when every spark of interest is dead and you can't face yourself or people!

He stepped across to the range with the razor still behind his back, and with a last desperate look at the dim glow of the fading coals placed his hand over his closed eyes and drew the razor across his throat.

He swayed, terrified and profoundly sick, desiring now with all his being to hold onto life. The razor fell from his hand and the blade struck the fender with a steely clink, toppling into the hearth, its broken edge jagged and bloodstained.

The small, unusual noise startled the deep silence of the kitchen and woke Mr Hamilton, always a heavy sleeper. He turned his grey head on the pillow and peered sleepily; 'Whit's the maiter, Donal'?' he said, 'why are ye no' in bed? Whit are ye staunin' like that for? Hae ye goat toothache? Then he saw the blood on his son's hands and the quick drip of blood splashing the bright steel fender with crimson drops. He threw aside the blankets and was standing by Donald's side in an instant with his arm round him. 'My Goad, whit hae ye done, Donal'? Whit hae ye done tae yersel' for Goad's sake!' He tightened the support of his arm as Donald sagged against him, desperately pressing his hands to the wound, convinced he had ended himself, that no help now could stop the warm life flowing away trickling over his fingers down through his open shirt on his naked breast. Donald tried to speak but it seemed as if his blood, like some thick warm liquid was pouring down his throat and he emitted only a gurgling whisper.

His father, barefooted and clad only in his shirt, sat Donald back in the chair and taking the roller-towel from the roller on the press-door quickly wound it round the ugly gash on his neck. Then he began to dress hastily while he called softly to the youth, still heavily asleep in the bed, 'Alec! Alec!' He had to lean over and shake him, doing it as quietly as possible for fear of waking the three girls sleeping in the front room. He saw the broken razor, picked it up, wiped it quickly and put it out of sight, then wiped the blood off the fender, throwing the cloth into the small cupboard under the sink, asking himself in distressed bewilderment what had come over Donald to make him do this to himself. Only two hours ago they had been joking and laughing together. The wound wasn't deep, wasn't fatal, he told himself, trying hard to believe his thought. Donald wouldn't be able to sit up like that if it was.

When he was dressed, with a raincoat buttoned up to his chin hiding the rough scarf he had put on to save time, he placed his trembling hand on Donald's shoulder: 'Whit made ye dae this tae yersel', Donal'? Whit made ye dae it for Goad's sake? Whit was worryin' ye? Thank Goad yer mother didnae live tae see this night!' He whispered to Alec, a youth of seventeen, stupified with sleep, leaning against the bedboard pulling on his trousers, to hurry up and get dressed and Alec frowned at them sleepily and up at the clock asking what was the matter, grumbling at being roused at this time in the morning. Mr Hamilton told him he would have to look after Donald while he went for the doctor. Donald was very bad.

He had regained control of himself and was hoping that the family doctor would do all that was necessary and hush the matter up. Why had this terrible thing happened so soon after his wife's death and Ian's imprisonment? Thank God she died before that too. He had reared his sons to be decent, hard-working and respectable and he felt that fate was treating him with savage cruelty.

Donald's sickness was passing. As his father put on his hat he sat up and told him to wait. He was aware only of a bitter stinging beneath the towel. His one desire now was to hold on to life and fly from the nothingness he had desired some moments ago. He wondered, terrified, if he had badly wounded himself. He knew his hand had faltered through fear, that he had maybe not cut deep. He told his father he would go to the doctor; he didn't want him brought here. He walked steadily into the lobby, proudly refusing his father's help; wrapped a woollen scarf round the towel, put on a raincoat and hat and called through the kitchen, 'I'm ready!'

As they went downstairs Donald told Alec to go back but his father said Alec would help him if he took sick in the street. They hurried through the streets, lightening towards summer dawn. A dreamy wind fanned them, the fast-fading stars gleamed fainter than far, small lights in mist and the softness of the unclouded sky was like a caress of pity for the three distressed humans.

Mr Hamilton was relieved that Dr Paterson lived in

Crown Street above his surgery and dispensary. He and Alec had to step out to keep pace with Donald who walked fast, looking straight before him, his face white and set. In less than ten minutes they wheeled out of Rowanglen Road and turned into a close in Crown Street near Cumberland Street. They went up to the first landing where Mr Hamilton pressed the bell of the door on the right. They waited and Mr Hamilton pressed the bell again, looking anxiously at Donald who returned his glances with a fixed mad stare.

Five minutes passed; Mr Hamilton was raising his hand nervously to ring again when they heard footsteps padding along the lobby, the door opened and Dr Paterson, a stout elderly man in a glistening blue silk dressing-gown, green pyjamas and red slippers glared irritably at the three men asking them indignantly what they meant by disturbing him at this unearthly hour. He had just returned from seeing a patient. He was dog-tired. Was he never to get any sleep? he said.

Mr Hamilton told him humbly and quickly what had happened. Instantly sleep fell from the old doctor and he looked keenly at Donald while Mr Hamilton asked if it would be possible to treat Donald and keep quiet what he had done. Dr Paterson went indoors and returned with the key for the door in the close opening into his surgery and told them to come down, saying half to himself, 'It a' depainds how much damage the laddie's done. It a' depainds! I doot there'll be complications. Ay, there'll be complications!'

The three drably clad men looking more sad and drab against the doctor's bright night-attire, followed him into his small surgery where he asked Mr Hamilton and Alec to wait in the waiting-room and led Donald into the surgery.

It was only then that Alec, after a few halting questions to his father, fully realised what Donald had done to himself and he sat staring miserably with tear-dimmed eyes while the next ten minutes seemed to them both interminable. They were inexpressibly relieved when the doctor came out with Donald and told them that Donald had not seriously injured himself. Dr Paterson had been attending the family for thirty years. He had read in the newspapers of the trial and imprisonment of Mr Hamilton's son, Ian, and he felt sorry for the little man. He had given Donald temporary treatment, but he would have to be taken to the Infirmary. If he was given private treatment there might be complications and no doctor could take that risk. He looked with deep sympathy at Mr Hamilton but he was sorry, Donald's case would have to be reported to the authorities. Then he turned to Donald, 'You're just a foolish young man,' he said severely, 'how will ye answer to your Maker for this night's work? It's only His mercy that stayed yer haun. Life bears hard on us a' but it's only God has the right to take it. I'm afraid you'll be detained and charged with attempted suicide.' He turned then to Mr Hamilton telling him he would ring for a taxi to have Donald taken to the Infirmary.

With his throat thickly bandaged, Donald sat white-faced and silent, desiring only to live no matter now bitter and shameful it might prove. All his former certainties, his cocksure atheism and materialism were now empty fallacies, beliefs he had acquired from the books and flaunted to make himself different. He was glad when the taxi arrived. He wanted to get away from his father and brother, from his whole family. Out of the world for awhile in a hospital or home he would see life more clearly and steady himself to face it again. 'Ye've been saved by the mercy o' Providence, young man, but don't do it again,' Dr Paterson said finally as they left his surgery.

Donald was given surgical attention and put to bed in the Infirmary, and for six weeks was detained in a Corporation Mental Home in an environment that struck him as likely to drive a man to suicide again. He was visited loyally and regularly by his father and every member of his family who cheered him all they could. On the day of his discharge the medical superintendent told him he hadn't a trace of VD. The assurance lightened his depression but he found the outside world still a grey place though it was preferable to the unknown he had almost plunged into.

Six months' unemployment with short spells of casual work, followed his discharge from hospital. When he was idle he seldom went out, when working he spent all his evenings indoors regretting the delusion that had caused him to make himself so conspicuous in the neighbourhood. He had lost the big hearty laugh and jocular manner that had made him so popular. When acquaintances stopped him for a talk in the street he believed they were only morbidly curious to have a look at the fellow who had tried to cut his throat.

He dropped all serious reading, convinced that thinking had driven him to the conclusion that life was futile. He had worked it all out according to materialist logic—life in the end signified nothing and we were all creatures of Blind Chance. Now, the very word 'philosophy' frightened him and he told his sister to sell all his books on economics, philosophy and literature to a ragman or a second-hand shop. She could please herself. He was finished with Thought for good and all. He would have taken a lodging away from the neighbourhood but the company of his family was more attractive that the loneliness of a bachelor room. Jeannie Lindsay, he told himself, would have saved him now. Married to her with a home and children, life would have been great. He heard she had gone to Canada with the other man who had given her a child and had been forced to marry her.

He applied for Corporation employment—that sure job which is the supreme ambition of thousands of Glasgow workers—and thought he was lucky when he was taken on after only a nine months' wait. It was a fairly comfortable job, slating the roofs of Corporation houses, buildings and tramway-depots for eight hours a day. Once he would have felt ashamed of his satisfaction at being in a steady job with a superannuation pension tacked on to it while over a million were unemployed, but he felt different about all that now.

He was surprised when Neil Mudge called on him one evening. They began to go about again and Neil never hinted by word or look that he knew of his attempted suicide. He and Neil had always been rivals, scoring off one another, never genuine friends, but Donald was grateful for his company and in the following summer he fell in with Neil's suggestion that he should join the ILP. Rambling

Club and Workers' Holiday Association and life apart from his job became normally interesting again. He began to forget what he had tried to do and people in the locality had also forgotten. His self-consciousness left him and he took up the study of Esperanto and began writing to foreign correspondents in that thwarted language. In the next summer he and Neil went to Denmark with the WHA. It turned out a holiday like any other. He was not impressed by being on foreign soil nor shaking hands and talking international brotherhood with comrades of other lands. His beliefs in a world-wide revolution and glorious Socialist international millennium were things of a distant, foolish past. The WHA and Rambling Club were merely ways of pleasantly spending Sundays and getting a cheap summer holiday.

When strikes, lock-outs and extremist agitations for shorter hours and higher wages were making Clydeside internationally famous round about the twenties after the War he kept away from processions and mass-meetings and eased his conscience by adding a trifle extra to his trade-union contributions. His comfortable job had become the most important thing in his life and he wasn't going to lose it by getting mixed up with a lot of Utopian agitators!

A year after his Denmark trip he and Neil Mudge tramped for a summer fortnight in Devon. It began as a hiking-tour with a lightweight tent for two but the sense of adventure had died an unnatural death in both of them. Their first night out proved too cold and the weight of the tent and haversacks became an irritation. Next morning they reckoned up their cash, found they had enough to lodge them comfortably under roofs and sent all their gear home by train. They proceeded by cheap hotels and cyclist touring club hostels, with generous helpings of bus and train, looking down on Devon for a hundred miles or so in the insular Scottish manner, finding the West Country superlatively inferior to the Scottish Highlands.

The tour ended at Dartmoor where they had a look at the prison which during the War had been a Government Work Centre for conscientious objectors. Donald had spent eighteen months in the grim building, with several hundred men of various religious creeds and political beliefs, when the cell doors were never locked, remaining open all day till late at night, when men worked in comparative freedom, without armed guards, and were allowed the run of the village and a generous radius beyond after working hours.

The companionships he had formed, the gaiety and talk which had rung these brutal walls, the study-circles, endless discussions and debates, the concerts and amateur theatre run by the young idealists all sworn to crusade for peace and world-betterment after the War—Donald remembered all that dimly without a thrill of emotion. It was all like a silly dream and meant nothing to him now.

An armed warder approached as they were trying to get into a good position to climb and look over the wall. 'You'd better keep moving. You're not allowed to loiter here!' he said.

A three days' stay in London, during which they sized up the Metropolis within the narrow compass of the back-street mind, deciding that it was considerably over-rated and by no means preferable to Glasgow, ended their English tour.

That year the Rambling Club became a weekend camping association in response to the craze for sun-bathing and the open-air that was infecting all communities. Membership rapidly increased and among the newcomers Donald met Annie Findlay, a sonsy, auburn, dark-eyed young woman of rugged well-padded proportion, whose prototype can be seen by the thousand in Glasgow any day.

He wenched her for a year of stolid, regulated courtship without any raptures or roses in it. In summer they met once a week on the same evening and again at weekends as campers; in winter they walked out on Wednesdays and Saturdays and dropped into the pictures. After some preliminary embraces in the close when he was seeing her home, Donald was introduced to her folks, but the effort of talking to her parents through a whole evening was so laborious that he was glad when he found Annie perfectly willing to try longer embraces in the close. Annie was all for Labour, but no revolution, and when she found that Donald was the sort of man who stayed indefinitely in the one job, she married him.

They began life in a single-end in a douce, cosy style never for a moment transported by love or gorgeously amorous play. One child came, a boy, and it stopped at that. Donald had hoped for several romping lads and lassies but when no more were produced and time went on he knew that the family were thinking things. He and Annie were regarded as a queer couple and he didn't feel happy about it. His married brothers and sisters were contributing offspring with decent but creditable speed. His father had contributed ten and Annie's father twelve, to the population. Donald had no such ambitions, he only wanted to be reasonable. But Annie had gathered humanitarian ideas from the Labour Movement. She wasn't going to bring bairns into the world to suffer. Donald thought her limitation was a wee bit too strict and suspected she was thinking of her own pains rather than those of the unborn, but Annie, shortly after marriage, began to complain of repeated headaches and her obvious frailty, though she became steadily more sonsy and rugged as her firstborn grew older. When Donald wanted to increase his family by another one Annie reminded him of her delicate constitution and acquired a habit of periodical nervous breakdowns which laid her abed for inconvenient periods when Donald had to go to his married sister's for his principal meals. If he really loved her he wouldn't persist. 'Ye ken fine Maggie died o' seventeen bairns' she said once, sarcastically referring to one of his cousins who had been an ace of fertility and silencing Donald for a long time on the subject.

Annie had her own way in all other matters of importance. It was she who decided that they must move into a new Corporation house in a northern district where she had been brought up. Donald was eager to return to the Gorbals where he had spent his boyhood and youth but Annie said the Gorbals was common, so they had to move up north. Donald was growing fat and disinclined to argue, 'Och, wan hoose is jist the same as another. Ah don't care what part we stay in,' he compromised lazily. But he sighed for his swaggering, youthful days when he could dominate women and pick and choose among the beauties of the tenements. But he saw that Annie would always have her own way and he accepted the fact as he was accepting most things. Mental and physical comfort had become the ruling ambition of his life.

Donald's wandering reflections over his life from his youthful days had gradually lessened his abysmal depression. He looked at the clock on the mantel and saw it would be a good hour still before Annie and the boy returned. But he wasn't going into that kitchenette again. He would sit tight by this roasting fire till he heard them at the door.

He regretted he had missed going to the class in mathematics at the Technical School. If he had said he wasn't going Annie would have insisted on his coming with them. It would have been nice and cheerful this minute sitting back in the Regal that they kept warm as toast, in the dozy way he enjoyed, smoking his pipe and thinking of nothing at all. Funny how he had come to like the pictures, looking forward to them twice a week, just like Annie herself. Wasn't that long ago that he used to talk highbrow and say the films were cheap and demoralising when she asked him to come? Ach well, they fill up the blanks in life!

His family and acquaintances thought him peculiar for studying mathematics just to amuse himself. Well, he supposed he was but he enjoyed working out the problems the way some people enjoy poring over jigsaw puzzles. Anyway, it wasn't leading him, like philosophy, to think that nothing mattered, even his comfort, his fireside and his job.

By juv, he had dabbled in some hobbies, and no mistake! He lit his pipe and considered them and the different people he had met through them. Ay, Esperanto was interesting, but it didn't seem to be leading anywhere. It soon became difficult to find things to write about to those foreign correspondents. Jings, his mind had got properly rusty on that subject by this time o' day! Who would have thought you could forget a language so easily in two years.

Then there was that year at the violin. Soon got the hang o' that! Ach, there wasn't much he couldn't learn as quick as the smartest o' them. It was just as easy to master the piano. Wasn't long before he was rattling away at jigs, reels and waltzes on that too. A proper Paderewski, they said he was. He thought of the violin stuck in a corner of the kitchenette in its dust-covered case. Six months since he had put a finger to fiddle or piano! Suppose he rattled off some reels right now to cheer things up a bit? He looked at the piano drawn across the corner by the bookcase and half-started up, but the idea of filling the room with sound suggested deeper loneliness and he sat back.

He gazed reflectively awhile at the fire then walked over to the small, glass-panelled bookcase on top of the small sideboard where his boy kept his playthings. The few books, leaving wide gaps on the little shelves, lay slopped and slanted in the neglected state of books that are never used. He turned idly the pages of an Esperanto grammar then pushed it back between a copy of Milton's *Poems* and Shakespeare's *Complete Works*. He looked at them, remembering proudly how once he could quote from memory long passages of Milton and Shakespeare. Ach, what's the use of stuff like that anyway? It doesn't get you anywhere.

Beside a massive volume of Karl Marx's *Das Kapital* lay a tiny volume, *Youth and Other Stories* by Joseph Conrad, which had strayed into his possession from somewhere—he couldn't remember. He must have had it for ten years. Maybe he'd read it for all he knew. He looked into it incuriously. 'They say this fellow Conrad's a great writer an' a wonderful stylist. Can't see it meself! What's the use o' literature an' poetry an' art anyway? They're all right for rich an' middle-class people wi' plenty o' leezure but nut for us workin' men!' He dropped the book back slackly and returned quickly to the armchair, yawning as he sat, huddling close to the fire. The fireplace, like a magic circle, seemed to shut him in from dismal thoughts.

Suddenly he recalled a desperate letter which Francie Macdonnel had sent him from the English Asylum, asking him to come and see him and tell him how he had got himself discharged from Hawkhead. He neither answered nor visited Francie, not even when he was transferred to Hawkhead and to the same ward where he himself had been for six weeks. No fear! He didn't want to see the inside of one of those places again as long as he lived. He had felt a bit sorry for Francie when he heard of his death, but he couldn't have done anything for him.

Fear of his thoughts overcame him again and he wished desperately that his wife and boy would return. Jeez, these two hours had crawled like a long miserable day. Thank God they'd be in in another ten minutes or so. As he rose to get more coal he heard them at the door and ran to open it.

Mrs Hamilton was extremely surprised by this unusual welcome and his bright smile of relief. 'Ah thoaght ye had forgoat yer key,' he said, a little foolishly, and took the hand of the boy who was telling him excitedly about Mickey Mouse as they entered the front-room. Little Donald, aged seven, had been the kind of boy familiar on posters advertising patent rusks or mild food, but his golden curls had lost their springy glint and his face, peaked by incessant bad temper, had lost the angelic innocence so valuable to commercial advertisers. He invariably threw his toys at every visitor, screaming hysterically, 'Ye're a bad man!' or 'wumman!' and his parents always excused his behaviour telling his victims he was temperamental. He began shouting that they must play a game of cards with him or he wouldn't go to bed.

Mrs Hamilton hung up her hat and coat and followed them, complaining, 'Ye've left the light oan in the kitchen. Ye ken fine the electricity bill gets heavier.' Donald lied, 'Och, it's only been oan five meenits!' He felt cheered, supported, stronger. Their coming had filled in the fathomless emptiness inside him. He watched, smiling, as his boy pulled a Hornby train from the sideboard and ran it up and down the floor, yelling imitation of a train-whistle.

Mrs Hamilton began letting down a double-bed settee, the bed of which was already made, remarking, 'Ah thoaght ye were gaun tae the night-school?' Donald yawned and stretched, then said, getting a light for his pipe with a paper spill, 'Och, Ah couldnae be bothered. Forbye, it's ma birthday an' Ah'm gie'n masel' a treat. Thirty-seven an' still goin' strong!' He gave a short mirthless laugh.

'Ay, ye'll soon be an' aul' man!' Annie said cheerfully, patting the bed tidy. She sat opposite him and laughed, 'My, whit hae ye done tae yer face?' He looked at her annoyed,

'Och, whit's the maiter wi' ma face?' She pointed, 'It's a' hairy oan wan side an' a' smooth oan the ither.' She stopped laughing, suddenly, frowned and held a hand to her heart. It was too soon to be laughing, only three days after her fortnight's nervous breakdown. Donald rose, drawing at his pipe, 'Och, Ah was cauld shavin' in there an' Ah came ben tae hiv a warrm. Ah'll away an' feenish ma shave.'

Janet Mudge frowned and did not glance from her book as Neil came into the kitchen. For a few moments he sat by the range then rose restlessly, stood against the dresser, looked at her as if he was about to say something, picked up a book, flicked idly the pages and as though driven out by her determined silence, dropped it noisily and, returning to the bedroom, sat at the window, gazing at the Clyde and Glasgow Green.

The Clyde here ran, narrow and sluggish, looking still as a canal and dark and cheerless as his thoughts. The sky was grey, the black waters deepened its darkness. There was nothing hopeful in the prospect of river, street or Green.

He hunched his shoulders, plunged his hands in his trouser pockets, and the corner of his mouth twisted in a sneering smile. He wished his mother was alive now. She wouldn't have been so hard on him because he was out of work.

His sisters had turned out a fine lot! During the War he was a hero because he had gone to prison as a conscientious objector. Janet had called him 'A Pioneer of World Peace.' Now his few months' unemployment had put all their grand principles to the test. Janet with her high-flown Christian pacifism and Mary and Margaret with their comradeship and uncompromising revolutionary Socialism. All men are brothers. Ach! He knew fine they were turning against him because he couldn't get a job. As if it was his fault when there were nearly two million unemployed. They had never said as much, but you could see they thought he was lazy, wasn't trying. Well, to hell, let them! His conscience was clear as to that anyway.

Their sympathy didn't last long. He was surprised at himself being taken in by their insincere affection when he applied to his old firm for a job and they refused to take him back because of his attitude to the war. 'Oh, you'll soon get work, Neil. Don't worry!' they said. But he never dreamed they'd turn like this.

They were carrying out a determined policy of ostracism because he wouldn't take the dole. He knew they were pinched but it wasn't so long ago that he had given them the last of his savings and it wasn't as if he intended to live on them indefinitely. It wouldn't take him long to pay them back. They were all lucky to be in jobs themselves, anyway. They'd be singing a different tune if he was the one in work! To hell, he'd be better off tramping the roads.

The vision of himself sleeping in barns and under hedges, getting odd jobs on farms, tramping the country from Land's End to John o' Groats, pulled at his heart for a moment, drawing him out to the majesty of sunsets and dawns and the call of white roads infinitely wandering, winding like rippling ribbons, lost now in dark avenues of trees, now drooping into valleys or the twilit hollows of hills. But the dreariness outside and within himself blotted out his dream; all its stirring colours faded and he recoiled timidly from the idea of leaving the uneasy security of home.

He knew that life on the road would never suit him. He believed he was superior to it and secretly looked down on those who took to it, though he had read much about road and adventuring life in the works of Jack London, Bart Kennedy, Stephen Graham and RLS. He had keenly enjoyed those books and he thought of them now. Och, it's all very fascinating in books but he hadn't seen much good come of those chaps who left the locality to 'pad the hoof' as they called it! They were all of the lowest type—hooligans and work-shirking corner-boys, who wouldn't come to much good anyway. In his heart he was afraid of the hardships he might meet.

He frowned and sighed heavily, wishing Andrew could find him a labourer's job in the engineering shop where he worked. Andrew had promised to call as soon as he heard of a chance but it was six dragging weeks since he had come to see them, though he only lived a penny tram ride away.

Of course, Andrew didn't hit it off very well with Janet. She thought Andrew's wife was beneath her, a dull, commonplace woman without a single interest in life outside of her tenement house and her children. Janet said all women should be devoted to Ideas, Freedom and Progress and professed to despise motherhood. She maintained that women should refuse to bear children until they were the economic and political equals of men.

Neil despaired of his brother turning up. Was it possible he was doing overtime? That would mean chances of a job. Neil caught at the hope then called himself a fool to imagine that overtime was being worked anywhere while the labour-supply was greater than the demand. He shrugged his shoulders and rose to go and visit Andrew when the doorbell rang. He heard Janet answer the door and Andrew asking 'Is Neil in?' So it had come at last! For six months he had waited for it and Andrew said it would be a pretty rough job at best, throwing him only fifty bob a week!

He strolled unhopefully into the kitchen telling himself he was being too optimistic. Maybe Andrew had no news for him. He had waited so long he could hardly feel excited even if it was word of a job. He had become demoralised through long idleness and was past caring, like thousands of the unemployed, he told himself, nodding to his brother who sat stiffly at the range with his cap on his knees, looking more like a messenger of calamity than a bringer of good news. Neil sat opposite him while Janet returned to her book. In better days she would have offered to make tea for her brother, but these were hard times. Suddenly Andrew's small dark features wreathed in a cheerful grin; he leaned forward, elbow on knee, 'Weel, Ah've goat a joab for ye, Neil! The gaffer says ye can start tae-morra.'

Neil could hardly believe it. He saw Janet look up, smiling from her book, taking a quick glance at him and he fancied her look was a trifle shamefaced. The news did not stir him, he had waited so long, but by God he would show her he wasn't afraid of work! 'By jeez, that's great!' he said, with false eagerness, 'a job at last. By crikey, Andy, you're a champion!' He shook his brother by the hand, thinking,

'That'll show her!' and said, 'When do Ah start? It can't be too soon.'

Andrew sat back with a show of self-importance, 'Ye start at six tae-morra. Be at the gate at five meenits tae an' Ah'll introduce ye tae Aul' McGovern. He's no' a bad aul' stick an' he says if ye're as good a worker as me ye'll dae fine.' Andrew grinned and Neil squeezed out the shadow of a smile. God, if only he could feel really glad, feel grateful to Andrew. Andrew had done his level best, he knew that. Neil nodded and smiled when Andrew raised a hand to his mouth and tossed back his head like a man draining a pint, then he went into the bedroom and put on his jacket and cap. The two brothers felt awkward with Janet who was possessed by one of her fussy intellectual periods, reading rapidly through several novels to prepare a paper on the English Novel for the Unitarian Study Circle. They bade her so-long and went out to discuss the amazing good luck of a job at fifty shillings a week, over a half-pint—which was all Andrew could afford—in a gruesome little pub.

Next morning they met in the same Scottish silence at the gates of the engineering shop and Neil, after a brief introduction to a greybeard foreman with watery eyes and a sharp chin, whom everyone called 'Aul' McGovern,' was given a heavy, unskilled job which left him at the end of the day a mass of strained muscle and sinew.

Neil's muscle soreness lasted for a fortnight. There were evenings when he fell asleep over his tea and he wondered if he had not gone soft with idleness. He hated the job and its whole atmosphere, regarding it as a comedown after his years of book-keeping. His Socialistic beliefs in equality and fraternity didn't help him to fraternize easily with his fellow-labourers and the workers at the bench; he was too much the clerk to feel at home among the whirr of driving belts and clang of metal, the foul oaths, the filth of sweat and oil-rags and the rust of iron and steel. But it was either this or another long spell of unemployment and the critical company of his sisters. He stuck it and stayed on.

At the end of two months he felt fitter and more physically equal to the job, though his loathing of it didn't lessen. Every day he examined the Situations Vacant columns of the *Glasgow Herald* and *Citizen* and wrote to all the firms advertising for a book-keeper. When he had been working for four months he reckoned he had paid his sisters back a big proportion of his keep when he was idle. He still nursed resentment for what he regarded as their uncharitable behaviour. He decided he required solitude in the evenings away from the trifling minds of women, to think out the problems of life and more in pride than anger, settled down in a bed-sitting room in another district, promising to send Janet money from time to time. He knew his sisters could manage without his help. With his pockets jingling his own money, life wasn't so bad.

He resumed interest in the Socialist movement, not as a fiery propagandist but as a theorist, an intellectual dilettante, dispassionately studying the political arena. He joined The Liberty Rambling Club, most of whose members were Socialists or were in process of conversion to Socialism and the majority of whom, like the rank and file of all religions, were unthinking accepters of its tenets. When they argued or debated about politics they seldom produced a really original thought, but whether they were followers of the Left, the ILP, or the Labour Party, they aired the opinions and slogans of the literature and leaders of their parties.

On summer Sunday rambles about Glasgow's neighbouring hills, Neil got well away, mentally and physically, from the engineering shop. He had tried to get work as a book-keeper and put his failure down to the fact that he was not an ex-soldier. He foresaw himself a labourer for a long time to come and realized he would be lucky if he kept this job for another six months. His firm were feeling the brunt of the industrial depression and he had heard talk of reduction of staff. One evening he entered his drab, cramped bed-sitting room, tired from an unusually hard day. Hanging his cap and overcoat behind the door he was figuring how long he could keep going if he was dismissed. With the dole and the ten pounds he had managed to save he would be fairly comfortable in this eight-bob-a-week room for a month or two, then he would tighten his belt like all the others. As he turned to make his tea on the gas-ring on the black-fendered hearth his eyes were startled by a letter, the second one he had received in his eight months here, lying on the battered tin ashtray on the narrow mantelshelf. He put on his pince-nez and read his name and address in erratic, blue typescript. It was a letter from an old Scottish Quaker, who had assisted and befriended conscientious objectors throughout the War and had visited Neil in Barlinnie Prison. He had written to Neil six months before and Neil smiled at the jumbled typing typed by the half-blind old man on his obsolete machine. It was probably one of his little sermons he spent hours typing to young pacifists all over the country, urging them 'in the name of God and Christ Jesus' to carry on the fight against militarism and 'bring in the reign of International Peace.' Neil marvelled at his invincible idealism. He was now over eighty but he still believed that men had fought their last war, that with its terrible example before them they would 'be filled with the Spirit of the True Christ' and would never again desire to war on each other.

Neil slit the envelope and stood up excitedly. It was a letter asking him to call tomorrow on a firm of electrical accessory manufacturers to whom his friend had recommended him for employment as a book-keeper. He read the letter twice again, placed it carefully in his pocket-book and went out whistling to fill his tin kettle at the sink in his landlady's kitchen. On the following Saturday he got his books with pay packet from the engineering firm and on Monday morning of the next week began work as a book-keeper. The job he had waited for had arrived in the nick of time.

He now felt more satisfied with life than he had been for a whole year. He called to tell his sisters of his stroke of luck and gave Janet five of the ten pounds he had saved. He could afford to be generous. Everything about his new job indicated that it would last indefinitely. A soldier's farewell to heavy back-breaking work! He walked briskly back to his room, flourishing the Gold Flake he was smoking, smacking his lips over the hearty supper Janet had cooked for him. His sisters were all smiles when he told them. Ach, lassies were all right! He believed now they hadn't meant to be unkind. They were just slaves of economic fear. Crikey, what luck! A real, civilized job at last. Nine to five and three-ten a week! Neil had written to his old friend and on the Thursday of the first week in his new job called to thank him personally. When he knocked at a door on the second landing of a two-storeyed lower-middle class tenement at the respectable end of Cumberland Street he almost stepped back with surprise when the door was opened by his old friend's wife dressed in mourning. She had always shuffled about the house when friends called on her husband, muttering and grumbling at his numerous visitors, telling every caller on the door-step that she never had his company and he was a silly old fool to be running up and down the country to his conventions and conferences at his time of life. She was a dark dwarfish woman, thin and flat-bosomed, looking always vague and faded in her plain Quaker dress. Her small dark eyes stared hard at Neil, as if she was trying to remember him, then she told him her husband had died on Tuesday. He was being buried tomorrow, she said, holding the door wide for Neil to come in.

Neil followed her cap in hand into a severe parlour, dense with Victorian horsehair furniture, where he used to sit talking with the old man. The little woman stood at Neil's elbow while he gazed at the old Quaker in his oaken coffin, resting on the solid parlour table. His white bushy eyebrows curled vitally, as they were in life, over his sunken, closed eyes, his long white hair, silvery and silkenfine, was beautifully combed, his small blue-veined hands, which had handed out hundreds of pacifist pamphlets at railway stations to soldiers coming home or leaving for the Front, were crossed on his shrunken breast.

Neil thought he was as small and frail as his own mother when she lay dead and, glancing up, he saw at the end of the sideboard the massive, out-of-date typewriter on which the dead man had typed hundreds of letters, sometimes filled with quotations from the Bible and religious books read to him by a neighbour's boy. Neil wondered if the letter which had got him this job was the last one typed, then he felt the old woman tugging his sleeve impatiently, telling him in a low, excited voice that she was not alone in the house.

Her sister was staying with her. She had just gone out for a message, and his brother, she nodded towards the dead face, was coming later on with his wife. When she said that she abruptly left Neil standing there and walked, muttering, into the kitchen.

Neil honoured his dead friend with a last look and followed her. While he stood for a second in the lobby he heard her through the half-open door walking up and down saying audibly, 'Robert, Robert, you're a silly man. Type, type, type, type, the lang day an' never a minute tae spare for me. Wearin' yourself awa' an' never a minute for me!' Neil went out and quietly closed the stairhead door, hearing in his mind the old man's canny tremulous laugh, full of sly friendliness when he argued with you and won his point. He would be eighty-three when he died yet to the last his mental faculties were clear, his optimism as sound as those of a young man. Neil would never see him again tapping his way home along Gorbals pavements, his long white hair vivid under a low-crowned, Quaker hat, always refusing assistance except when he had to cross a street.

Neil was sorry his letter had not reached the old man before he died. His triumphant feelings were eclipsed for awhile but they resurged in him next evening when he left the office with his first pay-packet. He scoured Govanhill for a respectable address appropriate to his improved position and found a comfortable room with board at thirty shillings a week. His rejoicings continued for some time when he found his employers were amply satisfied with his work and it was in this highly-charged condition of satisfaction that he committed the indiscretion which he ever afterwards regretted.

Neil always told himself in the resignation of advancing years, when what he called 'introspection's cancer' bit the acid of regret into his thoughts that if an inkling of the future which that mild November Saturday night began for him had glinted through his mind he would have thrown his dancing pumps in the gutter and finished the night alone getting wildly drunk. But he ran nimbly up the steps of the Saint Mungo Halls, his dancing pumps wrapped in paper, under his arm, a carefree, unsuspecting young man bouncing with eagerness to whirl into the gaiety of The Liberty Rambling Club's first winter Social And Dance.

When he had left his overcoat, hat and shoes in the cloak-room he retired in his glossy new pumps to the Gentlemen's to comb his romantic toss of hair into fascinating waves then hastened on shining feet, a short stocky figure in a dark brown suit, into the crowded hall. He had sold a dozen tickets for the Social and the fact that he had contributed to its success heightened his champagne feeling. Neil was an awkward, toe-treading dancer and women always left his arms with heated feelings and sighs of relief. He had hitherto scorned the pastime as a mere escape from reality for the unthinking multitude but lately had accepted it as an amiable method of propaganda and tonight he danced every dance with increasing cheerfulness, though none of his partners appealed to his poetic ideals. He never could, in spite of his romantic hair, fascinate attractive women, not even the tall slim types, who, he understood, were susceptible to short men, and he danced with the plain and pleasant, the middle-aged and motherly.

At the end of a dance through which he was hauled and hopped by a stout woman of forty who giggled girlishly and stifled him with voluminous breasts that dunted him like a marble bust, he made his way, in a condition of pleasant fatigue, to the temperance refreshment bar and ate and drank hungrily from its generous supply of cakes, pies, sandwiches, tea and mineral waters. He could still feel the dig of his last partner's whalebone corsets in his chest as he went to stand at the entrance for a smoke and a breath of fresh air while his arms ached pleasantly. When he had finished his smoke he threaded down the side of the hall between dancers and chairs and, deciding to sit out the next two dances, found himself seated beside Laura Redgrave.

Laura, a solid young woman of twenty-five with large, ungleaming brown eyes and auburn lustreless hair, was also a member of The Liberty Rambling Club. Neil had met her on several Club occasions but had seldom spoken to her. She had struck him as a densely silent young woman with a resentful, challenging expression who often blushed painfully when spoken to. Neil asked her if she was enjoying the Social. Laura, blushing, said it was great, while young men took partners from nearhand her but none of them asked her to dance. In after years, Neil wondered what dark influence had prompted him to do it, trying, like a psychiatrist, to unravel his tangled way back to beginnings, but he could never see clearly the motive for his impulse. Bowing and smiling he asked Laura out to the floor.

He danced a second and third time with her and in the third dance, a two-step, his warmth towards her had become sheer heat. He pressed her fiercely against him and felt her body respond to his daring clasp, and Laura's breasts tingled, shamelessly crushed against the waistcoat of the now amorous Neil, while she relished the unfamiliar tropical sensations in her spine. She have never been embraced in her life before tonight.

When the dance was over Neil asked her to come to the door for a breath of fresh air. It was a starry moonlit night flecked with thin racing clouds. Laura said she was tired and was going home. Neil did not propose to see her home but when she left him to get her things an unknown force impelled him in the direction of the gents' cloak-room and a few moments later he was walking, like a man in a dream, a dancing-pump in each overcoat pocket and his arm round Laura's waist, along the towpath leading to Oatlands where Laura lived in Rowanglen Road.

They walked very slowly, his cheek resting languidly on her shoulder, while he gazed at the skeltering scarves of cloud which the moon seemed to toss aside, emerging in full splendour to turn the sluggish Clyde to a bright silver road wandering like forgotten beauty through industrial ugliness. Neil was anticipating rarely sampled pleasure. He had never felt surer of anything in his life and he sensed those ultimate thrills as a connoisseur savours an old wine. In this dominant mood, before they were half-way to Laura's home he stood her against the high wall of a dyeworks alongside the tow-path and kissed her passionately again and again while his trembling hands fumbled and caressed.

When Neil had eased a little of his passion, Laura whispered to him her thumbnail biography. She was an assistant in a while-you-wait photographer's in Argyle Street, her father was dead, her mother was away in Manchester spending a week with her sister and Laura was all alone in a room and kitchen. Barely had she told him this than they were walking again, more quickly than before, and very soon leaving the tow-path they arrived on the stroke of midnight at a close opposite Oatlands Sewage Pump and Bowling Green.

They stood for a moment holding hands. Laura asked Neil if he'd like to come up for a minute—just time for a wee cup of tea before he went home—she would go up first and leave the door a wee bit open; he was to follow as quiet as a mouse and dart in unheard and unseen. For it would never do if the neighbours even guessed that she had brought a young man home for tea at midnight while her mother was away.

Neil heard Laura open her door and the silent close seemed to become full of watching eyes and listening ears. He followed the flight of the last tramcar, hurtling ablaze with light from the city to Rutherglen depot. He knew how Glasgow stairhead doors watched and listened. Many a time, going up his own stairs, deep in thought, he had been startled by a pair of old eyes peering through the crack of a slyly opened door. His next move required audacity and in time to come he was to regret his coolness and wish he had walked away that night, a coward and a free man. Instead, he took a last look at the luminous sky, walked impulsively to the end of the close, removed his shoes, gripped them tightly, darted on his socks silently up to the first landing and with his mind on the two other doors, slipped like a thief into Laura's house.

Laura was behind the door. She closed and locked it, hung Neil's hat and coat in the lobby and yielded to another masterful embrace, then she said the kettle was ready and with a peculiar, satisfied smile led him into a colourful kitchen. She had piled on coal before going out and a good fire burned in a glistening tiled range. Smiling her inward smile she made the tea while Neil reclined in an armchair, his anticipating grin fixed on a tastefully painted and curtained cavity bed, wondering whom he resembled most, Casanova or Mozart's Don Juan. He saw nothing queer in Laura's smile. It flattered him. His meeting with her tonight had revealed hidden powers. A man only needed irresistible maleness and the power to stagger them with the dominant approach at the right moment and he could conquer any woman. He did not think of marriage. He smiled possessively at Laura when she said tea was ready and pulled her on to his knee.

All that followed, leading to the cavity bed, was chaotic and blurred in Neil's memory. He slipped out unseen in the morning, however, a man of tremendous achievement and in the evening told his landlady he would not be home for a week. He would be staying, he said, in Milngavie with an old friend who had just returned, after long absence, to Scotland.

Until the following Friday Neil spent his after-office hours with Laura, slinking in and out her house unseen,—a week of delicious hours in the cavity bed, during which he prided himself that his virility was inexhaustible and his fascination improving. In fact, he smiled, he was relishing all the pleasures of married life free of its responsibility or wear and tear. He continued meeting Laura after her mother's return, but only on one or at most, two evenings each week. When it rained they went to Neil's favourite cinema in Argyle Street to hear classical interludes by a male pianist who, Neil said, had a poetically delicate touch and ought to be giving recitals in Saint Andrew's Halls, but he found to his disappointment that Laura had no musical ear and was always impatient for the pictures to start again. On mild, dry nights he took her his favourite walk over Cathkin Braes when they looked back at the lights of Glasgow and Neil with a grave, poetic sigh called it 'Sodom and Gomorrah' and 'a Hades of Industry where a million wage-slaves rot and decay,' then they walked the road to Carmunnock and returned to Glasgow by bus. These diversions always ended at the stairfoot in Laura's close where, after a short unsatisfactory embrace she left him at ten-thirty or eleven o'clock, because her mother always went to bed at that time.

Neil's carnal appetite was still very lively. He had imagined that Laura would satisfy that side of him, though he had soon discovered that she left him 'spiritually empty.' Her conversation was commonplace and limited; her silences had become irritating; she had no inkling of the meaning of Art and had read nothing worth mentioning. Laura would never inspire him. He decided he would finish with her, not with crude abruptness, but gradually, with finesse. Sitting in his modestly comfortable bed-sitting room in Govanhill, he closed Bernard Shaw's *The Perfect Wagnerite*, removed and breathed on his pince-nez and polished them with a new laundered handkerchief, replaced them and smiled in long reflection over that slim, lively young Irish typist in his office. He had never seen such strange, luxuriant hair. It was copper-coloured, burnished, and changing gleams that made you neglect your work to look at her; and her perfect, full lips and those astonishing, Celtic blue eyes made you think of clear summer days in the Highlands or of gazing far out over a calm, sunshot sea. 'Calm, sunshot sea.' Damn good, that! Jeez, he was in rare form tonight! He would write a poem about her and show it to her after she had been out with him for a few weeks. Her name was Noreen—Noreen Laverty. 'Noreen, my girl! Noreen.' He whispered her name and a wave of protective indignation flowed through him. That smutty old rascal, McDougal, the head book-keeper, with the drip at the end of his snuffling, whisky nose, called her Miss Lavatory. One of these days he'd tell the foul-minded old fool what he thought of him, head book-keeper or no head book-keeper. Och, Noreen had more life in her wee pinky than Laura had in her whole body! He hadn't passed more than the time of day with Noreen but he could tell by the way she looked at him that his personality had dazzled her. It was the psychological moment for the dominant approach. He mustn't let Noreen cool off. He was sorry for Laura but he had done his best for her. By God, the creative ferment was simply frothing up in him tonight! He'd lie awake composing that poem to Noreen till the landlady called him at eight. He stretched his legs luxuriously and his slippered feet toasted at the fire. Dreaming, he laid his head back with a complacent grin.

Soon after that night he began his process of 'tactful cooling off.' He had not seen Laura for a fortnight and his sense of power was flattered by a note from her one morning exactly three months after the night of the dance, asking him to tea on Wednesday evening to meet her mother. He smiled, Yes, he would go. It would be exciting to sit talking to the unsuspecting Mrs Redgrave in yon kitchen where he had lived for a week like a married man.

He stepped off the Govanhill car at the corner of Crown Street and Rowanglen Road on the following Wednesday evening and turned his steps towards Oatlands. He was due there at seven and it was nearly half-past. Och, well, he wasn't worrying. He would walk the rest of the way. It wouldn't hurt them to wait. They'd be impressed. He glanced at a sky that was uniformly grey as the massed tenements below and turned up his coat collar against the raw smoky air. On spring and summer nights he would lie on Cathkin Braes with Noreen Laverty, watching the sun setting over Glasgow while he read poems to her and gradually broadened her mind with the truths of Socialism. There was real intelligence in her intoxicating blue eyes. She only needed the right man to bring her out. Free Love! That would be the sexual relationship in a true Socialist society. Jings, it was a wonderful, mysterious power, the Life Force! Positive and negative eternally complementing each other. Man, the Positive; Women, the Negative. Some men hadn't a streak of the positive in them but, by jove, he had been positive in yon cavity bed! Laura Redgrave wouldn't forget him in a hurry.

Neil tripped up the stairs humming, 'What Can A Young Lassie Do Wi' An Auld Man?' and knocked at the Redgraves' door. He was surprised when Laura opened the door and didn't start quarrelling with him for not turning up two weeks ago. She was smiling her pensive smile and, blushing, she took his hat and coat while he deftly waved his hair with his pocket-comb, to impress Mrs Redgrave. He congratulated himself that Laura was pleasant because she feared to lose him but the moment he entered the kitchen his confidence completely vanished. Mrs Redgrave, a stout Englishwoman of fifty, was seated at the head of the table, at which Neil had dined night and morning like a husband with Laura, placing the cosy over the teapot with her big, red hands. She pushed out of the way a glass cakestand and arranged three cups and saucers for pouring. Neil, aware of Laura standing behind him, coughed nervously. Mrs Redgrave raised her large, florid face and frowned at him unflinchingly. 'Well, young man, you've turned up at last,' she said, 'we thought you were never coming.' She pointed to the chair opposite her and told him to sit there. Neil sat down obediently, stammering something about being kept late at the office, while Laura, blushing to her neck, sat down between them, her back to the fire.

It was not a mean table. There was cheese under a delf cover, a cake, jam, a glass dish of celery, another of tinned tomatoes. Mrs Redgrave handed Neil a cup of tea, frowning at him and told him to eat up, but his appetite had gone. He forgot how he used to rise from a strenuous night in the cavity bed, with the appetite of two men, to sit back, when he was shaved and dressed, while Laura cooked his breakfast. It was not the same kitchen. Its whole atmosphere had changed. He felt too unnerved to think and could find nothing to say. He was dominated by the feeling that a very unpleasant situation was impending from that detestable woman opposite him. He took a cream cookie from the cakestand, saying he was not hungry, and timidly nibbled, sipping his tea. Laura also said she was not hungry, looking with downcast eyes at a salmon sandwich on her plate while uncomely blushes mantled her face.

Mrs Redgrave said if they were not hungry, she was. She ate heartily, leaving only two sandwiches, taking with each one a stick of celery, beginning with the hearts, and the crunch of her eating sounded in the gloomy silence like a dog crushing a bone. Coughing, and fingering his glasses, Neil saw her coarse, red hand frequently rifling the crisp white sticks that glistened like purest ivory and each time he winced, waiting for the rasping crunch of her next bite. He stole scared glances at her, quickly turning his eyes from her determined frown. He saw an overgrown Laura. She had massive false teeth and the unpleasant habit of loosening the top plate with her tongue. Neil was now wearing a nervous frown himself. The noise of her eating was sawing through his nerves, when she stopped and asked him how he was off for tea. For something to do he passed her his cup, silently, and put an Albert cake on his plate. Mrs Redgrave cut herself a large slice of cake, ate it, and, without preamble said it seemed that he and Laura had been walking out for quite a time. They were at a nice, sensible age for marriage but they mustn't leave it too late. She understood from Laura that he was in a good steady job and she wanted to know what were his intentions towards her daughter.

Laura was crying. She rose to leave the kitchen with her handkerchief to her eyes, saying 'Oh, mother, don't!' Mrs Redgrave gripped her shoulder and roughly pushed her back in the chair telling her not to be a fool. She had allowed the harm to be done and was as much to blame as Mr Mudge but it wasn't too late to put matters right. Neil sat stunned, trying to think of a reply, wildly darting about in his mind for some loophole of escape. Had anything really happened to Laura? Were they conniving to trick him into marrying her? He felt like a physical impact Mrs Redgrave's frown fixed on his lowered head and he stammered desperately that he and Laura had only been acquainted a short time. They had never talked about marriage. They were good friends, that was all. Mrs Redgrave rose and banged the table, shouting that he had known Laura long enough for a certain thing to happen and that certain thing had happened and the best man that ever walked wasn't going to fool her daughter.

Neil's heart seemed to have left its natural position and was beating hotly in his throat like a padded hammer and the two cakes he had eaten lay in his tensed stomach like a ball of dough. He felt defeated and helpless. Almost inaudibly, he said he had no intention of fooling Laura. Mrs Redgrave said he wouldn't get the chance. There were ways of making a man stand by a woman he had got into trouble. A man up in Manchester in a good position had tried it on with her sister because her sister was a softy but she went and saw where he worked and threatened to expose him to his boss. He wasn't long in marrying her sister then. Mrs Redgrave paused, standing in the middle of the kitchen, her bunioned feet in unshapely shoes, her red hands folded across a blue print overall-apron, her florid face scarlet with righteous anger, the mean, unlovely symbol of Neil's destiny. With his hands on his knees, Neil took a white-faced glance at her, then with his chin up stared steadily at the window. Mrs Redgrave said she was going across the landing to talk to Mrs Molony for half-an-hour. They were old enough to arrange matters themselves and she hoped they would have everything settled when she got back. She went out, banging the door.

Laura came round the table and threw her arms round Neil, crying, asking him what he was going to do. She was going to have a baby. She was three months gone. It had happened the first night. She had been afraid to tell her mother but she was forced to. Was he going to run away? If he left her to face everything she would do something desperate; she would throw herself in the Clyde. Neil felt her hot breasts pulped against his shoulder, her breath on his turned face, and recoiled physically. She felt his recoil and clung to him and he patted her back, foolishly, telling her not to worry, everything would be all right while his hand felt the flabby flesh of her back sweating through her thin blouse. He winced as her hand touched his cheek. Her hands also were hot and moist, and as her wet brown eyes met his he thought, 'God, they're like boiled brandy balls!' He was a daftie, a stark staring madman. For the sake of a few, hot spasms of relief he had fated himself to live and sleep for years with this dull commonplace woman. That first night she told him it was her safe period. Afterwards he was careful. Was it possible that a plan could possibly form behind that heavy brow? She had tricked him! He pulled from her arms and rushed in desperation into the lobby and opened the door, with his coat and hat in his hand. She clung to him. He said he couldn't face her mother tonight. He wasn't well. He would come back. Talk things over. Tomorrow. He ran down the stairs, fumbling into his coat and she stood at the door crying, 'Neilie, come back! Don't leave me. On, Neilie!'

Laurie's silly, choked cry and her mother's indirect threat that she would go straight to his employers, dinged in his head as he walked blindly away from that loathsome close, hating the whole shabby, back-street locality where he had met with this abject misfortune. He was at the end of Rowanglen Road without realizing it. Laura's cry had faded from his ears; only her mother's threat jabbed insistently behind his incoherent thoughts, a cynical reminder that she would be there to bar any way of escape. He turned into Gorbals Main Street, his short, sturdy legs moving quickly, his head inclined and his clenched fists moving at his sides as if he was pushing himself along. He hurried past Gorbals Cross, passing the Irish navvies, the aged, done men and youthful failures, drifting home to verminous beds in the model-lodging-houses; the closed Jewish shops, the groups of Jewish youths at corners, the fried-fish saloons sending out their hot greasy smells into the cold night. He was seeing and feeling nothing of this familiar life as he crossed Stockwell Bridge and emerged from the semi-darkness under the railway-viaduct into Argyle Street, where the late crowds were thinning out. Disgusted with his folly, he saw clearly that he would have to marry Laura Redgrave or leave his job and face unemployment and dole-queueing for another year or two, in a mean lodging somewhere, hundreds of miles from Glasgow. That ordeal with Mrs Redgrave had shown him the sort of woman she was. If he refused to take Laura and stayed in Glasgow she would hound him out of his job and give him no peace. As he imagined her arrival at the office and his manager, a Quaker and a strictly moral man, sending for him, his heart failed him. But how could he marry and get a house with nothing saved? Only Mrs Redgrave could help him and she would have to if he married Laura.

Neil found to his surprise that he had walked unaware, beyond Kelvinhaugh Street and in misery at his predicament, he thrust impulsively into a pub on the verge of closing-time and ordered and drank quickly a small whisky and two pints of beer. He rarely entered a pub and the drink fuddled him. Musing gloomily he leant on the counter till the barman, closing the doors, called him and he stumbled out, swaying, guiding himself by dark side turnings towards the docks and the long way back through Broomielaw and over Jamaica Bridge to Govanhill. Life as expression and development was ending for him; he would remain one of the obscure millions, plodding the wage-earning rut, never achieving prominence in anything.

He walked on unsteadily, calling himself a clown and a moron, wishing he had been a soldier, one of the lucky ones to whom death had come swiftly. Better that than this dead-end marriage! He sniggered cynically, looking along Norfolk Street as he passed it, remembering the night long ago when he had read his essay on Individualism under the broken lamp, in the close in South Wellington Street, to Donald Hamilton and Eddy Macdonnel. That night he believed he could write anything—essays, novels, poems, a play—'Individualism we await thy glorious dawn!' His wonderful peroration! My Christ! he was making a fine show as an individual. What right had he to sneer at the unthinking multitudes when he was one of the least of them? He had sold himself into bondage for a taste of sensual pleasure without ecstasy or love! He was no better than the feckless husbands and wives of the slums whom he often despised. And he had fancied himself as one of the slim, wily Don Juans who go about fornicating and fathering all over the place among the freshest flowers of womankind! And what was he really? Nothing but a small-timer of the back-streets! An admission of his limitations, a profound awareness of his ungifted being, burdened him terribly for a moment, then he comforted himself with the reflection that perhaps Laura wouldn't make such a bad wife after all, that maybe her mother wasn't always so unpleasant as she had appeared tonight. He could plod along, like millions of others, and, by God, he might write something good yet, even walled-in by this sordid marriage his daftness was rushing him into!

It was midnight when he let himself into his lodging and slipped past his landlady's bedroom to his room. He did not light the incandescent mantle over the fireplace but undressed by the pale reflection of the streetlamp opposite his window. When he was half-undressed he sat on the edge of the bed in his semmit, trousers and socks, moodily dramatizing his fate. A favourite verse from Omar Khayyam came into his head and he muttered thickly:

The Moving Finger writes; and, having writ,
Moves on: nor all they Piety nor Wit
Shall lure it back to cancel half a line,
Nor all they Tears wash out a Word of it.

He stood up with folded arms and bowed head, his braces
hanging, seeing himself as a figure of tragedy and in that
posture he suddenly experienced the feeling of one sinking
into abysmal darkness and imagined he saw millions of
hands reaching up to seize him, to drag him down to the
dead level of obscurity. Chilled and depressed, he threw
off his socks and trousers, dropping them anywhere, and
lay down in pants and semmit, pulling the blankets over
his head, his knees up to his chin. Under that dark tent he
lay worried and anxious, wondering if Mrs Redgrave had
written to his employers tonight or if she would come to
his place of work tomorrow. In complete darkness he saw,
as clear as life, the shocked, reproving faces of his sisters
and the scandalized looks of neighbours talking about him
on the stairhead when he was married and Laura's child
arrived three months before it decently ought to have.
And he heard the sly, smutty jokes of old McDougal,
the head book-keeper and his fellow clerks. He writhed
in the darkness and lay for a long time drowsily awake.
But his short, rugged body had become warm with drink
that was simmering in his veins and his mind drowsed away
at last from every anxiety and towards three o'clock in the
morning, he fell into a snoring, alcoholic sleep.

CHAPTER SIX

A queue of six prisoners lined up, cap in hand, by the desk of the principal warder in the centre of the long prison hall, moved two paces forward as the principal warder beckoned with his finger and Eddy Macdonnel was placed at the end of the queue by the officer who had escorted him from his cell, where he had been kept in until the prison-doctor arrived. When the officer had delivered Macdonnel, he saluted his principal, turned smartly on his heel, and, jingling his chain and keys, went up the shining steel stairway to the third gallery to resume his guard over prisoners who were cleaning the lavatories and kneeling to wash the slate pathway between the cells and the rail.

The doctor was talking and laughing with the Church of England chaplain who had passed at that moment on his visits to groundfloor prisoners. The principal warder, a tall, broad kindly-featured man with a heavy grey moustache, frowned at their leisurely chat and shuffled the papers on his desk. He always had a pleasant word for every prisoner but this morning he tugged at his moustache and glared at the seven men waiting for medical attention.

Eddy Macdonnel's eyes were fixed on the bald skull of the chaplain which was red as a foggy sun and glazed like a polished apple. He was a podgy little man with tiny, pink hands and a bobbing walk who wore a continual jolly grin on his round face, but his small eyes were dark and contemptuous and he never brought any spiritual comfort to prisoners. His visits to them were hurried and they all referred to him as 'that fat little bastard.' Eddy Macdonnel had always gazed at his skull ever since the first day the chaplain entered his cell and now he trembled with desire to bring his open palm down on it in a hard, flat smack. A kind of nervous sparkling was going on in his own head;

under the right side of his skull, like a minute, electric wire sputtering, conveying almost uncontrollable nervous impulses to his arms. He gripped his cap tighter in his left hand, his right fist opened and closed convulsively while the arm jerked nervously against his side, and it seemed as if his eyes were leaving their sockets in their concentration on the chaplain's skull. What would happen if he suddenly left his place, darted round behind the principal warder and gave relief to his impulse? He knew he would let out a shrill laugh or a piercing scream as his arm shot up and his palm smacked the little man's red pate. And afterwards, locked in his cell, he would laugh, feeling the sleek warmth of that skull on his palm, and in body and mind he would know deep relief. But if he did it? Now! The chaplain would start back with his hand to his head, his cold eyes burning with rage, outraged at the indignity of this assault by one of these despicable conscientious objectors before his colleagues. Eddy Macdonnel saw that vividly and everything that followed—the wild scrimmage, the shouts. The principal warder would seize him roughly; perhaps a prisoner would leave the queue and assist him; the warder, apprehensive of an attack by another prisoner, would shout for help, 'Mister Potts! Mister Strang! Mister Blake!' his raucous voice booming through the hall. But Eddy knew he would not struggle. After doing that he would feel quiet. But two warders would run down from the galleries and hustle him, twisting his arms, into one of the punishment cells at the end of the ground floor. And maybe in the excitement of the doctor would dart forward to assist and use the opportunity to give him a vicious blow. Eddy believed that the doctor hated him.

Eddy Macdonnel was in a highly nervous state. When a warder came to take him to work after breakfast he had asked to see the doctor and was locked in his cell again. All night he had lain awake, in the grip of that recurring nightmare, which began as soon as he fell asleep and always wakened him. It was the dream of the cell door opening silently, with the slowness of a clock's minute-hand, until it lay flat against the wall. At the first tiny movement of the door he always leapt violently awake, springing into a sitting posture, his hands gripping the sides of the plank under his oakum-mattress, and then, with his gaze fixed on the door, he would gradually lie back, moving with cunning slowness, as slowly and silently as the moving door, until his head touched the oakum pillow and he lay, watching with terror-stricken eyes for the appearance of the doorway's black aperture through which would enter the unknown one, the faceless murderer, to strangle him with powerful hands or drive a knife deep into his heart. But his murderer never came. Only the threat of the doorway held his gaze, night after night as he lay, tense and utterly still, while sweat poured from his neck, his breast and back, wetting the green, coarse prison vest and shorts he slept in, while he listened to the rapid, suffocating beat of his heart and his mouth gaped as he tried vainly to scream, to shatter with a terrible cry the utter darkness and silence burdened with evil. Paralyzed with fear he waited, through tortured hours, powerless to move or cry, till the first morning glimmer touched his cell and he saw the top of the ugly door, with its eyehole for warders to look in, that it was shut, had been shut all the long night, and he relaxed, and tried to sleep. But he could never sleep. When more light entered his cell, he would rise an hour or two before the harsh rising-bell clanged through the hall at half-past six, and pour water into his small tin basin and wash himself at the table, fretfully rubbing the latherless soap, trying to dry himself with the stiff towel that rubbed like rough wood. Then he emptied the water from his basin into the chamberpot, hurriedly lifting and replacing the tight-fitting tin lid, filling the cell with the stench of the contents of his bowels, diseased with prison food and life. Then he would pace to and fro, cold and exhausted, or sit at the table with his head in his hands, trying not to breathe the tainted air that reminded him of his own feebleness and corruption and lingered, escaping so slowing, through the opening of one small sliding pane of the heavily-barred window. Sometimes he wanted to smash every pane in that window and let the air remove the indignity of the unnatural life, cleansing his solitude. And at last that long drab while would end with warders' heavy boots ringing the steel stairs, with jingling of keys and the clang of the rising bell, and he would troop out, with the other prisoners, carrying his chamber-pot to the big lavatory in the centre of the gallery, and wait his turn to empty it. What the prisoners called The Jerry Parade was the first Regulation duty of the day, followed shortly by a gruel and dry-bread breakfast. Then would begin, after his sleepless night, his long agony of debility and suicidal depression, when the ugly day lengthened unbearably, yet he dreaded the coming of the night.

There was another dream he hated and feared, though it came less often and did not last so long, nor leave him sleepless. It was the dream in which the roof and floor of his cell slid towards each other with infinite slowness, while he waited, unable to move, knowing they would crush him to death. But the dream he desired seldom came to him. Sometimes, waiting for sleep, he tried to recreate its warm brilliance, so that while he slept his spirit could live and wander. In this dream, the window and wall of his cell melted away and he found himself walking on a moorland where the clean Clyde rippled through sunlight and a solitary lark skirled his mounting song; walking alone, mazed by the glow of heather and the golden flames of gorse, smiling in simple pleasure at the beauty of the created world. From that dream he always woke refreshed and happy and nothing in the harsh penal life could irritate or hurt him.

How could a man grin so amiably and have such callous eyes? Was his grin a sanctimonious mask, a dutiful smile of 'A Servant Of The Lord' who had no real kindliness? A pale sunray from a skylight of the prison roof touched his skull and Eddy Macdonnel watched it twinkle, inclining slightly towards the doctor as he waved a fat hand, vivid against his black sleeve, telling his funny story. Was it of some poor, cranky prisoner he was telling? Eddy felt the throb in his head quicken. If the chaplain lingered another moment he would give way to his desire and land himself in solitary for another three months. His reason, not entirely clouded, warned him and he wished as strenuously as the principal warder, that the chaplain would continue on his way.

As if he had been struck by a stone, the chaplain turned in quick surprise as the principal warder dabbed a rubber stamp viciously at a paper on his desk. Seeing the latter's expression, he broke off his conversation briskly, with a jolly reference in Latin to the fleetness of time. The doctor smiled his wry, sneering smile and Eddy Macdonnel sighed with relief as the portly little man toddled away on his spiritual rounds. The principal warder coughed, and flushed with annoyance, fretting to get ahead with the day's routine and stood aside as the doctor commandeered his desk, hung his stethoscope from his neck and signed to his prisoner-assistant to draw near with the medicines.

The prisoners shuffled forward, one by one. Four of them were dressed in clothes of a dirty, stone-colour, signifying the third-division, two were second-division men in chocolate-brown suits, all of them marked from caps to trouser-hems like strangely-spotted animals with the broad arrow, painted black on third-division suits and white on the chocolate-brown. Eddy Macdonnel wore the political offender's garb of dark-grey stuff over which the arrows wandered, stencilled in white paint. As each man stepped up to the doctor and described his symptoms, he was given a pill or a draught of medicine, or handed a box of ointment, all taken from a basket-tray slung from the neck of a prisoner who accompanied the doctor on his daily visits to the four halls of the prison.

Macdonnel hated the doctor, whose irascible countenance aroused his most evil emotions, and he had suffered pain and sickness rather than ask to be seen by him. For months he had gloated, in his cell, over that bullying face with the pouched eyes and the thick, brutal lips. He had a small gallery of faces—the doctor's, and those of warders who had reported him for breaking prison-rules—at which he glared and shouted in solitude, upon whose persons he inflicted fiendish pain. Black moods like these, in which he invented ingenious tortures and imagined fantastic combats with his enemies, occupied many of his solitary hours. When these moods passed he did not speculate upon their origin nor try to dispel them as emotions inconsistent with his pacifist attitude; nor was he curious as to the evil effect they might produce in his own person. He lusted in these moods with all his strength until they were replaced by pleasanter emotions and he completely forgot them. Between the two extremes of emotional violence and tranquil happiness, he never slung the bridge of thought and in his murderous imaginations wasted an immense proportion of energy.

A tall, unhealthily-fat prisoner skipped away, grinning and shaking his head, at every few steps dancing lightly and gracefully on his toes and rattling a box of pills at his ear. He was serving a sentence for the crime of rape and they said he was soft in the head. It was now Macdonnel's turn and he stared nervously at the doctor who returned his stare with a look of indifference, from eyes burned dry of sympathy with many years of military service in India. 'Well, out with it! What's your trouble?' he said rudely and turned aside his face with an expression of boredom and contempt as Macdonnel, enraged and unnerved by his manner, became confused in thought, and stammered, trying to tell him about his nervous condition, his nightmares and insomnia. He had written down his symptoms on pieces of toilet-paper, the only paper allowed in the cells, trying to express them in the simplest words, then memorising them so that he could explain his condition briefly and clearly, hoping desperately that this time the doctor would listen and give him a powerful sleeping draught, something that would guard him, if only for a few nights, from those terrifying dreams. But the doctor did not wait for his reply. He had already signed to his assistant to pour a measure from a large medicine-bottle on the tray and was holding a full glass out to Macdonnel and Macdonnel's burning eyes stared into his, contemptuous and bored. 'Dammit, man! Take it! What are you waiting for?' A faint flush tinged the doctor's heavy face as he spoke and the principal warder, fingering his moustache frowned and exclaimed loudly, 'Come on, now, Number Ten! Do as you're told!' The pulse in Macdonnel's head throbbed and burned. He would have liked to throw the contents of that glass in the doctor's face and humiliate this bullying swine who abused his authority, finding pleasure in mortifying sick men. But he could not face again the long punishment of solitary confinement on bread and water. He reached out a trembling hand and took the glass, studying it for a moment. What was this they were giving him? Bromide? The stuff they give to lunatics to dull them, keep them quiet? Was he a lunatic and this pig of a doctor sane? He smiled ironically and the principal warder's voice rapped out again, "Urry up, Number Ten! Get it down. We can't wait 'ere all day for you!' Eddy Macdonnel tossed back the colourless liquid, his mouth twisting bitterly as he replaced the glass on the tray. The doctor, mockingly eyeing his averted face, half-inclining his head towards the principal warder, said with a dirty leer, 'You need a woman, my boy. You'd have done better at the Front!' and the principal warder sniggered and grinned knowingly, twiddling his moustache.

Eddy Macdonnel put on his prison cap and quickly walked away from the desk, blind fury hastening his steps, his footfalls ringing the steel stairs leading from the centre of the hall to narrow bridges connecting the three galleries on either side. When he reached the top gallery, he waited at the door of his cell for the landing warder to come and take him to his work in the bookbinding shop. There was no one in view. He stepped out and looked down through the canopy of wide-meshed wire-netting stretched from the first-floor galleries across the entire expanse of the hall to catch the bodies of prisoners who attempted suicide by launching themselves over the rail. He was trembling with rage and with insane fascination peered down at the distant figures, believing the doctor was still laughing at him, as he walked down the hall with the principal warder, who would unlock the door for him and his limping assistant.

The landing-warder issued from a cell at the far end of the gallery and shouted indignantly, 'Get inside, Number Ten!' Startled from his concentration of hate, Eddy Macdonnel stepped back hurriedly the yard of pathway between the door and the rail and stood within his cell. After a moment he cautiously stuck his head out and saw the officer disappear into another cell, but he did not risk looking over the rail again. He wanted no more of the punishment-cells; he had no enthusiasm left with which to make light of the debility of days on bread and water, confinement to a bare solitude and walking-exercise alone on the macadam ring of the prison-yard. He had had an impulse to answer the doctor back, but rage always struck him dumb or made him stutter stupidly. He was glad now that he had not. He was sick of the heroic attitude.

He sat down at his table, feverish with impatience to be taken to his work, to be marched across the prison-yard and get a breath of the flashing air of this Spring morning, to feel the sun's warmth on his hands, neck and face as he crossed from the hall to the bookbinder's shop. Another ten minutes passed and the landing-warder appeared suddenly at his door and faced him sternly as he stood up. He was a dark-featured man with a long nose and chin and a splay-footed walk. 'Yer know yiv no right to be a doin' of that!' he jerked his thumb in the direction of the rail. 'Don't yer? If I catch yer a doin' of that again I'll 'ave yer up afore the Guv'nor.' Eddy Macdonnel struggled to veil the hate in his eyes. Again and again this man had had him punished for the most trivial breaking of prison rules. While the other warders contented themselves with cautioning him for talking on the exercise ring or in the workshop this man had him brought before the prison-governor until it seemed to Macdonnel that the governor was as sick of the sight of his loutish face as he himself was. He would probably report him now. For leaning over the rail! Ah, well, for Christ's sake, let him! The execration exploded inside Macdonnel's head, bringing him some relief. He wouldn't be pleasant to this crawling dolt to win any favour from him. Their eyes had met many times on the exercise ring and in the workshop and Macdonnel's had never wavered in their expression of loathing. He turned his head to the wall and did not answer. The man's nasal cockney voice disgusted his ears and his oafish, equine face drove him to a madness of contempt.

The principal warder roared up from the groundfloor, 'Mister Potts! Keep Number Ten in today!' Mr Potts leant over the rail, touched his cap, nodded and answered, 'Righto!' and turned to Macdonnel. 'Now, me lad, there's no Association for you today!' He looked round the cell. 'Got plenty o' work? No, you hain't? All right, ye'll 'ave some mail-bags sent up.' Macdonnel's heart sank. To be locked in till seven next morning, all through this young, ardent day while the sun would be pouring into the book-binder's shop that caught so much of the light! 'But I don't want to stay in!' began Macdonnel. 'It's the worst thing for me. Haven't I had enough solitary confinement with all the punishment I've had? I . . .' Mr Potts cut him short, appearing more stupid as he drew himself up in an attempt to be dignified and officious, 'It ain't wot you want, it's wot the doctor orders an' the doctor 'as ordered 'as 'ow you've gotter be kept in. See?' He closed the door.

Eddy Macdonnel listened to his splay-footed stride slapping the slate flags of the pathway and cursed him with all the ferocity of his nature, clenching his fists, staring intensely as if he could burn through the iron door with the fire of his eyes. So the doctor was taking his spite out on him for his frank show of dislike? Holy God in Heaven, what sane doctor with any knowledge of his art, would treat with a whole day's confinement a man whose nerves were destroyed and his reason unbalanced by that same confinement? Did the doctor sincerely believe he was helping him by locking him up for a day when what he needed most was activity, outside, away from his cell; activity that might bring him one night's complete sleep? But perhaps the doctor didn't hate him. Perhaps he had only given him Regulation Treatment. Regulations! Rules! Tears of hopeless rage glazed Macdonnel's eyes as he walked to and fro from window to door, thinking of the dead weight of mental dullness around him—the minds that run all prisons, stifled by Rules and Regulations, biassed against any humane reform. Suddenly he noticed the two books the prison librarian had left on his table while he was downstairs waiting to see the doctor. On one he saw the hateful letters, SPCK, Society For The Promotion Of Christian Knowledge. He knew what to expect under that imprint. It would be a Victorian story of some unnaturally gentle young woman seduced by some utterly unreal scoundrel and sent careering into Prostitution to be received, at the eleventh hour, repentant and forgiven, into the broadcloth bosom of the Church; or the mushy epic of some moronic drunkard, rescued from delirium tremens by the love of Christ. Tcha! The stuff was no better than Salvation Army evangelism or sentimental tracts of back-street mission-halls. The librarian invariably left him one of these Christian Knowledge books, fit only for the minds of waitress and parlour-maids or the souls of respectable spinsters, blind to the harsh realities of life. He stopped his mad walk and picked up the book. It was entitled, '*Hetty's Sin*, by the Reverend Hiram Piggott.' He sneered at the name. How could good writing possibly come from a man with a name like that? The other book was a novel of the Australian bush by Rolf Boldrewood. God! How he loathed this writer's adolescent stodge! From cover to cover the ear was deafened by revolver and rifle shots and the fusillading hooves of horses driven to death by incredibly good mounted police in pursuit of utterly bad bank-robbers.

He shouted anathemas on both authors and hurled the books at the door, letting them lie where they fell, and began striding the length of the cell, bemoaning his luck. Once a fortnight they came round with books and this time he had hoped to get a fat volume of Dickens, a novel by Joseph Conrad, an engrossing book of travel or some contemporary writings which the conscientious objectors had succeeded in getting included in the library. He had waited six months for Prescott's *History Of Peru* which he had partly read, fascinated by the records of a vanished race, when he was rebinding it in the bookbinder's shop. Since men had been imprisoned for conscientious objection the prison library had widened its range of selection, but still there were not enough modern works or classics to meet the demand, and it was seldom that the librarian left the book a man pencilled on his slate when he was leaving his cell in the morning for association-work. Macdonnel regretted he had not been there to choose for himself from the book-basket. A whole morning of confinement lay before him with no work or new book to lighten his solitude. He cursed his luck and the stupidity of the entire prison system and imagined with disdain the ugliness of Mr Potts, slopping along the gallery with his flat-footed stride, his horsey face peering into cell after cell, hoping to catch some poor devil breaking the Rules. Macdonnel knew that another warder would not have locked him in. If only he had the relief of standing at the open door, merely to look at a long array of fifty similar doors, see an occasional warder pass or whisper a word to a fellow-prisoner as he went along, polishing the gallery-rail. To see some colour and movement, no matter how drab and familiar, lightened the intolerable hours. But Mr Potts was working for promotion and always strictly applied the rules!

Eddy Macdonnel picked up the two books, casting upon them a final imprecation as he placed them on one of two small fanshaped shelves fixed into the mortar in the left corner of his cell under the high window. They stood out, startlingly dull, in their dun official covers, against the green *Annandale English Dictionary* and his two volumes of Swinburne's *Poems*, which a friend had sent him. He took down the pale-blue, gold-lettered Swinburne and began to look through 'Songs Before Sunrise', though he had read them till he knew many of them by heart. He was praying that the inside works-master would bring him some mailbag canvas which would keep him occupied till lunch was served out at twelve o'clock. It was Wednesday—bully beef day. He liked that and imagined the taste of it greedily. The gruel that morning had been very thin, almost water. He felt empty, sick with a diseased hunger.

To turn his mind from thoughts of food and the bleak dragging time he began to read the poems of Swinburne aloud, walking up and down his cell, shouting them, gesturing, waving his arm. But he soon grew tired. Eighteen months on wartime prison-diet had worn down the young hopeful energy with which he had begun his two-year sentence. He sat on his stool and leant his elbow on the table, a legless, heavy, two-feet square deal board fixed solidly into the wall to the right of the door. He could not drag his thoughts away from food. He had heard intelligent men, university and theological students, men who lived more in the mind than himself, confess to this morbid preoccupation with food which controlled them after a short period in prison. Mealtimes broke up the monotonous days and lightened the burden of the implacable routine. Hunger incited the mind to unhealthy concentration on food in the hours between one scanty meal and another and stomach-craving became morbidly insistent.

Smiling, he leaned his two arms on the table and lost himself in recollection of friendly, uproarious dinners and

Christmas feasts in the novels of Charles Dickens, then he devised long menus for himself of rare wines and foreign dishes he had read of. His imagination became crowded with the life of the world and transported him from solitude into the company of beautiful women in a country mansion, then to a Viennese hotel, then a Paris restaurant. The table was crowned with costly flowers, artists and persons of inter-national repute and disrepute sat at every table, soft lights and the music of a faultless orchestra pervaded a continental atmosphere while he gazed soulfully into the mysterious eyes of his companion, a woman of rare, spiritual beauty, a poetess, a composite of Elizabeth Barrett Browning and Emily Bronte—two of his favourite women—passionately he held her slender hand that lay in his like a sunwarm rose-leaf while her other hand and divinely moulded arm delicately gestured with a perfumed cigarette. She was laughing at his talk; the music of her laughter inspired him and his flow of words poured, glittering with wit, style and wisdom, supple, easy and continuous as a sunlit stream. She adored him. A brilliant genius, she sat there dazzled by his superior power.

Suddenly, though his eyes had been fixed on it while he dreamed, Eddy Macdonnel saw the thick, frosted pane of glass behind which, in a recess of the outside wall, was the small gas-mantle that lit up his cell at night. He remem-bered the dead-whiteness of that midget mantle—which the night-warder lit with a taper—cold and inhuman, like his surroundings, and he foresaw with sudden fatigue and fear the night to come, wondering if the draught the doctor had given him would make him sleep, sleep as he had slept through a few blessed nights, not hearing the deafening summons of the rising-bell, dead to the clangs and roars of the awakening prison, till his door was unlocked and a warder roused him with a shout. He walked to and fro again, slowly now, feeling weak, thinking of his dinner, fancying he heard the clank of meal-tins. He smiled, glad that the time had passed so quickly and stood listening at the door, waiting to receive the tin of bread, potatoes and meat, which a warder, not glancing at him, would thrust hastily into his hands and close the door and pass on.

When he had listened a few moments the sounds he fancied he had heard ceased to echo in his head. Footsteps passed his door, then his cell and the prison-hall were again stone-silent. He had misjudged the time. Disappointed in mind and body, he sat again at the table, rested his chin on his palms and with head thrust forward, began to inflict dreadful torture on the bodies of the medical officer and Mr Potts, seeing them as vividly, feeling in his hands their hateful flesh, as though they were lying trussed up and helpless before him. These two, he believed, hated him, went out of their way to provoke him, make him break the rules and get himself punished. Now they were in his power and methodically, slowly, he subjected them to unbearable pain, with methods he had read of in books, with fantastic mechanisms be conceived himself, that maimed and twisted them. He stretched them on a medieval rack, squeezed their hands in the thumb-screw, pierced them with red-hot instruments and watched in fiendish pleasure the slow drop of the water-torture, smiting moment by measured moment, their foreheads, while their eyes bulged from their heads in apprehension of the glistening drop that cut more keenly at each fall. He heard with delight their shrieks and cries for mercy until his body and head were hot with revengeful lust, losing himself in his dream of hate, as he had lost himself in his sentimental vision.

At last he rose, muttering, clenching his fists, his eyes insanely staring, and prepared to look out of the window, and as he set about that, the ludicrous face of Mr Potts, the irascible face of the doctor, gradually faded until they became vanishing blurs on his mental horizon. The bottom of the window was seven feet from the floor. He placed his stool and piled on it all his books: first, the *Annandale Dictionary* and the Boldrewood novel, then *Hetty's Sin* and the two slim volumes of Swinburne's *Poems* and topped the pile with the obese prison Bible and the small, thick Book Of Common Prayer And Church Hymnal. On this he stood tiptoe, holding onto the transverse bars and, stretching his neck, looked out on a clear May morning of 1918.

Far away circled a common, glittering with Spring grass and ringed round by red, suburban roofs. Far down he saw a bend of the oval macadam pathway of the exercise ring and, distant to the left, a corner of the garden near the prison gates, where a cluster of daffodils glinted. Their sway and fragrance, their miraculous texture, so near his hungering mind brought them, filled him with painful longing to be free. In an unclouded sky, dreamy with the young azure of Spring, he saw three aeroplanes, small as swallows in that far height, black against the blue, then instantaneously glistening like a sudden-turning gull's wing. Their unfamiliar drone mocked him and droned through his head, like a jeer from those who believed in war at the handful of pacifists and objectors in all countries. The new weapon! Would they fill the sky one day as H. G. Wells had prophesied? The aeroplanes instantly were out of sight and earshot and he was aware of the supreme silence of the sky, pure and tranquil, untainted by the silence in which he was immured, a silence imposed, diseased, with the fear and resentment, depression and boredom, vice and cunning, emanating from a thousand minds. He imagined he heard a warder's key in the door and, quickly turning, almost lost his foothold. Being at the window he was breaking the Rules. The door did not open but he could no longer hold his strained position. He stepped down, replaced his books and, taking his stool to the table, sat there again.

Those aeroplanes reminded him of the Zeppelin raid when he saw from a cell window a stricken airship fall through the night like a burning rag. He was locked in with twenty prisoners in a dark groundfloor cell, while the raid was on, and he studied apprehensively the faces of habitual criminals, faces disfigured by vice and abnormal weakness, with one or two among them strong, dignified, quiet, the faces of men whom misfortune, perhaps, had brought here. Everyone crowded to the window; light from a brilliant moon faintly lit the cell and the faces moved fantastically through pale ray and deep shadow, unreal as faces in a troubled dream. From other cells conscientious objectors loudly sang 'The Red Flag' and pacifist hymns and Sinn Fein prisoners sang Irish rebel songs, their singing mingled with the hoarse shouts of warders vainly commanding silence. A white-faced little man, ex-bank clerk and forger, screamed hysterically, battering the door with his fists, then crouched on the floor,

crying like a child. Others sat, huddled and trembling while
the rest talked feverishly about the War, or their sentences,
the prison food, the time they had served or had yet to
serve, delighting in this macabre, social gathering after many
months of enforced silence. One man produced two cigarettes
and a single match. He was very fat and cheerful. He laughed
heartily, telling them how he brought the fags in under
his armpit, he said, when he was sentenced a week ago.
Two elderly men, old lags, cursing and swearing, said you
couldn't get anything past the Reception warder. The fat
man said angrily by Christ he would show them, beginning
to unbutton his jacket, saying he had more hair under his
arms than any man in the prison. He undid two buttons
and commenced laughing vigorously again, as though he
was laughing at some private joke, his fat cheeks, his double
chin and big stomach shaking. He stopped in a moment and
bent down to strike the match saying it would be napoo
to their smoke if it didn't light. They made room for him
and the match lit at the first scrape on the stone floor. The
man straining to look out of the window gave up the stool
to him and he stood on it tiptoe throwing out the burnt
match through the opening of the sliding-pane, drawing
hungrily at the cigarette and blowing the smoke through the
opening. The two cigarettes were quickly consumed among
six prisoners, who crushed round him and took their turn
on the stool. The other prisoners did not attempt to share
the cigarettes. Several of them had not smoked for a year or
eighteen months and said it was foolish and only started the
craving. All their faces were pale and strained. They were
thinking of the bomb that might fall on them crushed in this
dark cell and much of their excited talk hid their fear.

And he had argued vigorously, all through that ceremony
over the previous cigarettes, with three vicious-faced young
prisoners, who had threatened to set about him, saying the
warder ought to have shoved him in with the conchies and
not among decent Britishers. He forgot his fear of the raid in
his fear of them, believing they would stick at nothing, would
kick him senseless if they got him down. A stout, elderly man,
with abundant white hair and a venerable face stepped across
and supported him, intimidating the three young prisoners

with a torrent of obscene eloquence delivered in a lush cockney accent, telling them that conchies were right to keep out of a bloody capitalist war, while Eddy, relieved, listened astonished to the exuberance of curses spurting from the mouth of this saintly-looking old man. He told Eddy then that he had spent thirty out of his sixty years in prison. He was in for house breaking and was first sentenced when he was twenty. Then he led Eddy across to the window, pulled himself powerfully up by the iron bars and looking out, said you could see nothing and supported Eddy with his shoulder as he hung from the bars and stared into the thrilled silence of a moonlit London under a Zeppelin raid. At that moment the Zeppelin hurtled down through the moonlight, a whirling flame. The whole prison resounded with cheers. Eddy Macdonnel dropped to the floor, excited, trying to imagine the scene where the bomb had fallen, his mind back again in the bloody welter that was soaking the fields of France. Two of the young prisoners he had argued with were waltzing round madly at the door, some of the prisoners were shaking hands, the fat man squealed with delight, 'They got the bastard. Hooray, they gottim! Now you'll 'ear the 'ooter an' it's napoo to our chinwag.' But it was a long time before the siren blew and they heard the irregular tramp of feet, and they were let out to join the straggled march of prisoners through pitch-darkness up the steel stairs back to their cells, all loudly talking and singing, while the warders, flashing torches, shouted for silence.

Three men went mad that night, one of them a conscientious objector, but many prisoners welcomed raid-nights, when they could talk freely for hours. Eddy Macdonnel shivered, seeing again his companion of the unlucky night when he was shut in alone in the groundfloor cell of a powerful epileptic, his face crimson with high blood-pressure, a man with protruding eyes and a hook dangling from his armless right sleeve. Half-crazed with unused energy, he raved up and down the cell cursing 'the bloody Huns' and foully roaring what he would do to the Jerries if only he could get at them. He kicked the door shouting, 'Let me out! Let me out! Let me get at the bastards!' Then he tore off his jacket, pulled open his shirt baring a powerful, thick-haired chest and springing close to Eddy Macdonnel, shouted into his face, 'See that? Feel it!' He made Macdonnel feel his bicep, that was hard as the wall, with veins like thick string, then he roared, 'An' they keeps me in, the swine! They keeps me in 'ere w'ile the 'Uns is murd'rin our wimmen an' kids!' Macdonnel stood pressed into a corner, gazing in terrified fascination at the thick hairy arm, the knotted muscles and ham-like hand, expecting to have his face clawed by that hook or be laid out with a blow from the man's fist. He blinked, tried to look interested, and searched desperately in his mind for ways he had read or heard of, to pacify a madman. But he could remember nothing while the man grimaced into his pale, scared face then suddenly began pacing the cell madly, swinging his jacket from his armhook, whirling it round his head. For several minutes he paced, forgetting his companion, then, in one leap across the cell he seized Macdonnel's shoulder in a grip that seemed to be driving his nails into the shoulder bone, and shook the hook in his face. And as unaccountably, he exposed his shapeless yellow teeth in a horrifying smile and began a recital of his crimes. Macdonnel, trying to appear cool and friendly, gasped, 'And what are you in for this time?' The man's eyes protruded, roving insanely over Macdonnel's face, before he replied, 'A vanload!' Macdonnel's blanched face wreathed in a timid smile. He didn't care a tosser what a vanload might be, but it was safer to keep talking and he forced out, 'What's that?' and was sickened by a look of ferocious amazement, 'Gawdstruth! Mean ter sy yer don't know wot a vanload is? W'y it's a bleedin' vanload! Yer know. A vanload.' He gestured as if he was tugging reins, made a sound like a carter starting a horse, then he gripped Macdonnel's bicep, thrust him against the wall, pushed his enormous face close, 'Look 'ere! It was like this, see? It was dahn W'itechapel wy, see? A vanload was a standin' outside the ware'ouse, so up I jumps an' off I drives an' 'oo should come along but a nark—a plainclothes nark 'oo rekenises me an' it was napoo wiv yer 'umble! See?' He released his grip and stood back triumphantly as Macdonnel nodded and smiled eagerly. Yes, he saw! And he wondered when this eternal strain would end and the door would open to the welcome shine of steel keys and the blue uniform of a warder. It was a false warning and there was no raid, but Macdonnel was locked in for an hour with the lunatic and returned to his own cell, unnerved and sick, to toss sleepless through the night.

He walked the floor again, gazing up at the small square of sky-space, saw a bird flash by, chirping as if it had seen him. He laughed, hearing continued quarrelsome chirps. There must be a nest up there above him. The London sparrows, living their winged, free lives, feeding from the prisoners' crumbs under the eaves that roofed a thousand solitary men. They also, in their element, knew greed, cruelty and fear, but never this unholy solitude that brought no reformation of character or peace to the soul. Thirty years out of sixty spent in gaol. How had enforced solitude helped men like that? He piled his books on his stool again and, hanging from the bars, sucked in the sweet air through the sliding-pane, felt the bloom of the sky on his face. On the pathways of the common he saw solitary figures walking, the coloured dresses of children playing on the grass. The clean breeze entered into him, thrilling his veins like an injection of some exhilarating drug, piercing him like a sword with pain of desire for freedom. Oh, to be out, striding across that grass! What like was that London through which the military escort had hurriedly brought him? In that short journey from station to prison he was stunned by the great city's multitudinous life and noise, amazed by its gigantic novelty, so bewildering to his Northern eyes. He thought of homes out there, and people, free people, sitting down to meals in bright rooms, with friendly talk and laughter. People enjoying a freedom that was enviable even though it was the restricted, anxious life of war. He imagined the glamour of theatres and cinemas, money in his pocket and unlimited choice of books, companionship of men and women; love. Twice in eighteen months he had seen the blurred outline of a woman's face through the close-meshed grille of the Visiting Hall. When would the War end? News here was scarce and vague, gathered from an occasional chat with a warder, a whisper from a new prisoner. In six months his sentence would end. He had lost all his remission through breaking the Rules. He would be court-martialled and sent back for another two years' hard labour. Perhaps the War would last for several more years. Who could believe the rumours of its ending that filtered in here? His preoccupation deafened him to the sound of the warder unlocking his door and pushing his dinner across the table.

When he got down at last reluctantly, tired with hanging from the bars, he was surprised to see it there and glad that the warder had been too hurried to see him at the window. He tipped the stone-cold food onto his enamel soup-plate—precisely eight ounces of sodden, waxy potatoes, eight of tinned beef and four of bread all carefully weighed—and ate it with nervous greed. At times he suffered from attacks of voracity, when he lived from meal to meal, thinking only of food, alternated by periods of excessive lassitude and feeble appetite, when he passed his bread to his neighbour. After their first few days of disgusted rejection of prison diet, new prisoners were always hungry and were grateful for any extras which came to them only in this way. In a few moments his scant meal was over and he was still hungry, weak with a sickly emptiness. He washed his plate and tin knife in the tin basin. There was a box of sandstone powder and cloths lying in Regulation position on the floor under the shelves by the window. He killed some time scouring and polishing his tin basin and knife, applying the powder with a wet rag then rubbing the articles till they glistened, though they were already so bright he could see his reflection in them. Every prisoner was expected to keep these articles and the tin chamberpot-lid polished for periodical inspection and the trifling task of cleaning them became an enjoyable ritual, except to the most depressed, because it passed some time. He replaced the shining basin upright against the wall next to the polished tin lid of the tilted chamberpot, and the knife and plate on one of the shelves—positions demanded by Regulations—and repaced his cell miserably, too tired to hold his position at the window. His mind was wistfully wandering through the warm sunlight in the bookbinding shop that would be empty, locked up and silent now, through the meal hour, and the one small machine that printed ruled paper for the prison ledgers would be still. The bookbinding shop caught more sunshine than any other workshop. It was very pleasant to be out of the cell and doing that light absorbing work, rebinding books that had passed through the hands of hundreds of prisoners, tearing off the broken batters and the gummed bookspines, separating the book sections and sewing the leaves together again ready for the prisoners who rebound them. He was being taught binding himself and making quick progress. After his long punishment he had asked the prison governor to have him taken from the laundry and put to lighter, work and the governor, exacting a promise that he would behave himself, had asked him where he wanted to work and he chose the bookbinder's shop. He had now been three months there and regretted he had not worked there from the start. But in this matter prison was like the outside world. A man had to be in some months to find out which were the best jobs, and get one by luck, or find a way to get one. The prisoners in the bookbinding shop were six conscientious objectors and three Sinn Feiners. He could talk there, in a low voice, about the War and the Labour Movement, about books and work for the future peace of the world.

Mr Pritchett, the tall, limp warder who supervized them was not a callous or officious type. He always knew when they were talking but affected to be unaware and only stopped them when their voices rose to normal tones. He fell asleep regularly every afternoon in his chair on the raised platform from which he overlooked them. He was six feet two and slightly stooped with the weight of his lank body. When they had been working for half an hour after each dinner-time, he would begin to nod and they all smiled at each other watching sleep get the better of him. He said it was indi-gestion and when his superiors weren't near he swallowed bismuth tablets and mouthed chewing-gum. Sometimes his bilious-complexioned face would droop and he would start awake, sit up soldierly and exclaim, 'That's enough of that! Turn it in! Get on with it!' Unlike the other officers, he never said, 'Stop that talking there!' or, 'Less talking there!' but invariably, either on exercise-ring or in the workshop, called, 'Turn it in!' until he was nick-named by the prisoners Old Turnitin. He always woke at the grating of the Chief Warder's key in the door, sprang to attention, saluted and said smartly, 'All correct, sir!' as the Chief, in his spotless silver-braided uniform, walked in, took a quick look round and departed on his daily tour of workshop inspection. But there were days when Mr Pritchett did not hear the key and one of the prisoners would drop something heavy near his platform and wake him in the nick of time. An Irish prisoner swore that Mr Pritchett would wake up sometime, salute, and shout at his Chief, 'That's enough of that, sir! Turn it in!' They were all waiting for that day.

Och, it was a great job. To be able to read the books they were rebinding, sometimes get through half of an interesting book in a day's work. Pritchett didn't nose round or hurry them like Mr Potts and some of the others, and if a prisoner wanted to take a book and finish sewing it in his cell at night, Pritchett would let him. Eddy Macdonnel had managed in this way to get through several extra books which had come as a godsend. A wave of anger burned through him again at the stupidity of the doctor who had caused him to be locked in for a whole day. He listened for the prison to come to life once more. It should be nearly time for the collecting of the meal-tins. Ah, God, sometimes a mere three-quarters of an hour dragged like three hours in here!

Heavy footballs thudded the dead silence; some doors were unlocked and warders' voices called, 'Right! Right!' then along all the galleries sussurated the feet of the dinner-orderlies, in the slipperlike prison shoes, shuffling from cell to cell with a wooden tray, collecting empty food-tins, preceded by a warder. Again the strain of silence was broken and Eddy Macdonnel sighed, as he waited impatiently for the momentary pleasure of seeing someone and whispering a passing word. His door was unlocked; he stood in the threshold, holding the thick, heavy tins, watching the slow approach of the orderlies on either side of the gallery as they paused for a whispered talk at each cell, and the quick advance of the warders unlocking the doors. He placed his tins on the tray, smiling and nodding at the two orderlies, one of whom, a stout, dark little Jew, in for thefts from hotel rooms, whispered behind his hand, 'The Allies have entered Berlin. An armistice has been declared.' The warders had opened the last doors, and were keenly watching them from the end of the gallery, shouting, 'Hurry up with those tins, there!' The orderlies quickened their pace, a warder shouted, 'Get inside, Number Ten!' and Eddy Macdonnel closed his door.

He laughed loudly, standing with hands in pockets and straddled legs, looking up at the window. That news about an Armistice had been whispered through the prison day after day and the Allies had been entering Berlin for the past month! Ach, no one knew when the war would end! If the Germans really had their backs to the wall at last, anything might happen to turn the tide against the Allies. Time and chance happened in wars as they did in the peaceful life of men. There were no certainties in any existence. Ach, the sun must be hot out there today in that sparkling, midday world! Even through these thick walls the heat could be sensed. Sunrays, trembling, glancing, drawing fragrance from the life they inspired! A whole world of beauty laid waste in France! Man's twisted, obdurate heart responded only to the adventure of War. Was there no excitement in the adventure of Peace? Perhaps that ecstasy could only be known by philosophers, saints and poets. The millions always thought cynically of Peace even when staggering, exhausted and broken, out of the agony of War. That sun would be pouring through the slum tenements of Glasgow now, the crowded back-streets, blazing reflection from thousands of tenement windows, burning a roadway of gold down the Clyde to that wild estuary of mountains, noble gateway to the sea, guarding deep, blue lochs. There, above the moors, light would be trembling, golden ether wherein mountains seem to float! In six months he would be taken out into a dark winterworld, court-martialled and returned here for another two years. Soon he would forget how the world looked in sunlight!

He turned at the sound of feet tramping the galleries and rattling down the steel stairs. It was one o'clock. All the prisoners and his mates of the bookbinding shop were going out to Association. From seven this morning till seven next morning. Twenty-four hours of solitary confinement. A

punishment for being sick! His heart beat faster as he heard
steps outside. His door was opened and the inside works-
master appeared with his load of new canvas pieces over his
arm, his uniform dusty with blond fluff from the mailbag
cloth. He was an elderly man, with cheerful, glimmering eyes
and a thick, rusty-grey moustache. He slapped a bundle of
folds of canvas of various sizes on the table with his invariable
salutation, 'There you are sonny. That'll keep yer out of
mischief! Want any wax and thread?' He gave Macdonnel
a skein of thick white thread from the skeins on his shoulder
and two rough pieces of wax, one yellow, one black, from
his pocket, and Macdonnel asked if he could have his door
left open. 'Sure mate. Sure!' said the warder, pushing the
door right back and continuing along the gallery, humming,
giving the work out cheerfully.

Eddy Macdonnel hummed and grinned himself. If Potts
wasn't on hall-duty this afternoon his door would remain
open till the prisoners returned from Association at six
o'clock. He placed the canvas ready on the floor and for
a seat, took down his oakum-pillow from its regulation
position on top of the mattress and bed-clothes, the latter
folded strictly according to regulations and slung with the
mattress over the top of the bed-plank that was tilted end-up
against the wall. Sitting with his back to the wall, he waxed
thread until dozens of stiffened black and beeswax-yellow
threads lay beside him, then he put on the issued leather palm
for driving the heavy needle through the thick cornerfolds,
and began to make mail-bags.

He was happy now, with the open door, like a man from
whom tight cords have been unloosed. He sewed quickly and
neatly, making many bags, forgetting his fear of the coming
night. He sang in a low voice old Irish and Scottish songs,
filling his mind with sentimental and dramatic pictures.
This work tranquillized him. Images and thoughts ran on
clearly in his mind and his accustomed thought that perhaps
this mail-bag he was making might soon be carrying letters
through the streets of Glasgow, came to him, and at once he
was free. That fancy always liberated him. From this very
bag might be handed a letter to his mother in yon Gorbals
street, a letter from the Eastern or Western Front from his

brothers Jimmy and John. He was walking through Gorbals
streets as if he was there in body; past Gorbals Cross and
the spicy Jewish bakers' shops; under the railway bridge
and by Hospital Street, Thistle Street, Crown Street, Rose
Street branching off the lengthy Gowan Street; watching as
he passed the many groups of playing children from hundreds
of closes in the long, straight tenement streets; looking into
back-courts at bookies taking bets, dodging the police, the
singing beggars, the women at work in wash-houses, the lines
hung with coloured washing; seeing familiar faces, meeting
friends; entering well-known kitchens, those of neighbours
and his own mother's, seeing her making beds, cooking,
scrubbing, living out her life in that small space just as he
had watched her from his childhood; and from her kitchen
seeing the thousands of kitchens like it where the working
women of Glasgow had worked for men and families, continuing the generations there since the great industrial city
was a small, charming town. And he imagined that letter-
bag used for delivery in Glasgow's business centre; along
Saltmarket through Argyle Street by Glasgow Cross and old
Trongate and up and down those streets that still have memories of olden days when the Tobacco Lords swaggered the
pavements, Virginia Street, Candleriggs, The Fishmarket,
Stockwell, Miller Street, Oswald Street, historic High Street,
Cowcaddens, the Gallowgate, Buchanan Street; watching
the coloured tramways pushing up the hills of West Nile
Street, Renfield Street, Hope Street, northward and away
to the bourgeois West along Sauchiehall Street to the Dock-
land areas and the shipyards by the Great Western Road
where pearly festoons of street-lamps swing up and on to
Anniesland; looking up graceful Saint Vincent Street, rising
to its sunset ridge, down which at gloaming tonight, a flood
of sunlight would pour; seeing the lights of his city at
night: the foundry-fires of Parkhead; Dixon's Blazes glowing up the sky and the burning slag-heaps round Dalmarnock
and Rutherglen shading night-clouds with rose and golden
gleams; window-lights, lamplight and bridge-lights, the
lights of the great railway viaduct by Jamaica Bridge, in
wavering spiralled reflections on the seaward-flowing Clyde.
    London he could not roam in, though he was near it, but

while his fingers worked, like parts of a machine, his spirit came clear as a bright-winged creature comes clearly from a chrysalis, and hovered over his native town. A great part of his afternoon eased by in this absence and when he returned to the consciousness of his cell, he returned cheerfully, astonished at the number of mail-bags he had made. With less regret he thought of the walk to the bookbinding shop that took him near the gardens at the prison Gate. This long day would soon be over. The image of the daffodils bloomed in his head, symbols of airy freedom and intelligent creation and he repeated while he sewed, the daffodil poem of Wordsworth, seeing the grave, reverential features of the poet in age, unashamed of his ingenuous delight in the sudden vision of the flowers.

He laughed suddenly at the queerness of mental association. The golden vision had reminded him of Goldie, the handsome little sergeant-major who had befriended him while he awaited court-martial. Was Goldie alive still? There was a million-to-one chance against every soldier in a world-war. In every second of his thought men like Goldie were meeting death over there in France. Gratitude towards the good-natured NCO welled up in him. A gentlemanly soldier of the pre-War Army, up from the ranks, every man in the barracks loyally admired 'Good Old Goldie' for his merciful discipline and nicknamed him because of his blond hair and neat, waxed moustache. Eddy Macdonnel saw their meeting again. Goldie, from his desk in the barracks-office saying smartly, 'What's your name?' his direct, blue eyes amused at Macdonnel's youth. 'Macdonnel!' Goldie still smiled, unangered by his tone. 'First name! And stand to attention and say Sir, when you answer me!' Eddy Macdonnel found himself liking the clean-cut fine-complexioned face and the frank eyes shrewdly sizing him up. He could not maintain the defiance he had shown to the bullying type of officer. But he had to stand for his principles. Looking at the wall above Goldie's head he said somewhat lamely, 'I refuse to obey military orders! This is a capitalist war. A war of economic conquest. I refuse to take part in it!' The orderly-sergeant brutally kicked his heels together and shook him violently by the ears to make him stand at attention. Goldie fingered his blond moustache to conceal his amusement: 'All right! Stand him aside. I'll deal with him later.' When he had entered the new recruits he had Macdonnel marched into a small room where he faced him. 'All you objectors are damned cowards out to save your own skins,' he said. Macdonnel flushed, answering that he would fight in a Working Class Revolution but never in a Capitalist War. Goldie pretended a sneer. 'Will you fight one of my boys,' he said, and Eddy answered boastfully, 'I'm afraid of no one here!' Goldie signed to the orderly-sergeant, 'Bring in Private Murphy and the gloves.' The sergeant went out and returned carrying a set of boxing-gloves and followed by a tough young soldier, who began shadow-boxing, dancing nimbly on his toes, making ferocious faces as he upper-cut and jabbed. Eddy Macdonnel paled. They were going to try out his physical courage with this quick-eyed Glasgow hooligan, a type he had been reared among. He began to regret his foolish boast. This youth would bewilder him and lay him out in a couple of minutes. 'That'll do, Murphy. Don't frighten him off before the start,' said Goldie. Macdonnel said pugnaciously that he wasn't afraid. Goldie laughed sceptically, 'We'll soon see! Off with your tunics and roll up your sleeves. I'll referee, and no foul blows!'

Eddy Macdonnel had picked up a smattering of boxing. He faced the soldier in correct style but with quivering inconfidence, knowing he was facing a clever boxer and wondering how badly he would be beaten before the fight was stopped. He launched a straight right, missed, and was jarred through his whole body by a blow on the chin like the slam of a brick. He staggered with buzzing head and closed eyes, amazed at the striking power of the human hand, then he rushed ferociously at the blurred outline of Private Murphy and dizzily heard Goldie say, 'That's enough!' The sergeant caught his whirling arms and Goldie said, smiling admiration, 'Take him to the guard-room, sergeant. See he gets a good tea—plenty to eat.' Macdonnel rubbed his throbbing jaw as he was led out, thinking that Goldie was the finest man in uniform he had met. Goldie came frequently to the guard-room to argue with him and once in the nick of time he appeared and prevented a burly sergeant who was proceeding to manhandle Macdonnel. He shook his head sadly at Macdonnel's foolishness, told him he would have made a good soldier: 'Why don't you do as you're told, my lad? You're only butting your head against a stone wall. What you and your kidney are doing won't stop men fighting. Men and countries will always be fighting. They can't help themselves. I've soldiered since I was a boy. I know what men are.' Macdonnel returned his smile: 'You wouldn't admire me if I deserted my principles now, would you, sir?' Goldie looked at him steadily and Macdonnel produced his choicest arguments from books and pamphlets to prove that Britain was as culpable as Germany. But Goldie laughed at his propaganda while the other soldiers stood around listening, enjoying this unusual guard-room discussion and Goldie went out, warning the sergeant to report any insubordination to him but to keep his hands to himself in future. Macdonnel looked gratefully after the trim, upright officer, so harmlessly vain of his handsomeness and popularity, wondering what would be his fate; if that erect physique would be crippled for life or horribly smashed and killed. Gallant, generous Goldie! Where was he now? Dead, maybe, and rotting in some unsearched corner of a battlefield, his face mutilated beyond recognition.

Birds flashed minute shadows across the walls. He fancied himself catching one, taming it for company, as prisoners in ancient dungeons tamed mice and rats. He laughed out loud. That would be prohibited as unhygienic in a modern gaol! In these latter days of his sentence he could not hold deep pleasure long and depression darkened his spirit again. He thought of his brother Jimmy and the poor chance he had of seeing home again if that news about Gallipoli was true. Men mown down like grass! John Macdonnel had visited him one day on his way through London to the Front and they met after two years, in the visitors' cubicles, unable to shake hands, their faces blurs to each other through the close-meshed grille. 'It's like the confessional box,' said Eddy. John said that the family had received no news of Jimmy for nearly two years.

What would happen to Jimmy and John when the War was over and they returned to civilian life—if they came through at all? They would probably marry and have too many children, like their tragic parents, and be unemployed and wretched in a country recovering from the extravagance of war. He saw them, cleaving to the rut of the Glasgow back-streets, becoming old and grey without dignity, personality or accomplishments—nothing to show for their lives but a crowd of superfluous children.

What would his stand avail, or that of the few hundred conscientious objectors, against the millions to whom war seemed a necessity of life? War was older than the memory of man. All the arguments in the multitudes of books, the historic, organized attacks upon Capitalism had not prevented this war. Sentimental appeals to the spirit of world-brotherhood were futile. What education or organized appeals could ever destroy inborn racial antipathy? Those to whom war was a physiological need would fight till they wearied and find reasons for war again when they recovered. The interval would be similar to the aftermath of other great wars, with unemployment, hunger and strikes and the rank and file heroes of battle would be despised and rejected. The forms of society might change but would human oppression and distress ever vanish from the earth? Religious creeds had been imposed by prison, torture and the sword. Every creed had had its turn, then came the imposition of economic freedom, but the French Revolution had not stamped out poverty or oppression. He recalled the delight he shared with the other Socialist opposers of the War when the news of the Russian Revolution was heard in the prison. Could any freedom bid for in violence and blood ever end in freedom?

What good had he done here in prison for two years while other objectors were enjoying comparative freedom in Government Work Centres up and down the country? His gesture of electing to leave a Work Centre and return to prison to try and suffer as much for pacifism as soldiers were suffering for patriotism had been one of mere vanity. But the self-gratification he had enjoyed for so long had burned out of him and he regretted leaving that Home Office Camp in the

Highlands where the work of road-making that was hard for men more delicately reared had been easy and pleasant for him. Through the beauty of winter he had worked till snow left the feet of the mountains and gleamed remote on the peaks. Then Spring brought light to the hills and countless falls, and flashed new azure through the deep lochs, and he beheld a miracle of change such as he had never seen or dreamed of. That six months, distant from war-fevered cities, growing with the rhythm of altering Nature, passed as sublime music and colour through his adolescent senses. In his health and happiness he thought of the Absolutists, who chose to stay in gaol rather than compromise by accepting the Government's alternative of work in Centres till the War was over. Wishing to stand in with them, he wrote to the Home Office that he would cease work from that moment and lounged about the camp for a week awaiting his arrest.

He stopped sewing, like a woman thinking as she sews, the materials held pensively in his hands, and, looking up saw, in that patch of the sky he could see, the blue colour of Loch Leven as it shone on that immaculate Spring day he sailed down it on a motor launch with the Home Office Agent, to be handed over to a military escort at Stirling. His comrades had organised a whip-round for him and presented him with a gift of money when they crowded on the small jetty to cheer him farewell. That was a hard parting on that day when the Camp valley in the mountains glowed like an emerald bowl, with wild-flowers decorating its rim where it shelved up to the heights. The hundred men cheering him he had lived with for six months, sharing all their activities, the lectures and debates, the amateur theatricals and concerts. Among a hundred men of various social grades, differing in religious and political opinions, he had disagreed with many, but formed close friendships. In that six months the life his mind and spirit gathered was to return to him after long years. They waved to each other while the boat throbbed down the glowing Loch and they vanished from his sight as it turned a bend of the shore.

His sudden burst of laughter rang in the silent prison hall and he stopped in alarm, remembering his surroundings, waiting for a warder to appear and ask him if he had gone crazy and close his door. No sound of hurrying feet broke the stillness. His thoughts ran on again. He had laughed at the picture of the corporal and the sergeant waiting for him on the railway platform, at Stirling, scanning every carriage. He had dodged them by staying in the lavatory till the train moved out and wondered often afterwards why they did not search the train. But his escape then gave him a week's freedom with friends in Glasgow before he surrendered himself to the authorities. Soon he was back here! What had his foolishness and vanity achieved when he tried to stir up a mutiny among the conscientious objectors three months after he was back? He had whispered his plans to them at every opportunity on the exercise ring and in the workshop and twelve had sworn to follow his lead. They would all cease work then and hunger-strike till the Home Office ordered their release. One afternoon he conquered his inconfidence and leapt up suddenly on the laundry table to deliver his carefully memorized speech. His limbs trembled and, after his quivering shout of 'Comrades and fellow-prisoners!' he could only recall the first sentence of his magnificent opening. He stood on the steaming, soap-swilled table, while his comrades, with averted eyes, continued scrubbing at prisoners' underclothes, his mind empty, confused, his face crimson with mortification, staring open-mouthed at Mr Potts who gaped back at him, from his overlooking pulpit, astounded at this mutinous conduct. Then he saw Mr Potts' clownish face actually flush with indignation as he birled shrill blasts on his whistle, stepping down from his pulpit and birling frantically as he ran to the door. Within the minute another warder appeared while we was getting down from the table to stand sheepishly among the others, saying nothing when they told him he was foolish to bring heavy punishment on himself. He wanted to rush from their presence and was glad when he was led back to his cell by Mr Potts, who would charge him before the Governor in the morning and told him pompously, 'It ain't just three days bread an' water you'll get for this me lad!'

He was punished with three months' solitary confinement and three months of three days' bread and water and three days' ordinary diet alternately, in a gloomy groundfloor cell. Every morning, immediately his door was unlocked, he tilted his plank and made-up bedding outside the door, then washed in the lavatory, leaving his towel also outside before being locked in again. He could work at picking oakum if he wished, but he was given no sewing lest he should swallow a needle or open his veins with one. All books, except the black-bound prison Bible, were taken from him. The only furniture of his cell was a urinary pot of vulcanized rubber, stained and crusted, like the walls of a urinal, with salts and acids from prisoners' urine.

During that dark, long time he often recalled his ludicrous failure and, within himself, writhed in shame, walling himself round with inescapable inferiority, telling himself he lacked the talent and resolution to carry through that which he had attempted. He had acted from unworthy motives of pride and vanity, scorning the tameness of the other objectors, who, he saw now, were wiser than he. Never would he, in the humblest way, be a leader of men. He would day-dream of greatness in many ways, till advancing years deadened his power of dreaming and he would end, like his father and brothers, an obscure walker-on in the drama of life.

He looked up at the collection of letters in a letter-rack on the top shelf. He was allowed one each month and they had all been opened and censored before they reached him. He had a dozen letters; brief notes from his mother and John, well-written letters of several pages from the friends he had left in the Highlands. He had read them all so often that he could bring each one before his mind's eye and study its handwriting and contents. Every few days he arranged them and three different envelopes faced his eyes whenever he looked that way and he passed time by testing his memory of all they contained. The note from his mother and that from John were like their bewildered selves who could not understand why he had become an objector; the others complimented him upon his uncompromising stand. From where he sat he could read the prison address in Donald Hamilton's thick flamboyant hand and Neil Mudge's neat, clerical script. They both wrote that they disagreed with his Absolutist attitude but admired his courage and hoped the War would end soon when they would have a reunion in Glasgow. Ach, they also were wiser than he! Would he not have done more for Peace outside, even in the restricted freedom of a Work Centre? What did the attitude of all the world's pacifists represent? A tiny glimmer of reason in the oceanic mass-consciousness maddened again and again by the epidemic of war! Could any appeal to reason prevail against that recurring conflagration of the world which reason, as well as feeling, set aflame? All men were apprentices in the art of living; no man, rich or poor, derived from life a full, continuous happiness; all human life, from birth to death, was a dance of the apprentices. Perhaps in some future time, ages remote from now, men would be masters of themselves and life, finding excitement and adventure in the peaceful use and contemplation of themselves and this lovely, miraculous earth. Then would the ugly pastime of war no longer make a hell out of heaven. What had inspired his own weak opposition? Had not all his actions sprung from a vague sentimentalism, nourished on misunderstood poetry, propaganda pamphlets and revolutionary speeches? He had sneered at the unquestioning obedience of the millions who drilled and marched and gave their lives at last to end all war. But was his conduct more clear-sighted than theirs? He also was a unit in a minority mass-movement, with no clear individual view of a way of life. In gloomy prophecy he saw Neil Mudge and Donald Hamilton, released after the War and returning to wage-labour. Before long they would forget their adolescent, revolutionary ideals and marry and settle down to keep up appearances for approval of Glasgow respectability. Youth did not last. Ideals were the flowers of youth that drooped soon and rotted away.

He heard the prisoners return from afternoon Association work to be locked in till next morning. That was six o'clock. He closed his door, astonished at the swift passing of the last five hours. Then he thought of the long evening before him and began to work more slowly on the mail-bags that he might have enough to occupy him till the bell rang bedtime. Again the daffodils by the prison garden, bowing in the brilliant sun, glistened in his head. Soon night would enfold them and they would hang cold and still. One air-raid night in a crowded cell, a queer, thin man, tall and dark and stooped like a secretary bird, had tried to convert him to Theosophy, gravely assuring him that flowers were the highest forms of Creation. And Macdonnel, remembering that, saw those flowers as beings, and their life seemed to him richer and happier than the life of men. Their dance never lost gracefulness. Men danced and were happy for awhile, but they soon lost the magic of happiness. Their youth passed like a sunlit cloud.

Warders were unlocking some doors to let out the meal-orderlies for the serving of supper. That was a quarter-past six. He always knew the time from the relentless regularity of mealtimes. Five minutes later his door was opened and a warder handed him, from a wooden tray, a small square, two-compartment tin containing a half-ounce of margarine and one ounce of cheese and out of the white basket of bread slung round the orderly's neck, an eight-ounce loaf. He laid them on his table and took from its regulation position on a shelf in the window-corner, his vase-shaped, white delf mug in which he received his morning pint of gruel and his pint of ship's cocoa at night. He stood at the door, turning in his fingers the smooth, glazed vessel, thoughtfully studying the imprint, His Majesty's Prison, circled in black letters on its centre. Another warder came along with an orderly who supported on his knee as he shuffled from cell to cell, a four-gallon can of hot, steaming cocoa. The warder ladled a pint of cocoa into his mug and shut the door on him for the last time that day.

The cocoa was boiling hot, too hot to drink in this warm weather. Sometimes in winter it was lukewarm, when he would have been grateful for this scalding heat. He gazed a moment at the large circles of cocoa-fat floating on top of the cup. On darker evenings, when the cell was earlier lit, they gleamed like golden sequins. He walked his cell for five minutes till the strong-smelling liquid cooled. His stomach-sickness had eased and he felt a healthy hunger. Thank God the long day was almost over. As he walked he avoided looking at the door. If he remembered not to look at it he might not dream of it tonight. Would he sleep till morning? Yes. His nerves had been tranquil today and he had thought happily for a long time. Perhaps the draught the doctor had given him had steadied him.

He ate his meal hungrily, cutting the midget loaf into thin slices with his tin knife, trying to spread each one thinly from the half-ounce of margarine, laying them in a row on the glass-cloth he used as a table-cloth. These little ceremonies filled in time. Everything tasted delicious. The cheese, that was so often waxy and tasteless, was flavoursome and soft; it had been baking-day in the prison and the bread was fresh and sweet. When he had finished, smiling with pleasure in his hunger and well-being, he saw that light was dimming in his cell and hurriedly took his stool to the window and piled up his books to take a last look at the dying day.

For a long while he gazed hungrily till darkness filled his cell and his face sank into that darkness, away from the outside world, like the face of a drowning man disappearing for the last time. He heard the night-warder shuffling from cell to cell in his rope-soled slippers, lighting the gas mantles in the wall recesses. He stepped to the floor. He had concentrated so intensely on the daylight that his dazed eyes, staring at the shadowed wall, saw still a haze of celestial azure and flickering glints of sunlight. Clear in his vision the daffodils hung; against his face he sensed their satin coolness and in his nostrils their faint, vernal scent. Then the night-warder's taper wavered outside the square of frosted glass; the plop of the lighted mantle sharply struck his ears; gaslight flooded his cell; his vision of the earth and sky was blotted out and his aura of flowers faded away as he stepped once more on his stool and drew the blanket used for blackout, across the window.

CANONGATE CLASSICS
TITLES IN PRINT